MURDERED BY THE
BOOKS

ENDORSEMENTS

With meticulous planning and enviable skill in *Murdered by the Books*, debut author Jodi Casstevens-Short leads her readers down an ever-tightening path of murder and intrigue with a liberal splash of romance and several laughs to lighten the mood. With just enough clues and the occasional red herring, Short keeps us hanging until the very last chapter, where everything is tied up with a beautiful black bow. I wait eagerly for the next installment.
—**Paula Peckham**, award-winning author of the historical San Antonio series

Murdered by the Books is a great read. I especially enjoyed the authenticity with which the author portrayed the fire service and the camaraderie of the brotherhood. The author obviously understands and respects the firefighter lifestyle.
—**Greg Smith**, Fire Department Battalion Chief

Fantastic cozy mystery! From the engaging and charming characters to a grisly murder to a budding romance, the author has created in *Murdered by the Books* a story full of plot twists, cliff hangers, and laughs any cozy mystery fan will love. Throw in a group of close-knit women who support each other no matter what, the handsome, brave

men who inhabit their lives, and several furry companions, and the author has a hit on her hands—a page-turner from start to finish! Can't wait for the next book in the series!
—**Tracey Maxey**, Library Media Specialist

Jodi Casstevens-Short's debut promises more good reads to come. *Murdered by the Books* is a Miss Marple-style delight from start to finish with colorful, lively characters, blossoming romances, and a charming small-town setting. The intricate, page turning plot keeps you guessing until the very end. Beware! Red herrings abound. A highly entertaining read.
—**Cheryl Burman**, author of award-winning Amazon best seller of *Keepers*

MURDERED BY THE
BOOKS

JODI CASSTEVENS-SHORT

A Christian Company
ElkLakePublishingInc.com

COPYRIGHT NOTICE

Cover and Interior Design: Kelly Artieri, Deb Haggerty
Editor(s): Peggy Ellis, Cristel Phelps, Deb Haggerty

PUBLISHED BY: Elk Lake Publishing, Inc., 35 Dogwood Drive, Plymouth, MA 02360, 2024

Library Cataloging Data

Names: Casstevens-Short, Jodi (Jodi Casstevens-Short)
Murdered by the Books / Jodi Casstevens-Short

382 p. 23cm × 15cm (9in × 6 in.)
ISBN-13: 9798891341807 (paperback) | 9798891341814 (trade paperback) | 9798891341821 (e-book)
Key Words: cozy mystery; murder; romance; family relationships; children's bookstore; schnauzers; firefighters

Library of Congress Control Number: 2024936127 Fiction

DEDICATION

To my Mom—for her support and encouragement in all things and for teaching me the importance of faith, love, and family.

ACKNOWLEDGMENTS

Thank you. These two small words hardly seem enough to express the gratitude I feel for all the help and support I've received over the past few years as I wrote, edited, queried, and finally found a publisher for my first cozy mystery.

To Deb Haggerty and Cristel Phelps at Elk Lake Publishing, Inc.—thank you for taking a chance on a rookie author. Your faith in my book means the world to me. To Peggy Ellis, my editor, you've been a dream to work with and I hope we will work together again. You helped take "my baby" and polish her until she shined.

To my two fabulous critique partners—I'm so blessed to have met you both. Our Friday morning Zoom sessions have taught me so much about the do's and don'ts in the literary world. Thanks to your constant support and brilliant critiques on everything from characters and plot structure to formatting and grammatical errors, you've helped me grow and become a better writer. You're my literary cheerleaders who share with me the knowledge of how hard it is to write a book and get it published.

I'd like to thank Dr. Kurt Beaumont, DVM, for his expertise in veterinary medicine and for answering all my questions pertaining to Abbey and Hayley, both in the book and in real-life. You're the best, KB.

To everyone who inspired a character in this book (and those to come in the series), thank you for being a part of my life. I hope you will recognize bits of your personality and be pleased with your portrayal—you were all so much fun to write.

To my best girlfriends, who read the book in its original version and gave me their valuable feedback, I thank you for being my first critique partners before I even knew I needed one. I appreciate your belief in me, your honest opinions, and your helpful suggestions for the book, but most of all, your love and friendship.

And finally, I want to thank my wonderful husband, Trent. You've always been there for me, but never more so than in these past few years as I decided to jump in feet first and follow my dream. You understood when I needed time alone because I was in writer-mode. On nights I got caught up in a chapter and forgot to start dinner, you had it delivered without complaint. You patiently answered all of my firefighter-related questions to help make those scenes as realistic as possible. Thank you for giving me the space and time to write and for supporting me on my journey to the bookshelf.

CHAPTER ONE

Jillian sat behind the wheel of her car idling at the curb. The air conditioner blew in her face, cooling the beads of perspiration trickling down her temples. She attempted to still her racing heart and quiet the doubts wreaking havoc on her confidence.

C'mon, girl. This is not the time to fall apart.

She wiped her sweaty palms on the paint-spattered legs of her work pants. Several deep breaths calmed her nervous stomach.

As she stared at her reflection in the rearview mirror, a pep talk seemed appropriate. "Jillian Saoirse Edwards, this is it. The hard work, the sacrifices—everything comes together tonight."

She killed the engine and climbed from the vehicle. Jillian opened the passenger door and two frenzied, furry friends tumbled out, dragging her up the front sidewalk toward the house. They swirled around her ankles like autumn leaves in the wind.

As she climbed the steps onto the porch, a sudden movement over her shoulder grabbed Jillian's attention. An old man in grimy overalls marched from the dilapidated house across the street. He shook his fists and shouted words she couldn't make out.

"That guy moves fast for someone his age." Jillian shared the observation with her schnauzer pups, Abbey and Hayley. "He does not look happy."

"Hey, Book Lady." His voice shattered the quiet of the neighborhood. Even the pups stopped yipping. "You hold on one gosh darn minute."

Sidestepping her dogs and their leashes, Jillian ducked inside the door to her children's bookstore, Whimsy & Wonder. She silenced the alarm before facing her angry visitor.

"I been wantin' to talk to you, Book Lady."

Hmm, I guess there are worse things he could call me.

Jillian recognized this man. He'd skulked around her store the past few months—peering through her bushes, peeking around trees, and stealing glances in the windows. She pasted on a smile while muttering under her breath.

"Looks like I'll be meeting the infamous Mr. Erickson today." The neighbors had warned her about him.

Rumor was the bookstore had him all riled up. The other homeowners said he'd initiated a one-man mission to shut her down. No problem. She could deal with him.

"Good morning. I'm—"

"Don't 'good mornin'' me, missy." He shook a finger in her face. "This here's a quiet street. I—we don't want no crowds of people comin' here, makin' all kinds of noise, and drivin' down our property values." He gestured toward the other houses. "Pack yer books and git out. Me and these other folks ain't gonna tolerate no bookstore in our neighborhood."

Spittle flew from his mouth. His face grew mottled with red splotches. Jillian feared he'd suffer a heart attack if he didn't calm down.

"Don't listen to him, sweetie," someone shouted. "Your store will be great."

"Yeah, that old coot doesn't speak for us," another voice called out. "We're thrilled you're here."

Jillian hadn't realized her confrontation with this grouchy, old man had attracted a crowd. Several neighbors stood on the periphery of her yard. The noise and commotion worried her girls. Their unhappy whimpers drew Jillian's attention—only for a moment.

"Mr. Erickson, isn't it? I'm glad to finally meet you." She motioned toward two wicker chairs on the porch. Their colorful cushions begged one to snuggle in and read a good book. "Let's have a seat and talk. I could make coffee or tea. Which do you prefer?"

"I didn't come fer no tea party. I came fer action." He pounded his fist on the wooden porch railing. "Give me yer word you won't open this store, and I'll go on home. And would you make them dogs stop whinin'?"

To show his contempt, he kicked at the nearest pup with the steel toe of his work boot. Lucky for Hayley, he missed wide. Lucky for him too. His aggression didn't sit well with Jillian. Her grip on good manners slipped. Anger took charge. All intentions of sweet-talking her grumpy neighbor were lost.

"Mis-ter Erickson! You will *not* come onto my property and threaten to hurt my dog. I've been patient with you, listened to your concerns as you've expressed them very loudly. I draw the line when you threaten my girls."

She positioned herself between the man and the pups, fisting her hands on her hips.

"I've talked to the other neighbors. They're thrilled this house will be used after sitting vacant for five years. Empty houses drive down property values too, you know."

She paused to let her point sink in. He opened his mouth. Jillian cut him off before he had a chance to utter one word.

"I will open this bookstore with or without your approval." Her left foot tapped an angry rhythm on the whitewashed floorboards of the porch. "I don't understand the problem. Don't you like kids? Are you worried my shop will attract the wrong crowd?" Sarcasm dripped from every word. "Children, Mr. Erickson—sweet, innocent children—will come here looking for books to read. I'm sorry this has upset you, but ... well ... too bad."

Jillian's oldest sister, Cate, chose this moment to arrive with a signature blue box from her bakery, Sugar & Spice. Excited yips and yowls from the dogs, and nothing but stony silence from Jillian and her guest, greeted the newcomer.

"What's going on?" Cate directed the whisper at her sister. "I could hear you from my car. So did everyone else, it would seem." She motioned at the gathered crowd. "Offending your neighbors before you open is not a good business strategy."

Mr. Erickson caught a whiff of the delicious smells escaping from the blue box. His stomach growled with the ferocity of a wild animal, drowning out the pups' soft yipping.

"Excuse me, purdy lady." He placed his hand on his chest. "The name's Erickson. Whatever's in yer box sure does smell good. I ain't had no breakfast this morning. Would you be willin' to share some of them treats with a hungry, old man?"

"Now you turn on the charm? No way, mister. You're too late." Jillian waggled a finger at him.

Cate swatted Jillian's hand away. "Don't be rude."

"Me? You didn't hear the rude things he said to me. And he kicked at Hayley."

Cate seized the opportunity to help promote goodwill with her sister's neighbors. She addressed the assembled crowd. "Good morning. Please join us for some coffee and pastries."

As everyone moved onto the porch, Cate pushed Jillian toward the door. She lowered her voice. "Take the dogs inside and make some coffee. Come back when you're calm and civil."

"I can manage calm," Jillian mumbled. "Civil? I'm not sure."

Jillian left Cate to entertain her guests. She led the pups inside and let them off their leashes, watching them scamper around the store with their short, stubby tails wagging like tiny flags. The tension in her shoulders eased. She shook out her clenched fists—a few deep breaths steadied her.

She leaned down and spoke in a quiet voice. The pups hung on her very word. "I didn't count on company for breakfast today. The sooner they leave, the sooner I can get some work done." Abbey and Hayley gazed at her with their sweet, bearded faces and soulful brown eyes. Her heart melted. "C'mon, you two. Help me make the coffee." The dogs dutifully followed as she headed to the kitchen at the back of the house.

Jillian went through the motions of making coffee, her thoughts focusing on the evening's open house. "I have one chance to make a good first impression. I need Whimsy & Wonder to be perfect."

There were many people to impress, especially her sisters. They'd both been a huge help in her efforts to become a business owner. She'd lived rent-free for the past five years in Cate's finished basement, complete with kitchen, which was nicer than any apartment she'd ever leased. Her middle sister, Amanda, hired her as part-time help at her flower shop where Jillian worked on weekends, summer break, and during school holidays. She'd used this extra money, along with her teacher's salary, to make her dream of owning a bookstore a reality.

I couldn't have done this without them.

And, of course, there were her mom and dad. A daughter needs and wants her parents' approval no matter how old she gets.

Jillian gazed around the store, pleased with the way everything turned out. "I hope they're impressed with the finished product." Hayley offered an enthusiastic woof, earning her a scratch behind the ears.

"Thank you. I appreciate your vote of confidence." She gazed at Abbey. "What about you—any words of wisdom?" The shy dog planted a sloppy kiss on her mama's face. "Ah, the silent supporter. Works for me." She stroked Abby's soft gray coat.

"Did I hear you ask these two furballs for their opinions of the shop?" Cate strolled into the kitchen. "Being stressed is no excuse for asking dogs for business advice. Not a sign of fiscal confidence, Jilly."

"These furballs, as you call them, are smart enough to know when to speak and when to keep quiet. Unlike certain other people." She raised an eyebrow at her sister.

"Touché. Point Jillian." Cate drew an imaginary tick mark in the air. "I'm glad you've retained a sense of humor, but let's be serious a minute. How's everything coming together around here?"

"Good, except my to-do list has several things needing attention by tonight. I came in early to work—hadn't planned on this impromptu breakfast gathering." She gestured at the people congregated on her porch. "I wanted some quiet time in the shop. Working alone calms my nerves."

"Nervousness is normal before opening your own business. You know that, right?" Cate rubbed her sister's arm. "The week I opened the bakery, the term hot mess could've described me. I couldn't sleep. I couldn't eat. Lost my car keys three times! Poor Wes had to fend for himself since my overloaded brain could only focus on one thing. I didn't take time to enjoy the experience. Learn from my mistake. Relax and enjoy the ride. Your bookstore is going to be a huge success, sis."

Jillian blew a stray auburn curl from her face. "I will. I promise." She crossed her heart at her sister's dubious look. "Working will help. Being busy quiets the nerves in my stomach and the doubts in my head."

Cate brushed her hands together. "My job here is done. You have everything under control—except for this whole Doctor Doolittle thing." She pointed at the dogs. "Let's get the coffee outside and connect with your guests. Neighbors today, customers tomorrow."

Making nice with her visitors took forty-five minutes from Jillian's morning, but Cate's idea to reach out to them had been brilliant. They were wonderful people who'd banded together, telling Mr. Erickson they were excited to have the bookstore in the neighborhood.

A woman who lived three doors down was first to comment. "Look at these flowerpots filled with bright red, orange, and yellow fall blooms—such a cheerful entrance to the store." The woman addressed Mr. Erickson. "She's making our neighborhood more beautiful, Henry. You might want to do something with your shambles of a house."

The old man scowled. "My house is fine the way it is."

Mrs. Sanford, from the end of the block, jumped on the bandwagon. "This old house sat lonely for years. Ms.

Edwards has brought it back to life. You've done a wonderful job, dear."

"Please, call me Jillian. And thank you."

"Did you paint those children's storybook characters on the window?" This came from Mrs. Kirby who lived next door. "They're adorable and hint at the wonderful books waiting inside for all the kids who'll come in."

"I'd love to climb onto that antique wooden swing and enjoy the spectacular view of our neighborhood." Another lady offered her praises. "And those comfy wicker chairs— they're calling my name. You've created a happy place for children to come and read."

Their compliments thrilled Jillian. She hoped they'd take the wind out of Mr. Erickson's sails.

She'd chosen this spot for her bookstore because of its location in this neighborhood. The house sat on the corner of Sweetwater Avenue and Magnolia Street surrounded by trees of the same name. The homes on Magnolia had been built in the 1940s and were the perfect blend of styles— Cape Cod, colonial, and craftsman.

There was a beautiful park with a pond east across Magnolia Street, and the charming downtown area was reachable a few blocks around the corner. Jillian understood she'd been blessed when the city council voted to rezone this house, allowing for her bookstore. They'd readily agreed when she told them she'd be using the rooms upstairs as her own living space. Those renovations weren't complete, so she had yet to move in. Her priority had been getting the store ready to open.

When they'd devoured all the cinnamon rolls, the crowd wandered back to their own homes—except Mr. Erickson. He remained seated, glaring at them.

"The rest of them people think I should give you a chance with this here bookstore." He spit it out as if it was a four-letter word. "They're a bunch of idiots who are gonna be sorry. Mark my words, Book Lady. You got all them people comin' to this here open house thing tonight. That's when the decline of this neighborhood begins." He stood and hitched his pants. "They'll park their cars everywhere and hang around outside after dark, makin' a bunch of noise. Probably won't be able to hear the fight on TV with all their gosh darn racket. You better keep them rug rats outta my yard, missy." He scowled, shaking his finger.

Without waiting for her response, he pivoted military-style and graced Cate with a huge grin. "Pastry Lady, you bake a mighty fine cinnamon roll. Feel free to stop by my house anytime with a box of them tasty sweets. I live across the street—there." He pointed to his own dilapidated house. "Don't be a stranger." He winked at Cate, pivoted again, and marched off the porch.

"You've made a fan." Jillian bumped her sister with a hip. "I suggest you bring him some rolls, otherwise he'll show up at the bakery. Trust me, you don't want him camped out there. He'll drive away your customers with his sparkling personality."

"Oh, stop. He's not so bad." Cate stifled her laughter. "He's a lonely old man."

"Being old and lonely is no excuse for being grouchy and rude." Jillian snatched the food-encrusted napkin he'd left on the chair.

Cate sighed. "I've done all I can here, so I better get going. Poor Becca is drowning in cinnamon roll dough. Those things are flying out the door faster than we can bake them." Cate snapped her fingers in quick succession. "Don't worry. I still plan to let Becca off early, so she can be here to help you. She's reminded me every day this week—a bit annoying really."

She grabbed her purse from the chair. "If those dogs you love talking to offer any sound business advice, I'll expect you to share it with me." Cate waved over her shoulder and climbed into her car. "See ya."

"Your Aunt Cate thinks she's funny, doesn't she?" Abbey and Hayley responded with wiggly butts and quivering bodies. "She doesn't understand what great listeners you are. You're also better company than some people." Jillian glanced across the street at her new adversary's house.

"Come on, ladies. We won't let him ruin our day." She gathered the trash from breakfast and went inside to get a start on the day's to-do list. She worked in blissful quiet with two schnauzers and her own thoughts for company. After she finished one task, she considered her next.

"Maybe I should connect the computer and printer Mom and Dad gave me as a 'store-warming gift'. Or I could unpack a few more book boxes. What do you girls think?"

The slam of the screen door thwarted her plan and sent the dogs scrambling to greet their unexpected visitor.

"Guess who?" a familiar voice chirped.

Jillian watched her Aunt Grace breeze into the main room, catching a pleasant whiff of the flowery fragrance which had become her aunt's signature scent. This morning, Aunt Grace resembled the flowers of which she smelled. On this warmer-than-usual September day, she wore a pastel floral kaftan and bubblegum pink gladiator sandals laced around her toned calves. Both sculpted, tanned arms were adorned with her trademark gold bangles clicking together when she moved. Her auburn curls were swept into a messy bun showing off the large gold hoops in her ears.

At sixty-something, Grace wasn't afraid to wear bright colors and trendy styles despite the muttered disapproval from others, who believed her fashion choices were inappropriate for a woman of her age. Jillian disagreed with these judgmental cynics. She loved her aunt's confidence to wear what made her happy. In her opinion, Grace was flamboyant and fabulous.

"Good morning." She kissed her aunt on the cheek. "What brings you here this early?"

"Oh, Kitten." Her aunt had called her Kitten from the time she was a toddler. "There I was, seated at the kitchen table finishing my morning tea—Earl Gray, of course. I peered into the bottom of the cup." Grace paused for dramatic effect. "The leaves held an ominous sign. They told me you were in danger, so I rushed right over to help."

The Edwards family quietly accepted as fact that Aunt Grace had been blessed with the gift of prophecy. She claimed to read tea leaves, people's palms and auras, and often had visions, both good and bad. She believed God sent messages through her, and her responsibility was to use them to benefit others.

"Well, sure. I can use all the help I can get—still loads to do." Jillian ignored the part about the tea leaves.

"No, Kitten. The threat was for you, not the store." Grace shook her head, sending a few stray curls flying. "Your aura is pulsing an unusual shade of yellow—a warning color." These last words escaped in a whisper.

"Could it be I'm standing in a room *painted* a warm buttery shade of yellow?" She gestured at the walls around the main room.

"Oh well ... yes ... it is." Aunt Grace glanced around the room, her gaze focused on those painted walls. "But I know what I saw. The leaves were clear. They were shaped like a snake slithering around the letter J. The snake is an evil omen, and the letter J means you. This is bad, Kitten.

Really, really bad." She wrung her hands and rocked from one foot to the other.

Jillian sighed, knowing she must calm her aunt, or she wouldn't get any more work done that morning.

"Why don't we sit and have another cup of tea? Chamomile, perhaps. You always say an herb tea settles you." She guided her aunt down the hall to her office, offering her the overstuffed armchair in the corner of the cluttered room. Grace gnawed on her bottom lip when something troubled her. Jillian noticed she nibbled away like crazy today. "You relax. I'll get that tea."

Jillian stood at the antique gas stove and practiced deep breathing techniques she'd once learned at a teacher in-service. This had often helped her in the classroom, why not now?

The kettle whistled as Grace called out.

"Kitten, you should lock the shop and go home. You'll be safer there."

"I can't leave, Aunt Grace. Many people are counting on this store being ready and open on time." Jillian returned from the kitchen, carrying two steaming cups of tea.

"Kitten, please take my advice. I'd never forgive myself if something terrible happened to you." Grace's hand shook when she took the proffered tea cup.

The breathing exercises weren't helping. Jillian asked for a little divine intervention.

Oh Lord, I do love this woman, but time is ticking. Please help me get her out of here.

Like an answer to her prayer, the screen door banged again. The pups rushed to greet their latest guest, singing their usual canine chorus.

"We're in the office," Jillian called to the newcomer.

"Hello, sweetheart—oh, you have company." Joy strolled in carrying a huge bouquet. She shoved books aside to make space on the desk for the vase.

Help had arrived in the petite, yet mighty package that was Jillian's mother.

"Hi, Mom. This is a nice surprise." She hugged her mom and whispered in her ear. "I'm so glad to see you. Your timing is impeccable."

Joy nodded at the flowers. "I ran into Amanda's delivery boy on the porch. Whoever sent you these beautiful blooms did his homework. Pink roses and white jasmine—your favorites."

"Hmm, I bet I can guess who sent these." Jillian read the card aloud. "Good luck tonight, honey. Your store is going to be a HUGE success. These flowers will brighten the front counter. All our love, Dad and Mom."

"They're beautiful." Jillian stuck her nose into the fragrant bouquet and inhaled. "Smell amazing too. This was his idea, wasn't it?" Her father thought every special occasion deserved flowers.

"Yes, and he's right. They'll be perfect on the counter." Joy fussed with a rose in the center of the arrangement. "There. Even better now."

"Ahem." Aunt Grace cleared her throat.

"Hello, Grace." Joy greeted her twin sister. "Did you come this morning to help our Jilly?"

"Yes, I came to help *your* daughter, who won't listen to reason." Grace snapped at her sister.

Joy frowned. "Are you here because you had a vision?"

"No, I did not have a vision. God sent a message in my tea leaves, which was crystal clear. Something evil is coming. Jilly needs to go home and stay there." Grace dipped her head in her niece's direction.

Nothing short of a national disaster was going to make Jillian leave. She hoped her mom could get Aunt Grace to go home.

Joy moved around the perimeter of the room, picking her way among books, boxes, and furniture crammed into this tiny space.

"Sweetheart, you need to organize this room. A person can't move without bumping into all this clutter." To illustrate her point, Joy faked a stumble into the desk, knocking the outdated computer and printer onto the floor. The impact smashed them both to pieces.

"Oh, my goodness. How could I have been this clumsy?" Her mother hid her face to cover the devious expression.

Grace pounced on the opportunity to prove she'd been right. Her melodramatic personality went into overdrive. "There, you see. The bad is happening already." She wrung her hands. "I told you. Oh, I told you, Kitten. This. Is. Terrible. How will you print those adorable fliers and coupons you designed for the grand opening? This could ruin your business before you even open."

Jillian joined her mother's deception by picking a few pieces from the floor and trying her best to appear annoyed by the broken equipment.

I hope I'm half the actress my mother is.

"I track everything on my computer—inventory, future orders, vendor information—everything. Now it's ruined. When am I going to find time to install a new one?" Jillian made sure her voice quivered a little.

Her aunt cleared her throat again, raising her eyebrows. "I'm ready to listen if anyone wants to apologize for dismissing my concern."

Jillian knew there'd be no moving forward until they'd shown the proper contrition to Aunt Grace.

"I'm sorry, Auntie. I never should've doubted your tea leaves." She kissed the top of her aunt's curly head. "Thank you for trying to warn me."

"Tea leaves are never wrong, Kitten." A smug grin bloomed across Grace's face.

"I've made a mess in here." Joy apologized again. "Please let me make amends."

"Mom, it was an accident." Jillian put an arm around her mother. "Don't worry about it."

"I know." Joy snapped her fingers as an idea took shape. "I'll get lunch from the Corner Deli for you and your friends. Your Grandma McClaren always said it was good manners to offer food to your help. We can bring the meal, say, around noon. How many people should I plan for?"

"I hadn't even thought about food." She smacked herself on the forehead. "That would be great, Mom. If you two will join us, plan for seven people."

"Lunch for seven it is." Her mom hoisted Aunt Grace from the chair and guided her from the office. "C'mon, Sissy. Let's leave, so our girl can get busy."

Joy glanced back and winked. Jillian mouthed 'thank you'. Her mom's quick thinking had saved the day.

Or at least the rest of my morning.

The front door hadn't yet closed all the way when Jillian's work crew burst in the back, laughing and bickering. Her friends, Trixie, Becca, Ethan, and her cousin, Bryan, wore grungy work clothes and carried an assortment of tools. They were a rowdy, derelict-looking bunch, and she'd never been happier to see them.

"Are we ready for work or what?" Becca paraded the hall like a model at New York's Fashion Week. She'd chosen her favorite faded jeans and a navy T-shirt with a red bandana wrapped around her short brunette bob.

"What do you think of this lovely ensemble I threw together?" Trixie strutted her stuff. She wore cutoff denim shorts, a tie-dyed T-shirt knotted at the waist, and a pink baseball cap with her glossy black ponytail dangling through the hole in the back.

"Nobody cares what you're wearing." Ethan grumbled at his wife and Trixie. "This isn't a fashion show. We're here to work."

Both guys wore ratty T-shirts and faded blue jeans. Their leather belts loaded with tools dragged their pants low and threatened to show more of the men than anyone cared to view.

"Uh-oh." Bryan muttered as he spotted the two older women leaving out the front. "My mother was here, and it's before nine o'clock. Nothing gets her up and moving this early except a prediction of impending doom. Did she have one of her silly visions?" Bryan refused to believe in his mother's gift.

"Sort of."

Jillian gave a quick recap of Grace's vision in the teacup and her mother's scheme to shoo her aunt from the store. By the end of the story, Bryan's face sported a scowl, while Becca had tears streaming down her cheeks from laughing so hard.

"Oh, I love your aunt!" Becca swiped at her face. "She's smart, stylish, and quirky enough to be entertaining."

"This isn't funny," Bryan snapped. "My mother's embarrassing. Did you know she approached a stranger at Wal-Mart last week—said her aura was three shades of green? She suggested the woman go to a doctor as soon as possible because she might be terminally ill. The poor woman dropped her groceries and ran from the store, traumatized by my mother."

"Relax, Bry." Becca punched his arm. "Everyone in Willow Springs knows your mom means well with her prophecies. You're being too sensitive."

"Too sensitive—really? I think the woman from the store would disagree with you."

Trixie chose to add her two cents. "Some people are more intuitive than others. They're blessed with special gifts and talents. Maybe Grace is truly one of them."

Leave it to Trixie to champion the underdog. While she made a valid point, coming to Grace's defense set Bryan off on a rant. Jillian shouted to be heard.

"Hey, quiet down." She waved her hands in the air. "We have work to do. Bryan and Ethan, could you assemble and install the remaining bookshelves, please? Ladies, we'll finish decorating and staging the Main Room and the Arts & Crafts Corner. When the guys are done, we'll get the last books loaded onto the shelves. Our goal is to finish by noon."

"Why? What happens at noon? Do we change into pumpkins?" Becca snickered. "Shoot, I left my glass slippers at home."

Always the comedienne.

"Funny, but no. My mom will be here. She's bringing lunch."

"Sounds great. One question though—is she bringing my mother back?" Bryan grimaced.

"Yes, she is." Jillian rounded on her grouchy cousin and poked a finger in his chest. "I expect you to behave. No snide comments to upset your mother. I can't handle family drama hours before my grand opening. You hear me?"

"Yeah, I hear you." He crossed his arms. "She better not try to read my future in the chicken salad. If she does, I'm outta here."

"Great, that's settled. How 'bout we get some work done?" Ethan clapped Bryan on the shoulder and steered him toward the kitchen. "Let's roll."

"Let's roll—is that cop talk? Do I need to salute you, Officer Harden?" Bryan snorted at his own humor.

"It's *Detective* Harden, and yeah, a salute would be great. While you're at it, you should have the stick removed from your butt. Otherwise, you won't be able to bend over and help me assemble these shelves."

Ethan put his hands on Bryan's back and shoved him down the hallway. The two guys jawed back and forth the entire time. The women watched and shook their heads.

"Men—can't live with them, wouldn't want to live without them." Becca tilted her head to appreciate her husband's backside.

"Yeah, yeah. Your husband's wonderful, he's easy on the eyes, and you're a lucky woman ... blah, blah, blah. Let's get busy." Trixie dragged Becca into the Arts & Crafts room. "Let's start by hanging the twinkle lights. I love twinkle lights—they're so romantic ..." Trixie's voice tapered off as the two friends drifted into the next room.

Jillian hung back. She'd watched Becca watching Ethan. A pang of jealousy shot through her. She couldn't be happier Becca married the love of her life. She just wondered if she'd ever do the same. The past few years were a blur of work and more work. There'd been no time to meet anyone, let alone go on a date. Maybe once the store opened, there'd be time to find love.

She laughed at herself. Who was she kidding? Most new stores operate in the red for at least the first two years. She'd be working harder than ever. Plus, she hadn't exactly been lucky in love. Quite the opposite, in fact. A long sigh escaped.

Yeah, my love story won't be starting anytime soon.

"Earth to Jilly. I asked you a question." Becca snapped her fingers. "Why're you standing there with a weird expression on your face? What's wrong?"

Shaking herself from her musings, she looped an arm around her friend's neck.

"What could be wrong? My friends are here to help finish my store. The open house is in a few hours. All is right in my world."

The women worked side by side, talking, laughing, and singing with the radio. Jillian entertained them as she belted out the words to Gloria Gaynor's hit, "I Will Survive," a screwdriver as her makeshift microphone. Her encore stopped short when the screen door slammed open yet again, signaling another visitor.

CHAPTER TWO

Abbey and Hayley barked and raced to the door. Jillian followed and found a scruffy stranger standing in the center of the room. Her visitor wore a dirty, red plaid shirt and a puffy, black vest with a rip down the front. His greasy, reddish-brown hair needed a trim. A scraggly beard obscured a portion of his face yet failed to hide the ugly scar on his left cheek. He eyed her dogs with an angry sneer.

Jillian shooed her pups behind the counter where she joined them, securely latching the dog gate. This man and his sudden appearance made her wary. A voice in her head told her to put the strong wooden counter between herself and this unwelcome guest.

"May I help you?" She greeted him with her friendliest voice. "We aren't open for business, but I'm happy to answer any questions you might have."

The man approached and laid both hands on top of the counter, showing off the grime underneath his fingernails and the snake tattoo on his right arm.

"You should keep the door locked if you ain't open for business. Anyone could wander in." He leaned close as he spoke. The pungent stench of cigarette smoke on his clothes and the scary skull tattoo on his neck made Jillian recoil.

"Good advice. Thanks," she said. "What brings you in today?"

"I want to talk to the owner." His intense stare, creepy tattoos, and gravelly voice were unnerving. Jillian refused to be intimidated.

"I'm the owner. And you are ...?"

"Nobody important. I hear we have a mutual friend—Maggie Kiernan. You know her, right?"

"Yes, I do. How do you know her?"

Better yet. How does Maggie know this guy?

The man snorted. "Huh. She and I—you might say—we have a little business to attend to. I need to talk to her. Figured you might be able to hook me up."

"I'm not sure I can. What kind of business do you have with Maggie?"

He ignored the question. "Maybe you've got her phone number?"

His refusal to answer her questions set off warning bells. She decided to play his game and give her own vague answers.

"No. Sorry. I don't believe I have it."

"An address?" He wouldn't quit.

"No again. She moved a few weeks ago. I could give her a message—if I run into her." Jillian wanted this conversation done and him gone from her store.

"You give her this message. Tell her I want what's mine." He slammed his fists on the wooden counter, causing her to jump. The dogs growled. "You better talk to her soon. Because I'll be back if I don't get what I want. My return won't be pleasant for anyone."

"Are you threatening me?" She narrowed her eyes at her menacing guest.

"Why—do you feel threatened?" He leaned even closer.

"Not in the least." Jillian stood tall and met his stare. "You didn't tell me your name. I can't tell Maggie who the message is from."

"She'll know." He grinned, showing missing and blackened teeth. He stalked out without another word, slamming the door behind him.

Jillian watched him climb in a black vehicle parked in front of the store. She rubbed her arms, chasing away a cold shiver. She locked the front door as the unnerving stranger had suggested.

"Who was he?" Trixie popped from behind, startling Jillian.

"Oh, don't sneak up like that. You scared me!" She placed her hand over her racing heart.

"Did you chase off our first customer?" Trixie teased. "Doesn't sound like a good business plan to me."

"He wasn't a customer."

"Didn't think so. He didn't look like a children's book kind of guy." Trixie wrinkled her nose. "What'd he want?"

"He stopped in to ask a few questions. No big deal." Her gut instinct told her a different story. Jillian wondered why Maggie would be associated with a creep like him. She'd ask her tonight at the open house. He'd threatened to cause trouble, and she needed to know why. Aunt Grace had predicted evil was coming.

I think it just walked into my store.

Jillian double-checked the dead bolt.

The next few hours flew by in a haze of hard work and laughter. At noon, Joy and Grace brought enough food to feed a small army. In no time at all, they'd devoured lunch and finished the to-do list.

"This place is incredible. Your bookstore is going to be a big success." Becca drew Jillian into a hug.

"Thanks, Bec. I couldn't agree with you more."

The finished product exceeded Jillian's expectations. Twinkling fairy lights bathed each room with a soft glow.

Fresh flowers filled the Main Room with an aromatic scent. All the wood surfaces were polished to a warm shine, and the pillows and seat cushions provided pops of color.

And the books. They filled every shelf like little treasures waiting to be discovered.

Her eyes brimmed with tears. "Thank you, everyone. You've helped make this store perfect." She glanced at her own filthy clothes. "I, on the other hand, am a mess and need a shower before welcoming my guests this evening."

She ushered them to the door and waved goodbye. "I'll see you all back here at seven."

Jillian snapped leashes on the pups and grabbed her bag. "C'mon, girls, we need to go. I can't arrive at my own store's open house covered in dust and dirt. What would people think?"

Hearing the magic word *go,* Abbey and Hayley made a beeline for the door. After she shut off the lights and locked the door, she and her girls headed home.

After a long walk and a rousing game of tug-of-war, the dogs were ready for dinner. Jillian filled their bowls with their favorite food. While listening to their happy snuffs and snorts, Jillian broke the bad news to them.

"Ladies, my bookstore is opening for some special people this evening. I'm afraid you have to stay home. Sadly, not everyone enjoys dogs—even ones as sweet as you." She scratched their soft heads. "My guests will come and go all night. I wouldn't want you two to get trampled. Don't worry. I'll be home to give you your bedtime snack."

She left them to polish off their kibble and climbed into the shower. Jillian stood beneath the warm spray, letting the water wash away her fears and worries. As she was pressed for time, the shower was brief. She stepped out, dried off, and slipped the silky blue wrap dress over her head. She styled her wavy auburn hair into a French braid with a few loose tendrils framing her face. Her jewelry—a simple diamond pendant, small hoop earrings, and a slim gold bracelet Becca had given her on her birthday last year. Some blush, lip gloss, and a touch of mascara finished things off. She slid into her new, strappy gold sandals and was ready to go.

"What do you think?" She pirouetted for her dogs who perked their floppy ears. Abbey's tail wagged a quick rhythm while Hayley barked.

"Wow, two thumbs up. Or should I say paws?" She thanked her girls for their approval with a dog biscuit.

"I have to go. Wish me luck." As she left for the open house, she had a smile on her face, a bounce in her step, and butterflies the size of elephants in her stomach.

Standing in the Main Room full of nervous energy, Jillian busied herself fluffing pillows that didn't need plumping and wiping down tables which were already clean. Time refused to move faster—no matter how many times she stared at the clock.

A loud bang on the window startled her. After her unsettling morning visitor, her nerves were on edge. She spun around to see Becca and Trixie's eager, smiling faces pressed to the glass. Jillian opened the door, and her friends burst in, wrapping her in a fierce hug. Becca broke her hold first.

"Too quiet in here, Jilly." Becca disappeared behind the counter. Moments later, soft jazz filled the room. She swayed to the music. "Ah, there you go."

In the kitchen, they worked to fill trays with the appetizers Becca and Cate had prepared that afternoon at the bakery. They arranged glasses on the beverage table for the champagne and sparkling punch. Becca and Trixie had volunteered to serve as waitresses for the evening.

"I used to make good tips in high school when I worked at IHOP." Trixie carried a tray in each hand like a real pro. "Never dropped a thing."

Jillian left her friends to finish in the kitchen. She stood in the Main Room staring out the window. Almost seven o'clock. Her first guests would be here any minute. She hoped there'd be plenty of parking along Sweetwater, Magnolia, and the streets nearby.

A panicked thought flashed through her mind.

What if people didn't show up? Parking wouldn't be a problem.

"Are you ready to open your store?" Trixie bounced on her toes.

"*Our* store." She corrected her assistant. "And yes, I'm ready."

Jillian flipped the lock.

Among the first arrivals were her mother, father, and aunt, followed by her sisters, their significant others, and a few neighbors. Jillian welcomed them, while Becca and Trixie circulated the room offering refreshments.

"This place is wonderful, sweetheart." Joy beamed at her youngest daughter. "You've done an amazing job."

"We're so proud of you." Her dad planted a loud kiss on her cheek.

"Oh, the littles will love coming here. This house has a positive aura." Aunt Grace smiled and hugged her. "You've done something good here, Kitten."

"Thank you. I couldn't have done it without all of you."
She handed them each a glass. "Enjoy the evening. I have
to go be the hostess with the mostest."

Jillian welcomed new guests, including former students
and their parents. The children clamored for a tour of the
store, and she happily obliged. She began in the Lending
Library. The room had been designed for those children who
couldn't afford to buy books, because she believed all kids
deserved access to good reading materials The community
had stepped up and answered her plea for book donations.
"You come in here to borrow books from our small, yet
growing, collection. When you're done, bring them back
and check out more."

"So, this room is like the library at school," a tall boy
shouted out.

"Yes, Reid, like the library at school." This young man
had been in her class last year.

"The Arts & Crafts Room is this way." She led them
into the adjacent room. "I'll pick a book each month for
everyone to read. On the last Saturday, you can come in
and do a fun art or cooking activity related to the story."
This was greeted by a rousing cheer from the kids.

"This month, I've chosen one of my favorites, *Charlotte's
Web*—about a pig and spider who become best friends.
If this sounds interesting, get the book, register for the
activity, and come back on the twenty-sixth. We'll make
our own spiders and webs to take home."

"You read us that book last year. The story was good,
but sad," a girl in front piped up. "The art project sounds
cool."

"I hope you'll read the book on your own and join us for
all the fun, Anna."

Jillian excused herself to mingle with arriving guests and say thank you to those who were leaving. She repeated this pattern for the next few hours as people cycled through her store. She was headed for the refreshment table to get some punch when her aunt took her by the arm.

"Everyone loves Whimsy & Wonder, Kitten." Aunt Grace whispered in her ear. "I'm glad the ugly business from earlier is behind us. I hope that was the danger I saw coming, and nothing else will happen. We can all relax and enjoy the evening." Aunt Grace kissed her on the cheek and drifted away, a swirl of cream silk and floral perfume.

Her aunt's words sent Jillian's mind back to her strange visitor.

Is the ugliness behind us? Or is it dead ahead?

Her aunt approached a distinguished-looking gentleman and placed her hand on his arm, treating him to a coquettish laugh.

Mr. Handsome will be no match for Aunt Grace.

Maybe she should rescue him.

The poor man would have to fend for himself. Former coworkers from the elementary school waylaid her, offering hugs and congratulations.

"What's with the old guy outside?" one teacher complained. "He yelled at us to stay off his property and keep the noise down." The others laughed as she mimicked his cranky voice.

Jillian shrugged, biting her tongue, not wanting to say anything inappropriate in front of her guests. She'd deal with Mr. Erickson later. They chatted until she excused herself to tell other guests goodbye.

A few minutes later, a soft tap on the shoulder startled her. She spun around, coming face to face with Maggie.

"Can we talk for a minute—in private?" Maggie fussed with the black ribbon on a package in her hands.

"Of course we can." She hugged her friend and led her behind the counter. "I'm so glad you're here. There's something I need to share with you."

Maggie shoved the wrapped box at her. "I want you to have this. Please keep it safe. No matter what happens."

Those ominous words made Jillian's skin tingle. She placed the box on the counter and took Maggie's hands in hers. "Is something wrong? What do you mean ... no matter what happens?"

"Oh, don't mind me." Maggie pulled her hands back and began babbling. "I've had a stressful week. I'm exhausted. I get melodramatic when I'm tired. After a good night's sleep, everything will be better in the morning." Her eyes welled with tears. "Thank you for being the best friend I've ever had. I'm—" Her voice cracked. "I need some air." Without another word, she bolted for the front door.

"Maggie, wait."

Her friend ducked onto the porch and was swallowed by the darkness before Jillian could warn her about the weird guy and his threats.

I'll catch up with her before the night is over.

Jillian spied Maggie a few times in the crowd during the night, but never had an opportunity to talk to her. By ten o'clock, people began leaving, including Maggie and the other teachers. Family and friends waited for the last guests to leave, so they could help Jillian clean the store. She wanted everything spotless when her bookstore opened for business in the morning. She'd pitch in to tidy up as soon as she escorted Mrs. Daly to her car.

Everyone loved Mrs. Daly, the secretary from the grade school. She was an elderly widow who cared for each student and staff member at Willow Springs Elementary School. Since her husband's unexpected passing, everyone looked out for her too.

A loud racket disturbed the stillness of the evening.

"Goodness gracious, what's all the noise?" Ms. Daly protected her ears with her hands.

A black SUV pulled away from the curb and raced down the street, tires squealing. The elderly woman craned her neck, pointing as the vehicle passed. "The driver is going too fast. He should slow down before someone gets hurt." Mrs. Daly often said this same thing when students ran in the hallway at school.

Someone in the crowd shouted, 'Slow down, you moron.' The warning went unheard.

A loud thud, more squealing tires, and hysterical screams pierced the chilly night air.

Mrs. Daly had been correct—someone was hurt. A lifeless form obstructed the intersection.

The older woman grasped Jillian's arm. "Did someone hit a dog and drive away? Who would do such a heartless thing?" Mrs. Daly sniffled.

"I'm not sure, Mrs. Daly." Jillian took the woman's arm. "Let's get you into your car where you'll be safe."

Jillian said a quick goodbye, then moved closer to the intersection. She cringed at the sight of the unmoving figure.

Not someone's dog.

Ethan, who'd been outside talking on his phone, knelt beside the victim. He spotted Jillian and yelled at her. "I've called 9-1-1. Can you find a blanket?"

She spun on her heels and bumped into Becca, who steadied them both with her strong arms.

"I'll get him a blanket," Becca said. "You see if he needs another pair of hands."

Becca pushed her way through the crowd, heading for the store. Jillian moved closer to the victim. She stood behind Ethan, listening as he talked to the woman in the street.

"Ma'am, can you hear me? My name is Ethan. I'm a police officer. Help is on the way."

The poor victim mumbled something unintelligible. Every time the woman tried to move, she cried out from the pain of her efforts.

"Lie still. I'll stay here with you." Ethan held her bloodied hand.

Becca returned and shoved the blanket at Jillian while averting her eyes from the blood. "Here. I'm not getting any closer."

Jillian held the blanket out for Ethan, but he was preoccupied with the victim. His voice remained calm. "Ma'am, can you describe the car or driver who hit you? Is there anything you can tell me? Your name, perhaps."

The woman muttered the word black a few times before losing consciousness.

Ethan swore under his breath. He flinched when Jillian's hand touched his back.

"I've got the blanket," she said. "What should I do?"

"Lay it across her body." He scanned the street. "Where is the ambulance?"

Jillian leaned down, draping the blanket over the victim's body. The woman's clothes were torn, her right leg lay at an awkward angle, and her arms were slashed with deep gashes. When Jillian glanced at the blood-smeared face, she gasped and staggered back. Her legs quivered as she searched for balance, fighting the queasiness in her stomach.

"Um ... Ethan. I know ...she's ... that's ..." The words wouldn't come as her brain refused to cooperate.

He couldn't hear her. The fire truck's siren swallowed her words as the rig turned the corner and screeched to a halt. Three men jumped off, their arms loaded with equipment. They rushed to the victim. Jillian stood close enough to see the compassionate looks on their faces. Their hands were gentle, their actions calm and purposeful, yet they worked fast. Each time one of them moved the woman, even a little, she whimpered.

The firefighter who appeared to be in charge spoke to the victim the entire time, his voice low and soothing. His gaze never left the injured woman's face. An ambulance arrived, and the paramedics wasted no time. They loaded their patient into the back and whisked her away to St. Francis Hospital.

As the ambulance's wail faded in the distance, Jillian stood in the street, unable to make her legs move. Ethan touched the small of her back.

"Let's go. You can't stand here in the intersection." He steered her from the road onto the curb.

Her hearing became more acute as any effort to think or speak failed. The firetruck's powerful engine rumbled to life, and the air brake released with a hiss. Birds twittered in the trees. A dog barked on the next block. The cool autumn wind whistled through the dry leaves. She even heard the streetlights buzzing. So focused on these sounds, she jumped when Ethan touched her again.

"I need to ask you some questions, Jilly. Let's go sit down." He headed for Whimsy & Wonder's porch.

Jillian's brain felt fuzzy, disconnected from the rest of her body, but she managed to move her feet. With each step, the fog shrouding her brain lifted. The memory of someone she knew spattered with blood and sobbing in pain ripped at her heart. Warm tears trickled down her cheeks. She took a deep breath.

"Ethan, stop!"

His steps ceased. He turned to face her.

"I need to tell you something." Her voice wavered.

"I'm listening."

She inhaled deeply before her words came out in a rush.

"I know that poor woman, and I know who ran her down."

CHAPTER THREE

"The woman in the road—she's my friend, Maggie. This was no accident."

Jillian filled Ethan in about her encounter with the man in her store, the strange questions he'd asked, and the threats he'd made. Her words spewed like lava erupting from a volcano.

"Are you sure it's her?" Ethan rubbed at his temples. "Why didn't you say something?"

"I tried. You couldn't hear me above the sirens." Her voice quivered. "And *yes,* I'm sure it's her. I'm also sure that man hit her on purpose."

"Whoa, hold on there, Jilly. Take some deep breaths." He led her to a seat on the porch. "I don't need you to hyperventilate and pass out on me."

She took a moment and slowed her breathing before she continued.

"The man in my store drove away in a black vehicle. Mrs. Daly and I saw a black SUV racing down the street towards the intersection. Maggie mumbled *black* to you several times." Jillian ticked her points off on her fingers. "All of these facts point to the guy from my store. He hit her—I'm positive."

"Well, I'm not. Do you know how many black SUVs are in Willow Springs? I drive one myself."

"Yes, I know. But I don't believe you're on the suspect list, Detective." She lashed out at him. "I'm sure *you* didn't run Maggie down in the street."

"Why would your scary visitor try to kill Maggie if, as you say, he wanted something from her? If she's dead, he's not going to get what he wants."

Ethan's logic didn't sit well, since it contradicted her own theory. She jerked to her feet. "Fine. Will you at least agree to check him out?"

"I promise to do everything I can to find the person responsible for hurting your friend. They'll be held accountable whether it was an accident ... or not."

Think what you want, Detective. This was no accident.

Jillian got home much later than planned. After giving Ethan her statement, she'd stayed to make sure Whimsy & Wonder was perfect before it opened for its first day in a few hours. The store was ready—she was not. Her mind and body were exhausted—her spirit defeated.

As she shoved her key in the lock, the sound of Abbey and Hayley sniffing and snorting on the other side of the door comforted her. They were the balm needed to soothe her tattered nerves. She scooped them up for a quick cuddle and carried them outside.

In the wee hours of the morning, she hadn't expected to have company in the yard. Yet, she wasn't surprised when Cate joined her. The sisters stood shoulder to shoulder, whispering in the moonlight.

"You okay?" Cate broke the silence.

"I think so—out here soaking in the quiet night air while I give the girls a potty break before we try to get some sleep." Jillian yawned and rubbed her tired eyes. "I have to be on my toes when the bookstore opens at nine."

"Are you sure opening is a good idea—you know—after what happened? No one would blame you if you postponed things a day or two."

Cate's suggestion elicited an outraged response, hissed from between clenched teeth.

"I'm opening today. Nothing and no one is going to stop me. The doors will open, and I'll greet my first customers with a smile on my face." The anger in Jillian's voice cut through the dark like the blade of a knife.

"Calm down." Cate rubbed her sister's back. "You'll never fall asleep if you're upset."

"Sorry, I shouldn't have snapped at you." Jillian dragged her hands through her hair. She stared into the darkness. "I'm frustrated about tonight, but more importantly, I'm worried about Maggie."

"They'll take great care of her at St. Francis," Cate assured her. "How about those firefighters? They were amazing—the way they cared for your friend."

"Yes, they were. I was impressed with how calm and confident they were." Jillian blew out a breath. "I was a nervous wreck standing there watching."

"And the one in charge—whoa. Good-looking, close to your age." Cate elbowed her in the ribs.

"What?" She gaped at her sister's brazenness. "You checked out the firefighters while Maggie was bleeding in the street? You're unbelievable."

"Relax. I noticed him when they climbed back onto the truck to leave. I was standing on his side of the engine." Cate shrugged.

The pups had finished their business and headed toward the house.

"We're going to bed." Jillian yawned. "Talk to you tomorrow."

Cate tapped her watch. "Hate to tell you—it *is* tomorrow." She turned to go. "Good luck on your first day open for business."

"I don't need luck. I need customers."

Once inside, Jillian fed the dogs their bedtime snack and put on her softest pajamas. They climbed in bed and snuggled under the warm duvet, one dog tucked on each side. The soft sounds of puppy snores soon filled the dark room, yet sleep eluded Jillian. Every time her eyes closed, the body lying in the street popped into her head. She saw the blood matted in Maggie's curly red hair and splattered on her beautiful cream coat. She could hear her friend's soft moans.

Her mind raced with questions.

How is Maggie?

Who is the man in the black car?

Why would he do this?

Jillian prayed Maggie's injuries weren't as serious as they'd looked. She also prayed someone would come forward with information to catch this guy.

Two hours and no sleep later, Jillian threw back the comforter and swung her legs over the side of the bed. The girls lifted their heads. Their tired eyes stared at her.

"Sorry, girls. Too many things on my mind." She patted their heads. "Go back to sleep. We don't all need to be awake this early." They obeyed, falling asleep again in seconds.

Her Grandma McClaren had been famous for saying 'the best cure for idle hands and a busy mind is baking.'

Jillian believed there was nothing better to bake than her grandmother's triple chocolate chip cookies. She'd make a batch and take some to the store this morning—a treat for her customers.

Within thirty minutes, the smell of melting chocolate emanated from her oven. She sipped some hot tea, letting it chase off the morning chill while waiting for the timer to buzz.

Her last conversation with Maggie ran through her mind. Her friend had done all the talking and had appeared worried, scared even, before she ran out of the store. There'd been no chance later in the evening to warn her about the strange man and his threats.

Jillian gasped—the gift. She'd completely forgotten about the box Maggie had given her. "I don't remember where I put it."

She considered throwing on her clothes and rushing to the store. The absurdity of this idea hit her. Rushing off in the darkness by herself was silly, possibly dangerous. The stranger had threatened Maggie *and* her. She'd be at the bookstore in a few short hours and could look for the box then.

The timer beeped, signaling the cookies were ready. She removed the baking sheets from the oven and set them on the counter. She'd pack the goodies in a container after they cooled.

"All right ladies, I can't show up on my first day wearing these pajamas." She addressed her girls as she returned to the bedroom. Her tired pups struggled to raise their furry heads. "I need to look professional, yet I need to feel comfortable. Let's see what will work." She flung open the closet door.

She settled on black pants, a white button-down shirt, and a gray cardigan. Her flat black ballet shoes were a must because she'd be on her feet all day. Silver hoops and her Apple Watch completed her wardrobe.

Rousing Abbey and Hayley, she hustled them outside. "I need you to be quick this morning—can't be late today." Jillian noticed a movement out of the corner of her eyes. She spied Cate coming out her front door, juggling bookbags and totes, holding the hands of her two daughters.

"Talking to those furballs again?" Cate grinned.

Jillian ignored the teasing remark and greeted the two curly-haired cuties with her sister.

"Hello, Laney. Hi, Aubrey. How're my favorite nieces today?"

Her oldest niece wrinkled her nose. "Aunt Jilly, we're your *only* nieces, so, of course, we're the favorites. No one else could be." Laney was wise beyond her eight years.

"I wanna be the fav-rit." Four-year-old Aubrey pouted. "Please let me be your fav-rit, Auntie."

"You can both be my *only* favorite nieces, okay?" They sealed the deal with a pinky hook. "Where are the lovely Flaherty women headed this early?"

"To Mommy's bakery," Aubrey chirped. "Becca's makin' doughnuts. I'm gonna get one with lots of sprinkles."

"Sprinkles are for babies." Laney needled her sister.

"Mommy, are sprinkles for babies? I won't eat them if they're for babies 'cuz I'm not a baby anymore." Aubrey popped her thumb into her mouth.

Jillian chuckled.

You sure about that, kid?

"No sweetie. Sprinkles are for big girls too." Cate shook her head at Laney. "Don't tease your sister. You two get in the car. I'll be there in a minute."

The girls both yelled *shotgun* and raced for the front seat. Cate had to use her mom voice to settle their disagreement.

"Nobody rides shotgun—you're both too little." She scowled at her girls. "Get in your car seats in the back." She turned her attention to Jillian. "Aren't you glad you live in our basement and are a witness to these lovely family moments?"

Jillian winked at Cate. "Wouldn't miss it for the world." She continued with some sarcasm of her own. "Fancy meeting you here this morning. I can't remember the last time we stood in the yard and talked."

"Make sure Jilly is okay. Check." Cate made an imaginary tick mark on her hand. "You ready to open to customers today?"

"I sure am." Jillian smiled at her sister. "I'll be welcoming them with Grandma's triple chocolate chip cookies."

"What? When did you have time to bake?"

"When everyone else was sleeping." Jillian fluttered her hands in the air. "You know—the whole idle hands, busy mind thing."

"Yes, I do—been there myself many times." A car horn beeped twice, an alert that two little girls were waiting for their mom—and doughnuts. Aubrey's sweet four-year-old face showed through the front window. She waved at them before ducking out of sight.

Cate sighed. "I'm being summoned. I better go before she wakes the whole neighborhood. Talk to you later."

Jillian went into the house to gather the cookies, her purse, and the pups. With her mission accomplished, she loaded everything, and everyone, into the car.

"You two don't want to miss the first day of business at Whimsy & Wonder, do you?"

Several emphatic woofs answered back.

As she drove to work, her head and heart were filled with mixed emotions—anxiety, yet excitement, for this first day, along with concern and worry for her friend. She made a mental note to check with Ethan on Maggie's condition. The hospital wouldn't give her any information if she called. Talking to a cop about a victim's condition—that was a different matter. She prayed there'd be good news to start the day.

After parking her car in the garage behind the bookstore, she unlocked the door and silenced the alarm. Abbey and Hayley wandered and sniffed all the special nooks and crannies while she flipped on lights.

"Here are the ground rules for the day, ladies. No excessive barking. No jumping on customers. Stand still when the children pet you. And stay behind the counter when you're not being loved on by our young friends." They each received a scratch under their bearded chins. "There'll be extra treats at the end of your shift."

With ten minutes until her store opened for the first time, Jillian took a moment to search for Maggie's missing box. If memory served, she'd placed it on the counter. No luck finding it there. She checked behind the counter and all around the Main Room followed by the Lending Library and the Arts & Crafts Room with no success. Someone who helped clean must've moved the box. Trixie maybe.

At nine o'clock on the dot, Jillian flipped the deadbolt and raised the blinds, smiling at the sign in the window that read, "Two sweet dogs often in attendance here."

She took a deep breath and murmured, "This is it. I'm finally open for business."

Jillian was standing in the kitchen plating cookies when the doorbell jingled, sending her girls into their usual canine chorus. She shooed them behind the counter, giving them the command to be quiet and lie down. Brushing off her hands, she hurried to greet her first customer. She guessed it might be her mom or her aunt or maybe even Trixie showing up early for her workday.

Her first visitor was not anyone she'd expected. Entering the Main Room, she found a handsome, dark-haired man standing inside the door. Unlike the stranger who'd barged into her store yesterday, this man wasn't the least bit threatening. He didn't make her want to climb behind the wooden counter to protect herself. Quite the opposite. This guy was clean-shaven, dressed in nice clothes, with not a scary tattoo in sight.

Taking a deep breath, she rattled off her rehearsed greeting.

"Good morning! Welcome to Whimsy & Wonder. I'm the owner, Jillian Edwards. I'm glad you stopped in today. How can I help you?"

"Good morning, Ms. Edwards. Or is it Mrs.?" Her visitor asked.

"Oh … um … It's … Ms." His question caught her off guard. She stammered like a silly schoolgirl.

"I do have another question." He flashed a warm smile in her direction. "How many times did you practice that speech?"

He grinned, causing the corners of his eyes to crinkle and his left eyebrow to rise.

"A fair few, I guess. Was it obvious?" Her cheeks warmed.

"Yes, but your delivery was flawless. Practice makes perfect." He stepped closer. His proximity gave her a chance to notice a few more things—his deep brown eyes dotted with gold flecks, the way his damp hair curled around his collar, and the musky smell of his aftershave that reminded her of the scent her father wore.

"I'm sorry to intrude so early in your day. I hoped to avoid a store full of customers. Oh, wow, cute dogs." He squatted down and rubbed them behind their floppy ears. Abbey and Hayley wiggled from head to toe.

Those little stinkers had snuck from behind the counter without permission.

I don't know who this guy is, but he's making a good first impression on my girls.

"You're not a customer?"

"No, I'm not. And I wish I were here under different circumstances." He stood and retrieved a paper bag she hadn't noticed he'd placed by the door. "I'm sure you don't remember me. I was here last night."

"You were at the open house? I'm so sorry we didn't get a chance to talk." She couldn't believe she'd neglected one of her guests. "I hope you enjoyed the evening."

"No, you don't understand. I wasn't a guest at your party." He fiddled with the paper sack.

"You crashed my party?" Jillian frowned.

He chuckled. "No, I don't make a habit of going to parties without an invitation. As my mother would say, 'I was raised to know better.' Let me start again." Her tall, dark, and handsome stranger cleared his throat.

"My name is Travis Stevens. I was here last night *after* your party. My crew and I responded to the accident." He lifted something from the bag. "This blanket was draped over the victim and somehow got placed on our rig. Someone mentioned it might be yours." He held it out for her to take.

She swallowed the lump in her throat. "Yes, it's mine."

"Yeah? Great." A smile lit up his face. "I washed it at the station. You wouldn't have wanted it back in the shape it was in. Had blood all over it—" Travis froze. He blushed. "I'm sorry. Poor choice of words."

Jillian struggled to process what he'd said. This guy was the firefighter who took care of Maggie. Judging by his handsome face, he could be the cute one Cate mentioned. He'd come to bring her blanket, which he'd taken the time to wash.

He waited, holding the blanket out for her to take. She reached for it, and her hand brushed his, sending a shiver down her spine.

What was that? Did he feel it too?

Looking into his face, she thought she saw a flash of surprise in his eyes. Whatever it was extinguished quickly. She snatched the blanket from his grasp, breaking the physical contact between them.

"Returning this wasn't necessary, but thank you." She averted her eyes from his gaze, not wanting him to see the tears she held at bay. "I wish I could've done more than cover Maggie with it."

"Her name was Maggie." He shoved his hands deep in his pockets. "I asked several times. She couldn't tell me. You two were friends?"

"Yes. We worked together at the elementary school— teaching." One tear managed to escape. She brushed it away.

"I'm sorry. You must be shaken up after last night. I mean—the hit-and-run right outside your store." He ran a hand through his hair.

"Yes, of course. The whole thing was terrible." Jillian's breath caught, a tiny gasp escaping. "You wouldn't know how Maggie's doing today, would you?"

His head snapped up. Those deep brown eyes she'd noticed earlier filled with sorrow—or was it pity? "I'm so sorry, Ms. Edwards. I thought someone would've told you. Your friend's internal injuries were extensive. She didn't make it through surgery."

Jillian grabbed a hold of the counter as she started to sway. "Maggie's dead?" The room spun. She wobbled.

"Easy there." Travis reached for her arm. "Maybe you should sit down. Can I get you something?" Easing her into the nearest chair, he kneeled in front of her. Their eyes locked. Neither said a word. The silence was broken when the bell above the door tinkled. Ethan strolled in.

"Good morning." His friendly tone changed as he took in the scene. "Everything okay in here?"

Travis jerked to his feet.

Fearing she'd choke on her tears if she spoke, Jillian shook her head. Travis answered in a reverent tone. "I brought Ms. Edwards her blanket. She asked about her friend. I thought she knew ..." His voice trailed off.

"And you had the misfortune of breaking the news." Ethan pulled Jillian from the chair for a brotherly hug. "I was bringing the news myself—looks like the lieutenant beat me to it. I'm sorry about this—couldn't have been easy for either of you." Taking a step back, he stared into her face. "Maybe opening the store today isn't a good idea. People will understand—under the circumstances."

His kindness threatened to unhinge her, so she threw up a defensive wall and lashed out. "Stop telling me what to do. I'm tired of hearing opening my store isn't a good idea. In case you haven't noticed, I *am* open. Many of my former students are coming this morning. I won't disappoint them."

"Let's call Trixie. She could come in early for her shift. And your mom—she'd be happy to help too." Ethan still held her arms. "You're not safe here by yourself, Jilly."

"I won't be alone. My customers will keep me company."
She straightened her shoulders, managing a weak smile.
"Hearing Maggie is gone stunned me. She was a good
person and an even better friend. I'll never understand why
someone did this to her. Everyone, including me, will need
time to deal with her loss. But I can't sit and do nothing. I
need to stay busy."

"We'll find the person who did this." Ethan steeled his
features, showing his hard cop glare to the world. "We're
canvasing the neighborhood, interviewing Maggie's friends
and coworkers. Someone will point us in the right direction.
We'll find her killer."

Killer. The word sent a chill creeping across Jillian's
skin. The cold, hard truth her friend was dead had sunk in.
Sorrow and anger battled for control inside her.

"I know you will, Ethan. You're a great cop." She gave
him a chaste kiss before stepping behind the counter. Both
men watched her—Ethan with his critical cop stare and
Travis with a sympathetic expression.

"What? Are you two waiting for me to break down or
become hysterical?" She fussed with the floral arrangement
still sitting there from last night. "Don't worry. I'll be okay."

If she were honest, she knew the tears would come later.
In private.

Knowing when he'd been beaten, Ethan turned to Travis.
"You guys have a quiet night, LT?" He smacked Travis on
the back, jerking his attention away from Jillian.

"Hmm? Sorry. Did you say something?"

"Yeah." Ethan laughed. "I asked if things were quiet at
the station last night."

Travis shook his head like he needed to clear cobwebs
from his brain. "No, it was rough. We were out all night.
There was a three-car accident on the interstate."

"That sounds awful." Jillian frowned. "I hope no one was seriously injured."

"A few cuts, bumps, and bruises. Maybe a couple cracked ribs," Travis said. "Thank goodness for seatbelts."

Ethan mumbled around a mouthful of cookies he'd snitched from the plate on the counter. "That couldn't have kept you out all night. What else happened?"

"Somebody backed into a fire hydrant on Washington Street—knocked the sucker clean off its base. Created the world's largest water fountain. We couldn't get the water main shut off and had to babysit the mess until someone from the water company arrived." His spontaneous yawn interrupted his story. "We didn't get back in the station until six this morning. I stopped here on my way home." He yawned again. "I should probably get going."

He scooped the empty paper bag from the floor and folded it under his arm.

"Thank you again for returning the blanket," Jillian said.

"No problem." Travis stopped when he reached the door. "Hey, I have a niece who loves to read. Her birthday's in a few weeks. Maybe I could come back and find a gift for her?"

"Come back anytime."

"Great, it's a date ... I mean, not a date. I'll be back. To buy books. Because this is a bookstore. I should go."

Travis headed for the door and muttered, "What an idiot," under his breath. The screen door banged shut behind him.

Jillian smiled. His nervous stammering was adorable.

Ethan watched the lieutenant hurry to his truck. "Smooth. Real smooth." He laughed.

"Don't be mean." She nudged him with her hip. "Travis seems like a nice guy. He brought my blanket—even washed it first. That was thoughtful, don't you think?"

"Mm-hmm, very thoughtful." Ethan cocked his head at her.

"Why are you staring at me?"

"You two were pretty cozy when I came in. Did I intrude on an intimate moment?"

"An intimate moment? Don't be ridiculous. I met the man for the first time twenty minutes ago." She shook off his comment. "He had just told me Maggie was gone. I was shocked—got a little woozy. He helped me into a chair. End of story."

"Who are you kidding—end of story? I'm a trained investigator, Jilly. My job is to observe people's expressions, their demeanor and actions. The way you two looked at each other, your body language—there was electricity in the air." He rubbed his hands together. "Wait until I tell Becca. You can expect a visit from her. She'll want all the juicy details."

"There are no de—this is silly. I have work to do, so unless there's something you need." She motioned toward the door. He stood his ground.

"I do have a question for you." He took out his notebook.

"I'm free to talk until a customer comes in." She gave him a one-shoulder shrug.

"You probably know both Maggie's parents were killed in a car accident a few years ago, and she had no siblings. Did she ever mention an aunt, an uncle, cousins, any other relatives?"

Jillian leaned on the counter, placing her chin on her clasped hands. "Yes, I knew about her mom and dad. Their deaths devastated Maggie. She talked about her grandparents quite often, but they're deceased too. She never mentioned anyone else."

"I did a search for relatives and found nothing." Snatching a pen from the counter, he made a note. "There's no next of kin to notify of her death—sad, you know?"

"Maybe Maggie has no relatives, but she has a lot of people here in Willow Springs who cared about her." Jillian nibbled on her bottom lip. "With no family, who'll be responsible for her funeral?"

Ethan opened his mouth as she answered her own question. "Never mind. The other teachers and I will plan the memorial service. We were her family."

"Sure. If no one comes forward in a few days, the coroner will release her body, and you can make the arrangements. But who will pay for it?"

"Don't worry. We'll figure it out. Maggie will be laid to rest with respect and dignity. I'll make sure of it." A tear fell onto her collar.

"I appreciate your help." Ethan closed his notebook. "This can't be easy."

Jillian shook off his concern. "I'll do whatever I can to help find the monster who murdered Maggie. He stood there ..." She pointed at the spot. "... and threatened her life."

"We don't know your visitor was the one." He put up his hand to stop her interruption. "There's not enough evidence to draw any conclusions yet."

"Evidence. Are you kidding me? He came in my store asking questions. He threatened Maggie and me, then hours later she's dead. Of course, this guy is guilty." She clenched her fists to keep from grabbing Ethan and shaking him.

"Jilly, I promise to track this guy down. If he's responsible, it'll be my pleasure to throw him in jail. If he's not guilty, you can bet it will be someone Maggie knew—someone you might know too."

Nausea swept through her as the enormity of his words hit home.

Someone I know could be a murderer.

She shook the notion from her head. "No, Creepy Tattoo Guy did this. He's responsible for Maggie's death."

"Jilly, listen to me." He jiggled her arm. "You need to be careful."

"I heard you, and I will." She pushed him toward the door. "Now get out there, Detective, and ... detect. If you need me, I'll be here, trying to run my new business."

Thinking of poor Maggie.

CHAPTER FOUR

Jillian stayed busy all morning. She helped customers, rang up sales, and comforted former students who stopped in. Most had heard about Ms. Maggie and struggled with the loss. They shared hugs, tears, and memories of their favorite kindergarten teacher. After the tears were dried, the kids were solemn as they picked out books to buy and borrow. She watched the littles with a broken heart. They were too young to have death touch their lives this way.

She took Abbey and Hayley outside during a lull in business. Standing in the front yard, Jillian gazed around the neighborhood, looking from her perfect corner spot on Sweetwater and Magnolia Avenue. There were seven neighbors across the street and five more on the same side. She'd invited them all to the open house, and if memory served, every one of them had stopped by at some point in the evening.

Except for Mr. Erickson, the old coot.

He'd spent the evening camped out in his yard, yelling at her guests—"Keep off my lawn." He threatened to call the police on one poor woman who, according to him, parked too close to his grass. Even though the man had proven to be a handful, Jillian wanted the support of all her neighbors, including him. They'd gotten started off on the wrong foot yesterday. Maybe she would pay him a visit and try mending fences.

Her grumpy neighbor had a huge sweet tooth, judging by the way he'd inhaled three cinnamon rolls from Cate's bakery.

"That's it!" Jillian snapped her fingers. "I'll win him over with Grandma's triple chocolate chip cookies."

If I'm lucky, I can ask him a few questions about last night.

Maybe he saw something while sitting out on his lawn.

She urged the dogs toward the bookstore. "C'mon, you two. Who wants a treat for being good girls?"

Hearing the word *treat* elicited happy yips as Abbey and Hayley strained against the leashes. Dog biscuits were gobbled and naps resumed in record time.

She'd gone to the kitchen to box the cookies for Mr. Erickson when the screen door banged open. A raucous chorus of yips and yowls ensued. Who needed a bell above the door with those two in residence?

As her girls raced to greet friends and receive belly rubs, Trixie and Aunt Grace waltzed in arm-in-arm, giggling like schoolgirls.

"Hello, boss. How's business?" Trixie's eyes sparkled. Her friend and assistant knew she hated the way the word *boss* sounded. Her feisty assistant used it when feeling sassy to get a rise out of her. Jillian refused to take the bait.

"You two are awfully chummy—makes me think you're plotting something."

"Don't be suspicious, Kitten." Aunt Grace placed the greasy brown bag in her hands on the counter. "I came for a visit and ran into this sweet girl out front. Nothing more sinister."

Gathering her voluminous yellow skirt and dropping her matching purse, Grace plopped on the floor to shower attention on the two squirming dogs.

"Yeah, Jilly. Chill. Your aunt stopped by with lunch." Trixie pointed at the sack which emitted the most delicious smells. "Unless my nose fails me, we're having meatball subs from our favorite pizzeria."

"With extra parmesan and provolone." Aunt Grace stood, straightening the pleats in her skirt.

Jillian smelled the spicy sausage and garlicky tomato sauce from across the room. Her stomach grumbled. Ashamed for assuming the worst, she smiled and thanked Grace for the thoughtful surprise.

"I sensed you'd been too busy to eat, so I brought lunch to you, Kitten."

"That's so cool to have an aunt who can sense your needs." Trixie steepled her hands at Grace. "Can you adopt me, please? I'd love to be part of your family."

"Don't be ridiculous. You are family. You're the daughter I've always wished for." Grace hugged her. "Now, come. Have lunch while there are no customers. Can we eat in your office, Jilly?"

Trixie ducked her head, trying to hide the tear on her cheek. Jillian saw it, though. She knew being considered part of their family meant the world to her friend. Trixie had been adopted as an infant. She loved her family, but often felt like a square peg in a round hole. They were tall, blonde, and athletic. She was petite, dark-haired, and more cerebral than physical. Trixie had once tried to contact her birth mother, only to be harshly turned away. That kind of scar left its mark.

"Thank you for saying I'm like a daughter—means a lot." Trixie shuffled down the hall.

"Face it, Cupcake. You're one of us." Aunt Grace had chosen the nickname Cupcake for Trixie soon after they'd met, and she only gave family members these endearments. "I am confused by your current aura though—light pink with a slight tinge of blue. So, you're happy and sad at the same time."

Jillian cringed at her aunt's latest aura reading. Trixie's mouth dropped open.

"You're amazing. I am happy—happy to be working in this store and happy to be considered an honorary Edwards. There are times though when I get sad and have no idea why. My life is good."

"All will become clear." Grace patted her cheek. "In good time."

The three women chatted while enjoying their meatball subs and garden salads from Manelli's Italian Ristorante. When the bell above the door rang, Trixie popped up and ran to wait on the customers.

With a smug smile on her face, Aunt Grace munched on her sandwich.

"What's with the goofy grin?" Jillian eyed her aunt. "You look like a cat who swallowed a canary."

"I have no idea what you mean." Grace took a sip of tea.

"Oh, I'm sure you do. You've had a ridiculous smile on your face from the minute you sat down. What's going on? Does it have anything to do with a certain handsome man I saw you flirting with last night?"

"I saw him too." Trixie walked back in. "He was handsome—for someone his age. Good for you, Grace. Flirt away."

"I beg your pardon. A woman of my age does not flirt. That would be unbecoming and tacky." She adjusted her bracelets. "We socialize in a mature, adult manner."

"I stand corrected." Trixie stifled a snort. "Who was the handsome man you maturely socialized with?"

Sly glances passed between the younger women before they burst out laughing.

"Doctor Robert Madison is an oncologist from New York. He moved to Willow Springs to head the new cancer center at St. Frances. He's an ... interesting gentleman." Grace dabbed at her mouth with a napkin. Jillian and Trixie pounced on the chance to pelt her with questions.

"Where did you meet?"

"Is there an ex-wife spending his fortune somewhere?"

"Is he a good kisser?"

The final question sent Trixie into another fit of giggles.

"Girls, please. You're being absurd." Grace acted put out. "I met the doctor last week at the Corner Deli. We got there at the same time and asked for a table. They were crowded, so the waitress asked if we'd mind sitting together. We did and had a delightful time."

"Delightful, huh." Trixie waggled her eyebrows at Grace. "This will be a great story to tell your grandkids when they ask how you and grandpa met."

"Grandkids? Don't be silly." Grace patted Trixie on her knee. "Bryan will be the only one giving me grandkids someday. At least I hope he does."

"What happened next?" Jillian prodded.

"We talked, enjoyed breakfast, and parted ways. I didn't see him again until your party last night."

"Shoot." Trixie cursed in frustration. "You have nothing juicy to share? No steamy kisses or clandestine meetings?"

"You, my dear girl, read too many cheesy romance novels," Aunt Grace said. "He's a nice man. I may have more to tell you after our date on Wednesday."

"A date!" they shouted.

"Yes, He's taking me to a fancy French restaurant in the city."

"Good for you," Trixie congratulated her. "A hot date with a hot dude. You go, Grace. I wish I could get lucky and find a man for myself."

"You're such a sweetheart," Grace said. "I can't believe there's no one you're interested in."

"Well, there is one guy." Trixie's full red lips formed a pout. "He looks at me more like a sister than a girlfriend. Kind of frustrating really."

News of her friend's interest in someone shocked Jillian. She had so many questions about the mystery guy, but Aunt Grace jumped in first.

"Don't worry, Cupcake. You'll find Mr. Right. So will you, Kitten," she assured them. "The tea leaves have sent me a clear message. Wonderful things are in store for you girls. I'm glad I'll have a front row seat to watch romance blossom."

Trixie and Jillian exchanged wary looks, both choosing not to comment. Jillian would find out about Trixie's mystery man later.

This latest pronouncement from Aunt Grace left them shaking their heads. They finished their lunches in relative silence, each lost in her own thoughts. After they'd devoured the food, Grace cleaned the lunch mess, while the younger women waited on customers in the store. Grace came up front, wiping her hands on a cloth which she tossed to Trixie.

"I'm headed to book club at Marion Snyder's house. I hope she remembered to clean the litter boxes—there are six of them. The smell almost asphyxiated us last time we were there." Grace wrinkled her nose.

"Wait a sec, Aunt Grace. I'll walk you out." Jillian ducked into the kitchen and grabbed the cookies she'd boxed for her neighbor. "Trixie, I'm running across the street for a bit—won't be gone more than a half hour."

"Don't let the old guy get under your skin," Trixie called over her shoulder. "I hear he's a mean one to tangle with."

"No worries. I'll be fine." Jillian hoped this was true.

She took her aunt's arm. "Thanks again for bringing lunch. Have fun at book club."

"You're welcome, Kitten. And I'll have fun—if I'm not gasping for air." Grace giggled. "You behave yourself this afternoon."

"Who, me?" Jillian fluttered her eyelashes. "Of course, I will."

Bring on Mr. Erickson.

Jillian checked both ways before stepping into the street. They didn't need another tragedy on their hands. She plastered on her brightest smile. Reaching out to knock on Mr. Erickson's door, it was wrenched open as her knuckles met wood.

"Well, if it ain't the Book Lady." Mr. Erickson spat a chunk of tobacco onto the ground, missing her shoes by an inch. "What do you want? I ain't gonna change my mind— still don't want yer store disturbin' my neighborhood, so don't even bother."

Her first impression of her neighbor had been less than positive. This second encounter wasn't off to a great start either. The elderly man met her at the door wearing nothing but a wrinkled white T-shirt, dingy boxer shorts, and a scowl. His greeting was nothing short of rude. Jillian continued to smile, offering a reason for her visit.

"Good afternoon, Mr. Erickson. I was leaving the store and thought—"

"I don't give two toots what you thought." The old grump glared.

"Sir, we got off on the wrong foot yesterday. I came over this morning to try—"

"Stop right there, Book Lady. I said everything I had to say to you yesterday." He placed his arms across his scrawny chest as if he were drawing a line in the sand and daring her to make a move. "Go on back to yer shop and make sure all those loud, obnoxious kids stay the heck away from me."

Jillian took a deep breath. "Mr. Erickson, I brought you some cookies I baked. I noticed how much you liked my sister's cinnamon rolls, and she uses this cookie recipe in her bakery too." She offered him the box. "Since we're talking, let me assure you, Whimsy & Wonder will not cause a disruption to this neighborhood. As they told you themselves, your friends and neighbors are thrilled with my store."

"Them people may be my neighbors. You can bet they ain't my friends. Don't have use for any of 'em except maybe the lady who lives a couple of doors from yer shop—a real looker, she is." Mr. Erickson scratched himself in a place a person shouldn't scratch in front of others.

Jillian decided to retreat to avoid more uncomfortable moments like this one. As she took a step back, he grabbed her by the arm.

"Wait a minute, why'd you bring me these cookies? You can't buy my cooperation with a few cookies, ya know. Bet they're hard as hockey pucks." He snatched the box from her hands and tried to slam the door shut, almost catching the hand she placed on the door frame.

"Uh, Mr. Erickson. Could we chat for a moment about the accident last night?"

"Accident? Huh." He snorted. "That wasn't no accident. The black car came speedin' down the street—ran over the lady in the white coat. Never made no attempt to stop."

"You saw the car hit Maggie? Did you tell the police?"

"Po-lice! I ain't talkin' to no po-lice. They came knockin' on my door. I didn't answer. Nothin' good comes from talkin' to them." He spat another glob of tobacco in the dirt.

"Please, Mr. Erickson. The woman who died was my friend. She didn't deserve to be run down like that—no one does. The police need help finding the person who killed her." She pleaded with him, hoping to change his mind.

"Killed her? That poor girl is dead?" The old man's face paled. His voice cracked. "I watched 'em load her into the ambulance and take her away."

"Yes, she was alive when they left but died during surgery at the hospital." As the bad news hit home, his features softened slightly.

What'd you know? There might be some compassion under his crusty exterior after all.

"My best friend's husband is a detective on the police department. Would you speak with him about what you saw? Who knows, you might have important information to help solve this case."

"Me? Help the cops solve a case? Well, wouldn't it be somethin' if I did?" She could tell he'd warmed to the idea of working with the police. "I'll talk to this friend of yours— nobody else. And you better come with him. I ain't talkin' to no po-lice without a witness. Bring him here tomorrow mornin' at eleven o'clock. No promises though."

Jillian turned to go. He stopped her.

"Book Lady? Uh, thanks for the cookies." He slammed the door with a bang.

Go figure. He does have some manners.

Jillian scooted back across the street to check on the store. Things were quiet when she walked in. Trixie popped her head up from behind the counter.

"Today's bottom line is looking good, boss. Books are flying off the shelves. I'm busy ringing up the sales. Cha-Ching."

Things were under control. Jillian liked how that sounded.

"Hey, Trixie. I set a small box wrapped in gold paper with a black bow on the counter last night. Have you seen it?"

"Nope, sorry. I'll keep my eyes open." Her assistant scurried to help another customer.

Trixie didn't need her, so Jillian took the dogs outside before retiring to her office. The *Willow Springs Herald* had asked her to write a 1,200-word piece on the store. Jillian wrote several drafts before producing one she was satisfied with. She'd just hit 'send' to submit her article when Trixie knocked at the door.

"Excuse me, boss. Abbey's pacing and whining at the front door."

"I took the girls outside an hour ago. I can't believe she has to go again."

"You've been back here for almost three hours." Trixie pointed at the clock on the wall. "It's after five o'clock."

Peeking at her cellphone, she gasped. "Oh my gosh, poor Abbey. No wonder she's waiting at the door. Hayley, let's go find your sister."

Saying goodbye, Jillian gathered her things and headed out the door. Time had gotten away from her. She'd meant to call Ethan about their meeting with Mr. Erickson tomorrow.

I'll call him as soon as the pups and I get home.

While in her driveway unloading the girls, Jillian noticed a car pass by at a snail's pace, like they were lost or searching for an address. The car made a U-turn and came back by her house. She wondered why they didn't stop and ask for directions. As this car—a black SUV—went by a third time, a dark thought slithered through her mind, sending a chill skittering down her spine.

Her creepy visitor had driven a black SUV. Jillian wasn't sure what model. She'd never been good with cars. She'd never cared enough to learn. Maggie had been hit by a black SUV. Could it be a coincidence, or was this car trouble? She urged her girls toward the house.

The black car went around the corner, only to reappear a few seconds later, headed straight at her. She hoped her snap decision wasn't ill-advised as she headed toward the unfamiliar vehicle. As she approached, the driver rolled down the window. Her initial reaction was to duck and run—in case they had a weapon—until she saw the driver's face.

"Hello, Jillian. I hope you don't think I'm some crazy stalker driving by your house." Travis stared at her with a sheepish grin. "I left a friend's place down the street, spotted you and the dogs. I didn't want you to think I was some weirdo, so I drove on past. But I did want to talk to you, so I drove back around, which really made it appear—I don't know why I'm rambling—I'll stop now." He clamped his lips shut.

I'm glad I'm not the only person who babbles when nervous.

"Don't worry about it." She flashed a weak smile. "I freaked myself out. You drive a black SUV. The man who hit Maggie drove one too. I let my imagination run amok."

"Oh my gosh, I bet you were scared to death—uh—bad choice of words *again*." He smacked himself on the forehead. "I don't know what happens when I'm around you. I come off sounding like a big idiot. I should go." He started to raise the window.

"No, wait." She knocked on the glass. "You wanted to talk. Why don't you come in? My pups are tuckered out, and I'd like to lose these shoes. We could have something cold to drink."

"I don't want to bother you." He remained in his car. "I'm sure you're exhausted after your first day."

"No bother. I'd love the company. Coming home to an empty house isn't the most exciting way to end a day."

"If you're sure?"

"Positive." She headed for the house, hoping he'd follow.

Travis parked and joined them in the yard. Abbey and Hayley greeted him with enthusiasm. He sat on the grass, rewarding the dogs with belly rubs.

"They really like you." Her eyes widened in surprise. "That's a huge compliment, especially from Abbey. She's shy around most strangers."

"They must smell my dog, Blaze."

"You have a dog," she said. "What kind?"

"She's a six-month-old German shepherd I rescued from a fire at that abandoned warehouse out on Route 36. She and I hit it off. Now we're roommates."

Once inside, Abbey and Hayley scurried around, checking their territory to make certain it was undisturbed. Travis followed them, leaving his shoes at the door. He caught Jillian glance at his socked feet and rushed to explain.

"Sorry, force of habit. My mom insists no shoes in the house."

"Mine are coming off too." She placed her small ballet flats next to his very large work boots. "Please sit down. Make yourself comfortable. Can I bring you some iced tea?"

"Sounds great, thanks. Only if it's no trouble."

"No trouble at all." Jillian's exhaustion disappeared as she floated toward the kitchen.

Travis called to her from the living room. "I like how you've decorated this place. It's not girly or fussy like some women's places I've been in—not that I've been in many women's places."

She'd chosen soft shades of gray, cream, and blue throughout the apartment. The craftsman-style furniture was simple, yet comfortable, with pillows and a few blankets in darker shades of her chosen colors. Family photos were scattered amongst the books on her shelves, and a vase holding fresh flowers sat on the coffee table. Her favorite watercolor painting hung above the fireplace.

"Thanks. I filled it with colors and things I love." Returning with a tray of cookies and iced tea, Jillian was unnerved to find Travis looking so comfortable on her couch. Her hands shook when she handed him the glass.

"How long have you lived here?" He sipped his tea. "Is that peach I taste?"

"Five years, and yes, it is." Jillian curled on the loveseat covering her shoulders with a gray blanket. "This is my sister Cate's house. When I decided to open the bookstore, she and her husband, Wes, let me move into their finished basement to save money."

"That's great they could help you out. Even in a small town like Willow Springs, rent can be ridiculous. Plus, it's nice you get to live near family."

"Nice until you need some privacy." Jillian pointed toward the ceiling. "Having a sister living right upstairs can be a blessing and a curse."

"I wouldn't know—no sisters." He shrugged. "I have a younger brother who lives in the city. We don't get together as much as I'd like. He's a cop, and our schedules don't mesh."

"A cop and a firefighter? Wow, your parents must be proud."

"My mom brags to anyone who will listen. Dad rolls his eyes behind her back, but we know he's proud. He's a retired firefighter."

"You followed in his footsteps, which makes you— what's the phrase?" She snapped her fingers, trying to retrieve the correct words.

"A second-generation firefighter. Yeah, I am."

He hadn't yet helped himself to any cookies, so she held out the plate. "I baked these for my customers this morning. I left a few here. Please try one—unless you don't like sweets."

"I wouldn't say that." A grin spread across his face. "Ah, chocolate chip—my favorite." He bit into one and his grin got bigger. "These are amazing. I thought my mom's cookies were the best. You've proved me wrong—please don't tell her."

"I won't and thank you. I use my grandmother's recipe. She was the best cook I know. Cate uses this one and many others at Sugar & Spice."

"Wait. Your sister owns that bakery? I love her place. I stop at least twice a week for the incredible cinnamon rolls." He patted his stomach. "I have to work out for an extra hour after I eat them, but I can't help myself. They're so good."

The two of them sat in comfortable silence for a few minutes, enjoying the tea and cookies.

"You wanted to talk to me about something?" Curiosity forced Jillian to broach the subject.

"Right." Travis set his glass on a coaster. "After I left your store this morning, I remembered something I hadn't mentioned to you and Ethan. Your friend, Maggie, mumbled all the way to the hospital. She repeated, *black, red line, black, red line* several times. Do you have any idea what she meant?"

"No clue." She shook her head. "Ethan needs to know about this."

"Already told him. I talked to him earlier—at my friend's house." He popped the last cookie morsel into his mouth. "I ran into him there."

"Wait a minute. Your friend lives on my street?" She inched to the edge of her seat, letting the blanket fall from her shoulders.

"Yeah, the gray house with a red door on the corner."

"You've got to be kidding me." She heard the disbelief in her own voice. "Your friend is Bryan?"

"Yes, do you know him? He owns McGuire's, the Irish pub and restaurant over on Main Street. You ever been there?"

"Yeah, I've been there." She stifled a giggle.

"Did I say something funny?" His confused expression tickled her.

"McGuire's is my family's favorite place to eat. Great food, great service, and never-ending pints." She recited the pub's motto in her best Irish brogue. "Doesn't hurt the restaurant's been in my family for three generations."

"You're related to Bryan. How did I not know this?" Travis scratched his chin.

"Bryan and I are cousins. He's my Aunt Grace's only son. He's also known for being tight-lipped about his personal life."

"I've met your aunt. She once predicted I'd meet my soulmate on one of our fire calls." Travis smiled, shaking his head. "Hasn't happened yet. I'm still waiting. She makes Bryan nuts, but I think she's one spunky lady."

Jillian appreciated his assessment of her aunt, raising her opinion of him even higher.

He glanced at his watch. "Oh my gosh. I better get home. Blaze will need to go out before I have a mess to clean." He placed his empty glass on the tray. "Thanks for the tea and the amazing cookies. This gives me two excuses to go to your sister's bakery."

"I'll tell Cate to expect you." She walked Travis to the door. "I'm glad you stopped by. Your company was a wonderful surprise at the end of what's been a couple of long days. Thank you for that."

"My pleasure. Wish we could've solved the mystery of your friend's clue—you know—black, red line."

She wished the same. "That was an odd thing for her to say—must mean something. I pray Ethan has some luck finding out what she meant."

Ethan. She still hadn't called him.

Travis stepped closer and patted her arm. "He's a good cop, like you said earlier. He's got a solid reputation on the streets. He'll solve this case and find out who killed her."

"Thanks. That's nice hearing you have faith in him too."

He cleared his throat. "Well, I guess I should go. I'll stop by the store soon to pick out a birthday gift for my niece."

"Anytime." She smiled.

Standing in the doorway, Jillian waved as he drove away.

He reminds me of Bryan. No wonder they've become good friends.

CHAPTER FIVE

Jillian had trouble falling asleep for the second night in a row. She yawned from weariness, while her mind replayed her conversation with Travis. He'd been attentive to her girls, interested in her family, and easy to talk to. She'd learned he liked dogs, had a younger brother, a niece, and impeccable manners. Maybe she'd consider dating him if they'd met under different circumstances.

"What am I thinking? He didn't act the least bit attracted to me." She snorted at her own foolishness. "He was more interested in you two cuties."

Rubbing her sleeping pups' soft, warm bellies, Jillian snuggled deeper under the covers.

The next thing she knew, her alarm sent her straight up in bed. Seven o'clock. Silencing it with one hand, she marveled at how Abbey and Hayley slept through the noise.

She dragged herself from the warm bed, her thoughts on the day ahead. Arranging a visit between Ethan and Mr. Erickson was at the top of her to-do list. Her pleasant evening with Travis had lasted until after nine o'clock, making it too late to talk to Ethan. She'd take care of his call this morning along with ones to Cate and Amanda.

She hadn't spoken to her sisters in more than twenty-four hours—they never went this long without talking.

After a quick shower, she dressed and went into the kitchen for breakfast. A surprise waited at the table.

"What's the deal, Jilly?" Amanda said. "You too busy being a successful business owner to find time for us?" She tsked, tsked in mock disappointment.

"You could show more gratitude for everything we've done for you." Cate's eyes sparkled as she teased. "There's not one missed call from you on my voicemail."

"Why am I on the hot seat this morning? Did both your cell phones stop working? I don't believe I missed calls from you two, either." Jillian placed her hands on her hips and waited for their witty response. When none came, the three sisters burst out laughing. Once the giggles subsided, they got down to enjoying the breakfast Cate and Amanda had brought.

Cate arranged blueberry scones, cinnamon rolls, and banana bread fresh from the ovens at Sugar & Spice onto a blue and green platter she found in the cabinet. Amanda produced three steaming cups of chai tea latte from a cardboard carrier on the chair next to her. The scent of cinnamon filled the room. The sight and smell of the goodies brightened Jillian's morning—as did the ladies who brought them to her kitchen. She wouldn't give them the satisfaction of admitting it aloud.

"You two just barged in and made yourselves at home. Did you ever think to knock?" she baited them.

"Made myself at home? This *is* my home, or did you forget you live in my basement? Cate acted put out, but Jillian knew she was teasing.

"What if I had company? That could've been uncomfortable for you," she fired back.

"Who would you be with this early in the morning?" Amanda scoffed. "The only living, breathing things in your bed besides you are those dogs. And you're welcome. I took them outside, so they wouldn't pee on your floor."

"You mean my floor," Cate interjected.

"Keep talking, you two, and I won't tell you about my handsome visitor." She flashed a secretive grin in their direction.

"What handsome visitor?" Amanda frowned. "Have you met someone and didn't tell us?"

"Never mind." Jillian bit into her blueberry scone. She'd make them grovel first before telling them about Travis. "C'mon girls. Let's take a lap around the yard. Your aunties need time to adjust their attitude."

She stood in the cool autumn air and let her thoughts wander back to Maggie. Her friend would never enjoy another crisp fall morning like this one. She'd never meet a handsome man, fall in love, or get married and have children. Someone took those chances away from her. This made Jillian sad—and angry.

Her inner musings were cut short when Becca's car screeched to a stop in Cate's circle drive. She hopped out and slammed her door.

"Some friend you are, Jillian Edwards. You've been canoodling with a gorgeous guy, and I hear about it from my husband. Un-be-lievable." Becca paced the driveway.

Amanda came into the yard, struggling into her jacket. Cate trailed behind. "Geez, Becca. We could hear you all the way inside. Why are you yelling?"

"And who's canoodling with whom?" Cate asked.

Becca greeted them both before pointing at Cate. "Don't say a word. The morning baking is done. Your part-time employees can hold down the fort. This one ..." She jerked a thumb at Jillian. "... is holding out on us."

"Time to come clean, Sis. What's going on with you?" Amanda said. "Who's this guy Becca is yelling about?"

All three stared at Jillian.

"Fine. Can we go inside for this discussion? My tea is getting cold." Without waiting, she brushed by them and headed to the door—both dogs and her breakfast guests right behind her. They settled around the kitchen table with lattes and pastries, ready to hear about her mystery man.

Becca jumped right in. "C'mon, we aren't getting any younger waiting on you."

"I suppose you're talking about Travis." A sly grin spread across Jillian's face.

"Wait, who?" Amanda said. "How does Becca know this guy?"

"Ethan told me." Becca said. "He caught them having a cozy moment in the bookstore yesterday."

"Who is Travis?" Cate drummed her fingertips on the table.

"He's the cute firefighter you saw." Jillian pointed a finger at Cate. "Yes, he came into the store yesterday. No, we did not have a cozy moment."

Her sisters and friend wanted all the details, so from his driving past her house multiple times, to taking off his shoes, to snuggling with her pups, she left nothing out. There were gasps, sighs, and questions as the story unfolded.

"Wow. The open house on Friday, the first day of business on Saturday, and this. You've been a busy girl." Amanda gave Jillian a pat on the back.

"What? We've had two conversations. No big deal." She cringed, hearing herself make excuses.

"You should ask him out for dinner." Cate rubbed her hands together.

"I'm not asking him on a date."

"Why not?" Amanda demanded. "You haven't dated anyone since He-Whose-Name-Shall-Never-Pass-Our-Lips. I know he did a number on your heart making it tough for you to trust, but c'mon, Jilly. Don't you think it's time?"

"We'd be happy to help if you need a few pointers," Becca said. "We can get you through a first date."

"Me take advice from you?" Jillian shook her head. "Two old married women and my sister ..." She looked sharply at Amanda. "... who can't commit to her boyfriend of five years. No thanks. Besides, I don't even think he's interested in me."

"Ethan would disagree. He said and I quote, 'He was staring into her eyes. You could feel the sizzle in the air.'" Becca mimicked her husband's voice.

"Still not asking him on a date." Jillian stood her ground.

"Suit yourself," Becca said. "But you should know that when this date happens, and it will, we'll be here for breakfast the next morning for all the juicy details. I'll bring the pastries."

They finished breakfast, laughing and talking. Jillian gazed at her sisters and friend. She was blessed to have these amazing women in her life. They always had her back.

"Ladies, if you'll excuse me, I need to get to work. Unlike you three, I don't have the luxury of lazing around. I have a new business to run."

She gathered her things, whistled for her girls, and headed out the door. Unlike usual, it wasn't Amanda who delivered the parting shot—this time.

"Don't accuse me of being Aunt Grace," Cate called after her. "But this guy sounds perfect. You deserve to have the love of a handsome man in your life."

Jillian closed the door behind her, their laughter echoing in her ears.

Trixie had scored the nine-to-three shift today, but Jillian needed to work off some nervous energy. She planned to search for the elusive box Maggie had given her. With any luck, she'd find it and still have time to organize the last storage room before her shift began at one. Both activities would keep her hands and mind busy.

She called Ethan after parking in the garage behind the store. He didn't hide his displeasure that she'd questioned an eyewitness or waited so long to tell him. He balked at her tagging along on his interview. She assured him she hadn't searched for the information that had fallen into her lap.

Well, sort of.

"I'm sorry, Ethan. If you want to get anything out of him, I have to go with you. Mr. Erickson won't talk to you without a witness—his words, not mine. And he wants me. He's expecting us at eleven. He insisted on this time because it's after breakfast with his buddies at the Corner Deli and before his poker game at the VFW."

Ethan agreed to the meeting and ended the call.

Apparently, Mr. Erickson wasn't the only cranky one. Watching those two men lock horns would be entertaining.

Bringing the girls into the Main Room, Jillian was thrilled to find the store crowded. Children swarmed Abbey and Hayley clamoring to pet them. The sweet pups stood still and accepted all the love and affection being heaped on them by many pairs of small hands. With their tails wagging and bodies quivering, they sought cheeks to lavish kisses on with their tongues. Released from their leashes, they headed for their blankets behind the counter.

"I think it's cool you bring your dogs to the bookstore, Ms. Edwards." Levi, a former student, eyed the pups as they scurried away. "Wish I had a dog—my mom says I can't. My brother is allergic."

"You're welcome here anytime to love on mine, Levi. They enjoy the attention." She winked at him. "Let's find that *Dragon Master* book you wanted."

They pulled the book from a shelf in dire need of restocking. Grabbing some other books from her office, she filled the empty spots, while showing a little girl where the Dr. Seuss books were located. The young lady chose *Green Eggs and Ham* and took it to a cozy chair under the window. She pulled her little brother onto her lap and read to him.

Jillian watched the siblings together and put her hand on her chest, a warmth spreading there. This was how she'd pictured it—a store full of kids discovering the joy of reading. Her heart was full.

"Trixie, let me know if you get swamped and need help. I'll be upstairs."

When she'd bought this house, Jillian's plan was to put the bookstore on the first floor and to remodel the five rooms upstairs for her apartment. Until time and funds were available for that project, she used two of the spare bedrooms for storage.

She stepped into the room dubbed *The Book Bin*, marveling at the rich walnut cabinets and shelving units Ethan and Bryan had built. Someday, this would serve as an amazing walk-in closet. For now, it was crammed with boxes of books waiting to be unpacked and entered into inventory. She'd torn into her fourth carton when she heard heavy footsteps clomping on the stairs along with happy whistling.

"Hi, Ethan." She marked three books off the invoice and put them into the cabinet before shutting the door. "You're in a good mood."

"For now." He checked his watch. "Are you ready to go talk to this friend of yours? It's ten to eleven."

"Let me wash my hands." She took a deep breath. "I should warn you. Mr. Erickson is ... he—"

"What? He's a senile old man who thinks he knows more about the law than the police? If that's the case, I'm not sure I have the patience for this interview." He scowled.

She hesitated, not eager to share Mr. Erickson's less-than-positive qualities. "Yes, he's an old man. I don't believe he's senile, just gruff and grouchy." Jillian frowned. "He does have an aversion to the police and only agreed to talk to you because of me. Maybe you should handle him the way you would a hostile witness."

"Great. Perfect," he said. "This is not how I envisioned my day." The happy, whistling Ethan morphed into the cranky, irritable Ethan she'd spoken to on the phone.

"Suck it up, Detective. The goal is to get some information to help your case." She brushed past him into the hallway.

At eleven o'clock sharp, they knocked on Mr. Erickson's door. Within seconds, he jerked it open and glared at his guests. Unlike the last time he'd opened his door to her, he was fully dressed, wearing khaki pants and a blue plaid shirt, both wrinkled as if he'd slept in them. This was at least an improvement over yesterday's dingy skivvies.

"Mornin', Book Lady. And this must be your friend, The Cop. Well, don't stand there. Come in. I ain't got all day."

He stepped back, allowing them entrance. "My poker game starts in an hour. If I'm late, I don't get the good seat at the table. That rat, Harvey, will plant his fat behind in it."

Jillian cringed at the old man's crudeness, but chose to ignore him. Ethan let out a chuckle.

Grumbling the whole way, the old man shuffled into his dark living room, which smelled of cigars and stale food. He plopped into a well-worn leather recliner and motioned for them to sit on the couch. Everything—his chair, the couch, the carpet, the curtains—was brown. She wondered whether this was by choice or due to years of foul smoke from his cigars. Ethan chose a seat across from his host, shooting a dubious look in her direction.

"I'm Detective Harden." He stuck out his hand. The old man ignored the gesture. "Not a handshaker. Got it. Thank you for agreeing to answer some questions."

"Save your breath." Mr. Erickson leaned forward, putting his hands on his knees. "I'll tell you what I saw. You write it down in yer notebook. You got one, don't ya? All the cops on TV do."

Ethan took one from his pocket and showed his witness. Mr. Erickson smirked.

"So, it happened like this. I was sittin' out in the yard makin' sure none of her guests parked on my grass." He gestured at Jillian with a gnarled finger. "She was havin' that shindig at her store—what's it called—Wimpy & Worthless?" He snickered at his joke.

"Whimsy & Wonder," Jillian corrected him in her best teacher voice.

Act like a child. I'll treat you like one.

"Yeah, whatever. She sent me an invite to her little get-together. I didn't go. I don't care to be around people."

"Hmm, I never would've guessed." Ethan mumbled under his breath. The older man didn't notice. Or he didn't hear.

"I'll admit I was bein' nosy watchin' the comin's and goin's of yer party." Mr. Erickson winked at her. "Yer guests were more interestin' than the fight on TV. TKO in the first fifteen seconds—bunch a baloney. By ten o'clock, her party was breakin' up, and people was leavin'."

Ethan scribbled as fast as the man talked. Jillian applauded his efforts, as this might be his only shot at an interview.

"I was watchin' some purty ladies sayin' goodbye. One was a real cutie—curly red hair wearin' a white coat—she left the others and started across the street. All of a sudden, this black car, parked a few houses down and across from mine, come speedin' down the street. The redhead froze in the road. I hollered, 'Move, lady. Move'. She didn't and then—BAM! The car plowed right into her. She flew in the air, legs and arms flailing. Her body landed in the intersection. The bum didn't even stop—turned the corner and took off down Sweetwater. End of story." The old man stood, heading for the door.

"Um, sir, I have a few more questions," Ethan said.

"Better make it snappy. We may not have a lot of time." He chuckled and patted his belly. "The spicy breakfast burrito I ate this mornin' is startin' to talk back."

Ethan huffed out a breath. "The black car was parked down the street. Do you have any idea how long it had been there?"

"Yep. I saw it park at the curb at the beginnin' of the party around seven."

"Did you notice anything unusual—with the car, I mean?" Ethan said.

"You mean other than sittin' there for three hours without movin'?" Mr. Erickson snorted. "The right headlight was out and there was a red stripe down the driver's side."

"Great." Ethan made more notes. "Is there anything else?"

"What kind of detective are you, son? Ain't ya gonna ask me if I saw the guy sittin' in the car?"

Ethan clenched and unclenched his jaw. "Are you saying you *did* see him? You're sure a man drove the car?"

Jillian could tell the men were losing patience with each other. Ethan better finish soon, for both their sakes.

"Yes, I saw him." Mr. Erickson took a moment to light a cigar. "And yes, it was a man—well—I'm almost sure the driver was a man. Hard to tell with the baseball cap and sunglasses. Don't know why the heck he was wearin' them at night." Mr. Erickson mumbled. "Somethin' felt off—him sittin' there for hours. I wanted to figger out what he was doin', so I took a little stroll past him and his car."

The elderly man's hutzpah amazed Jillian. He was a tough old bird who'd probably been a force to be reckoned with back in the day. And his memory. Ethan should be thrilled with all this information.

"I walked by. He looked my way. I nodded at the young man who shot me a nasty snarl. I hightailed it back home—not because he scared me or anything." Mr. Erickson tapped his temple. "I made a lotta mental notes. He was a white guy—I'm purty sure—kinda scrawny, red ball cap, sunglasses, and wearing one of them puffy vests the kids wear these days. He was smokin' and drinkin' somethin' from a gray thermos." Mr. Erickson slammed his fist down on the coffee table. "The bastard ran down that poor girl and killed her. You best find 'im and make 'im pay."

Ethan shoved the notebook back in his pocket. "Sir, you've been an excellent witness. You have my promise we'll find the person who did this. If I need to come back and ask more questions as the investigation progresses, I'd appreciate you answering the door."

"Only if you bring this cutie with ya." He winked at Jillian. "And only if she brings some more cookies. They were mighty tasty."

His attitude toward me sure has changed. I knew those cookies would do the trick.

"I'm so glad you liked them, Mr. Erickson. I promise to bake for you again soon." His flirtatiousness amused her.

Ethan stood to leave with Jillian following his lead. Her feisty neighbor grabbed Ethan's sleeve and tugged him backward. The older man whispered in the younger man's ear. She went ahead and gave the men their privacy.

Ethan came out of the house chuckling.

"Do I detect a smile on your face, Detective? I thought you'd be a royal grouch after you interviewed Mr. Erickson."

"He's a grumpy, old dude with a wicked sense of humor." He took her arm and ushered her across the street.

She wondered what Mr. Erickson had done or said, but decided it was best not to ask. Some things were better left a secret.

CHAPTER SIX

Jillian checked in with Trixie, making sure her pups were asleep. When all proved well, she pushed Ethan into her office before exploding with excitement.

"Mr. Erickson was incredible—remembering so many details—and his description of the driver sounded like my creepy guy."

"Hold on a minute. Slow down." Ethan waved his hands. "Yes, the old man gave me some information I hadn't heard, and I'll check out everything he said. His description of the driver disappointed—a bit too generic. He didn't mention any tattoos or scars like you saw. He couldn't even be sure the suspect was a man."

Her enthusiasm deflated. She searched for a solid lead to grasp.

"Mr. Erickson saw a red line on the side of the black SUV. That tip should help identify the vehicle, right?" She paced in the cramped space. "Travis said Maggie mumbled 'red line'. She must've seen the one on the car that hit her."

"Could be. Anything is possible, I guess." He scrubbed at his face. "However, I need *solid* evidence. A dying woman's ramblings aren't enough to go on."

Jillian sucked in her breath at his 'dying woman' comment.

Trixie poked her head into the office.

"Excuse me, boss. There's a cute guy out front asking for you. What should I tell him?"

A cute guy. "Tell him I'll be there in a minute." Jillian hoped she knew who waited for her.

Trixie nodded and ducked from the doorway.

Ethan's soft chuckle caught Jillian's attention. "Why are you laughing?"

"We both know who's here and why." He waved her toward the door. "Go on, get out there. He's waiting. Maybe he's here to ask you on a date."

"If you're talking about Travis, he's here to pick out a birthday present for his niece. Not to ask me on a date." She did take a minute to add some lip gloss—just in case.

"That's a matter of time, in my opinion." Ethan leaned back against the wall. "I told Becca there's a spark between you and the lieutenant. We're wondering when the two of you will figure it out."

"Thanks, by the way." She fisted her hands on her hips. "Your big mouth sent Becca flying to my house this morning, ranting and raving at me. Couldn't keep it to yourself, huh?"

"Nope. Marriage Rule #36—a husband must tell his wife when her best friend is making googly eyes at a handsome man. Wait until I tell her you've had two guys hitting on you this week."

"Travis wasn't hitting on—wait—two guys? What do you mean?" Jillian frowned.

"Old man Erickson admired your backside as you left the room. He told me if he were only twenty years younger ..."

"Twenty?" Jillian shuddered. "More like sixty. He must be in his nineties." She stalked out of her office to greet her visitor. Her heart skipped a beat when she saw Travis.

He leaned over the oak counter, whispering to Abbey and Hayley. She imagined them wiggling and wagging their tiny tails, hanging on his every word. As she entered the Main Room, his gaze rose to meet hers, sending goosebumps skittering down her arms.

"Hey." His deep voice wrapped around her like a warm blanket. "Would this be a good time to find a gift for my niece?"

"Perfect," Jillian said. "Tell me a little about her. That will help me pick the right books for her."

"Her name is Emma. She'll be nine next week. My sister-in-law says she's reading well above her grade. She's a self-proclaimed tomboy and loves animals."

"Great. Let's find chapter books with animals as the main characters."

She showed Travis shelves on the back wall stuffed with books to interest Emma, pointing out a few personal favorites—*Ralph S. Mouse, Mrs. Frisby and the Rats of NIMH, Mr. Popper's Penguins*, and of course, *Charlotte's Web*.

He chose them all, plus a couple he found on his own.

"Emma might also enjoy the arts and crafts activity—since she'll have the book." Jillian tapped a fingernail on the picture of Wilbur, the pig. "Entering her in my art class could be part of her gift and would be a fun surprise for her birthday. I mean, if she lives close enough."

Travis didn't hesitate to write Emma's name on the class roster. "I'll check with my sister-in-law, but I'm sure she'll let Emma spend the day with me. I can bring her to the store. She'll love this place."

"With these books and the arts and crafts activity, she'll love you and tell everyone you're her favorite uncle."

"I'm her only uncle."

Jillian led Travis to the counter. "We can gift wrap the books and print out a gift certificate for the class if you'd like."

"I'd appreciate it. I'm not good with wrapping paper. Or tape. Or bows," he added with a laugh. "My gifts look like my three-year-old nephew wrapped them."

There'd been no other customers in the store while she'd helped Travis. Ethan and Trixie had stood at the counter watching them the entire time. Trixie ogled the lieutenant while Ethan grinned like the Cheshire Cat. Placing the books on the counter, Jillian gave them both an irritated stare.

"Trixie, this is Travis Stevens. He's a lieutenant on the Willow Springs Fire Department. He responded to the 9-1-1 call when the car hit Maggie."

Her comment hit its mark and wiped the smile from Trixie's face. Friday night's event was enough to upset anyone. "Travis, this is my assistant, Trixie."

"Nice to meet you," he said. "You two have a great place here."

"Thanks, and it's nice to meet you too." Trixie offered her brightest smile. "I'd be happy to wrap these gifts for your niece."

"Nothing too girlie," Jillian instructed Trixie. "Please print a certificate for the art class and tuck it inside the book."

"Sure thing, boss." Trixie grabbed some wrapping paper. "I'll have everything ready in a jiffy."

"Take your time," Ethan said. "I need to talk to Jillian and Travis for a quick minute."

He motioned for them to follow him into the Lending Library. The room was empty—perfect for a private conversation.

"This is a great idea, Ethan. Maybe we could share what we learned when we chatted with Mr. Erickson." Jillian's eyes locked on Ethan's face. "I mean, Travis was one of the last people to talk to Maggie before she died. Maybe hearing our information will help him remember something else she might have said."

"Taking charge of my investigation, Jilly?" Ethan growled.

"Absolutely not. Trying to be helpful is all, Detective."

He hesitated only a moment. "I hate to admit this—especially to you, Jilly. Sharing our info is exactly why I brought you both in here."

Between them, they made quick work of bringing Travis up to speed. He listened, stopping Ethan once to clarify something.

"You think Maggie muttered 'red line' because she saw one somewhere on the car that hit her?"

"It's a possible theory," Ethan said. "I'll ask the local garages and custom shops if anyone owns a vehicle fitting the description."

Travis rubbed his forehead with his eyes scrunched shut. Jillian moved a step closer, putting a hand on his arm.

"Are you all right?"

"There's something I should tell you." He took a deep breath and cleared his throat. "Some guys at the fire department took our vehicles to Shorty's Garage about a month ago. He detailed a red stripe down the driver's side of our cars. He stenciled the guy's Engine Company number at the end of the stripe as a show of solidarity, you know, to the brotherhood."

Jillian's heart went out to Travis. Sharing this detail, which pointed the finger toward someone he cared about, couldn't have been easy.

"Travis, I hate to ask. Could any of these guys have had a problem with Maggie? Anyone who could be capable of this?"

"No way." Travis shook his head. "Absolutely not. We take an oath to save lives. We risk ours to keep other people safe. No brother or sister in the fire service would take another life."

"I hear you. I still have to check out this lead. How many cars were detailed?"

"I don't know—a dozen, maybe more—including mine," Travis said. "Put me on the list if you're investigating all the guys with black SUVs."

"Don't be silly." Jillian's tone sounded defensive, even to her own ears. "Ethan won't do that. You couldn't be a suspect. You were on duty and responded to the emergency."

"Sorry, I have to check his vehicle too." Ethan contradicted her. "Everyone's car has to be examined if only to rule them out. This is how it works, Jilly. I have to investigate all possible suspects before they can be eliminated." She opened her mouth to protest. His intimidating cop face stopped her. "Nope. Department policy—like it or not."

"I don't expect special treatment. If Ethan investigates the other guys, it's only fair I'm included." Travis held his head high. "I have nothing to hide. I'm fine with the official investigation."

"LT, the information we shared is part of an ongoing case," Ethan said. "I have to ask you to keep it to yourself, please."

"I won't say a word." Travis moved to face Jillian. His tone was formal and stiff. "I want to say—again—how sorry I am your friend was killed. I promise you no one on the department was responsible for her death."

He gathered his niece's gifts and left the bookstore without another word. Jillian watched him go.

"I hate that your investigation has led a trail straight to the people Travis cares for. Facing the possibility a friend is involved can't be easy for him."

"I'm sorry, Jilly. Trust me, I don't like prying into the firefighters' private lives. There's an unspoken code of cooperation and respect between us. We work scenes together. We have each other's backs. Some will consider this investigation a betrayal of trust." He stared at the floor for a moment, then shook himself out of his funk. "I better go—lots of leads to check out."

She patted him on the back. "You can do this. I know you'll find Maggie's killer soon."

"From your lips to his ears." Ethan motioned skyward. "Because I'm going to need all the help I can get on this one."

"I'm here if you need me," she said.

"I didn't mean *your* help."

"Okay, I just thought—"

"No. Stay out of this." He pointed his finger as he delivered his warning. "I don't want you involved."

Too bad, buddy. I became involved when someone killed my friend.

He stalked out, bumping into Trixie on his way.

"Whoa, what's his deal?" She grimaced.

"He's being a typical stubborn male," Jillian said.

"Mm-hmm. What did you do to aggravate him?" Trixie cast an accusing stare.

"Me?" She placed a hand to her heart. "I didn't do a thing."

CHAPTER SEVEN

With Ethan and Travis gone, Jillian grabbed the dogs' leads. The sound of the jingling leashes caused a flurry of movement as Hayley and Abbey rushed from behind the counter.

"I'm taking the girls around the block." She herded them to the door.

"No worries, boss. I have everything under control." Trixie winked.

"Ugh. I hate when you call me that."

"I know." Trixie giggled before flitting off to help a customer. "Enjoy your walk—*boss*."

Jillian sighed, mumbling to herself. "Some things never change."

She zipped her jacket against a cool breeze, heading east on Magnolia. As the trek took them south onto Sweetwater, a chill permeated her body, having nothing to do with the temperature in the air. Her current steps traced the same path the driver of the black SUV took after hitting Maggie, causing Jillian to consider the recent information they'd found.

The driver's description might not get them far, but there could only be so many black SUVs with the red stripe both Maggie and Mr. Erickson mentioned. Travis had given Ethan a place to start on the next leg of his investigation. She hoped the trail didn't lead to any fellow firefighters. She refused to believe someone sworn to save lives would do something this heinous.

The pups urged her back toward the bookstore as soon as they rounded the block. Still lost in her thoughts, it took a few moments to realize someone was calling out to her.

"Excuse me, Ms. Edwards." A petite silver-haired woman in a navy velour jogging suit rushed from the white, colonial-style house a few doors down from Whimsy & Wonder, waving her arms.

Jillian stopped the pups, making them sit. In their exuberance to meet and greet people, Abbey and Hayley sometimes forgot their manners and jumped onto the poor unsuspecting person. A light wind could knock down this diminutive woman. She'd be no match for their enthusiasm.

"Hello." She searched her memory for the woman's name. "I'm happy to see you again, Mrs. Taylor."

"Oh, you're sweet to remember an old lady." The woman smoothed down her flyaway hair. "I'm glad I caught you. I wanted to thank you for the invitation to your open house. Everyone seemed to have a wonderful time, myself included. The children are going to love your store."

"We hope so." Jillian smiled. "And please let me assure you, we intend to be respectful neighbors. A few residents have concerns about noise and traffic—"

"Dear girl." Mrs. Taylor raised a hand to stop her. "You've been listening to cranky old Mr. Erickson. He does not speak for the rest of us on this block. We aren't the least bit concerned with noise or traffic. Most of the homeowners on this block are older folks. We could use some excitement around here." A mischievous grin crossed her face.

I'm going to like this sweet lady. She has spunk like Aunt Grace.

"Speaking of excitement—oh, that's a poor choice of words." Mrs. Taylor's grin faded. "I heard a young woman was killed Friday night outside your store. Word has it she taught kindergarten at the school, and you two were friends. I'm very sorry for your loss, dear."

"Thank you. Maggie was a good friend. She will be missed by so many people."

"I'm not sure, but I may have witnessed something Friday night—I don't know—it might be important." The older woman took a deep breath. "You're friends with the handsome police officer. I thought I could tell you what I saw, and you could share the information with him."

"Mrs. Taylor, that's not how it works. The police will want to speak to you themselves. I can let Detective Harden know you'd like to talk."

"I don't want to bother your young man. I'm sure he's busy. You can tell him for me, all right?"

"I'm sorry, Mrs. Taylor." Jillian shook her head. "My friend, Ethan, will need to talk to you himself. I'd be happy to arrange a meeting."

He probably won't be happy with me for doing this again.

"I ... don't ... know." She twisted the hem of her jacket. "Talking to the police makes me nervous. Maybe if you brought your young man to my house for tea this afternoon—say three o'clock?"

"I'll call him right now." Jillian took out her phone, waiting three rings for him to answer.

"You've got to be kidding. Another elderly neighbor has come to you with information. When is this going to stop?" He complained in her ear.

She waited him out.

93

"Fine. I'll be there."

He ended the call without another word.

Hmm, someone's grumpy today.

"All set," Jillian said. "I'll bring Ethan for tea at three."

"Wonderful. I'll hurry home and straighten the living room. A messy home when guests are expected is bad manners." The prospect of company for tea had soothed Mrs. Taylor's nerves. "I'll steep a pot of lavender tea to go with the lemon cookies I baked this morning. Oh, this will be such fun. See you soon, dear."

Watching her kind neighbor hustle into her house, something she'd said struck Jillian. She called Ethan her young man—twice.

"Oh my gosh, she thinks he's my boyfriend." Jillian doubled over with laughter. "I'll have to set the record straight. But I will tell Becca. She'll love holding this over his head."

She turned the dogs toward the store. There was work to do before any more of this day got away from her.

Lord, please let this tea party yield clues to Maggie's killer.

Jillian sat behind her tidy desk in her office thumbing through children's book catalogs. She glanced up as the door creaked open. She greeted Ethan.

"Hello there, my young man. I'm glad you're on time for tea with my sweet neighbor." She chuckled at the puzzled expression on his face.

"What's so funny?" He narrowed his eyes. "Why did you call me your young man?"

She let out a heavy sigh. "Sorry, I'm being silly. I do need to explain something before we visit Mrs. Taylor for tea."

"Yeah, about that. Do I really have to drink tea?" He made a face, sticking out his tongue.

"Oh, quit being a baby. You'll sip the lavender tea—and listen."

"*Lavender*? That's a color, not a tea."

Jillian controlled her laughter, and her firm teacher voice slipped out once again. "You should also know Mrs. Taylor made lemon cookies." Her hand flew up to stop him. "I know—you *hate* lemons."

"This lady better have some helpful info. I'd hate to sacrifice my taste buds for nothing."

"I have no idea what she's going to say. You should know she thinks you're my *young man*. She said it several times when we spoke earlier." She laughed out loud when his mouth dropped open.

"The old lady thinks we're dating? Did you tell her I'm married to your best friend?"

"Don't call her an old lady—that's rude. And no," Jillian continued, "I didn't tell her. Mrs. Taylor is a sweet woman. Contradicting her would be like correcting your grandmother." She grabbed her jacket from the back of her chair.

"My grandmother wouldn't make me drink lavender tea and eat lemon cookies," Ethan grumbled under his breath.

"Let's go, Detective." She grabbed his sleeve. "Being late to a tea party is considered poor manners."

They stood at Mrs. Taylor's door at two fifty-nine. The older woman opened the door as if she'd been watching for them. She'd changed from her blue jogging suit into a trim yellow dress reminiscent of June Cleaver.

"Hello there, you two." Mrs. Taylor ushered them into her home, which smelled like moth balls and lemon Pledge. "I appreciate young people who value being punctual." She invited them into her sitting room and showed them to a burgundy velvet love seat under the window—faded and worn, yet surprisingly comfortable.

"Mrs. Taylor, your home is lovely." Jillian motioned around the room. "I adore these older houses. They're filled with such character."

"Character? Well, that's one way of putting it. My home is old—falling apart in some places and needs work—much like me." Their hostess chuckled. "All of that really doesn't matter. The house is mine, and it suits me."

"Your home is warm and charming. When I searched for the right location for my store, I was drawn to this neighborhood. The houses on this street have good bones and wonderful curb appeal. This one was perfect—right on the corner and close to Main Street and all the other businesses."

Ethan cleared his throat, a reminder of his presence in the room.

"Oops, sorry. Where are my manners?" Jillian introduced him to Mrs. Taylor, mentioning he was the detective on this case and her best friend's husband.

"Aren't I a silly goose?" Mrs. Taylor fluttered her hands. "I thought you two were—what do you young people call it—an item. I've noticed you together on many occasions. I'm sorry I made the wrong assumption."

"Not a problem, Mrs. Taylor," Ethan assured her.

"Please call me Lizzie. Mrs. Taylor sounds too formal." She busied herself pouring their tea, adding small amounts of honey and cream. She placed their delicate cups on saucers with two lemon cookies on the side. Ethan sipped his tea and nibbled a cookie as instructed. He wasted no time with small talk.

"Mrs. Taylor ...

She tsk-tsked him.

"I'm sorry—Lizzie. You saw something Friday night?"

"I'm not sure—maybe." She fidgeted with her teacup.

"Take your time and tell me what you saw."

Ethan's attempt to put her at ease appeared to work. Mrs. Taylor took a steadying breath and began her story. "I left the bookstore's open house a little after eight. A black SUV sat parked in front of my house. The man in the driver's seat smoked a cigarette and watched the people coming and going from the party. He made me nervous." Her words came out in a tumble.

"Could you describe him?" Ethan said.

"Oh yes. He was thin, had a scruffy beard, and wore a ball cap with some kind of dark puffy coat." The older woman sipped her tea. "When I passed the man's car, I tried being friendly, smiling at him. He ignored me. When he wouldn't make eye contact, I knew he was up to no good. Plus, people with snake tattoos are suspicious in my book."

"He had a snake tattoo. On which arm?" Ethan asked.

"Let me think. Hmm ... yes, it was on his right forearm. The snake was red and black, coiled like it was going to strike." Mrs. Taylor shuddered. "I don't like snakes."

Hearing the tattoo description match the one her unwelcome visitor sported caused Jillian to choke on her tea. She grabbed a napkin and dabbed at the dribbles on her shirt.

"Are you all right, dear?" Mrs. Taylor's voice oozed concern.

"I'm fine. Please go on." Jillian perched on the edge of her seat, dying to interject herself into this conversation.

Nope, I can't. Ethan won't appreciate the intrusion.

"This is all helpful, Lizzie. I'm curious, though. By the time you left the party, it was dark out. How could you notice the snake in such detail?"

Mrs. Taylor pointed out the window. "The car sat right under that streetlamp."

"You were on the passenger side of the car?" Ethan scribbled something in his notebook.

"Why, yes, the sidewalk is on that side. I'd never walk in the street—it's not safe."

"Did you notice anything else?" Jillian couldn't hold the question in.

Oops, I couldn't help myself.

She mouthed *sorry* to Ethan.

"I'm afraid not. I wish I'd thought to write down the license plate." Mrs. Taylor shook her head. "Sometimes, I can be so scattered."

"Lizzie, I have one more question." Ethan cocked his head. "Why didn't you share this with the police officer who knocked on your door Friday night?"

"I wasn't home. My daughter, Lily, came to get me at eight-thirty to spend the weekend with her in Stonefield. I arrived home this morning and read about the accident in the paper. I'd already decided to speak to Jillian when I saw her with those sweet dogs of hers."

Small talk ensued for a few more minutes. When the teacups were empty, they thanked Mrs. Taylor for her hospitality.

"This has been lovely, Lizzie." Jillian put her arm around the woman's shoulders. "I'm afraid I have to leave. This is my night to close the store, so I need to relieve my friend Trixie."

"I should go too." Ethan put his cup and saucer on the table. "I appreciate you bringing this information to me,

Lizzie. Call me if anything else comes to mind." He handed her his business card.

Ethan made a hasty retreat as they left Mrs. Taylor's house. Not a word to Jillian.

"Hmm, someone's in a hurry to check out those new leads. He could've at least said thank you," she muttered.

Climbing the front steps to Whimsy & Wonder, Jillian crossed her fingers and whispered a prayer.

"May wherever he's headed yield positive results. We need a break in this case."

CHAPTER EIGHT

Expecting her bookstore to be calm and quiet, Jillian pushed open the door to anything but a peaceful scene. Aunt Grace, a vision in deep purple, sat in a child-sized chair weeping into a lilac handkerchief while Joy patted her back. Bryan towered above his mother, yelling at the top of his lungs. A rack of paperbacks lay scattered across the colorful carpet. The pups, frightened by Bryan's shouting, paced and whimpered. Trixie sat on the floor doing her best to calm them.

On the bright side—there were no customers to witness this family drama.

Jillian exhaled a deep breath before yelling above Bryan's tirade.

"What's going on? I leave for an hour and chaos breaks loose." She planted her fisted hands on her hips. "Somebody tell me what happened."

Everyone spoke at the same time.

"Hey, hey, hey." She waved her arms to attract their attention. "Knock. It. Off. If a customer comes in, they'll get scared away by my crazy family."

Her outburst stunned them into silence. She'd never raised her voice to them. Her mother sank into a chair next to Grace, who tried her best to stifle future sobs. Bryan jammed his hands in his pockets and paced the floor. Trixie excused herself from the situation by taking the dogs outside.

"I need you to tell me what happened—one at a time. Who wants to go first?" She searched their faces.

"I will." Her mom volunteered. "Grace and I stopped in to say hello. We were only going to stay a few minutes. I stopped at the counter to talk to Trixie and pet my grand puppies. Grace searched for some books for Aubrey and Laney. That's when it happened."

"What happened?" Jillian held out her hands.

"A woman tapped my shoulder and asked me a question." Aunt Grace jumped into the story.

"Sounds harmless enough. What did she want?"

"You," her aunt said. "She wanted to talk to you."

"What did you say to her?"

"Nothing. The moment I saw her, I screamed—thought I was face to face with your friend Maggie's ghost. My scream startled her, and she backed into the bookrack." Grace pointed to the mess on the floor.

"Your screaming startled everybody." Bryan snarled at his mother. Facing Jillian, he said, "I stopped by to fix your screen door, to keep it from banging so hard. When I walked in, Mom was yelling at some woman. Poor lady couldn't escape from here fast enough. She's one customer who'll never darken your doorstep again."

"I'm sorry, Kitten. She was the spitting image of Maggie. I thought I was having a vision—your friend communicating with me from the beyond. I've never been contacted by the recently deceased, so I freaked out." Grace wiped away a stray tear.

"Did you talk to this woman? Did you see her?" Jillian stared at her mother and cousin.

"Aunt Joy had her back to the lady. She ran by me so fast I couldn't tell you what she looked like." Bryan shrugged, letting his arms drop to his sides.

Jillian could understand her aunt's reaction. Seeing someone resembling Maggie in her store would be unsettling. She'd have freaked out too. There was no way this mysterious woman's appearance in town was a coincidence.

"Who is she? Why does she want to talk to me?"

No one answered.

Jillian bent to pick up the books strewn all over the floor. "I need to put this room back together and get some work done. Trixie's shift is over, and I'm sending her home. Bryan, I'd appreciate it if you'd stay to fix the door. You two ..." She pointed at her mom and aunt. "... thank you for checking in. Everything is under control." She motioned to the door.

"We can't leave, Kitten. We need to find out who this woman is *if* she wasn't the spirit of your friend." Aunt Grace objected to leaving the store without solving this mystery.

Bryan tensed and opened his mouth, shut it, and stalked from the room.

"Grace, we should go—Jilly has a business to run." Joy moved toward the door.

Aunt Grace refused to budge. "But that woman—"

"I'm sure the resemblance to Maggie was a fluke. After her death, we're all a bit on edge. Perhaps you overreacted," Joy said.

"I most certainly did not overreact." Grace stamped her foot. "She was the spitting image of the poor dead girl. They could be twins. And another thing. Her aura was black.

This means unreleased anger and grief. She came here for answers, and she thinks you have them." She pointed a finger at Jillian.

Grace slung her purple hobo bag over one shoulder. Before opening the door, she stopped to give one last warning to Jillian. "Mark my words. The woman will come again. She'll bring nothing but trouble. You watch your back, Kitten."

Grace jerked open the door and marched out with her signature floral scent and Joy trailing behind her. Trixie chose the same moment to bring the pups inside and had a near collision with the departing duo.

Trixie whirled out of the way. "Your aunt is madder than a hornet."

"She'll recover," Jillian muttered. "My aunt can create drama wherever she goes."

"You weren't here. The lady who spooked your aunt looked exactly like Maggie. Uncanny resemblance. Creeped me out." Trixie shuddered.

"Wait, you saw her?"

"Sure, I greeted her when she came in. She ignored me and approached Grace, tapping her on the shoulder. Your aunt took one look and screamed bloody murder."

"So, you agree she resembled Maggie?"

"They could've been twins. Spooky." Trixie rubbed her arms. "Maybe she read Maggie's obituary in today's paper."

"Her obituary is in the paper?" Jillian grabbed their copy off the counter.

"Page eight," Trixie offered. "I'm telling you. This woman has to be a relative—same red curly hair, same green eyes, and same porcelain skin. No doubt in my mind."

Had this woman read the article, seen Maggie's photo? Could she be a relative? So many unanswered questions.

Jillian hated to add one more thing to his plate, but Ethan needed to know she'd had another strange visitor. She called, getting his voicemail. She pushed End without leaving a message.

"Ethan didn't answer?" Trixie said.

"How'd you know I called Ethan?"

"Stands to reason. He'd want to hear Grace's ghost story."

"I'll call him when I get home from work. He should hear this from me, not on his voicemail."

CHAPTER NINE

Jillian unlocked her door at half past eight and called Ethan. She dreaded disturbing him since bedtime came early at the Harden house. Becca's day at the bakery started at five in the morning. Ethan's phone rang three times. Becca surprised her by picking up.

"Ethan is unavailable to talk. My husband is exhausted from a brutal day at work, and he's sound asleep in his recliner. Please leave a message at the tone. He'll get back to you tomorrow. Beep." The line went dead.

A few seconds later, Jillian's phone rang. Caller ID showed Ethan's number.

"Hi, Ethan. Sorry I bothered you. Go back to sleep. I'll talk to you in the morning."

"No, wait. You wouldn't call unless it was important. What's going on?" His voice sounded flat. "Another neighbor drop a clue in your lap?"

Not too tired to be a smart aleck.

"No, but I believe a clue waltzed into my bookstore today."

Bet I have your full attention now.

"I chased leads all day starting before eight at Shorty's Garage and ending at Lou's Tattoos thirty minutes ago.

Twelve hours of police work and all I have to show for it is heartburn from my greasy lunch at Del's Diner. Tell me your news, so I can go back to sleep."

Becca's voice chastised Ethan for being rude. Jillian heard the words *neanderthal* and *insensitive jerk*.

"I'm rude? You're the one who wouldn't let her talk to me in the first place."

"I didn't know who it was. I didn't check caller ID. Give me the phone."

Jillian heard a scuffling sound, then Becca got on the phone, out of breath.

"You're on speaker, so my boorish husband can apologize to you."

"No need. I shouldn't have called. Tell Ethan I'll talk to him tomorrow."

"No, no, no." Ethan shouted. "I'm not waiting until tomorrow to hear how a clue walked into the bookstore. Ask her to meet us at Manny's for pizza."

"Ooh yes. Meet us for dinner, Jilly."

"Are you sure about this, Becca? Eight-thirty is pretty late when you have to be up early in the morning."

"Are you kidding? I can eat a Manny's three-meat-extra-cheese pizza anytime." Becca smacked her lips. "You have perfect timing, Jilly. Ethan came home ten minutes ago, we haven't had dinner yet, and I'm starving." We'll see you in fifteen minutes." She ended the call.

Jillian gave the girls fresh water and a bowl full of kibble. She ran a brush through her hair, added some sheer lip gloss, and grabbed her purse. If she left now, she should make it to Manny's on time without exceeding the speed limit.

Must stay on the right side of the law. He's already annoyed with me.

Aromas of fresh baked dough, spicy Italian sausage, and garlic teased Jillian's nose when she stepped into the warm pizzeria. Ethan and Becca sat at a cozy table in back sipping their drinks from frosty mugs. A glass of unsweetened iced tea waited for her. She sat in a red vinyl chair across from her friends, noticing they held hands and sat as close as possible without being inappropriate in public.

"Hey, guys. I'm sorry for intruding on your evening." Jillian lifted her iced tea and took a drink. "Thanks for this."

"You're not intruding," Becca said. "We love having dinner with you, sweetie. Tell her, Ethan."

"I'm the luckiest man in this place tonight." He raised his own mug in a toast. "Two beautiful ladies, a cold one, and—if you'd hurry and order—a pizza on this table in less than twenty minutes. Yes, I'm a lucky man." All was said in his sincerest voice.

No one needed a menu. They ordered their usual—one large pepperoni, one large three meat, extra cheese, and an order of breadsticks with marinara sauce. The waitress jotted down the order and promised to be back with refills.

Ethan wasted no time getting down to business. "What's this about a clue, Jilly? I hope whatever you have helps break the case. Hitting dead ends is getting on my nerves."

"Nothing new today?"

"Nope. Shorty did all the red stripes on the firefighters' cars pro bono, so there are no receipts for who got work done. I'll have to talk to every firefighter who owns a black SUV. Lou at Lou's Tattoos does lots of snakes matching the description, so he'd need to lay eyes on the actual tattoo to verify whether he did the work. So unless our suspect decides to turn himself in—another dead end." Ethan slumped in his chair.

The waitress arrived with drink refills and a basket of piping hot breadsticks.

"Let's eat these while they're still hot." Ethan grabbed the nearest one. "Besides, on second thought, I'd like to enjoy my dinner without any murder talk. We can do that after."

The women agreed to his suggestion with a subtle nod to one another.

"I didn't realize I was this hungry," Becca mumbled around a huge bite. "We were so busy at the bakery, I never took a lunch break. I baked for three birthdays, a baby shower, a wedding anniversary, and a bar mitzvah." Becca winked across the table at Jillian. "Your gorgeous new friend came in for my amazing cinnamon rolls." Bryan's unexpected arrival at their table interrupted further comments about Travis.

"What's this? A night on the town and I wasn't invited? Some friends and family you are." Bryan shoved his chair closer to Jillian's.

"Sit down. Stop your whining. Eat a breadstick." Becca pushed the basket at him. "Any cousin of Jilly's is welcome to dine with the Hardens."

"I'm her only cousin." He snatched a breadstick and dunked it in marinara, splattering a bit on Jillian's arm. "Thanks for this though."

"You're such a slob—always have been." She wiped off the blob of sauce with her napkin.

"Gee, sorry. Someone's a little touchy this evening." Bryan elbowed her in the side.

"Cut it out, Bryan. We're not kids anymore." She pushed back. "Or I'll tell everyone in this place drinks are on the house at McGuire's tonight."

"You wouldn't. That would cost me a fortune. There are fifty people here tonight. My bar can't afford to lose money." He began to sound panicked, so she took pity on him.

"Relax, I'm teasing. I'd never mess with your pub's bottom line. We business owners have to stick together." She gave her cousin a nudge. With that, a truce was sealed.

Their waitress came with a pizza to-go for Bryan. She leaned in, placing her chest in his face. She gave him his pizza with one hand and caressed his shoulder with the other. She gave him a sultry wink before leaving the table, swinging her shapely hips.

"Uh, Bryan." Ethan chuckled. "I'm not sure you noticed. Our waitress wants your attention in the worst way. Is there something you've been hiding from us?"

Bryan's face was beet red.

"C'mon, you guys. No big deal. Gigi and I dated in high school for a few months. She moved away at the start of our senior year." Bryan scratched at his five o'clock shadow. "She's back in Willow Springs and wants things to be like they were ten years ago. I've tried to let her down easy. She's persistent and won't take no for an answer. I'd stop coming here, except Manny makes the best pizza."

"He makes the *only* pizza in town." Jillian pitied her poor cousin. "You're in a bad spot, buddy."

"What kind of a name is Gigi?" Becca hooted. "Sounds like a poodle to me."

"Don't let the women get you down." Ethan gave him a fist pump. "Men can live without chicks, not pizza."

Becca smacked her husband lightly on the back of the head.

"Hey, watch it." Ethan rubbed the spot she'd whacked.

Bryan managed a weak smile. "Thanks, dude. I gotta dash. Mike's waiting for this pizza back at the bar. You guys enjoy your evening."

They watched him pick his way across the room, steering clear of the waitress's path.

"Poor guy," Ethan said. "He'll never be able to eat pizza in here again."

"You may not eat again either. What's with the 'men can live without women, not pizza' nonsense?" Becca glared at her husband, who wrapped his arms around her.

"I wasn't serious, babe." He planted a loud kiss on her cheek. "Bryan needs to know I've got his back."

The waitress appeared with the rest of their order. Peering down her nose at them, she scowled and dumped their pizzas on the table, stomping away without a backward glance.

"What's wrong with her?" Ethan said. "She almost dropped the food in our laps."

"If I'm not mistaken, our waitress considers Jilly and me competition for Bryan's affection." Becca grinned. "Maybe we could help Bryan out by making her think one of us is dating him."

"One of you?" Ethan held up his left hand, pointing to his wedding ring. "Do I need to remind you we're married? I don't like my wife having a boyfriend."

"Don't be jealous." Becca patted his cheek. "I'd still love you best. Besides, I wouldn't have to be the one to pretend to be Bryan's girlfriend."

They both stared at Jillian.

"Uh-uh, no way." She waggled her finger. "Your idea is weird and creepy on so many levels. I'm not pretending to be my cousin's girlfriend. He's on his own."

They nixed plans to save Bryan from the romantic clutches of the jealous waitress and got busy enjoying their pizzas. Ethan made quick work of his, and the ladies shared the other. With only crust left, Ethan was ready to discuss what had brought them here.

"The food is gone. My glass is empty. Let's hear about this new clue, Jilly."

She described the scene at the bookstore with her Aunt Grace and the mystery woman, careful not to leave out any details. Ethan listened, saving his questions until she finished.

"Your aunt and Trixie were the only ones who saw her?"

"Yes."

"Did anyone get this woman's name?"

"No. She left in a hurry after Aunt Grace yelled at her."

Ethan sucked in a deep breath and blew it out. "I agree she's connected to the case and more than likely related to Maggie. We need to find out who she is—only it won't be easy. Without a name, my regular avenues of identifying someone won't work."

"Willow Springs is a small town," Becca said. "A stranger looking exactly like a murder victim won't be able to hide."

"She'll be back—to the store—to talk to me. I'm certain of it." Jillian met Ethan's stare. "When she does, I'll call you and hold her until you get there."

"Do you hear yourself?" Ethan snapped at his wife's best friend. "You cannot hold someone, Jilly. You're not the police."

"No, I'm the best chance you've got to figure out who she is. I'm sure I can keep her there talking—woman to woman."

They glared at each other from across the table. The silence was palpable When Ethan's chin hit his chest, Jillian savored the sweet thrill of victory.

"I can't believe I'm saying this," he muttered. "I expect you to call me if this woman comes back. Keep her talking. If she wants to leave, you let her go. Do you understand?"

"Yes, Detective. I hear you. However—" She paused for dramatic effect. "I promise you she'll be there when you arrive. My aunt may have been frightened by Maggie's lookalike. This lady won't scare me."

"And if she's involved in this murder? You should be scared." He pushed back from the table, throwing money on the table. Without another word, he stomped to the front door, leaving Jillian in stunned silence.

"Sorry, sweetie. He's cranky when he's tired." Becca stood, grabbing her purse and coat. "I better go after him. Can you take care of the bill?"

"Sure. Go on. Please tell him I'm sorry."

Becca waved as she weaved through the labyrinth of tables and chairs.

Jillian regretted making Ethan so angry, ruining their lovely evening, but she wouldn't apologize for one thing.

I am his best shot at identifying this woman. No doubt in my mind.

CHAPTER TEN

Snuggled in bed, Jillian worried. She'd never seen Ethan explode like he had at dinner. She feared she'd pushed him too far. Would he forgive her?

Solving this case obviously weighed on him. This would be his first murder investigation since he'd left the Chicago police department.

He moved home to get away from all the murders. And now this.

Ethan's frustration was understandable. She needed to give him some space—let him do his job. She'd help discover the identity of the mystery woman, then back way off.

Won't stop me from wondering though.

Was this woman related to Maggie? Probably. Grace and Trixie agreed the resemblance was striking. Why hadn't her name popped when Ethan tried to locate any relatives?

"Someone has to know if Maggie had extended family," she said aloud to her empty bedroom. "Maybe one of the other teachers knows." She could stop by the school tomorrow for a visit. That would also give her a chance to check on her former coworkers—see how they were coping after Friday night. If she were lucky, maybe one of them knew if Maggie had a distant cousin or something.

Jillian made her mental to-do list—identify the mystery woman, back off Ethan's case, talk to the other teachers.

I can do all that. Not necessarily in that order.

The alarm beeped at seven. Her girls circled the bed like sharks, a clear sign they needed to go outside. Jillian stepped onto the chilly hardwood floor and shivered in her thin nightgown. She put on a warm, oversized sweatshirt, slipped into a pair of old shoes, and led the girls outside. As Abbey and Hayley sniffed every blade of grass in the yard, she stretched and rubbed her tired eyes. Her sister's voice startled her.

"How're we all doing this morning?" Cate greeted the pups who strained at their leashes. She scratched their furry faces and doled out a few smooches. They wiggled their behinds in appreciation of her attention.

"You furballs can come live with me if your mommy isn't treating you right. There are two girls who'd love having you sweet things upstairs with us."

"You don't want eight muddy paws on your new beige carpet." Jillian reminded Cate why the dogs stayed in the basement. "You're off to the bakery pretty early. Everything okay?"

"Wes is taking the girls to school. The PTA is sponsoring Daddy/Daughter Donut Day. The girls insisted their daddy had to go, and of course, he said yes. They've got him wrapped around their little fingers."

"They're like us when we were their age," Jillian said. "Dad didn't stand a chance against his three persuasive daughters." She winked at her sister.

"Still doesn't," Cate agreed. "Since I don't have to feed the girls breakfast, I'm going in to help Becca. We've got a big order to fill. Plus, I'm sure she's busy developing new recipes. Our customers wait in line for the doors to open to get the first taste of her latest creations. They loved yesterday's new s'mores muffin recipe."

"They were amazing." Jillian could still taste the graham cracker, chocolate, and marshmallow flavors. "I should know—ate two of them." The memory made Jillian's stomach growl. "Could I take some of Becca's delicious concoctions to the elementary school this afternoon?"

"Sure, I'll make a box and set it aside for you. Come in whenever you're ready." Cate tilted her head. "Any particular reason for the visit today?"

"I want to check in on everybody—make sure they're all right. I also hope they could help me solve a little mystery."

"You mean the identity of the woman in your store?"

"Good grief." Jillian threw her hands in the air. "How did you hear?"

"Aunt Grace was distraught. Mom dragged her to the bakery for sweets to calm her. Three cups of chamomile tea and two chocolate chip scones later, I'd heard the whole story of the mysterious stranger. Sounds intriguing." Cate rubbed her hands together.

"Intriguing? I guess you could say that. Also, weird. In the six years I worked with Maggie, she never mentioned anyone other than her parents and grandparents." Jillian bent down to pull a stick away from Hayley. "According to Trixie, this woman was the spitting image of Maggie, so they have to be related. It can't be a coincidence she appears days after Maggie is killed. I hope someone at school will know who she is."

"Good luck." Cate crossed her fingers on both hands. "By the way, what's Ethan think of you poking around in his case?"

"Who said I'm poking into his case?"

"Come on, Jilly. Willow Springs is a small town where everybody knows everybody else's business. The gossip mill says you've talked to Mr. Erickson and Mrs. Taylor. Now you're going to pump your former coworkers for information. You can't deny you're involved. I'll bet Ethan isn't happy either."

Jillian ducked her head, not wanting to see her sister's reaction. "He tried to make me promise to stay out of it. I never agreed—sidestepped the issue with some double talk. I have decided to back off after today's outing and give him space to solve the case."

"Good idea." Cate gave a firm nod. "You also need to be careful. Someone murdered your friend. You could be in danger next if they find out you've uncovered clues for the police."

"I'm asking a few harmless questions, nothing more. Anything I find, I'll take straight to Ethan."

"Don't do anything reckless." Cate pointed a warning finger.

"I would never be reckless."

"Yeah, right." Cate's voice dripped with sarcasm. "And on that note, I'm out of here before Becca gets worried and reports me as a missing person. Come and get those treats for your teacher friends. I'll have them ready." She blew an air kiss and hopped into her minivan.

Her sister's concern was touching. She made a silent promise to be careful so Cate and Ethan wouldn't worry.

The morning flew by as Jillian ran errands. Wherever she went, people asked how things were going at the store. Many asked for details on the hit and run. Unsure of what she should say, her response to their questions was 'the police have asked me not to discuss the case.'

Ethan should be happy with the way she handled those awkward questions.

The next stop was Amanda's flower shop, Blossoms & Blooms. As soon as she opened the door, her senses were assaulted by vibrant colors—blues, purples, reds, oranges and more—and the amazing scents of roses, jasmine, freesia, and plumeria. She admired the artistic way Amanda displayed the blooms with the lightest, the most subtle colors from white to light pink to pale lavender on the left, circling around to the deepest, darkest shades of fuchsia, violet, scarlet, and indigo on the right. The showroom was like the color wheels in a paint store.

"Hey, you." Amanda came from the backroom, wiping her hands on the green apron she wore while she worked. "C'mon back and talk. I'm finishing a few bouquets for delivery this morning."

Jillian followed her sister into the workroom. Watching Amanda create her bouquets was like watching an artist paint a masterpiece. Perched on a stool, she prepared for the floral magic to happen.

"This is Monday—your day off. What're you doing out and about so early?" Amanda clipped the tiniest leaves from the stem of a rose. "I'd still be in bed at this hour if I didn't have to work."

"I've run errands, avoided awkward questions—you know—a typical morning." She shrugged.

Amanda reached across the table and squeezed her hand. "I can't imagine how hard this is for you. Losing your friend is horrible enough. For it to happen in front of Whimsy & Wonder during your open house—unthinkable. Have people stayed away because of the accident?"

"No. Business is good."

"Great news." Amanda snipped the bottoms off some pink roses. "You've worked hard getting your place opened. You deserve a great start."

Amanda's praise lifted Jillian's spirits. She wished she could stay at the flower shop all morning, but she had a purpose for this visit.

"Could you throw together a bouquet for me?" She gestured at the cheerful fall blooms in the cooler. "Something simple with vibrant colors like those."

"No problem. Do you want them in a vase or a box?"

"Neither. I hoped for some fresh cut blooms with a ribbon wrapped around the stems." She opened the drawer where Amanda kept the ribbon spools, pulling out a green one.

"Not green—yellow." Amanda returned the green one to the drawer.

"I'm visiting my friends at the elementary school. There's a memorial for Maggie outside the school fence. I'll leave some flowers to show my respects."

"Are you sure you should go so soon after the accident?" Amanda reached into the cooler for asters, marigolds, and dahlias.

"I need to do this. Maggie was our friend—my friend. We should come together in our grief." Jillian toyed with the fallen leaf of a dahlia. "I guess you haven't heard. This was no accident. Ethan and I believe she was killed on purpose."

"You mean *murdered*?" Amanda dropped the yellow marigolds on the worktable. She ignored the ones which slid onto the floor.

"Yes, murdered."

Jillian watched a scowl spread across her sister's face. She wasn't surprised at what came next.

"The rumor around town is you're investigating this case." Amanda fussed with the flowers. "Ethan can't think this is a good idea."

"He did warn me to mind my own business." Jillian shrugged. "I couldn't promise I would."

"You are so infuriating sometimes." Amanda shook her clippers at Jillian. "You're not a trained investigator. Please let Ethan do his job."

Much like Cate's, Amanda's concern moved Jillian, but she knew in her heart she wouldn't step aside. Not until she'd talked to her former coworkers and discovered the name of Maggie's look-alike. Taking a deep breath, she made the only promise she could. "I'll be careful and call Ethan the moment I learn something important."

"Is that the best guarantee you can give me?" Amanda snipped a piece of shimmery yellow ribbon and tied the fall stems she'd arranged neatly together. She shoved the blossoms into her baby sister's hands. "Here."

"Amanda, these are gorgeous." Jillian breathed in their scent. "Maggie would love them. How much do I owe you?"

"Nothing. They're on the house, you stubborn mule."

Ignoring the name-calling, Jillian thanked Amanda. "I appreciate this. As always, you did a great job."

"Of course I did."

"And as always, your modesty astounds me." Gathering her things, Jillian headed for the door. "I'm stopping at the bakery to pick up pastries for the staff at school. I'll talk to you later."

Amanda opted for a parting shot. "Remember your promise. I plan on holding you to it."

Jillian acknowledged her sister's admonition with a wave, dismissing her warning with a flick of her hand.

Her next stop was the bakery. Sugar & Spice bustled with customers clamoring for Becca's mouth-watering goodies. Jillian didn't want to disturb her friend while she basked in the glow of her culinary success. A quick hello to Becca, and she was back in her car, headed for the school. Classes let out in ten minutes. She wanted to be there to check in with a few former students. Running her store brought her happiness, but she missed the daily challenges and joys involved in teaching.

Three red lights and a funeral procession slowed her trip. All the students were gone when she got there. As she drove into the visitor's parking lot, Maggie's tribute came into view. Balloons, flowers, stuffed animals, posters, and handwritten notes were piled against the school fence. The outpouring of love and grief saddened her at first until anger replaced this emotion.

This memorial shouldn't be necessary. Maggie should still be here.

Outrage further fueled her desire to make sure the killer was brought to justice.

Jillian placed the floral bouquet among the others lying on the pavement. She whispered a prayer for Maggie before carrying her packages toward the school.

As she entered the office to sign in, she greeted Mrs. Daly, who came around the desk and enveloped her in a hug. The woman's perfume—a subtle citrus and vanilla combination—comforted her. Jillian stepped back. A tear trailed down the secretary's cheek.

"Mrs. Daly, I hope this isn't a bad time. I know how busy the end of the day can be here in the office." Jillian handed her a tissue. "I brought you some lemon tarts from my sister's bakery. I recalled how much you like them."

She handed her a small blue box.

"You're a sweetheart." Mrs. Daly peeked inside. "I can't believe you remembered. My mother's had a flaky, buttery crust and tart lemon curd. Your sister's recipe brings back childhood memories."

"Cate uses our grandmother's recipes. She was a stickler for using fresh ingredients. Her baking mantra was 'fresh is best'. Grandpa made her a sign for her kitchen."

"I'm not surprised your sister's bakery is so popular if she's using tried-and-true family recipes." The secretary took a small bite. "Mm, I'm going to savor every one of these little beauties. Thank you, my dear."

Mrs. Daly enjoyed another bite. Jillian hated to interrupt this pleasant moment for her but wondered how to broach Maggie's death. The problem was solved when Mrs. Daly mentioned it first.

"All right, enough with the niceties. Rumor is you're helping the police investigate Maggie's death." Disapproval shrouded the older woman's face. "You're being reckless, not to mention irresponsible. You never struck me as irresponsible, young lady."

Everybody at Willow Springs Elementary knew one thing about Mrs. Daly. The student in question was in big trouble when Mrs. Daly referred to them as young man or young lady. Like an eight-year-old called to the principal's office and chastised for her behavior, Jillian attempted to downplay her involvement by laughing off the accusation.

"I wouldn't say I'm helping the police. I stumbled across a few clues and shared them with the lead detective, that's all. He's my best friend's husband."

"That's not what we've heard. Word around town is you've been working with Detective Harden interrogating witnesses." Mrs. Daly's steely glare made Jillian flinch.

Never being good at thinking on her feet, she decided the truth was her best means of defense.

"The rumors are true. I was with Detective Harden when he questioned neighbors around the bookstore. Those people came to me with their information, which I took straight to him."

"You've always been easy to talk to. I understand why people are comfortable sharing sensitive issues with you." Mrs. Daly twisted the tissue in her hand. "I have something to tell you too."

Jillian's curiosity went on high alert.

Did she see something the night of the open house?

Eager to hear Mrs. Daly's news, she was disappointed when several teachers strolled in, interrupting their conversation. The women were ecstatic to see Jillian—the famous blue box of pastries didn't hurt either. They shared hugs and tears and checked on each other's well-being. Questions about Maggie's death took center stage. Jillian promised to tell them what she could after her visit with Mrs. Daly.

Her former coworkers left with the sweet treats in hand, giving her the privacy needed to chat with the secretary.

"Mrs. Daly, what did you want to tell me?"

"Something strange happened this morning. Maggie never mentioned any relatives, so I assumed she had none. However, a woman—who could've been our Maggie's twin—waltzed into the office soon after we opened. She demanded I show her Maggie's classroom." The older woman's voice shook. "She gave me an uneasy feeling. Mr. Burch was out of the building, and I wasn't comfortable with some stranger wandering around. I told her I'd check with the principal and get back to her."

"Did she introduce herself to you? Did she want anything else?"

"I didn't get her name. The woman claimed she'd known Maggie since they were kids. She said Maggie was holding onto something valuable for her, and she needed it back. She thought maybe Maggie'd left it in her classroom. The whole story sounded fishy to me. I can't imagine Maggie would bring something valuable to school." Mrs. Daly wrinkled her nose. "Not a pleasant woman, by the way. She got ugly when I wouldn't let her into the room, but I stuck to my guns."

"Good for you, Mrs. Daly." Jillian put an arm around the other woman's shoulder. "Someone can't barge in here unannounced and expect entrance into someone's classroom. You did the right thing. Is she coming back tomorrow?"

"I'm not sure. I guess it depends on what Mr. Burch has to say. She asked me to call her with his answer."

"Call her? She gave you her phone number?" A tingle ran down Jillian's back.

"Yes, and I promised to call her with an answer in the morning."

Ethan needed to know about this. He'd be irritated she'd stumbled on yet another piece of information. She couldn't help that these clues kept falling at her feet.

"Mrs. Daly, you should give that number to the police. Let them handle this woman."

"I was thinking the exact same thing." She pulled a paper from her desk and dropped it in her purse. "I'll take care of it on my way home from work."

After thanking Mrs. Daly and promising to come back soon, Jillian scurried to the teachers' lounge for a quick visit and some probing questions. No one remembered

Maggie mentioning any relatives. Her fact-finding mission was a bust.

They did discuss and agree to take care of the funeral arrangements.

"We'll make sure Maggie is laid to rest with dignity," said the librarian.

"The community will come together and help pay the expenses, don't you think?" Maggie's co-kindergarten teacher looked hopeful through her tears.

Jillian promised to keep them posted about when they could begin planning the services. She also reminded them to stop by Whimsy & Wonder anytime to visit and take advantage of the teacher discount she offered. They thanked her for the pastries, promising none would be wasted.

Jillian had exited the building when a sad thought struck her. The last time she'd been inside the school, Maggie had been alive.

Life can change so suddenly. And not always for the better.

She drove home with a heavy heart.

CHAPTER ELEVEN

Jillian called Ethan—no answer. She left a message asking him to call. She chose not to leave any details. She'd rather share Mrs. Daly's news in person, even though the thought of facing his wrath made her cringe.

She needed a distraction. A beautiful fall day like this was perfect for taking Abbey and Hayley on a walk.

Jillian took the last turn toward home. And there he was—in the driveway—leaning on his car, arms crossed over his chest. Waiting. The scowl on his face said it all.

Uh-oh, someone's not happy with me.

She pulled her car next to his.

"Hey, Ethan. I guess you got my message." She climbed from the car. "I need to take this dry cleaning into the house. The girls need a walk. Would you care to join us? We can talk along the way."

"Yep." He reached for the clothes in her arms and followed her to the door.

Always a gentleman. Even when he's mad at me.

Two exuberant dogs greeted them. Their wiggling bodies and wagging tails exhibited their enthusiasm at having two pairs of hands rubbing them at the same time.

"Wow, are they always this excited when you come home?" Ethan scratched Hayley's belly and received a lick on the hand for his efforts.

"Yes, they are. They soak in all the love and affection they can get." She stroked Abbey's soft ears. "There's nothing better than their company and unconditional love. You and Becca should get a dog. That big house you bought has plenty of space."

"Not you too." He rubbed his neck and grumbled. "Becca's pestered me for months to get a dog. She wants something big like a German shepherd or a Labrador retriever. She claims they'll be protection for her when I'm working late."

"She has a good point. Both those breeds make great guard dogs. But the best reason to get one—your wife wants a dog."

He watched her clip on the leashes and grab a plastic bag.

Ethan made a face. "There's the biggest reason I don't want a pet. Picking up after them is disgusting."

"Oh, stop being a baby. You'll make your wife happy. You'll get a dog, and you *will* pick up poop."

The four of them headed off, allowing the pups to take the lead. Jillian zipped her coat against the brisk breeze and yanked her hat down over her ears.

"Some dogs tug like crazy on their leashes. Yours are well-behaved." Ethan waited while they rustled through the leaves. Abbey emerged with one hanging from her beard. He reached down, plucked it off, and threw it into the air. "I can picture Becca and me walking a dog together like this. Maybe when my case is solved, I'll revisit the subject."

"She'll be thrilled." Jillian rewarded her pups' good behavior with treats from her pocket.

"Becca will have these two to thank when she gets her own dog." With that, Ethan brought their discussion back to his case.

"Talk to me, Jilly. What's going on?"

She relayed Mrs. Daly's story of her unexpected visitor. When she finished, she waited for Ethan to speak. He said nothing, and his silence infuriated her.

"Are you kidding me? You don't have anything to say?"

"I suppose Mrs. Daly gave you this woman's phone number." His tone accused rather than asked.

"No, she didn't. I told her she should share the number with the police. In other words, you." Insulted by his accusation, Jillian lashed out. "I'm not an idiot, Ethan. I'm aware how information on a case should be handled. I wouldn't want the killer to get off on a technicality because I made a mistake. Give me a little credit, will you?"

"You're right. I'm sorry." He ran his hands through his hair. "I've had a crappy day. I shouldn't take it out on you."

"Apology accepted. " She urged the dogs around the corner. "I'm sorry you've had a rough day. Does this mean the case isn't going well?"

"I spent the day interviewing fifteen Willow Springs firefighters, including Travis. They had their black SUVs detailed at Shorty's with the red stripe. They were polite—cooperative—even let me examine their cars. Not one vehicle showed damage from a hit and run."

"This is good, isn't it? None of them are responsible for Maggie's death. Why don't you sound happy?"

"Yeah, they're all in the clear, which is good." Ethan blew out a deep breath. "I'm back to square one with no more leads on the vehicle. There's one more firefighter to interview. He's been out of town since Friday morning. I doubt he'll shed any light on this case."

"You have moved forward in the investigation by proving our first responders aren't involved in this mess." Jillian switched both leashes to one hand and hooked her arm through his. "Now you can focus on the other clues—the snake tattoo and the mystery woman." Ethan gave no response, so she continued her pep talk. "Stop by the police station. Mrs. Daly should have dropped the phone number off on her way home from school."

Their walk had brought them full circle to her apartment. Jillian smiled at the familiar car sitting parked at the curb. Travis climbed out along with a guy she didn't recognize. Despite his paint-spattered work pants and grungy tee shirt, the sight of Travis sent her pulse racing.

Be still my heart.

Jillian frowned at the somber expression on his face.

"Glad we found you." Travis shook hands with Ethan and introduced the other man.

No greeting for her. No acknowledgment she stood there. She bristled at being ignored.

"This is my friend and engineer, Jack Olsen," Travis continued. "He and his wife left on Friday to visit family. When he returned this morning, he found a nasty surprise in his garage—one requiring some police assistance. I'll let him tell you." Travis squatted down, giving some love to Abbey and Hayley.

Another snub. He couldn't be bothered to speak to her, but the dogs received VIP treatment.

All three men acted is if she weren't standing right there with them. Their disregard irritated her, and a caustic remark popped into her head. She refrained from letting it loose because of the set of Jack's jaw and the pained expression on Travis's face.

"Go ahead, Jack. Ethan needs to hear this." Travis stood and patted the man on his shoulder.

Jack cleared his throat. "Like Travis said, my wife and I got back into town this morning. We'd been to Ohio visiting her parents. She wanted to take her new car, so my SUV sat in the garage all weekend. When we got home, I pulled her car into the garage and parked next to mine." He stopped, taking a few deep breaths.

"When I carried our suitcases into the house, I brushed against the front of my truck. My pants hooked on the bumper and ripped." He fingered the three-inch tear in his khakis. "I couldn't figure out how they got caught until I bent down, took a closer look at the car."

Jack's agitation grew. He paced, and his voice grew louder. "The entire front is destroyed. The fender's crumpled, one headlight is busted, and the hood's got a huge dent." He ticked the offenses on his fingers. "How could something like this happen when my car sat in the garage all weekend?"

Obviously not all weekend.

"Jack rushed across the street—we're neighbors—and dragged me over to see the damage," Travis said. "I suggested he come straight to you. The officer at the front desk at the cop shop told me you'd left for the day, so I figured you'd gone home. We were headed there when we saw you with Jillian." Travis finally met her gaze and smiled. She did a mental forehead slap.

Those eyes. One look from them and her anger melted like butter.

"I'm glad you did." Ethan addressed Jack. "Is there anyone who could access your truck or the keys? Anyone stop by to check on the house while you were away?"

"Only my wife and I have keys. Travis kept an eye on the house from across the street."

131

Ethan scribbled down a note in his book. "Sounds like someone broke in while you were gone, stole your car, and brought it back. We'll check things out to be sure."

Jack shook his head. "Why would someone steal my car, wreck it, and put it back in my garage? That makes no sense. They should've dumped the mess somewhere."

"There may be a bit more to the story." Ethan steered them toward Travis's car. "I'll be able to tell you more once I see your vehicle. I'll follow you guys to Jack's house."

Ethan climbed behind the wheel of his department-issued car. He checked the rearview mirror and noticed two furry faces peering at him from the backseat. The passenger door opened, and Jillian slid in.

"What do you think you're doing?" Ethan said. "Get out, and take your dogs with you."

"Please let me come with you. This could be the car that killed Maggie. I'd like to see it for myself." She pleaded with her eyes as she clicked her seatbelt. "Aren't you excited? This could be the big break we've needed."

"There's that *we* again." Ethan adjusted the rearview mirror. "Did you become a cop without telling me? If not, please get out and let me do my job."

"I'm not trying to do your job, but you can't deny I've been helpful in your case. I brought you leads from Mr. Erickson, Mrs. Taylor, and Mrs. Daly. If it weren't for me, you wouldn't have their information. They were all hesitant to speak with the police, but me—well—what can I say? I'm easy to talk to." She gave him what she hoped was a sincere smile. "I promise to be quiet and stay out of the way." She steepled her hands and waited.

"You sound just like Becca—can't say no to her, either." Ethan huffed out a breath. "Fine, you can come. There's really no harm as long as you say nothing and touch nothing. Understand?"

"Yessir, Detective." She gave a military-style salute. "I'll be on my best behavior."

"You'd better be. I don't need any more complications in this case. And you, Jilly, could be a huge complication."

CHAPTER TWELVE

Ethan clenched his jaw. He had a white-knuckled grip on the steering wheel. Not one word was spoken between them. Jillian knew she'd pushed his buttons. She hadn't meant to be a problem. She knew in her heart she could help, and she needed to know if this was *the* car.

"Thank you for letting me ride along." Jillian hoped heartfelt appreciation would soften his irritation with her.

"Mm-hmm."

So maybe too soon.

They followed Travis a few blocks to a cul-de-sac off Riggs Road. They parked in front of a two-story, red brick house with a beautifully landscaped yard and a porch swing. The neighborhood struck Jillian as a great place to live and raise a family. Yet something sinister had insinuated itself into this quiet neighborhood.

Ethan cracked the back windows for the pups. Without a word, he climbed from the car and went with Travis and Jack to the garage. His thoughtfulness toward her dogs, despite his anger, lessened her irritation with him. Following them up the driveway, she doubled her commitment to be quiet and unobtrusive.

Jack punched in a code on the keypad. As the door rose, the black SUV came into view. They left the warm sunshine for the dark, cool garage. She rubbed her arms to ward off the chill.

"I sent Shelby off on a few errands." Jack stared at the empty side of the garage. "I haven't told her yet—didn't want to alarm her before I knew something myself."

"Good idea," Ethan said. "Also makes it easier to check out your car without hers parked in here." He snapped on some gloves and approached the front of Jack's vehicle.

Jillian hung back and observed, noting things were as Jack had described—busted headlight, crumpled fender, dented hood. Realizing Maggie's body had likely caused the damage, Jillian shuddered and wrapped her arms around her body.

Ethan checked every inch of Jack's car. He opened the driver's side door and examined the inside, running his hands under the seat, across the dashboard and the floor, lifting the floor mats as he went. Shutting the door, he went around to the passenger side and repeated the process. Next, he focused his attention on the front of the vehicle, running his latex-covered fingers across the damaged surface. Ethan pulled his hand back, examining something stuck on the glove. He removed them inside out and stuffed them into a plastic bag.

"Hold this." He shoved the baggie into Jillian's hands.

While his attitude annoyed her, she decided not to press her luck by confronting him. He'd allowed her to come to the scene, so she could stand there and hold this bag for him. She took the opportunity to sneak a peek at Ethan's evidence. He'd turned both gloves inside out rendering it impossible to make out the substance. Her imagination filled in the blanks. A shiver crawled down her spine.

Blood. Maggie's blood.

He stepped behind the vehicle and jotted down the license plate number. A weary sigh escaped his mouth. Ethan approached Jack wearing his grim cop face. "As we all suspected, your car was probably used in a hit-and-run incident on Friday night where a woman was killed. The damage to the front of your vehicle is consistent with the injuries suffered by the victim. We'll need confirmation from the forensics team, though. I'll call this in. Your SUV will be towed to the lab for further testing."

"What ... how ... I don't ..." Jack stammered, running his hands through his hair. "We weren't even home. You can't think I did this?"

"No, someone wants me to *think* you did. They stole your vehicle, ran down Jillian's friend, and returned it to cast suspicion on you. I don't know who or why yet, but I promise I'll find the answers." He dangled a set of keys. "These were still in the ignition. You're going to be without your wheels for a few days—can't be avoided."

"No need to apologize, Detective. You're doing your job." Jack jammed his hands in his pockets. "Take it. Do whatever needs to be done. If someone used my car to kill someone, I don't want it back."

Ethan stepped away with his phone out, calling the forensics team and a tow truck. Jillian left the garage behind Travis and Jack. She wasn't sure if it was the darkness inside the garage, the thought of Jack's truck being used in Maggie's death, or both making her so cold. She welcomed the warmth of the sunshine on her face and arms.

She hadn't realized she'd shivered until Travis draped his jacket around her shoulders, letting his hands linger for a moment. For the third time in as many days, she was struck by his thoughtfulness. Her growing attraction to this man surprised, yet excited her.

Could he be feeling something too?

Ethan returned. He announced he'd wait for the tow truck and forensics team. She and Travis were free to go. Without waiting for an answer, he retreated to the garage. Jack's wife, Shelby, came home from the market and parked on the street. She searched for Jack through the window, a worried look on her face.

"I'd better explain things to her. She'll freak out when she sees my car." Jack trudged down the driveway, his shoulders hunched forward.

Jillian and Travis sat on the front porch swing, swaying in the warm breeze.

"Thanks for your jacket. I didn't realize I was cold until we stepped out of the garage." She wrapped the coat tighter, noticing the same musky scent she'd smelled the first day Travis came into her bookstore.

"No problem," he said. "Are you okay—I mean—your face in there …"

"I'm fine. Staring at Jack's car got to me, I guess. Holding that bag Ethan handed me didn't help. His gloves are inside—with dried blood on them."

A lone tear trickled down her cheek. Travis reached out, wiping it away. He jerked his hand back immediately. Jillian dared a glance into his eyes. Something flickered in his, extinguishing right away. Was it attraction—or embarrassment? He dropped his gaze.

"I'm sorry. I shouldn't have touched you like that." A flush crept from the collar of his shirt. "A woman's tears get to me. I act before I think. I was way out of line." He raised his head to look her in the eyes. She met his glance with a smile.

"There's no need for an apology. Your gesture was sweet." She rested her hand on his chest before placing a quick kiss on his cheek. She felt more than heard him suck in his breath.

Caught you off guard, huh? Surprised myself a little.

Travis scooted closer, putting his arm around her shoulders. She leaned into him and closed her eyes, enjoying his warmth and the soothing motion of the swing. They sat in silence until Jack and his wife joined them. Jack introduced Shelby.

"Jack says his car was stolen. The thief ran someone down in the street—killed her. That poor woman—so awful." Shelby's blonde curls bounced as she shook her head. "Why would someone do this?"

No one could say.

"We're going out for dinner—don't want to watch our house ransacked for evidence." Jack took Shelby's hand in his. "You two care to join us?"

"Thanks for the offer, but we're waiting for Ethan. Jillian's holding some evidence for him. Her dogs are also still in his car. We'll need to take them home soon."

There he goes, thinking about my needs—and my girls—again. Does that mean he's interested in me or just a nice guy?

Jillian's own growing attraction toward Travis and her uncertainty about his feelings were mentally exhausting. Jack's voice snapped her out of the cerebral ping-pong going on inside her head.

"No worries. Give me a call when the coast is clear. Shelby and I will come home." The two friends shook hands.

"Will do," Travis said. "Enjoy your dinner."

"Nice meeting you, Shelby. I'm sorry it was under these circumstances." Jillian smiled at Jack's wife.

"Nice meeting you too. I'm sure we'll be running into each other—I mean—since you're dating Travis." Shelby pointed to the white bungalow across from their house. "He's Jack's friend *and* our neighbor."

At the word *dating*, Jillian sucked in a deep breath, setting her on a coughing fit.

Jack cleared his throat. "They're not dating, honey."

Jillian noticed how Shelby's face turned red from embarrassment. "Oh, I'm sorry. Jack told me ... I assumed ..." Her voice trailed off.

"Sweetie, let's go. I'm starving." Taking his wife's arm, Jack led her away from the awkward situation.

Jillian watched Jack and Shelby leave hand in hand, whispering to each other.

That was odd. I can't believe she thought we were dating.

She stole a glance at Travis. He wouldn't meet her eyes.

The forensics team arrived moments later. They combed the garage, the house, and the surrounding yard for evidence. One tech found something in the grass and placed it in a baggie, which they marked and put into a box.

"What do you think they found?" Travis said.

"I have no idea. Whatever it is, I hope it helps Ethan solve the case."

The sun sank toward the horizon as the forensics team gathered their tools and loaded the van. The tow truck arrived and backed into the driveway. Jillian's focus on watching the 'murder weapon' being removed from the garage kept her from noticing Ethan had retrieved her pups from his car. He brought them to the porch.

"Can't believe you two hung around—figured you'd get bored and leave." He handed the leashes to Jillian as the girls greeted their mama and her friend. "I brought you some company. They peed for me."

"Thanks, Ethan." She buried her face in their soft fur. "The girls thank you too."

"Did the forensics team find anything helpful?" Travis slowed the swing as Hayley climbed into his lap.

Jillian shook her head at the little black dog.

You little traitor. I can't believe you'd dump me for a handsome face and a scratch behind the ears.

"I'm not at liberty to say anything about evidence. Forensics will run tests and send me the report." Ethan scrubbed at the stubble on his face. "I've crossed Jack off the suspect list. His alibi in Ohio checked out."

"He'll be relieved you cleared him of any wrongdoing. He was weirded out when he came and banged on my door. Thanks for your help, Ethan."

"No problem." The men shook hands. "I'm headed to the station. Have to wrap up some paperwork."

"Um, before you go ..." Jillian handed him the evidence bag with the bloody gloves.

"Thanks." Ethan shoved the plastic bag into his coat pocket. "I'll need to check this into evidence."

They watched him trudge down the drive to his car. He moved as if the weight of the world rested on his shoulders.

Enjoying the beautiful sunset for a few minutes longer, Jillian and Travis sat without talking. The two sleepy pups snuggled between them on the swing. She ended the silence.

"How long have you and Jack been neighbors?"

"I bought the property two years ago. The house needed renovating, so I got it for a steal. Hard work and elbow grease have made it a nice home." He stroked Hayley's black fur. "Even though the place is too big for one person, I can't bring myself to sell it. I keep thinking someday I'll have a family, so the space will be great."

Talk about renovations and having a family caused her heart to skip a beat. The butterflies fluttering in her stomach made her nauseated.

What's happening? How can I be falling for him so fast?

Travis squeezed her shoulder. "Earth to Jillian. Did you hear anything I said?"

"I'm sorry. My mind wandered for a minute." She blushed at being caught not listening. "What did you say?"

"Nothing important." He ducked his head, focusing on the concrete under his feet. "Funny how Shelby thought we were dating, huh?"

"An honest mistake."

"What she said got me thinking. Maybe you and I could go out?" His glance was hopeful.

Looking into his warm brown eyes made her insides go soft. Her pulse raced. "You mean a date?"

"Yeah. It'd be fun, don't you think?"

"Yes," she said. "I'd love to." She told her heart to behave.

Bring it down a notch, Jilly. You don't want to scare him away.

"Does Wednesday night work for you? I'm on duty tomorrow."

"Sounds perfect." She smiled.

"Six o'clock?" Travis reached to scratch Abbey behind her ears. Hayley nudged his arm to bring his attention back to her.

"It's a date. Now, could I ask you a favor?"

"Sure, and the answer is yes." His eyes never left her face.

"You might want to hear the question first." She pointed at herself and the dogs. "We rode here with Ethan. We have no way to get home."

"No problem. Let's load 'em into my truck." Travis scooped Abbey and Hayley into his arms and carried them to his car. He put the girls on an old blanket on the back seat. Jillian settled herself in the front passenger seat with his jacket still wrapped around her. She enjoyed both the warmth and his smell.

Travis distracted her with a constant stream of conversation on the way home, careful, she noticed, to avoid mentioning Maggie's death. He told her about a fire call they'd had a few days ago.

"The flames were shooting through the roof when we arrived on scene. A neighbor thought someone might be home. We searched and found no one inside."

"Are you ever afraid going on a call? I'd be scared out of my mind."

"This might sound dumb. I've never thought to be scared." He shrugged. "The tones go off—we jump on the rig. The adrenalin kicks in, and we do the work we've trained for. There's no time to be scared. People's lives depend on us doing our jobs."

Staring at his profile, she found his confidence attractive. She fought the urge to throw her arms around him.

Travis parked in front of her house, saving her from doing something irrational and making a fool of herself.

Relax, Jilly. You don't want him to think you're crazy.

He opened the back door and let the pups out, holding their leashes until Jillian reached for them.

"Here you go." He handed her both leads. "They're great car riders. Never made a sound."

"I taught them to be quiet and polite in cars. Nobody wants the headache of riding with two yapping dogs in the back."

Abbey and Hayley tugged her toward the door. Travis followed with his hands jammed in his pockets.

"I appreciate the ride home. We'd have been stranded if it weren't for you. Ethan left me without a second thought."

She unlocked the door. Her girls rushed inside to search the premises for anything amiss. She removed Travis's coat, handing it back to him. "Thanks for lending me your jacket."

"Anytime." He reached to take his coat.

Their fingers touched. There it was again—that familiar electric zing coursing through her body. If Travis felt it, he gave no indication. He shrugged into his coat and zipped it.

"Will you be all right here by yourself?" he said. "Today's been another rough one. Maybe you could call your sisters and spend the evening with them."

"No, I'm fine. If I need something, Cate and her family are upstairs. I'll fix a bite to eat, take a warm bath, and settle on the couch with a good book. Sounds like a perfect evening to me."

Jillian sensed he had something else on his mind as he lingered at her door. When he remained quiet, she filled the awkward silence.

"I'll be ready at six on Wednesday." She held her breath, hoping he hadn't changed his mind.

His face broke into a wide grin. "I can't wait."

She exhaled the breath she hadn't realized she'd held. "Any idea of our plans—so I know what to wear?"

"If you don't mind, I'd like to keep my plans a surprise. Our date will be low-key. Wear something comfortable."

Comfortable was not a helpful suggestion, but she let it pass.

"Not helpful, huh?"

Could he read her mind?

"My sister-in-law once told me women worry about what to wear on a first date."

"Your sister-in-law is wise," Jillian said. "I'm sure I can make comfortable work, and I love surprises."

"Great. I'll be here at six."

She met his smile with a brighter one of her own. "I'll be ready and waiting."

Reaching forward, she intended to give Travis a quick hug. He leaned in at the same time. For a hug? Or a kiss? Jillian couldn't be certain.

They both went right, then left—an awkward teenage move by both. They finally managed to get their arms and heads leaning the right directions for a friendly hug. She took one last sniff of his cologne she liked so much. Travis stepped back, placing a chaste kiss on her cheek as she'd done to him on Jack's porch.

"I should go." He released her arms, placing them at her sides. "Take care and don't get into trouble with Ethan." He waved as he drove away.

"'Bye, Travis," she called even though he couldn't hear.

Wednesday couldn't come soon enough.

CHAPTER THIRTEEN

Jillian shut the door and leaned back, steadying herself. Her legs quivered. She didn't think they'd hold her if she tried to move. This attraction to Travis was happening hard and fast, which both excited and scared her. She hadn't felt like this since college—with Scott.

They'd met their sophomore year in an economics class. Like now with Travis, her feelings for Scott had been immediate. Jillian fell hard. Scott had too, or so she thought. After dating for three years, she'd thought he was the one. They'd discussed marriage and having a family. She expected an engagement ring before graduation.

Her life was all planned until she caught Scott having an intimate moment with one of her roommates. This behind-the-back relationship had been going on for over a year. The betrayal crushed Jillian. She moved home to teach and be near family, swearing never to let this happen to her again. She couldn't go down this same road with Travis. Sure, he seemed to be a great guy, but what did she really know about him?

Maybe I should cancel our date.

"I'll sleep on it—make my decision in the morning." This she announced to her pups who sat at her feet. They each cocked their head at the sound of her voice. "Good idea, right?"

Taking a deep breath to calm the jitters, she found her legs did carry her—to the kitchen. She fixed a quick chicken pasta dinner and ate it on her patio, wrapped in a warm blanket to ward off the chill. She loved sitting outside. She enjoyed the light autumn breeze ruffling her hair, a nearby firepit's smoky smell, and the sound her pups made crunching their bones. Her frayed nerves and troubled thoughts were soothed by these comforts.

Travis was right. This had been a rough day. She shuddered, thinking about the vehicle responsible for her friend's death. Maggie must've been so frightened when the SUV headed straight at her. Too scared to get out of the way, according to Mr. Erickson.

A not-so-gentle knock at the door disturbed her musings. With Abbey and Hayley on her heels, they walked to the door to welcome their visitor.

"Hey, Becca. What brings you here so late? I'd expect you'd be in bed at this hour."

"Maybe I would be if you'd told me the news yourself. But no, I had to hear from my husband you snuggled with a hunky fireman all afternoon. And there was a kiss involved? Some friend you are, Jillian Saoirse. This is twice you've kept vital information from me."

Becca stomped inside, threw her coat on a chair, and flopped on the couch. The pups jumped next to her and begged for attention. Experience had taught them Becca would give belly rubs and kisses. To their extreme pleasure, she did not disappoint.

"Wow, you threw in my middle name. You must be really mad at me." Jillian tried teasing her friend into a better mood. Becca scowled back.

"I'm sorry." Jillian raised her hands in surrender. "I should've called you."

Before Ethan tattled on me.

"Yes, you should've." In her current mood, Becca rubbed the dogs harder than they liked. Abbey and Hayley took refuge in their fuzzy bed by the fireplace.

"Again, I'm really sorry."

The heartfelt apology cooled Becca's anger. She switched to playful teasing. "We're best friends, Jilly. Besties are required to share details like this ASAP. I mean, who did I call after Ethan kissed me in the eighth grade? Who was the first person I told when he asked me to the movies? Wasn't it you I ran to when Ethan asked me to give our relationship another try? And, again, when he proposed to me?"

"The answer to all the above is me." Jillian hung her head. She'd been so absorbed in her own thoughts and worries, she'd hurt Becca's feelings. Another apology was in order.

"Becca, I messed up," she said. "I have no excuse. I should've called you as soon as Travis left this evening. Can you please forgive me?"

"Wait? He was *here* tonight too?" Becca patted the cushion next to her. "Sit. Talk."

"Can I get you something to drink first? Tea? Hot cocoa? Wine—anything?" She wanted to be sure her friend was well-tended.

"Let me hear your story first. I'll decide what beverage I need once I've heard the details."

Jillian curled up on the opposite end of the couch, pulling a soft, cream afghan over her shoulders.

"Well, Travis's friend Jack's SUV was used in the hit and run incident on Friday. Someone stole it from Jack's garage. We went over to—"

"Yeah, yeah, I know all the cop info. Don't get me wrong, it's awful. But get to the good stuff." Becca wriggled deeper into the couch cushions.

"Travis and I watched the forensics team collect evidence while we waited for Ethan. We sat on the porch swing so we'd be out of their way." She toyed with a stray curl escaped from her braid. "I'd forgotten to bring a coat, so Travis gave me his jacket."

"Yes, very nice. Chivalrous as well. Continue." Becca waved a hand urging her on.

"My emotions got the best of me." She shrugged at her perceived weakness. "I cried. He touched my cheek—wiped away a tear."

Jillian shivered at the memory of his thumb stroking her skin and the intensity of his stare. Her pulse quickened.

"Now we're talking." Becca rubbed her hands together. "What happened next?"

"I kissed him—"

Becca squealed.

"—on the cheek. I caught him by surprise."

"On the cheek?" Becca's shoulders drooped. "Okay. He brought you home. What happened next?" She leaned forward.

"He walked me to the door where we chatted a few minutes. We shared a clumsy hug, and he left."

"A kiss on the cheek and an awkward hug? I was expecting so much more when Ethan told me you two were snuggling on the porch swing."

"I wouldn't say we were snuggling—sitting close maybe." Jillian gave a one-shoulder shrug, an attempt to downplay the event. "Travis seems like a very thoughtful guy. I enjoy spending time with him."

"That goofy grin on your face says you think he's a whole lot more than thoughtful," Becca teased. "Are you falling for this guy? You just met him a few days ago."

"I'm not *falling* for him." Jillian's emphatic denial left Becca shaking her head.

"No. No. No. We're not going down this road again, Jilly." She scooted closer and took her friend's hands. "I know you too well. Your body language is screaming how much you like Travis. That's exactly how it started with He-Whose-Name-Shall-Not-Pass-Our-Lips. Don't do this to yourself again, please."

The fact her friend had so little faith in her hurt Jillian. "I'm well aware of what happened with Sco—"

"Ah-ah. Don't say his name." Becca waggled a finger. "Not now, not ever."

"I won't let that happen to me again." Jillian pulled the afghan—a true security blanket—tighter around her shoulders. "Don't you think it's time to let go of the old hurt and move ahead with my life? I don't want to end up old and alone. I want someone to share my life with, make a family. Don't I deserve that?"

"Of course, you do, sweetie." Becca pulled Jillian in for a hug. "You deserve that and so much more. I'm simply asking you to take it slow with Mr. Thoughtful and be careful."

"That's a promise I can make." She gave Becca a squeeze. "Now, what can I get you to drink?"

"Hot chocolate sounds good."

"You got it." Jillian scurried into the kitchen, filled two steaming mugs, and hurried back to the couch to continue the conversation.

"Tell me what you know about Mr. Wonderful," Becca said.

"He has a name—it's Travis."

"Yeah, whatever. I'll bother to remember it if he treats my bestie well. C'mon, fill me in."

Jillian gave her the basics about his job, his family, and what he looked like." She twisted the silver Claddagh ring on her right hand. "I've only known him a few days, yet every time we're together, he does or says something to make me like him more. He's sweet, thoughtful, brave, strong—everything I want in a guy. Am I crazy to be having romantic thoughts about a man I met on Saturday?"

"You're not crazy." Becca held up a hand in front of Jillian's face to stop her next words. "You want to find the perfect man and fall in love. I want you to take your time getting to know him. I don't want you to get serious and have another relationship end like your last one."

"You mean like a train wreck?" Jillian shuddered at the memories.

"Travis sounds like a great guy, but relationships take time. If this thing with him is meant to be, if he is the one, he won't mind taking it slow. A first date might be a good place to start."

"We're going out on Wednesday."

Becca let out an excited shriek. "Way to bury the lead. I've been here for thirty minutes, and you waited to tell me he'd asked you on a date?" She pointed toward the ceiling. "Man, he has your head in the clouds. Give me the info on date night."

"Wednesday night, six o'clock."

"What are the plans? You need to know what to wear."

"It's a surprise. He said to dress comfortably."

"I can help you with comfortable—that's easy. And you love surprises. This sounds like a recipe for a great first date." Jillian saw the spark of excitement in Becca's eyes.

"I'm glad you approve." Jillian smiled.

They drank a second mug of hot cocoa and chatted until Becca got a text from Ethan.

"My hubby is done with work and coming home. I better go and make sure he eats." Becca carried her empty mug to the kitchen sink. "If I'm not there, his dinner will consist of a beer and pretzels."

"Thanks for coming and kicking me in the pants." Jillian stood as Becca returned to the room. "I promise not to withhold any more information. You'll be the first call I make after my date."

"I'm holding you to it." Becca pointed at her. "And know this. I won't hesitate kicking him where it counts if Mr. Hunky Fireman gives you any grief." She grabbed her purse from the couch and hugged her friend. "I'll be back to help you find a fabulous first date outfit."

Jillian watched her climb into her car.

She was blessed to have Becca's friendship. Life wouldn't be the same without her.

She headed to the bathroom for a warm, relaxing soak in the tub. The new work week would be busy, and this might be her last chance to unwind. Gazing in the mirror, she piled her hair into a messy bun and smiled.

A busy week, which now includes a date with Travis. She couldn't wait.

Her alarm beeped at seven, like it did every morning. Today felt different. Jillian gave herself a few minutes lounging in bed to consider what the difference might be. In less than a minute, she knew.

Travis.

A shiver ran through her.

Oh, how her life had changed since they met.

Recalling how they'd met, guilt replaced happiness. Maggie would never fall in love with a great guy. She'd never experience love's first kiss or the excitement before a first date. Anger warred with sadness as Jillian thought of her friend's senseless murder.

The pups decided their mama should get moving and nosed her hands for attention. She rewarded their efforts with soft rubs. Putting on a robe and slippers, Jillian shuffled to the kitchen. The dogs' clicking toenails on hardwood trailed behind. Clipping on the pups' leashes, she opened the door to find a surprise someone had left for her.

A small bouquet of pink sweetheart roses—her favorites— lay on the porch. They were wrapped in pink floral paper with a note stuck among the blossoms. She slid the card out from the envelope and read the messy handwriting.

Looking forward to our date—Travis

Short, sweet, and to the point. She breathed in the flowers' scent. Once again, Travis made her weak in the knees with a simple gesture.

How did he get them here so early this morning? And how'd he know pink sweetheart roses are her favorite?

The B & B logo from her sister's flower shop, Blossoms & Blooms, adorning the blush pink paper answered both those questions.

Jillian winced at the thought of how relentless her sister could be. She hoped Amanda hadn't been too rough on him. Poor Travis.

"Looks like we'll need to stop and see Amanda today before heading into the bookstore," she informed her pups. "She'll want to talk to me—uh—interrogate is more like it."

The Waterford crystal vase her great-grandmother brought over from Ireland would be perfect for the petite pink blooms. As she arranged the flowers, Jillian wondered how she should respond to Travis's kind gesture. Was there protocol on how to thank a man for flowers when you haven't even been on a date yet?

While Jillian had no idea of the social etiquette, she knew someone who would. Not to mention, she'd promised to keep Becca apprised of all things having to do with Travis.

Grabbing her bag and promising Abbey and Hayley she'd be back soon, Jillian headed out the door. She prayed it wouldn't be too early to knock on the Hardens' door. This was Becca's one morning off.

Perhaps they'll forgive me if I bring breakfast.

Parking in front of Sugar & Spice, she stepped from the car, leaning back in to grab her purse. A man's voice shouted, "Jillian! Watch out!

CHAPTER FOURTEEN

Jillian jerked toward the voice as a silver sedan careened around the corner, heading straight at her. She slammed the door and bolted for the curb, escaping the car's path by inches. The sedan sideswiped her car, knocked off the driver's side mirror and left deep gouges from front to back. Without slowing, the car sped away down Maple Avenue.

Her heart raced. If someone hadn't shouted her name, she would've been killed—just like Maggie. With this realization came lightheadedness, nausea, sweaty palms, and blurred vision. She reached out, grabbing for something to steady herself.

Someone, not something, stopped her fall. A pair of strong, muscled arms grabbed her waist and drew her back against a rock-hard body. She leaned into the safety offered by this stranger. The arms held her, giving her time to stop shaking. Jillian took some deep breaths. Her vision cleared, and the nausea passed. As things returned to normal, she again heard someone calling her name.

"Jilly, oh my gosh. You could've been killed." Cate swooped in and grabbed Jillian away from the strong arms that had saved her, crushing her younger sister in a hug.

"I'm fine," she muttered. "You can let go. Please. I can't breathe."

Cate relaxed her grip but kept a hold of Jillian's arm. Her attention shifted to Jillian's rescuer, thanking him for saving her sister's life.

"Your heroics ruined your breakfast." Cate pointed to the spilled cinnamon rolls strewn across the ground. "Don't worry. I'll get you a new box. We're taking some fresh ones out of the oven."

Jillian turned to offer thanks to the man who'd saved her life. She gazed at him, noting how handsome Travis looked in his uniform. His smile unhinged her. Choking back a sob, her eyes filled with tears.

"Hey, hey, what's this?" He wrapped his arms around her and reeled her in. "Everything's fine. You're not hurt. Your car can be fixed. No permanent damage." His attempt at lighthearted humor did little to stem her flow of tears.

She let him hold her close—a safe harbor in a storm. After a moment, she stepped back enough to see his face. "If you hadn't shouted, I would've stepped into that car's path." There was more she wanted to say. Her voice cracked and her soft thank you escaped in a whisper.

He gave her an extra squeeze. "No thanks are necessary. I'm just glad you're all right."

The commotion caused a small crowd to gather. They gawked at the couple's display of public affection.

"Maybe we should move this party inside the bakery." She gave Travis her hand.

Approaching sirens drowned out his response. Ethan screeched to a stop. Leaving his unmarked car in a 'No Parking' zone, he slammed the door and marched toward Jillian. Without a word, he grabbed her in a bear hug and held on for a few seconds.

He shook hands with Travis. "I hear you're the hero of the day. Our girl is lucky you were around and paying attention. Glad she's all in one piece."

"Excuse me. I am standing right here," she chastised Ethan. "And how did you ... who told you ... I had a—"

"Attempt on your life." His face changed from concerned friend to serious cop in an instant. "Someone called 9-1-1. Said a car almost ran a woman over. I came to investigate. As I turned the corner, I saw it was you."

Ethan gestured at the people who'd gathered. "Maybe we should take this conversation somewhere private. Travis, I know you're on duty. Is it possible you could stay for a while? I need to take your statement."

"Sure. I can take the rig out of service for an hour or so. Let me call dispatch." He stepped away, talking into his radio and giving directions to his crew. "You two come on in. I'm buying breakfast—again."

Jillian and Ethan were seated at a cozy table near the back when Travis joined them. Cate placed steaming cups of coffee on the table.

"This man gets all the cinnamon rolls he can eat for free for the rest of his life. After all, he saved my sister's life." Cate squeezed Travis's shoulder. "I'll make a tray of treats for your crew too. I hope they're hungry." She pointed to the table where his engineer and firefighter sipped their morning brew.

"They're always hungry. And thank you, but free rolls aren't necessary." Travis gave her a bright smile. "Please make sure I get the bill for my crew. Give them whatever they want."

Ethan pushed his coffee aside. Wasting no time, he whipped out his trusty notebook and fired his first question.

"Can you describe the car?"

Jillian and Travis agreed it had been a silver, four-door sedan. Neither could remember anything else.

"Driver?"

Travis admitted his attention had been on Jillian. Her focus had been on getting out of the way.

Ethan cleared his throat. "Did you notice anyone following you on the way to the bakery?"

Jillian wrinkled her nose. "No. Why would you ask?"

"I don't mean to scare you, but we have to be realistic," Ethan said. "The odds of this being a random incident are slim to none in light of Maggie's death."

"I had the same thought of course." She fidgeted with the sugar bowl on the table. "There's no way this is a coincidence. The car made no effort to slow down or miss me. I'd bet anything the driver is the same man who killed Maggie. I wonder whose car he stole this time."

Cate arrived with a platter of fresh-baked cinnamon rolls, offering them to Travis first. He helped himself to one of the warm gooey treats. Jillian smiled as she watched a wide grin spread across his face.

"I can't help myself. These are pastry perfection."

Ethan declined a sweet treat. "Now that I know everyone's okay, I have to leave—get some work done." He faced Jillian. "Sorry about your angry visitor last night, but I can't hide these things from Becca." Ethan closed his notebook. "I'll be in the doghouse if I don't tell her about this morning's incident, so I imagine you'll hear from her soon. Please take care, Jilly." He dropped a kiss on top of her head before leaving.

"Funny he mentioned Becca," Jillian said. "I was on my way to see her this morning for some advice."

"Advice about what?" Cate asked.

"Someone left a bouquet of beautiful sweetheart roses on my porch this morning. I wanted her advice on the best way to say thank you." She raised an eyebrow at Travis, who blushed the same color as the rosy blooms he'd left at her door.

Cate opened her mouth to give her own advice. "Well, you could—"

Jillian interrupted. "Thank you, Travis. The flowers are beautiful. Pink roses are my favorite."

"Your sister told me—your other sister—after she gave me the third degree when I asked what flowers you liked best."

"Well, a man we've never met comes in to buy flowers for our baby sister ..." Cate let her voice trail off.

"I apologize for Amanda's cross-examination." Jillian glared at Cate. "Both my sisters tend to fuss because I'm the youngest. They think it's their job to watch out for me."

"Someone has to," Cate blurted out. "You keep getting yourself into trouble."

Her attention turned to Travis. "I can tell she's in good hands with you." Cate winked at him. "Nice to meet you. Don't be a stranger." She walked away, cloth in hand, to wipe down a few tables.

"Don't be upset with your sister, Jillian. Everybody needs someone like her in their life," Travis said. "I think it's nice you three sisters are close and take care of each other."

"Like the way you did for me today." Jillian hesitated for a moment. "If it weren't for you, I could've been—"

"Stop." The harsh tone of his voice shocked Jillian. "I don't want to hear what you're about to say. I'm glad I was there, and you weren't injured. Nothing else needs to be said." He waved off further attempts at discussion.

They sat and talked a bit longer, enjoying each other's company. One glance at her watch, and Jillian realized her pups would need her home soon.

"I'm sorry. I need to go." She stood and pushed in her chair.

"No problem. I should get our rig back in service." He laid two twenties on the table.

She smiled at his generosity, knowing Cate would never accept his money. The cash would somehow find its way back to him.

Travis walked Jillian to her car, which thank goodness, was drivable. She ran her fingers down the deep gouges and sighed.

"I'll call my insurance agent and a mechanic as soon as I get to the bookstore. I don't want to drive around in a damaged car."

She hugged Travis, thanking him again for everything he'd done. He held on to her as if he were afraid to let go. Everyone in the bakery and on the street stared at their embrace. This included Cate, who'd been spying on them from the store's window. Jillian gave her an exaggerated wave. Cate grinned and went back to work.

Travis made sure Jillian got into her car safe and sound. As he crossed the street and climbed onto his rig, she watched him in her rearview mirror.

This day started rough, but things are looking up. Thanks to that wonderful guy.

She felt herself smiling at the memory.

CHAPTER FIFTEEN

The dogs weren't the only ones waiting at home. Becca stood on the front porch with her hands on her hips. For the second time in less than twenty-four hours, Jillian prepared to face the full force of her friend's anger. She was shocked by the response she received.

Without saying a word, Becca launched herself at Jillian and wrapped her arms around her—tight.

Oof. Is she trying to hug me or crush me? And why isn't she yelling? Becca always yells when she's mad.

Jillian soon realized why Becca was mute. Her body shuddered with heart-wrenching sobs.

"Hey, sweetie, calm down." She begged her bestie to take some deep breaths. "I don't want you to hyperventilate."

Becca loosened her grip. She sucked in a few huge gulps of air and slowed her breathing.

"There you go. Much better." Jillian patted Becca's back. "Wow, I'm not sure I've ever seen you this upset."

"I've never been this upset because no one has ever tried to kill my best friend before today." Becca's nostrils flared, a sure sign her anger was in hyperdrive.

"I understand." Jillian stuck the key in the lock. "Let's go inside. Maybe rubbing the pups will calm you down—always works for me."

Once they were inside, two enthusiastic schnauzers accosted them, demanding attention. Their exuberance made Becca smile. She dropped to her knees and loved on them until their mutual needs were satisfied.

"I want a dog." She gave each pup a kiss on their furry heads. "Ethan needs to get with the program."

Soon, my friend. Very soon.

"If you're done smooching on my dogs, go on inside. I'll take them out for a quick spin around the yard." She clipped on their leashes.

Back inside in under five minutes, Jillian found Becca settled on the couch, sipping a glass of white wine. She lifted it in salute.

"Don't you dare judge me. I'm sure it's five o'clock somewhere." She patted the couch, inviting the pups to join her. They happily complied. "Ethan filled in most of the details. Now, I need to hear your version." Becca motioned for Jillian to join her on the sofa. "Don't leave anything out."

Following her friend's directions, Jillian relayed the horrible episode from the beginning.

"The story is even more chilling the second time around. If Travis hadn't shouted at you, we wouldn't be here enjoying this wine." Becca shuddered and wrapped an afghan from the couch around her body. "And may I say, I'm liking this hunky fireman of yours."

"Becca, stop. He's not *my* fireman, and you're the only one drinking wine at ten in the morning. Second, I'm aware of what would've happened. The driver would've hit me like he did Maggie. Whoever this guy is, he needs to be caught, or he'll succeed in killing again."

"He's a lunatic," Becca declared.

"No, he's evil." Jillian hurled a pillow across the room. "Ethan has to arrest him soon."

Hearing their mama's voice getting louder, Abbey and Hayley ran to her side to provide comfort. She reached down and cuddled them both. Their nearness soothed her.

Who needed to drink wine when they had dogs?

The women chatted until Becca had to leave for the bakery to prep for the lunch crowd.

"Promise you'll watch out for yourself." Becca sounded tough. The fresh tears filling her eyes betrayed her. "I have one best friend. I don't intend to lose her, you hear me?"

Jillian promised to be vigilant. They shared a hug before Becca made a hasty exit.

"Girls, it's time to head for the bookstore. Let's go." She needed a distraction. Showing up early for her shift would take care of that.

Hearing the word *go* sent the dogs scrambling for the door, their toenails clicking out a rhythm on the hardwood.

Jillian used the drive to work to rack her brain for any detail she might have missed from this morning's brush with death. Everything happened so fast—the car, Travis yelling, her struggling to get out of the way—it all blurred together.

Wait a minute. There was something.

She banged on the steering wheel—the license plate. There was some kind of fruit—an apple? A pear, maybe?

"A peach!" Her triumphant shout startled the sleeping pups in the back seat. "The plate had a peach on it! That car is from Georgia."

She grabbed her phone to call Ethan only to find it dead, and the charger was on her desk at work. The call could wait until she got to the bookstore.

Jillian drove past the store on her way around back to park. A bunch of cars on the street grabbed her attention. A neighbor must have company, or better yet, Whimsy & Wonder was doing a brisk business this morning. The latter made her smile, thinking of the store's bottom line.

Stopped at the intersection, she inspected the cars more closely. She realized they were familiar—her father's black Ford F-150, Amanda's new red Mustang, and Aunt Grace's white hybrid filled the spots in front of the shop while Cate's minivan sat parked in front of Mr. Erickson's house.

The gangs all here.

Turning her head, she spotted the rusted gray truck parked around the corner.

Oh, for heaven's sake. Even Bryan's here.

The whole family must've heard about this morning's excitement. In true Edwards' fashion, they'd come to check on her for themselves. After she parked in the alley behind the bookstore, she unloaded the pups and steeled herself for what awaited inside.

"C'mon, girls, time to face the music."

The moment Jillian stepped into the store, her father wrapped her in his arms and whispered in her ear. "Hey, Peanut. Heard you had a rough morning."

His words threatened to unravel the tight control of her emotions Jillian had clung to since leaving Travis's arms. She leaned against her dad's broad shoulder and allowed herself a minute of self-pity.

"Hi, Dad." A single tear left a trail down her cheek. "I've had better days."

Everyone else clamored to hug her before the barrage of questions erupted. She tried her best to answer, assuring everyone she was unharmed.

"I knew something bad would happen. I saw it in the tea leaves on Friday.

"You were right, Aunt Grace. We should have listened."

"Hmm, I don't know." She pursed her lips. "I'm a bit ashamed. How *could* I have thought the problem would end with the smashed computer and printer?" Aunt Grace berated herself. "Some horrible woman comes to town bringing her negative aura. Our Jilly is almost killed like her friend. Why didn't I see it?" She moaned, dropping her head into her hands.

"Aunt Grace, please stop. Everything's fine. I'm not hurt. My car can be fixed. No harm, no foul."

"No foul? You can't be serious." Bryan growled through clenched teeth. "I don't usually agree with my mother. In this instance, she's right to be worried. Someone targeted you—tried to kill you."

"And we know why." Amanda joined the conversation. "You've stuck your nose into Ethan's investigation. The murderer isn't happy. What will it take to get you to back off?"

Jillian saw their faces cloaked with worry and fear. Her actions had caused this concern. Guilt radiated through her.

"I'm sorry, everyone." Jillian averted her eyes from their apprehensive stares. "Sometimes I get carried away. My curiosity gets the best of me."

"Now, there's an understatement."

Jillian ignored Cate's sarcasm. "I'm sorry I've caused you concern, I really am. You can't deny I've been instrumental in finding information relating to this case though." Groans went up around the room, causing her to become defensive. "Well, it's true. Without me, Ethan would be in the dark."

"He's an experienced detective, Jilly. He'd have found those clues without you." Bryan pounded his fist on the counter.

"Yes, but I found them sooner rather than later." She shot a smug glance in Bryan's direction, noticing her mom wiped at tears. Her heart broke. "From now on, I promise to stay alert. I'll be on guard until Ethan solves this case and puts the killer behind bars. Okay?"

A few bobbed their heads. Others mumbled a half-hearted agreement. The deal was sealed. She would watch herself while her family tried not to worry.

Who am I kidding? Knowing them, they've already planned a twelve-step intervention.

"I'm glad we got this settled." Jillian motioned to the door. "I need to get busy on a project."

Taking the hint, Trixie went to wait on new customers. Bryan gave Jillian a one-armed hug and headed out the door. Amanda hid in the store's office while Jillian convinced her parents, Aunt Grace, and Cate she'd be safe here with Trixie. Everyone drifted off, agreeing to a late supper at McGuire's after Jillian closed the bookstore. Aunt Grace called it a 'therapeutic' family dinner, a chance for them to relax and try to forget the recent tragedy.

"I'll be with Amanda if you need me," Jillian told Trixie before trudging down the hall.

"Sure thing, boss. I have everything under control." Trixie let out a shaky breath. "I'm glad you weren't hurt. We were all so scared when we heard about your accident."

"Thanks for the concern, Trixie. Sorry for the worry." She headed down the hall to face Amanda.

But my near-death experience was no accident.

Jillian knew her family would object. That couldn't be helped. This case had become personal. Because of this morning, she was more determined than ever to help find information to solve this case. She'd have to be more covert with her efforts.

Opening the door, Jillian found Amanda sitting in the comfy chair wedged in the corner, texting someone like crazy. She put her phone down to give Jillian her full attention.

"The family is gone. Now, tell me how you're really doing? You're holding back—aren't you—so they won't worry even more?"

"I'm fine." Jillian leaned back against the door. "Yes, it was scary. For a minute, I thought I might die—I didn't. I'm here in one piece. Can we give it a rest?"

Exhaustion crept into her body. She didn't have the energy to fight with Amanda.

Maybe she'll drop it now.

No such luck.

"Fine. Change of subject. Let's chat about Travis." Amanda raised her eyebrows to greet her hairline. "I met him this morning—early. He banged on my door before I'd even opened, wanting to buy you flowers. What's the deal with him?"

Jillian plopped into the leather captain's desk chair she'd inherited from Grandpa McGuire. The worn, brown leather and the lingering smell of his pipe tobacco made her think of simpler times. She sighed and addressed her sister's question.

"There's no deal. Travis and I met a few days ago. Fate keeps pushing us into each other's path. We hit it off, and we have a date tomorrow. Satisfied?"

"Not even close." Amanda's soft blonde hair swung as she shook her head. "Cate said you two shared a lengthy hug in front of the bakery after being snuggled at a back table. Then, there are the flowers. Your first date isn't until tomorrow, and this guy has already bought you my most expensive roses. And how is it he happened to be at the bakery today just when your life was threatened? This is all a bit too coincidental for me." Amanda's blue eyes didn't blink.

Jillian's shoulders slumped. She didn't want a face-off with her sister.

"Travis is a sweet guy. We've spent time together in the past three days because of Maggie. He's been in the store twice. We had some iced tea together at my place. And we helped his friend with a problem related to the case."

Amanda cleared her throat to speak. Jillian's open palm and angry stare stopped her.

"No. You wanted answers. Let me finish." She paused, trying to rein in her anger. "Travis was at Sugar & Spice this morning because he loves the cinnamon rolls. He was there to buy some for his crew. Thank goodness he was, or I might not be here sparring with you. Happy?"

Jillian rested her head in her hands and waited for the snarky remark she anticipated. Instead, Amanda shocked her with an apology.

"I'm sorry," she said. "I shouldn't have snapped at you. It's just ... the man who killed your friend is coming after you. This guy, Travis, appears out of nowhere, showering you with flowers and saving your life. How do we know he's not involved in Maggie's murder somehow?"

"Are you kidding me?" Jillian stared at Amanda in disbelief.

"Maybe. I mean ... how well can you know the guy in a few days?"

Funny. I've asked myself that same question.

"I know he's the firefighter who tried to save Maggie's life. I know he's a fierce friend and a thoughtful guy. I know he saved my life today. And I know my middle sister reads too many suspense novels." Jillian pointed a finger at Amanda. "You're crazy if you think Travis is involved in this."

"I'm sure you're right. I just think it might be a good idea to hold off on this date until the case is solved." Amanda held her palms upward and shrugged. "And please stop interfering in Ethan's case. Let him finish this investigation on his own."

Jillian regretted her part in making everyone worry, including Amanda, but there was no way Travis was involved in Maggie's murder. She wouldn't postpone their date, but she could agree perhaps it was time to let Ethan take care of things without her intrusion. Everyone's lives would be easier, including hers and Ethan's, if she stepped back from the case.

Jillian let out a tired sigh. "I promise not to stick my nose into Ethan's case if I can help it, but the information I've found thus far has fallen into my lap. There's no guarantee it won't happen again." She shrugged, hoping to put an end to this discussion.

"I'm going to hold you to that weak promise. You know this family will stage an intervention if you go back on your word." Amanda spoke into her phone. "Did you guys hear what she said?"

Jillian's mouth dropped open when she realized what Amanda had done. "You had your phone on this whole time. Who heard us?"

Better question—did I say anything inappropriate or embarrassing about Travis I may be sorry for later?

"Everyone—Mom and Dad, Aunt Grace, Cate, Becca, Bryan. Oh, and Ethan, of course." Amanda waggled her phone at Jillian. "They all heard you promise to stay out of this investigation. They'll hold you to it, Jilly."

"You're unbelievable. All of you." She grabbed Amanda's phone and shouted at her family. "I can't believe you listened in on our private conversation."

"Nothing's private in this family." Amanda grinned at her sister's outrage. "Did you really think we'd be pacified in under thirty minutes after you were almost killed? You should know better."

Yes, she should. Her family had left with little argument after a brief assurance about her well-being. If she'd given any thought to the family meeting in the store, Jillian would've realized how uncharacteristic their behavior had been. Her mother hadn't fussed. Her father hadn't offered his advice on handling the problem, and Aunt Grace hadn't asked to sit down and read her palm.

Cate's flimsy excuse she needed to get back to the bakery didn't hold water either. It was Becca's day to close the shop. Even Bryan left without much drama. His usual MO was to stomp around and threaten to kick someone's butt.

Jillian had pushed her family away when they'd needed her promise she'd be careful, not take more risks. She owed them that much. Her next words were chosen carefully.

"Again, I'm sorry. From here on out, I'll try my best not to interfere in the investigation."

"Thank you," Ethan's voice shouted from Amanda's phone. Everyone laughed. The tension had broken.

"Are we still on for dinner at McGuire's?" Amanda asked everyone who was listening. A unanimous round of yeses answered back. "Should we say eight o'clock?"

"I'll be there after I close, which means the girls will be with me. Maybe Bryan will be a nice guy and let Abbey and Hayley hang out in his office." Jillian eyed the phone.

"Fine," Bryan called out. "We'd better pray the health inspector doesn't choose tonight for a surprise visit. If he finds those hairy mutts in my place, he'll shut me down in a heartbeat."

Aunt Grace reminded Jillian to invite Trixie. With their plans confirmed, the phone call ended. Amanda shrugged into her coat and dropped her phone in her pocket. She made a move for the door, then stopped.

"Are you mad at me for not telling you they were listening? I admit it was a dirty trick."

"At first, but I've moved on." Jillian dismissed it with a wave of her hand. "I understand you're all concerned for me. I didn't handle it well. Now it's done—forgiven." She grabbed her sister by the arm. "Don't pull a stunt like this again."

"Don't make me need to," Amanda snapped back. "And Jilly, you need to clean this office— what a mess."

When Amanda left a room with a parting shot, all was truly forgiven.

CHAPTER SIXTEEN

Trixie stayed past her normal shift, listening to Jillian's family's latest antics.

"You really should've known they wouldn't be easily pacified. What were you thinking?" Trixie chuckled, shaking her head. "They love you and want you to be safe, you know."

"I do, yes." Jillian straightened a shelf of books near the counter. "In my defense, I had just been nearly run down in the street! My brain wasn't functioning at its best."

"True. A *valid* defense in my opinion."

"They want you to join us for dinner—stop shaking your head no. You said it yourself, they won't be easily pacified."

After much coaxing, Trixie agreed to come.

"Okay, I'll be there. I appreciate the invitation."

"Thank goodness. You would disappoint everyone if you didn't come. They'd blame me for not trying hard enough to get you there. I'd rather not hear more grief from anyone today."

"I do love your family gatherings. You guys can always be counted on for dinner and a show." Trixie giggled at something.

"What's so funny?"

"Remember when your dad burned down the tool shed in the neighbor's backyard as we sat down to Easter dinner? That was classic Edwards' holiday entertainment."

"Yes, I remember." The memory brought a smile to Jillian's face. "Dad tried to put out the flames with a garden hose—only made matters worse. My mom warned him it was too windy to burn leaves. As usual, he didn't listen."

"Let's hope McGuire's is still standing after tonight's dinner. We should keep all things flammable away from your dad." Trixie snickered as she grabbed her bag and headed for the door.

"Oh hey, before you go—I still haven't found Maggie's gift. Are you sure you didn't put it somewhere?"

"I never saw the box Maggie brought you, but I'm keeping an eye out for it. Don't worry, it'll turn up." Trixie waved as she breezed out the door.

Jillian searched for the elusive box. She didn't get far with her efforts, as customers needed her attention.

Darkness had fallen outside when the bell above the door jingled for the umpteenth time. Travis's solid frame filled the doorway.

"Hi there." Leaning in, he kissed her cheek. "Oh, was that okay?"

"Absolutely." Jillian picked lint off his shirt—wait—a red flannel shirt. He wasn't wearing his uniform. "Aren't you supposed to be on duty today?"

He wouldn't make eye contact as he shifted from one foot to the other, twisting a ball cap in his hands.

"Um ... I ... well. I'm here to ... "

"Travis, what's going on?" Jillian squinted up at him. "You're acting strange."

"Bryan and Ethan were supposed to tell you."

"Tell me what?" She sensed she wasn't going to like his answer.

"Well, we decided ... that is ... we thought—"

"Spit it out. Whatever grand plan you three hatched must involve me by the way you're fumbling your way through this conversation." Jillian's foot tapped out an impatient rhythm.

He sucked in a big breath and blew it out. "Can you try not to get mad? We only want to keep you safe."

"I'm sorry. Keep me safe?" Her emotions waffled between anger and amusement.

"Yes, safe. We're worried the guy from this morning will come back. We don't like you being here by yourself at night. Ethan says it makes you an easy target. We'll be here on the nights you close to keep an eye on things." He clamped his mouth shut.

He rambled, which she'd learned meant he was nervous. *They should all be nervous.*

A small part of her was touched these guys cared enough to devise this ridiculous plan. The bigger, more vocal part of her was insulted.

"So, I'm a helpless female who needs three big, strong men to protect her, and you geniuses plan to camp out here keeping guard." She motioned to the room they stood in. "This is my business. You can't skulk around here watching my customers. You'll make them nervous and chase them off."

She waited for him to say something. He stood silent, returning her glare. Rather than explode again, she let off steam straightening books on the shelves.

When Travis found his voice, he came back with a few strong words of his own. "Bryan said you'd be mad—we don't care about that. Your safety is more important than your anger toward us. We don't think you're a helpless female. What we do think is the killer is escalating. Ethan said criminals like this won't stop if they believe they have nothing to lose. We're willing to face your wrath, not your death." He shoved both hands in his jacket.

Stunned by his forcefulness, yet touched by his fervor, Jillian wrapped her arms around his waist and placed her cheek against his chest. He held her, resting his chin on her head. They stayed together until the bell on the door signaled a customer. She winked at him and went to greet the new arrival. Travis leaned against the wall in the Reading Room, giving him a clear view of the front door and anyone who might come in.

At eight o'clock on the dot, Jillian flipped the lock and closed the wooden window blinds. She straightened the rooms—pushed in chairs, replaced books on the shelves, and shut off lights. Her final task was to close out the register and prepare the day's deposit.

"I'm done. Let's go." She grabbed her bag and whistled for the girls, who scampered from behind the counter. They dashed to the door with their mama in tow.

"Are you coming?" She stared at Travis.

"Yeah. I'll make sure you get into your car before I leave." He held the door open.

"Do you have to go back to the fire station?"

"Nope, I used comp time to be here tonight."

"I have no idea what comp time is." She placed a hand on his arm. "But I'm guessing it means you're free for the night, right?"

"Yes—"

She cut him off again. "Great. You can follow me to McGuire's and have dinner with my family. I owe you a good meal for using your comp time to keep me safe."

The color drained from Travis's face.

Oh yeah. Payback's going to be fun.

"I don't want to intrude on your family's evening. Besides, they'll think it's odd I'm there. I mean ... we haven't even been on our first date yet." He gaped like a mouse trapped in the corner by a fat cat licking its chops.

"Fair is fair." Her saccharine smile could've sweetened Aunt Grace's tea. "You thought making plans for me was fine, so I'm making plans for you."

Even though her anger toward the guys for their idiotic plan had cooled, she didn't plan to let them off the hook yet, including Travis.

"I'll meet you at McGuire's in a few minutes." She set the alarm and locked the back door, stepping into the alley separating the store and its garage.

"Jillian, please. Wait a minute. This isn't a good idea." His face had taken on a green hue, like he might vomit.

"Newsflash. You three amigos camped out in my store isn't a good idea, either. You're still going to do it, aren't you?"

"Yes, we are. We're trying to protect you, keep you from being killed." He argued, almost begged. "This isn't the time for me to meet your family."

"Relax. You already know my Aunt Grace, Bryan, and Ethan. You met my sister, Amanda, this morning, and you know Cate from the bakery. Trixie will be there too. The only people you haven't met are my mom and dad. Oh—and Becca. You'll be fine. I won't let any of them bite you." She continued toward her car. "I'll call ahead and tell Bryan there'll be one more for dinner."

"Fine." He hung his head in defeat. "I can admit when I've been outmaneuvered. I hope I don't have to say, 'I told you so' if this evening is a disaster."

"There won't be a problem." She knew her family. They'd

welcome him with open arms after his heroic actions this morning. There might be some sideways glances and one or two awkward questions from her dad or Amanda, but nothing he couldn't handle.

Jillian and Travis arrived at McGuire's at eight fifteen. The huge dinner crowd made finding two places to park difficult. After she circled the block, a spot became available for Jillian. Travis parked around the corner. Jogging the two blocks to the pub, he helped unload her dogs. They'd arranged with Bryan to use the back door so his regular customers wouldn't witness two furry patrons being smuggled in.

Using the agreed upon signal, Jillian knocked five times—fast, fast, slow, fast, fast. Bryan opened the door, making no effort to hide his pleasure at Travis's presence at this family gathering. The two men shared a bro-hug and a firm handshake.

"Hurry and get the dogs in here." Bryan held the door open wide for the foursome. "I put some blankets under the desk, and I got them each a bone to keep them occupied." Hearing the word *bone* sent Abbey and Hayley into a frenzied fit of wiggles. "Max even heard the girls were coming. He's prepared a snack for them." Max was Bryan's cook and avid dog-lover who spoiled Abbey and Hayley any chance he got.

"My girls will love you and Max forever." Jillian hugged Bryan, whispering in his ear. "I'm really mad at you right now. You being nice to my girls could work in your favor." She smacked him on the chest and led Abbey and Hayley into the office.

Bryan wheeled around on Travis. "She's not thrilled

with our plan, huh?"

"Correct. She gave me an earful before guilting me into dinner. This isn't the time to meet her family, dude."

"Aw, it won't be so bad. You know me, Ethan, and Trixie. You've met my mom and survived. The rest will be easy." He winked and punched Travis's arm.

"He'll be fine." Jillian herded the men toward the back of the restaurant.

The crack of pool balls being broken and Garth Brooks singing about his friends in low places welcomed them. The mouthwatering scents of tangy barbecue sauce, grilled meat, and garlic assaulted their noses as they found their chairs.

The family sat at one long table. They'd been served drinks and appetizer platters piled high with jalapeno poppers, antipasto skewers, and stuffed mushrooms. Loud talk and laughter quieted at the latecomers arrival, causing a moment of awkward silence.

"Everyone, this is Travis." Jillian made the introductions. "Travis, this is my family." Going around the table, she helped him put names to the people he was meeting for the first time.

She was thrilled to introduce him to Sam, Amanda's boyfriend. His presence at dinner was a pleasant surprise. Sam's career as a professional photographer kept him away from home weeks at a time. He traveled to exotic places around the world on photo shoots. Most recently, he'd been in Fiji on assignment for a travel magazine.

Absent from tonight's dinner was Cate's husband, Wes, who was home on kid patrol. Tuesday is, after all, a school night and her nieces had a nine o'clock bedtime.

As expected, Jillian's family welcomed Travis with open

arms. Her dad patted him on the back every chance he got. Sam and Becca offered him the chair between them. Her mother and Aunt Grace fussed over him, bringing him an icy cold drink and a plate heaped with appetizers.

With all the attention being lavished on Travis, Jillian pulled up a seat between her sisters—close enough to Travis in case he needed rescuing. She'd browbeat him into this family dinner as punishment for his part in the guy's plan to protect her. She'd keep an eye on him and make sure he wasn't nervous or uncomfortable. Her anger at her protectors had cooled somewhat, but she wasn't willing to forgive and forget.

Ethan tried several times to catch her eye. She avoided making direct contact.

I'm not ready yet, Detective Harden.

Bryan attended to her beverage refills and rubbed her shoulder every time he passed.

You know you put your foot in it, don't you, cousin?

And Travis. He sat there, enjoying his conversation with Sam and Becca.

And you were worried this wasn't a good idea.

"I can't believe you brought him tonight." Amanda nodded toward Travis.

"He sure looks at ease at our family dinner." Cate glanced over at him. "How in the world did you get a guy you met four days ago to agree to come?"

"I manipulated him—a payback of sorts." Jillian shared the scheme hatched by Ethan, Travis, and Bryan to keep her safe from the killer. Both sisters sat with their mouths open.

"You've got to be kidding me," Amanda said. "I can't believe those three came up with such a great plan. Why didn't I think of it?"

Jillian smacked her sister on the arm. "I don't need to be

protected. I'm capable on my own, thank you."

"You needed Travis's help this morning." Cate sipped her iced tea. "If it weren't for his quick thinking, things could've been worse than a missing mirror and some scratched paint."

Cate made a good point. If Travis hadn't shouted Jillian's name, she would've been killed in the street. This reminder of her close call made her glance at the faces around the table—the faces of the people she cared for the most.

Did this now include Travis? As if reading her mind, he met her gaze across the table and smiled. Her heart betrayed her with a skipped beat.

Why does he have this effect on me?

"Oh. My. Gosh." Becca punctuated each word, rushing around the table and plopping in a chair next to Jillian. "Travis is amazing. He's smart, funny, and gorgeous. Sam and I are having a blast with him. In my opinion, he's a keeper. Did I mention he tells great stories? Oh, gotta go—don't want to miss his next one." Becca dashed back to her seat next to Travis.

"Becca's given an enthusiastic seal of approval." Cate watched her pastry chef settle back into her chair, hanging on Travis's every word. "I may have to agree with her on this one. Every time the guy comes into the bakery, he's friendly, polite, and likes my cinnamon rolls. Not to mention, he saved our baby sister's life." Cate slapped something down on the table. "He left this money at the bakery today. Make sure he gets it back please." She slid the folded bills to Jillian, who slipped them into her pocket.

"I'm not ready to jump on his bandwagon yet," Amanda cut in. "I will say when he came in my shop this morning, he complimented the remodel and asked my opinion on which flowers to buy. Unlike most men, he followed my advice and bought the pink roses, despite the fact they're pricey this time of year. So, at least he appears to have good taste. And he's not stupid."

From Amanda, this was something close to a rave review. She didn't hand out compliments freely. Instead, she reserved her excitement for her flower shop, Sam, dogs, and St. Louis Cardinal baseball.

"Thank you both for your evaluation of my choice in dinner guests, but you can relax. We've known each other four days. Our first date isn't until tomorrow. We may find we have nothing in common."

Please, don't let it be true. I really like this guy.

She couldn't wait for the date to find out if he felt the same.

"Hey, Peanut." Her dad put his arm around her and kissed her cheek. He gestured toward Travis. "This young man who saved your life—think I'll have a chat with him."

"Dad, be nice," Jillian whispered through gritted teeth. Her father winked and headed toward Travis.

Cate said something, yet Jillian didn't hear a word—her attention was focused on the woman who'd walked through the door. From the short, curly, red hair to the light green eyes and petite frame, this woman could be Maggie's ghost. Jillian forgot to breathe.

There she was—the mystery woman from the bookstore. No wonder Aunt Grace had freaked out. This woman was an exact replica of Maggie.

The stranger stood less than twenty feet away, leaning against the bar and laughing with Mike, Bryan's bartender. Without a word, Jillian jumped from her chair and crossed the room to confront their visitor.

Jillian tapped the woman on the shoulder. "Who are

you? Why are you here?"

"I came in for a drink and something to eat. This is a pub, isn't it? What's it to you, anyway?" The snarky response infuriated Jillian.

The women's raised voices attracted the other patrons' attention. Utensils and glasses were set down. All eyes were trained on them. No one wanted to miss a moment.

"I'm Jillian Edwards. I understand you came into my bookstore and frightened my aunt. I've also heard you've gone to the grade school where I used to work asking questions. Now you show up here—my cousin's restaurant—where my family is having dinner. What do you want?" She jabbed her finger in the woman's face.

Rather than answer, the woman broke down. Her shoulders heaved. Large tears dribbled down both cheeks. She twisted and untwisted the flowered scarf she wore to the point she almost strangled herself.

This woman's mood swings could give me whiplash.

"Everybody, calm down." Ethan stepped between them, facing Maggie's doppelgänger. "Ma'am, my name is Ethan Harden. I'm a detective here in Willow Springs. Your arrival in our small town has caused quite a stir. Let's go in back and talk—maybe clarify a few things."

With all the pub's patrons watching, Jillian and the stranger followed him to Bryan's office. When the door opened, two excited pups catapulted themselves at the humans. The weeping woman, startled by their appearance, dropped to her knees and showered them with attention. Their unexpected presence quieted her sobbing.

Impatient to discover this woman's identity, Jillian herded Abbey and Hayley onto their blankets, luring them with a treat. She chose one chair in front of Bryan's desk and motioned for their visitor to sit in the other. Ethan positioned himself behind the desk, keeping his trained eye on the door and their guest.

The woman took some tissue from her purse and wiped her eyes. "Those pups are adorable. Do they live here?"

"No, they're mine. They live with me." Jillian's response was clipped.

"I can't believe the owner allows animals in here, even ones as adorable as those two." She smiled at both dogs.

"As I said before, my cousin owns McGuire's, so it's no problem." Jillian snapped out her words. "I've answered your questions. I'd like answers to mine."

"Ahem." Ethan cleared his throat. He shook his head, which Jillian knew meant 'I'm in charge and will do the talking.' She silenced the questions running through her head.

Fine, I'll be quiet. For a while.

"Ma'am, let's start with your name," Ethan said.

"Moira Flannery." The words came out on a whispered breath.

"Nice to meet you, Ms. Flannery." He offered his hand, which she ignored. "I'm glad you stopped by tonight. Our town's rumor mill has talked about you for days."

"Due to the resemblance to my sister." Fresh tears rolled down Moira's cheeks. She grabbed another tissue as her bombshell pronouncement hung in the air like a storm cloud.

"You can't be Maggie's sister." Jillian couldn't hide her shock. "She didn't have any siblings."

"She and I are twins. I mean ... we were." Moira dropped her gaze and let the tears fall, making no attempt to brush them away.

"Twins, hmm." Ethan scribbled in his notebook. "Ms.

Flannery, can you tell me why you wanted to speak with Ms. Edwards?"

"I read in the paper my sister died in a hit-and-run accident outside her bookstore. The paper listed her as the owner. I thought she—you—might've known my sister." The scarf twisting started again.

"I'm sorry you found out your sister had passed from the newspaper," Ethan said. "When I searched for relatives, there was no record of Maggie having siblings. How do you explain that?"

"That's a complicated story." She crumpled the tissue in her hands. "A long, complicated story."

"I have time." Ethan sat without saying another word. He let the uncomfortable silence drag on. Jillian writhed in her seat, using all the self-control she possessed. She kept silent when she would've preferred to pepper this woman with questions of her own.

Moira finally blew out a breath and began her tale. "Maggie and I were born in a small town in southern Illinois. When we were four, Mama was diagnosed with a Stage 4 brain tumor. There was no hope for treatment or recovery. Mama wanted to make sure we'd be taken care of when—you know. She hired an attorney to find us a home, but she died before the lawyer found a family to adopt us. We were put into foster care. The state became responsible for finding us an adoptive family. No one wanted to take on two active four-year-old girls. We were separated and went to live with different families."

Moira stopped to compose herself as the flood of tears threatened to choke her. Jillian found herself pitying Moira.

"After my adoption to a family who lived not far from here, I never saw or heard from Maggie again. I had no idea what happened to her until I read the obituary in the paper.

I can't believe we've been living so close to each other all these years." Her voice cracked. More tears rained down.

The regret she heard in Moira's voice tugged at Jillian's heart. She handed Moira more tissues and a bottle of water from the mini fridge. Ethan stopped questioning Moira to give her time to compose herself.

Jillian wished to ease Moira's pain—give her something of comfort. "Maggie and I met six years ago when she was hired for the kindergarten position. We became good friends." She inched forward and took Moira's hand. "Your sister was kind, compassionate, and funny. She loved her students, and they loved her. She finished her master's degree last spring and hoped to be a principal someday."

Moira sniffed and swiped at her eyes. "I'm glad to hear she had a full life. Was she married? Kids? I'd like to meet her family. And her adoptive parents, too."

"She wasn't married, had no children." Ethan hesitated before delivering the next bit of news. "I'm sorry to say her parents were killed in a car accident five years ago."

"A car accident—how awful." Moira clutched both hands to her chest. "That's eerie, all three, dying the same way, I mean, because of a car. Did they live here in Willow Springs?"

"No, Maggie's parents lived in Ohio."

"Oh. I assumed she was raised here," Moira said.

"No, she moved here when she started her teaching job." Jillian's chest tightened. "I'm sorry for your loss."

"I'd hoped to reunite with her someday. I guess her life will remain a mystery to me." Moira sniffled and sipped her water. "I can't believe this happened."

"If I find anything during my investigation, I'll keep you informed," Ethan said. "What's the best way to reach you?"

Moira handed Ethan her business card. "Here's my

number. Please call me if you learn anything new."

He read Moira's card. Jillian moved behind to peer over his shoulder.

BODY & SOUL
1110 N. Prescott Court, Stonefield
Moira Flannery, Owner
Body massage, body art, & spiritual guidance
555-897-4543

"You have your own business in Stonefield?" Ethan directed his gaze at Moira.

"Yes, I do." Her mood brightened. "I've managed Body & Soul for over a year. We offer different massages and body art, plus a line of spiritual guidance products including books, CDs, crystals, homemade incense, and essential oils."

Jillian noticed Ethan's wrinkled brow as he squinted at Moira while she gushed about her store.

Uh-oh, I know that look. That's his serious cop face.

"Um, body art." Ethan flipped her card and found the backside blank. "Can you elaborate?"

"Body piercings, implants, henna, full body painting," Moira said. "And tattoos. Would you be interested in any of these, Detective?"

"Tattoos, you say." He jotted something in his notebook. "Do you specialize in any particular type?"

"No, we do whatever the client wants. My tattoo artist is a rare talent. His creations are works of art. If you're interested, please call for an appointment. We'd be happy to help you." Moira batted her eyes at Ethan. His face remained expressionless.

Jillian knew his wheels were spinning. She couldn't wait to hear what he thought.

"One more question, Ms. Flannery. When you learned

your sister had been killed, why didn't you go to the police? They'd have been helpful in answering your questions." Ethan's gaze never wavered.

"The police?" Moira blinked at him several times. Her hands fidgeted with her purse straps. "The thought never occurred to me, Detective. I suppose I'm not thinking with a clear head—you know—losing my sister and all." Standing and smoothing the wrinkles from her skirt, she thanked them for their time.

"Please give Maggie's coworkers my condolences. I'd like to meet them sometime." Moira shot a simpering smile in Jillian's direction. "I went to the school and asked for a peek at Maggie's classroom. Some awful woman in the office wouldn't let me. So rude."

This assessment of the beloved secretary rankled Jillian. "Mrs. Daly followed school protocol. For the safety of our children, strangers aren't allowed to wander in off the streets. She's a lovely lady who was doing her job."

"Hmm, I'm sure." Moira wrinkled her nose.

"She mentioned you were looking for something in Maggie's classroom. What was it?" Ethan asked.

"Oh, it's silly. Our mother wore a silver locket she kept our pictures in. Since I don't have it—" A grimace flashed across her face, only for a second —"I hoped Maggie did. The necklace is a sentimental family heirloom—no monetary value, just memories."

What's with the face? Is she annoyed Maggie might've had the locket?

"And you thought it might be in her classroom?" Ethan said. "A strange place, don't you think?"

"Honestly, I wasn't thinking. I didn't know where Maggie lived. The paper said she was a teacher, so the school seemed as good a place as any for me to look." Moira rubbed at her temples as if a headache was imminent. "I'd just learned my sister was dead—again not functioning with a clear head. Was the locket in with her personal effects?"

"No, she wasn't wearing a necklace," Ethan said.

Moira blinked back new tears. "She probably didn't have it either. We were shuffled around to several places right after Mama died. The locket must have been lost in the system—along with us."

As she prepared to leave, Ethan promised Maggie's killer would be caught.

"I hope so, Detective. What a shame it would be if someone got away with murder." Moira left out the back door. He continued staring long after she disappeared from his sight.

"Well, one mystery solved." Jillian stood to return to dinner. "I wish we could help Moira. She's suffered so much tragedy and loss."

"You believe her?" Ethan asked.

Jillian whirled around to face him.

"You mean you didn't? You think she's lying."

"C'mon, one minute she's crying her eyes out, and the next minute, she's giving an impassioned sales pitch. She's hiding something." He chewed on his bottom lip. "I get a weird vibe from her."

Jillian had recognized the grief etched on Moira's face. Her tears had seemed real. On the other hand, she respected Ethan's instincts. He'd been a cop for ten years and handled many cases.

"You think she's concocting this story. Why go to the trouble?" Jillian needed to hear his reasoning. She struggled to believe Moira had been less than honest with them.

"No, the bulk of her story is probably true, but I believe

she's either leaving out pertinent details or embellishing some facts—not sure which."

"I believed her." Jillian shook her head. "If she's lying, she should win an Academy Award."

"Don't sweat it. Her story sounded plausible. My cop instincts tell me not to trust her. Moira's sudden appearance days after Maggie's violent death leaves me wondering. Why is she here and what, if any, are her ulterior motives?"

"I'm impressed, Detective Harden. I sat here, hanging on her every word. Not you. You were being all analytical and rational—two qualities which make you a great cop."

Ethan shrugged. "Part of the job."

"What're you planning next?" She checked on her pups, doling out a few chin scratches and belly rubs.

"I'll do a background check on Moira to verify her story. There's a woman I know at the Department of Children and Family Services. Maybe she can give me information on Maggie's adoption. I'll visit Body & Soul tomorrow with more questions for our sketchy friend—surprise her on her own turf. Who knows, maybe I'll get inked while I'm there."

"Ha. You better check with Becca." Jillian gave him a pointed stare. "She's not a fan of tattoos, you know."

"Yeah, I know. She's made her opinion on the topic crystal clear." He grimaced. "Multiple times, in fact."

"So no to the ink." Jillian chuckled. "I'll keep my fingers crossed you uncover new facts to help us solve this case."

"Us again?" He shook his head. "You swore to your entire family and me you'd leave my investigation alone. Breaking your promise?"

She remained quiet rather than make another promise she wasn't sure she could keep. Her silence didn't go unnoticed.

"Yeah, I didn't expect an answer. C'mon, Nancy Drew,

let's get back to dinner. I'm starved and everyone's waiting to hear what happened with Moira." He opened the door, ushering her out with a hand at her back. "You can retell her story. You'll do it well."

CHAPTER SEVENTEEN

Questioning eyes followed Jillian and Ethan as they took their seats, drawn to their chairs like magnets by the aroma of Max's pulled pork sandwiches and barbecue ribs. Baskets of crispy crinkle-cut fries and hand-battered onion rings were scattered around the table amid the bowls of creamy coleslaw. Unable to resist the mouthwatering smells, Jillian filled her plate and dug in.

Max's food didn't disappoint. Never did.

While the entire table savored their meal, she regaled them with Moira's tragic tale. The women sighed, tsked, and gasped at different points throughout the story. The men just listened. Story complete, Jillian waited for comments she knew would come. Her family and friends did not let her down.

"Poor, sweet girl." Aunt Grace fussed with her gold bangles, a nervous habit everyone recognized as her personal distress signal. "She loses her sister when they're babies and loses her a second time as adults. Sometimes fate is cruel. Her dark aura makes sense."

"So sad," Jillian's mom said. "Their poor mother tried to find a home for her daughters, knowing she'd never watch them grow into women. I can't imagine." Gazing at her own three daughters, she swiped at a tear.

"Why didn't Moira's story include years of searching for her sibling?" Bryan tossed out this idea. "If she loved her long-lost sister like she claims, where were the stories about looking for Maggie and failing to find her? How hard could it have been considering how close they lived to one another these past few years? Why does she come—after her twin is dead?"

Trixie spoke with a somber tone in her voice. "Most adoption records are sealed by the courts and are difficult to get reopened. Maybe Moira tried with no luck." Being adopted herself, Trixie knew the heartbreak of being denied access to information. "Maybe she found it too difficult to talk about."

"Could be." Ethan huffed out a breath. "There are too many other things off with her story. She's hiding something— something big."

Bryan stopped with his fork in midair. "I knew it. You have suspicions about her too." Popping the slaw into his mouth, he shook the empty fork at Ethan. "You're planning to check her out, aren't you?"

"Yes, I am. Tomorrow morning, I'll make a call to DCFS to confirm this adoption story and run a background check on her. My schedule might include a visit to Body & Soul to chat with this mysterious woman." Ethan raised his frosty glass in salute. "Here's to finding the clue to break this case wide open."

Jillian didn't want to believe Maggie's sister could be untrustworthy, yet Bryan and Ethan's points were valid. Some things didn't add up.

Why didn't Moira search for Maggie? Even more puzzling, why hadn't Maggie ever mentioned she had a twin sister?

"Ethan, I know it's not my place to interfere, but I have a deep feeling about something—call it a divine impression. Will you hear me out?" Grace stared, wide-eyed, into his face.

He folded both arms across his chest. "Go ahead. I'm listening."

"Jillian should go with you tomorrow when you go to Stonefield. She could be a second pair of eyes and ears. Plus—" Grace raised her hand to stop whatever he'd started to say. "Moira might be more willing to talk if Jillian is there. I mean, she did seek *her* out at the bookstore." Grace stopped, letting the suggestion hang in the air.

"Are you crazy?" Bryan banged his fists on the table. "There's a nutcase out there who tried to kill Jillian this morning. Going with Ethan on his investigation could make things worse. C'mon, everybody, tell her."

"Calm down, Bry-bear." His mother's use of his childhood nickname sent laughter rippling around the table. "This woman sought out Jillian because she had a connection to Maggie. Maybe Moira would share more information with her there. Besides, Ethan will watch out for our girl. I could even give her a circle of protection amulet." Aunt Grace smiled and winked at her niece.

"Mother, be serious." Bryan scoffed at her suggestion. "Will your silly necklace keep Jilly safe from another car?"

"Don't you get smart with me, Bryan Aiden. You may not believe in these things like I do, but I'm still your mother. You'll be respectful, or I'll put you across my knee like when you were five." She gave her son a light smack on the back of his head.

Ethan intervened in their family squabble, surprising Jillian with his response. "You're going to be shocked—I agree with Grace. Jillian's relationship with Maggie interests Moira. This could work in our favor. However, you have to agree to my conditions." He dipped his head and favored Jillian with one of his hard cop looks.

"What would those conditions be?" She suspected she wouldn't like what Ethan said.

"One, you listen, and let me do the talking. Two, you tell Moira nothing." He counted his rules on his fingers. "And three, if I tell you to do something, you do it without question."

Time stood still as he waited for her answer. Everyone at the table waited. She glanced at Ethan and at her family and friends, who stared back with anxious faces. She'd caused them enough worry, so this was an easy decision.

"I understand your conditions and accept them." She stuck out her hand to shake on it. "What time do we leave?"

"Not before I give you that pendant." Aunt Grace dug through her purse. "Maybe I have one with me."

After the dinner dishes were whisked away and the coffee poured, Max brought out the dessert he'd created. He liked dabbling as a baker, trying out new recipes on Bryan's family. Tonight's masterpiece starred a rich, decadent strawberry swirl cheesecake with a warm chocolate sauce drizzled on top, served with chocolate-dipped strawberries on the side. His presentation elicited oohs and aahs making the often-surly Max smile.

Maggie loved cheesecake.

The thought popped into Jillian's head. When memories like this surfaced, their timing and intensity surprised her.

Maggie loved chocolate and strawberries too.

Jillian shook her head, trying to clear her mind like you'd erase an Etch-a-Sketch.

Pulling herself from her reverie, she watched Max slice and serve cheesecake to his eager taste testers, waiting for their honest feedback. The opinions were unanimous. They showered his new creation with their highest praise and told Bryan he'd be an idiot if he didn't add this dessert to the menu. Max smiled as he served a second slice to those who asked.

They'd enjoyed the evening and lost track of time. Maggie's identical twin sister's arrival had been the evening's entertainment. At close to eleven o'clock, everyone gathered the containers with their leftovers and put on coats.

"Another Edwards' dinner and show." Trixie clapped her hands. "As always, I've had fun, but I need to get going if I want to be on time for work tomorrow. My boss can be a real bear if I'm late." Trixie giggled and dashed out the door.

Cate had ridden with her parents who were parked right out front. Bryan walked Aunt Grace to her car down the block. Amanda and Sam had parked in the alley behind the bar. They exited through the back door, leaving Jillian, Becca, Ethan, and Travis gathered inside the front of McGuire's. Bryan returned and wrenched open the door, grumbling to himself.

"Hey, you all right?" Becca grabbed his arm to slow him down.

"Yeah, yeah, I'm fine." He shook off her concern along with her hand. "I'm annoyed with the wacky woman I'm forced to call Mom. She said the strangest thing on the way out to her car. She had another vision, I guess."

"Don't keep us in suspense," Becca said. "What'd Grace say?"

"She said 'The red-haired girl knows more than she's saying. Ethan should ask her where the silver car is hidden. She knows where it is.'" Bryan reached into his pocket.

"My mom said to give you this." He dropped a silver necklace with a cylindrical charm into Jillian's open hand.

"She pulled it from the bottom of her purse—said you should wear it for protection." Bryan snorted as she placed the chain around her neck. "Amulet of protection—give me a break. Anyone can see it's a tiny canister of pepper spray."

Pepper spray could come in handy.

"I don't suppose Grace saw the location of the car in her vision?" Ethan said.

"Nope, only *the girl* knows where it is. You've met my mom, bro. Take this with a grain of salt."

"Maybe. Since we're going to speak with Moira tomorrow, I'll be sure to ask." Ethan winked at Bryan.

Travis retrieved the pups while the others thanked Bryan for his bar's hospitality. Zipping their coats, the four friends stepped into the cool night air, heading for their cars.

"Wait, I need to say something." Travis stopped them as they crossed the street. "My gut's telling me Jillian shouldn't go to Stonefield with Ethan. Something about this doesn't feel right."

"Standing in the street isn't a good idea either," Becca mumbled behind Travis's back.

"I understand your concern." Ethan headed toward his car, moving the conversation to safety. "In this situation, I'm going to disagree with you, Travis. Jillian's presence could be helpful. Moira may be more comfortable talking with her there. Let's face it. I need all the leverage I can get in this case. She'll be with me the whole time. I give you my word I won't let anything happen." Ethan clapped Travis on the shoulder.

"I'll hold you to your promise." The concern in his voice warmed Jillian's heart.

He really is the kindest man I've met in a long time. Is he too good to be true?

Ethan and Jillian agreed he'd pick her up at two o'clock the next day at Whimsy & Wonder for their adventure to

Stonefield. With their plans set, the Hardens headed home. Travis made sure Jillian and the dogs were safe in her car.

"Maybe I should follow you."

"That's not necessary. My place is only a five-minute drive." She noticed the dark circles under his eyes. "Please go home and get some rest. I'll be fine with my two bodyguards in the back seat." As if on cue, Hayley demonstrated her loudest bark, her snout pointed at a rabbit she'd spied hopping through the grass.

"Text me when you're inside the house." He tucked a loose curl behind her ear. "I need to know you've made it without any problems."

"Ethan left. Bryan is closing the bar. I'm guessing you're still on watch duty, huh?" She expected a teasing reply, yet received the exact opposite.

"Yes, this is my night to watch out for you." His clipped words came through clenched teeth. "I know you don't like it, but we're afraid for you. Until this guy is caught and put behind bars, you're a target. We're not taking any chances. Deal with it."

Jillian recoiled as if he'd slapped her.

"I'm sorry." Travis ran his hands through his hair. "I'm frustrated."

"I'm the one who needs to apologize. I shouldn't make light of the situation. Sorry to say, that's how I deal with stress." She gave him a soft kiss on his cheek before stepping off the curb and getting into her car. Rolling down the window, she intended to ask if their date was still on for tomorrow. Travis beat her to the punch.

"Don't forget, I'll be at your place at six." He leaned in the window. The tanned skin around his gold-flecked eyes crinkled when he smiled at her. "Please go straight home and don't forget—text me." He reached out, touching the silver chain around her neck. "Maybe you should *always* wear this thing your aunt gave you. At least until Maggie's killer is caught. Extra protection can't hurt." He stepped away from the window, his face pinched in a concerned frown.

As Jillian pulled from the curb, she glanced in the rearview mirror. He waved as she drove away.

As promised, she got home within five minutes. Not wanting Travis to worry or have him banging on her door, Jillian texted him as soon as she got the pups inside.

> **JILLIAN:** Am home. Locked in for the night. Can't wait until tomorrow.

His reply was immediate.

> **TRAVIS:** Glad you and the girls are safe. Thanks for the invite to dinner. Your family is great. Sleep well.

Staring at his text, she paused. She gave thanks for the three men who'd sworn to protect her without concern for their own safety—both the two she'd known for almost a lifetime and the new one who'd entered her life only days ago and who was making a huge impression.

"I'm blessed to have them in my life," she muttered. "I pity anyone who dares go up against them."

As she crawled into bed with her dogs, exhaustion seeped through every inch of her body. She stretched out, stroking her sweet girls' fur. After a few minutes of this calming motion, her eyes closed. Her breathing slowed. In minutes, Jillian and her pups had drifted off.

A restful night wasn't in her future. A car backfiring startled her and once awake, her mind wouldn't take a break. Thinking about her date set her heart racing. Replaying their conversation with Moira made her head hurt. The flashbacks from her brush with death—the silver car racing toward her,

Travis's voice calling out, and the squealing tires made her heart pound. She could even picture the driver's red hair sticking out from underneath a ball cap.

Jillian bolted up in bed.

Red hair—the driver had red hair.

Why hadn't she remembered this detail before? She could picture it now and was shaken by this revelation and its possible implications.

Because who do I know with red hair?

CHAPTER EIGHTEEN

The alarm clock display glowed in the dark.

Four o'clock? I can't lie here for three more hours.

With a dramatic sigh, Jillian tossed aside the blankets and swung her feet onto the cold floor. Her dogs slept, undisturbed by her movements.

Slipping on her robe and shoving her feet deep into her favorite fuzzy slippers, she shuffled into the kitchen and put the teakettle on the stove.

Maybe some chamomile tea would help her relax.

Aunt Grace swears by its calming properties.

Seated at her kitchen table, she pondered the newest clue.

Was the memory real or a figment of her tired brain? Either way, she had to tell Ethan today.

If the driver did have red hair, this could be the piece of information he needed to solve the case. He also needed to know about the peach on the license plate. With all the excitement at dinner, she'd forgotten to tell him that latest revelation.

Waiting for the teakettle to whistle, the facts as she knew them so far rattled around in her head. The driver who killed Maggie was most likely a man with a shaggy reddish-brown beard and a coiled snake tattoo. Had his hair been red? No one knew because he'd worn a ball cap pulled down over his face. If this new memory was correct, the driver who'd tried to hit her had red hair and wore a ball cap too. Could they be the same person?

Her inquisitive mind didn't stop there. Was it a coincidence Moira had red hair and breezed into town days after her sister's death? Was Aunt Grace's latest vision about the silver car a fluke?

Probably not.

Over the last few days, Jillian had become suspicious of everything and everyone. The creepy visitor and Moira's appearance set off her spidey senses. Everything about the pair had fired warning signals in her head. She couldn't wait to tell Ethan her news, hoping hers would be the clue to crack the case.

The teakettle's whistle startled Jillian from her mental musings. She poured a mug full of hot water, steeped the tea bag for her usual four minutes, added a drizzle of honey, and stirred. With her hands wrapped around the mug for warmth, she sipped the amber liquid, letting the tea slide down her throat, waiting for the soothing effects to kick in.

As she enjoyed her tea and the early morning quiet, her thoughts wandered to her date with Travis. A wave of panic set in.

What should I wear?

What if we have nothing to say to each other?

She hadn't been on a first date in years. Worry over what to do and how to act threatened to overtake her.

Relax, you're going on a date—not marrying the guy.

Someone tapped on her door.

Only one person would visit this early, so she went to the door to let her in.

"Good morning." Becca greeted her friend with a one-armed hug. The other arm carried a brown paper sack. "I'm on my way to the bakery—saw your light on."

Becca threw her jacket onto a chair in the kitchen, making herself right at home. She rummaged around in the cabinets, taking out a mug and serving platter.

"Good morning to you too." Jillian peeked into the sack, finding some delicious-looking breakfast treats. "Please, come in. Take off your coat. I'm having some tea. Don't be shy—make yourself some."

Becca's response to the sarcasm was to stick out her tongue, which set the two friends giggling like when they were little girls. This shared laugh with her best friend melted away Jillian's exhaustion. She settled into a chair and sniffed Becca's goodie bag. "What delectable creations do you have in there, and why aren't they on my table yet?"

"You know me so well." Becca grinned and made a production of opening the sack. "I've been wide awake for hours working on these. Max's amazing dessert last night inspired my newest recipe."

Becca removed four golden-brown muffins from the bag, placing them on the plate she'd snatched from the cupboard.

"Ta-dah." She presented them with a flourish. "These are my Strawberry Chocolate Cheesecake Muffins. Try one. Tell me what you think."

Jillian didn't wait for a second invitation. If those muffins tasted half as good as they smelled, Becca would have a hit on her hands at Sugar & Spice. She peeled the paper from the muffin and took a big bite, moaning as she savored her first taste. The moist and creamy inside, still warm from the oven, melted in her mouth.

"Oh Becca, these are fabulous. You're a magician with muffins."

"The Muffin Magician—love the name. Do you think I should put it on my business cards?" She watched Jillian savor the treat. "I swirled strawberries, small cheesecake pieces and tiny bits of chocolate throughout the batter. I wanted the combination of flavors to explode in your mouth."

"Mission accomplished." Jillian finished that first muffin and couldn't stop herself from picking another.

"Well, I guess you do like them." Becca beamed, watching Jillian munch muffin number two. "Maybe I should throw together a bigger batch at the bakery for today's morning crowd to sample."

"Best idea I've heard today." Her praises were mumbled around a mouthful of muffin.

Becca tapped her watch. "How many ideas could you have heard by five o'clock in the morning?"

They sat in companionable silence while they sipped tea and polished off the remaining treats. Becca broke the silence. "My culinary creativity woke me early this morning. What's your excuse?"

"I've been awake for hours—couldn't block unwanted thoughts." Jillian yawned. "Yesterday's incident replayed in my head. I'm not sure, but I may have remembered some information on the driver and the car."

"I'm all ears." Becca placed her chin in her hands and leaned forward.

"The driver had red hair—I think—and the license plate was from Georgia. There was a peach." She waited for Becca's reaction, which did not disappoint.

"You did it again!" Becca jumped in her seat. "I've been here twenty minutes. You should have said something sooner. We have to call Ethan."

"Calm down. I'm driving to Stonefield with him, remember? We'll talk about my new clues this afternoon.

Your husband's working plenty of other leads. Besides, maybe I'm wrong. What if I imagined all this?"

"Jilly, if this memory is correct, we have two suspects—your uninvited guest at the bookstore and the awful woman who claims to be Maggie's sister."

"Claims to be—Becca, get serious. Moira and Maggie are carbon copies of each other. Of course, they're sisters. She couldn't have been the driver. She wasn't even in town yet. Not to mention, Mr. Erickson and Mrs. Taylor said the person in the car outside Whimsy & Wonder was a man."

"They *thought* a man drove the car." Becca corrected Jillian. "Too hard to tell with the ball cap shading their face. Don't forget it was pretty dark out."

Two sleepy pups wandered through the kitchen, heading for the front door. Hayley let out a single woof, her alert for all who could hear that she desired to go outside. Jillian and Becca put on their coats to oblige the dogs' needs. At five in the morning, the quiet, cool September morning—no cars passing by, no dogs barking, not even a bird twittering in the trees—created an eerie shroud around the two friends. They stood shoulder to shoulder, whispering in the dark, a faint light coming from the nearest streetlamp.

"Yes. They look alike, so the sister thing is on the level. But Ethan's instincts tell him she's hiding something." Becca blew into her hands. "Don't forget your aunt's vision. This red-haired woman must be involved—no doubt in my mind."

"Oh, I agree. The timing of Moira's arrival raises many questions. I hope our drive to Stonefield this afternoon will provide some of the answers."

"You two be careful." Becca waggled a finger. "Call me when you're on the way home. I'm keeping tabs on you both. Moira messes with you or him, she'll have to deal with me." She puffed out her chest.

Jillian laughed. "Calm down, Rambo. Can we change the subject? I have more pressing concerns at the moment."

"What could be more important than a red-headed psycho killer on the loose?" Becca gawked in horror.

"My date with Travis." Jillian threw her hands in the air. "I don't have a clue what to wear because I have no idea where we're going. I haven't dated in years. What if I'm no good at it? This could be a disaster in the making."

"Sweetie, breathe." Becca rubbed Jillian's shoulders. "The guy is already falling for you—in case you hadn't noticed. The clothes you wear won't matter to him."

"That's easy for you to say. You've found your forever guy who wouldn't care if you wore a paper sack." The goofy, lovesick grin on Becca's face made Jillian smile. "I get one first date with Travis. There are no do-overs, so I need a great outfit. Can you help me figure out what to wear?"

"Follow me." Becca led the way into the house. "Has Travis given you any hint where you're going?"

"Nope. He said the plans are a surprise, and I should wear something comfortable."

Jillian stood in her bedroom and watched in wonder. Becca tossed clothes from the closet onto the unmade bed, assembling outfits as she went. Within minutes, there were five choices for the date.

"How did you do this—and so fast?" She shook her head at Becca. "I would've been here for hours staring into the closet and still have found nothing to wear."

"Easy." Becca snapped her fingers. "Start with a piece you love and are comfortable in. Build around it with other pieces you like. If you look good, you'll feel good."

She made the impossible look simple. Now the challenge was to pick one.

Jillian tried each outfit, checking her image in the mirror. After much deliberation, she decided on her favorite dark wash jeans paired with a crisp white T-shirt under a soft blue cardigan and her new ballet flats. Simple hoop earrings, a gold chain, and her yellow handbag would finish the look.

"Thank you, Becca, I would have struggled with this for hours!"

"Oh, please, it was nothing." Becca blushed, downplaying her praise. "Now, I have to run, or I'll be late for the bakery. There are customers waiting to sample this new muffin recipe." She gave Jillian a quick hug. "You be careful today. Keep an eye on my hubby and get home safe, so you can have that first date with your hunky fireman. I want to hear the details." She blew Jillian a kiss and sailed out the door.

CHAPTER NINETEEN

Becca's departure left Jillian with time on her hands. She vacuumed, dusted the living room, and straightened the kitchen.

"If Travis comes inside at any point this evening, my house should be presentable." She rationalized her cleaning spree to the pups. "Grandma McGuire always said a clean home is a welcoming home."

A quick shower, a blow dry, and a change of clothes, and Jillian was ready for work. With Abbey and Hayley prancing around her ankles, she stepped onto the front porch and found a plain brown envelope lying on her doorstep. She noticed it wasn't addressed to anyone.

"Your Auntie Becca must've dropped this on her way out." Jillian turned to lock the door. "We don't have time to run by the bakery. I'll give it to Ethan this afternoon."

She slid the envelope in her bag for safekeeping and hustled the dogs to the car.

Jillian made the short drive to the bookstore in less than five minutes. She parked in the garage behind the shop and unloaded her girls. Their usual morning routine began as she unlocked the door and silenced the alarm. Off their leashes, the dogs roamed the store, sniffing every nook and cranny, making sure everything remained as they'd left it. With the blinds opened, the morning sunlight reflected off the warm yellow walls, giving the room a bright, cheerful feel.

A small rush started the day—a grandma who needed a birthday gift for her grandson, a mother who searched for books for a reluctant reader, and an aunt who bought the entire Harry Potter series for her niece. Jillian's mood soared each time she swiped a credit card.

This would be a good day.

After the early morning customers cleared out, she started on her to-do list. Sitting on a stool behind the counter was the perfect place to work. As she was knee-deep in an order for board books, her mind wandered. What if Becca needed the contents of the envelope? Might be the recipe for those divine muffins. She couldn't let Becca spend all morning thinking she'd lost it.

Jillian pulled the envelope from her bag, making sure it wasn't addressed to anyone. There was no postage either.

No address. No stamp.

No foul if I open it, right?

She used a fingernail file to slice it open. A single sheet of paper wafted onto the floor and landed face up. The bold, typewritten words seemingly jumped off the page.

YESTERDAY WAS A WARNING.
STOP ASKING QUESTIONS, OR YOURS WILL
BE THE NEXT BODY TO TURN UP DEAD.

Jillian froze. The reality of the threat on her life caused an involuntary shudder, followed by a surge of anger.

This envelope was meant for her.

Someone was on my porch, lurking outside my home.

They know where I live.

The store bell jingled. All ominous thoughts were shoved aside as she took a deep breath to settle herself before greeting her customer. A sigh escaped her lips when she saw Travis. Something about her demeanor must've alerted him. He crossed the room in three quick strides and grabbed her hands.

"What's wrong?" His gaze never left her face. "Don't insult me by saying nothing."

She handed him the note. "I found this on my apartment doorstep when I left for work."

Travis's shoulders tensed. He narrowed his eyes as he read the message. She could see the anger in his face, yet still flinched when he erupted like a geyser spewing out threats.

"Who does this guy think he is? He had no business outside your house this morning. I'm going to find this psycho, so Ethan can throw him in jail. When I'm finished with him, he'll be sorry he ever stepped foot in this town." Travis breathed hard, his nostrils flared.

"You do that, and you'll be the one in jail." Jillian put her hand on his arm, only to have him shake it off.

"Fine. We'll go somewhere far away from here until he's caught."

"While an impromptu getaway is a lovely thought, do you think it's appropriate for us to go away together? We haven't even been out on a date." Her flippant rebuke of his suggestion only inflamed him more.

"Why are you being so nonchalant? Someone has threatened your life. Again, you make jokes. I don't get it." Travis jammed his hands in his pockets. "I don't get you."

"Why should I be mad? You're getting angry enough for both of us." Jillian lost the battle with her mouth. She became defensive. "Why don't you calm down so we can talk."

He ignored her and took out his cell phone.

"Who are you calling?" She grabbed at his arm to stop him.

"Ethan—maybe he can talk some sense into you. I'll tell him you found this note."

"I'll show him this afternoon." She snatched at the note he held above her reach. "You don't need to do this for me. I can take care of things myself."

He disregarded her wishes and continued scrolling through his contacts in search of Ethan's number.

"Travis! Put the phone down. I don't want you calling him." She stood facing him toe-to-toe, glaring up at him. Her cheeks grew warm. "You can't swoop in here and take charge. I'm a grown woman, not some child who needs your protection."

His face crumbled. Placing his phone back in his pocket, Travis took a deep breath "Are we having an argument before our first date?"

"Could be." Jillian fisted her hands on her hips. "Why were you calling Ethan? You stepped over the line."

He searched for a response to defend his actions. "Your face. You looked so—scared. I wanted to help."

While his intention was thoughtful, it infuriated her even more. "Are you serious? You presume I'd become too distraught to think for myself? Poor little woman, too scared to have a coherent thought. I'll have you know I don't need some man rushing in and saving me."

Jillian could hear her voice become shrill. She didn't understand why she was having such a strong reaction to his gallant gesture of help.

He was protective. Most women would love this. What was wrong with her?

She'd overreacted and knew an apology was in order. She opened her mouth to deliver one, when the bell announced new arrivals. Her mother came through the door with her youngest niece, Aubrey.

"Hi, Auntie Jillian." The little girl bounced toward her aunt. Her blonde curls swung as she talked a mile a minute. "Grandma promised I could come to your store and get a book if I was good at the dentist's office." She leaned and whispered in her aunt's ear. "I was *very* good, so maybe she'll let me get two. Are your puppies here?"

Jillian wrapped Aubrey in a hug and kissed the top of her head. The sweet smell of baby shampoo made her smile. She still considered her niece a baby—Aubrey disagreed. And if someone slipped and called her one, they got a stern talking to from this precocious child.

"Sweetie, if you can't convince Grandma to buy you two books, I'll get you the second one." The two shared a secretive smile. "Yes, Abbey and Hayley are on their blankets. Go give them some love." She kissed Aubrey on the head one more time and sent her off. Girlish giggles and puppy snuffles could be heard behind the counter.

Jillian's heart skipped a beat, watching Aubrey rush around the store oohing and aahing at every book and toy she found with the dogs scampering behind her. Her bubbly visitor helped chase away the anger—anger she'd misdirected at Travis. She'd deliver an apology as soon as they were alone.

Racing around a bookshelf, Aubrey ran smack into Travis's legs. He reached out to steady the tiny girl. She grabbed both his arms. As her gaze traveled the distance to his face, she scrutinized her savior with her light, blue eyes.

"Who are you?" Aubrey cocked her head as she looked up at him. "Do you work here with my Aunt Jilly?"

Jillian jumped in to save him from having to answer.

"Aubrey, this is my friend, Travis. No, he doesn't work here," she said. "Mom, you remember Travis from last night. He stopped by to check on me. Isn't he thoughtful?" Her words—chosen with care—served as an olive branch for her previous rude behavior.

"Good morning, Mrs. Edwards." Travis extended his hand.

"Travis, so nice to run into you here. Checking on my daughter, huh?" She looked at Jillian, then Travis, clearing her throat as she spoke. "Did we come at a bad time? We'll hurry, so you two can get back to—whatever you were doing."

"Everything's fine, Mom. Let Aubrey enjoy the store. She doesn't get to spend enough time here."

Her mom ignored the plea, calling out to her granddaughter. "Aubrey, sweetie. Hurry and find your book. I promised your mother I'd have you to school by eleven."

"Grandma, you're not going to believe this." Aubrey held a book in each hand. "I found two I'd like to read. Both have a girl character like me. And she loves the color pink like me. I can't decide which one to pick. Please, could I, maybe, have them both?" The curly-headed cutie unleashed her brightest smile.

"Yes, sweetheart, I can manage two books today. Hand them to Aunt Jillian so we can pay. If we don't hurry, you'll be late for preschool." Aubrey rushed to the counter and placed her purchases on top.

"Ring me up, Aunt Jilly." She giggled.

The things coming out of this kid's mouth—where does she get them?

Aubrey was wise beyond her four years, having mastered the art of manipulation. She would give her parents a run for their money when the teen years hit.

I can't wait to sit back and watch.

The little girl's twinkling eyes returned to Travis. "My name is Aubrey. Jilly is my aunt. You're tall. How old are you?"

"I'll be thirty next month." Travis squatted eye-level with the little one. "How old are you?"

"Four." She displayed her age on her fingers. "I'm not a baby anymore."

"Oh, I agree. Babies don't shop at bookstores for something to read."

She shook her head, laughing. "No, silly. Babies can't read. Mommy says you should read *to* babies, so they'll grow up smart."

Jillian enjoyed the easy rapport between her youngest niece and her date for the evening. He was good with kids, seemed to like her niece. Until—

"Do you have babies?" Aubrey's innocent question made Jillian chuckle and Joy gasp.

Travis's face paled. He coughed to clear his throat.

Joy chastised the four-year-old for her bold behavior. "Aubrey, it's not polite to ask someone such a personal question."

"I'm sorry." She stuck out her bottom lip. "I didn't know babies were personal."

"Don't worry—no harm done." Travis recovered quickly and winked at Aubrey, letting her know all was forgiven.

"Were you talking about something personal, like babies, when we came in? Your face wasn't happy when we opened the door." Aubrey's interrogation of Travis continued. Jillian swooped in.

"Here you go, sweetie." She handed her niece a shopping tote, using it as a distraction from the topic at hand. "You enjoy your new books and the extra surprises I dropped inside." She kissed Aubrey on her pert nose, shooing her on her way. "Go with Grandma, so you get to school on time. We don't want Mommy to be mad at me for making you late."

Aubrey kissed her aunt back. "Thanks for letting me pick out books. Mommy told me to tell you how nice your store is. She's wrong—it's not nice. It's fabulous, dah-ling." With this, she snapped her fingers and tossed her hair.

Watch out, Cate.

This one is going to give you gray hairs. And laugh lines.

Aubrey squatted on the floor to give the pups one last love. "You two be good for Auntie Jilly. You're lucky she lets you hang out in here because most stores have No Dogs Allowed signs. I know because I can read them."

"Aubrey, let's go." Joy hurried her toward the door.

"In a minute, please." Aubrey shook her blonde curls in exasperation. Rather than heading to the door, she moved closer to Travis and shook her finger at him. "I know who you are. You're Aunt Jilly's boyfriend. Have you kissed her? I heard Mommy say you're a hunky fireman. Do hunky firemen put out fires like regular firemen?"

"Au–brey–Ann," Joy enunciated the three syllables. "We need to go."

"Let's roll, Grandma. If I'm late for school, Mommy will get mad, and it won't be pretty." She waved goodbye and skipped out the door, holding her grandma's hand.

Jillian smiled, watching them leave. That little one was a ray of sunshine everywhere she went.

I hope her special brand of happiness worked its magic on Travis.

Ready to face him and set things right, she caught him staring through the front window. He watched her mother buckle Aubrey into the car seat with an odd expression on his face—regret, sadness perhaps. This puzzled Jillian. Before she could ask, his attention reverted to her, and the look vanished.

"I'm sorry I snapped at you. The note freaked me out more than I thought." Jillian cleared her throat. "The threat made me furious. I lashed out at you instead of the person who sent it. You were caught in the line of fire. Can you forgive me?"

In a surprise move, he gathered her in his arms and kissed her. His mouth lingered on her lips for only a moment before traveling to whisper in her ear.

"There's nothing that needs to be forgiven. I'm the one who's sorry for rushing to take charge. I blame my job where taking charge is what I do. I apologize for coming in like a barbarian thinking you needed rescuing." He kissed her hand and stepped back, gazing into her eyes.

Lifting that same hand, she touched his face. "Not a barbarian. Let's say an overzealous knight in shining armor."

Travis took her hand from his face and placed it over his heart. "I promise I won't ride in on my white stallion to save the day. Or the beautiful maiden." His smile faded. His face grew serious, the mood intense. "Will you make me a promise too?"

Fearing she'd get cornered into making a promise she couldn't keep, Jillian's response was vague. "I can try."

"Promise me you'll ask if you do need my help," he said. "I'll be there for you anytime."

"I promise." She stretched on her tiptoes to seal the deal with a quick kiss on his cheek. The bell on the door jingled again.

"I'm glad we made up." She gave him a sly wink. "We can't go on our first date angry at each other—sets a bad precedent." Jillian spun around to face her newest visitor.

Mrs. Taylor entered the store, out of breath and frazzled. Her usual neat appearance had been replaced with windblown hair, a coat misbuttoned, and mismatched shoes.

She must have dressed in a hurry. Or in the dark.

"Mrs. Taylor, please come in, sit down." Jillian led the older woman to a chair. She refused the seat. "Let me make you some tea."

"N ... n ... no, dear. There's no time. Please come outside with m ... m ... me." Grabbing Jillian's arm, she tugged her toward the door. "He's out there. We need to catch him before he does anything else."

Not only did her sweet neighbor appear unkempt, she was agitated and had difficulty speaking without stuttering.

Is she having a medical emergency like a stroke or seizure? If so, Travis's medical training could help the poor woman. She signaled him over.

"Mrs. Taylor, this is my friend, Travis. He's a firefighter and a paramedic. Maybe he can help you." Once again, a chair was offered. The older woman wouldn't be distracted.

"You don't understand. He's out there watching this store." Mrs. Taylor pointed out the front window. "He's been watching you, my dear. Please come right away. Bring your young man with you."

"Who's here, Mrs. Taylor? Who's watching the store?" Travis said.

"The man with the black SUV. The one with the snake tattoo. He's standing across the street in front of Mr. Erickson's house, staring over here. Please come with me."

She urged Travis and Jillian to the door, jostling each other in their haste to check on the man outside. As Travis wrenched open the door, they ran headfirst into the cantankerous Mr. Erickson who shouted, "The bastard took off."

CHAPTER TWENTY

As everyone scrambled to get outside to catch a glimpse of the tattooed stranger, Travis accidentally knocked the three of them sideways through the door and onto the porch. The two petite women and the frail old man were no match for his six-foot-five frame. Jillian reached out for something to stop her fall and caught Mr. Erickson by the arm. He tried to shake her off but only succeeded in dragging them both down to fall in a heap on the porch floor. They bumped Mrs. Taylor who landed in a flowerpot filled with fall-colored chrysanthemums.

Travis rescued Mrs. Taylor from the flowerpot, helping her stand and brush dirt and flower petals from her clothes. This gave him an opportunity to make sure she wasn't injured. Except for a smudge of potting soil on the pants of her pale blue jogging suit, she appeared unscathed.

Amid loud protests, Mr. Erickson struggled to his feet with a death grip on the porch's railing. Jillian let him help himself. She wouldn't want to bruise his male ego too much.

Only time would tell how many bruises their bodies suffered during this scuffle.

Disentangled from each other, they scanned the street in every direction. Her hopes for the creepy stranger's capture were dashed. The man was, in fact, gone. Inviting her neighbors into the store for tea, Jillian hoped they'd give more details.

Leading her guests to the Arts and Crafts Room, she seated them around a table in the biggest chairs she could find—which wasn't easy. Most of her seats were for the pint-sized people who attended her classes. Mrs. Taylor perched on the edge of a bright yellow chair while Mr. Erickson grumbled something about his adult-size behind not fitting in a child's seat.

Lord, give me strength. Does that man ever say anything positive?

Jillian scurried to the kitchen to make tea while Travis occupied her elderly neighbors. Poor Travis. She wondered how the two men would get along. Scrounging for snacks for this impromptu tea party, she opened the Tupperware container with yesterday's treats from Sugar & Spice which included a few blueberry muffins, two chocolate chip scones, an apple tart, and a cinnamon roll. A few seconds in the microwave warmed and softened them. Once arranged on a pretty tray, along with teacups and a teapot, they looked perfect.

Mr. Erickson and Travis were laughing when she returned. She stood in the doorway, enjoying the camaraderie between the men.

"I can't believe you were on the fire department in the Marine Corp. I'll bet you've got some great stories to tell."

"Son, you have no idea." The older man slapped his own knee. "We ARFF Boys were a tough bunch of Marines. Nobody messed with us."

"I'm sorry," Mrs. Taylor interrupted. "ARFF Boys?"

"ARFF stands for Air Rescue and Fire Fighting. We used the initials to name ourselves." A wistful expression spread over Mr. Erickson's face. "We were a force to be reckoned with. I sure miss them days."

Jillian cleared her throat. "I didn't know you were a Marine. Thank you so much for your service to our country, Mr. Erickson. We owe a huge debt to veterans like yourself." He blushed at her praise, turning the reddish shade of the chair he sat in.

"I threw together what I had in the kitchen. I hope everyone can find something they like." She placed the tray on the table. The nervous clinking of china betrayed her calm exterior. Anxious to question her guests, Jillian made quick work of serving the treats she'd gathered.

"Please help yourself to these pastries."

Reaching for her tea, Mrs. Taylor declined any sweets. "Nothing for me, dear. I have to watch my figure."

"I'd like to watch your figure," Mr. Erickson muttered under his breath, helping himself to a muffin and the apple tart.

They ignored his crass remark in favor of the subject of the man outside.

"Mrs. Taylor, can you tell me who you think you saw?" Jillian said.

"I don't think, my dear. I know who I saw. The man in the black car with the snake tattoo—the one who killed your friend—that's who it was. He stood across the street, watched everyone who came in and out." Mrs. Taylor patted her disheveled hair, smoothing it down. "When I saw him, I came to warn you."

"Did you speak to him? Did he say anything?"

"Good heavens no, dear. I don't associate with criminals. But I needed to warn you about him. Staring at your bookstore like he was—up to no good, I say."

"If anybody cares ..." Mr. Erickson spit crumbs as he spoke, "I did go out and talk to the guy. Didn't like the way he was standin' there in front of my house, plus he was starin' at your store, creepy-like. I asked if he was lost or somethin'."

The old man stopped his story long enough to snatch the cinnamon roll no one else wanted. Taking a big bite, he took his time, enjoying the sweet, sticky treat.

"And? What did he say?" Jillian burst out, impatient with the speed, or lack thereof, at which Mr. Erickson told his story.

"Hold yer horses, I'm gittin' to it." He licked the gooey icing off his fingers and took another bite. He talked around his mouthful. "At first, he shook his head. Said nothin'. I asked him a little louder for his name and purpose for bein' in my front yard. The guy snarled, and said, 'Go away, old man. This is none of your business.' Well, that ticked me off. Nobody calls me an old man. I know I'm old! Don't need some smart aleck pointin' it out. I threatened him with the cops. Told him to get off my property, or I'd be callin' 9-1-1. He stepped toward me, musta thought better of it. 'Cuz he backtracked and hightailed it down the street. He hopped in a car—not the one he drove Friday night— and raced off, 'fore I could get a gander at the plate."

After hearing this latest twist to the mystery, Jillian's next move was obvious.

"Everyone, relax. Have more tea—or sweets." She eyed Mr. Erickson. "I'll be right back."

Calling from her small office, she told Ethan about the recent excitement in front of Whimsy & Wonder.

"I'll be right there. Don't let anyone leave." Their call ended abruptly, and Jillian found herself talking to dead air.

Yes, sir.

Those orders wouldn't go over well with a certain curmudgeon out there. She dreaded sharing Ethan's instructions with the group, not wanting to hear Mr. Erickson's complaints. Jillian grabbed the container of cookies Cate had dropped off yesterday and hoped they'd soften the blow.

"Detective Harden will be here in a few minutes and wants to speak with all of us. He asked everyone to stay put. His orders, not mine." Jillian shot a pointed stare at her cranky neighbor before handing him an oatmeal raisin cookie.

"Ooh-wee, these are my favorite." He snatched three. "Book Lady, where do you get all these dee-lishus baked goods? You're at this here store all the time, so I know you ain't got time to bake." He grinned around a mouthful of cookie.

"Don't you remember? My sister, Cate, owns Sugar & Spice, the bakery on the corner of Maple Avenue." She gave his memory a gentle nudge. "You met her a few days ago when she brought cinnamon rolls to my front porch."

You inhaled three of them.

"I guess I fergot. I'm old, you know." He chuckled and shook his head. "Now you've reminded me, I plan to be goin' there a lot in the future. The grub shore is good." He shoved a large bite in his mouth, letting crumbs rain down on his wrinkled shirt.

Jillian made a mental note to warn Cate again about this one coming into the bakery.

The bell above the door jingled as Ethan marched in with a scowl on his face. He gave curt greetings to the elderly pair and got right down to business. Mrs. Taylor recounted her story first, then Mr. Erickson. The old man retold his take on things, grumbling at each repeated detail.

Ethan directed his first question at Mrs. Taylor.

"Ma'am, would you happen to know what time you noticed this man outside the bookstore?"

"Yes, as a matter of fact, I do. I'd finished watching my favorite daytime program, *The Price is Right*, which ends at eleven. I went to fix some tea, glanced out the window, and there he was—staring at the store. Eleven o'clock on the dot." She tapped her watch to emphasize her point.

"Thank you." He pivoted in his chair to Mr. Erickson.

"Sir, can you say what time you went out to confront the man in your yard?"

"You betcha. The purty lady and I watch the same show, 'cuz I went outside to talk to the guy as soon as the showcase showdown ended. Some guy won a brand-new car. Eleven o'clock for sure." He winked at Mrs. Taylor, who cringed, cheeks flushing bright pink.

"Great. Is there anything else you can recall?"

"How 'bout the scar on his face?" Mr. Erickson said. "Across his left cheek, a thin jagged line from his ear to his mouth. Hard to miss."

Ethan made a note, waiting in case either of them would add anything else. He wasn't disappointed.

"When I threatened to call the po-lice, he ran like the coward he is—watched him hop in a banged up four-door silver car. Looked like it'd been in an accident—no sideview mirror on the passenger side, big dent in the door and the paint was scratched." Mr. Erickson slapped his hands on his thighs. "That's all I got."

Jillian shuddered at the description of the silver car—the same one used in the attempt to run her over.

"I appreciate your help—both of you. If I have any more questions, I'll give you a call or stop by." Ethan stood. "Ms.

Edwards has a few customers out front. I'll escort you both home."

"I sure as heck don't need the po-lice escortin' me home." The older man glared at Ethan. "The neighbors'll think I broke the law or somethin'. I'll escort this purty lady home and make sure she's safe inside."

He offered his arm to Mrs. Taylor. The old couple shuffled out of the store. Jillian, Travis, and Ethan watched them through the front window.

Travis couldn't hold back. "Is it my imagination or does Mr. Erickson have a thing for Mrs. Taylor?"

"Yes, he does." Jillian and Ethan answered together. Sharing a quick glance, they burst out laughing.

"Poor lady." Travis shook his head and blew out a breath. "She doesn't stand a chance against the old coot."

Jillian pointed in the old couple's direction. They all watched as Mrs. Taylor removed Mr. Erickson's hand from her backside. "She may be old and petite, but she's one tough lady."

CHAPTER TWENTY-ONE

After the elder pair left, Jillian showed Ethan the note she'd found. Less than thrilled with this latest turn of events, he put the paper and the envelope into a plastic evidence bag he grabbed from his car.

"I'll drop this at the station. The forensics team will get right on it—check for prints. I've flagged this case as a top priority." He flattened the bag letting all the air out and sealed it. "I shouldn't have to say this"—He zeroed his stern gaze in on Jillian—"since it's you I'm talking to, please be extra careful."

"We'll *all* keep our eyes on you." Travis drew her in with one arm and gave her a squeeze. "The next shift is yours, Detective. I have a few last-minute details for our date tonight to take care of while you two are off investigating. I'm counting on you to keep her safe this afternoon."

"Yeah, yeah. She'll be ready on time and all in one piece, Romeo."

As the front screen door slammed shut behind Travis, Trixie sailed in through the back, thirty minutes early for her shift and in a sassy mood.

"Never fear for I am here, ready to take charge." She pointed two finger guns at them. "You can go be Scully and Mulder and find the clues to this mystery."

"We're not chasing aliens, Trixie. There's a flesh and blood murderer out there." Ethan blew out a frustrated breath.

"I know, Detective." Trixie wrinkled her nose at him. "That was meant to be a compliment. Mulder and Scully always get their man. And you will too. Sue me for binge-watching the *X-Files*."

"Can you two kids please stop bickering?" Jillian shook her head at their childish behavior.

After they agreed to a truce, Ethan put on his cop face and asked Trixie if she'd noticed anything strange outside when she'd arrived at the store.

"Nope. Same old, same old." She placed some books on the shelf as they talked. "I parked in my usual spot out back, went around front to grab the mail, and here I am. Why?"

They filled her in on the morning's excitement. Trixie's mouth hung open.

"He was here—the guy who tried to kill you. And he left a note on your porch?" Trixie rubbed at her temples. "This whack job is out of control." She stabbed a finger at Ethan. "You better find him before anyone else gets hurt."

"He *will* catch him. We hope our trip this afternoon will yield the clue he needs." Jillian heard the confidence in her own voice and could only hope Trixie and Ethan believed it.

Right before two o'clock, as she prepared to head out with Ethan, Jillian realized the death threat had rattled her more than she'd ever admit out loud. She took a deep breath to silence her fears.

"Hey, Trixie, are you good with me leaving the girls with you this afternoon? I don't want them underfoot if anything unexpected happens in Stonefield."

"Sure thing. Your sweet girls are no trouble at all—love having them in the store, so do the kiddos. You two, on the other hand, better hope nothing bad happens." Trixie gave them her best 'mom' look. "You'll have to answer to your date and your wife."

"Agreed," Jillian said. "I wouldn't like facing either one."

Ethan mumbled his agreement. He rubbed his temple as if the very thought gave him a headache.

Jillian settled Abbey and Hayley on their blankets behind the counter and promised Trixie she'd get them in a few hours.

"No worries. You be careful out there. I can't run this store without you." Trixie gave her a serious look.

"Everything'll be fine. We're just talking to Moira, nothing dangerous. If you need anything, I have my cell phone, fully charged." She closed the door and stepped out into the September sunshine.

If nothing else, this trip would be interesting.

Jillian settled onto the uncomfortable leather seat of Ethan's unmarked police car. She marveled at all the bells and whistles on the dashboard, which reminded her of the control panel on an alien spaceship Scully and Mulder might encounter.

I'd love to play with all those knobs and buttons.

The thought made her giggle. She shook her head, thinking how angry Ethan would be if she pressed even one of them.

Get serious, Jilly. We're on a mission to question Moira, not play cops and robbers.

Jillian also wondered if she'd been silly earlier this morning when she'd slipped her aunt's protection amulet around her neck. She didn't believe in these things like her aunt did, but what could it hurt?

As they drove, she relayed her memories of the Georgia license plate and the driver's red hair. "I'm positive about the peach and ninety percent sure about the hair color. The driver was again wearing a cap, though."

"Still gives me solid tips to follow. Good job, Jilly. Thanks for letting me know and not investigating on your own."

"Why, Detective Harden. You gave me a compliment—good thing I was sitting down." Jillian batted her eyes at him.

Ethan made a quick stop at the police station to enter the brown envelope and its contents into evidence, so the techs could process it for fingerprints and other clues. He was back in the car in less than five minutes.

"You were in and out fast," she said. "They'll be able to get fingerprints, won't they?"

"Maybe. There's no way of knowing how many people touched the envelope besides you, Travis, and the sender. I'll need you to stop in and give your fingerprints—for the purpose of elimination." He backed out of the parking lot, hung a left on Magnolia, and headed toward the highway.

"I'll stop tomorrow on my way to the bookstore." Jillian put a note in her phone so she wouldn't forget. "Travis touched the envelope and the note, so they'll need his prints, won't they?"

"His are on file with the city. When he was hired on the fire department, fingerprints and a full background check were done—standard procedure for new hires."

"Makes sense people in emergency services would be checked out before they're hired."

This included Travis. Thinking about him made her smile.

"Knock it off, will ya?" Ethan grumbled.

"What'd I do?" His annoyance caught her off guard.

"You've got a sappy grin on your face, so I know you're mooning for Travis. I'll get you home in plenty of time for your big date with T-bone."

"T-bone?" She laughed so hard she snorted. "You call him T-bone?"

"Everybody does—the guys at the firehouse, the police station, dispatch. Everyone in EMS has a nickname."

"How'd he get that nickname, dare I ask?" Jillian feared what she'd hear.

"When a rookie gets off probation, tradition is he or she provides a nice dinner for the others on their shift, a sort of thank you for helping them get through their first year. Travis must have wanted to impress everybody. He brought T-bone steaks, twice-baked potatoes, sweet corn, and homemade apple pie for his probationary dinner. From that day on, Travis became T-Bone at the firehouse."

"That's a great story. Thanks for sharing." She thought of something else. "What would your nickname be, Detective Harden?"

"You don't want to know. Trust me—it's a guy thing."

Jillian noticed the tips of his ears were red. "C'mon, tell me. You know I'll ask Becca if you don't." She goaded him a bit. "She knows your nickname, doesn't she?"

"Yes, she does. And knowing my wife, she'll tell you." He mumbled through gritted teeth. "Let's just say my nickname is a play on words using my last name and leave it at that. I need to focus on our visit with Moira." Ethan took the ramp onto Route 36. "We'll be in Stonefield in twenty minutes."

The mention of Maggie's twin sister had a sobering effect. Jillian considered the possibility Moira was involved in Maggie's death, which frightened and angered her. Ethan's voice broke through her meditation.

"I hope to catch Moira off-guard with this unannounced visit. Maybe she'll slip and give us information on her estranged relationship with Maggie or the real reason she's in Willow Springs. She arrived at McGuire's on a fishing expedition last night. Now it's our turn."

As they continued in companionable silence, Jillian reviewed everything she knew, struggling to understand why anyone, including her twin sister, would've wanted Maggie dead. None of this made sense.

"The address on Moira's business card says 1110 North Prescott Court. GPS says we should arrive in five minutes." Ethan checked the time. "Two o'clock in the afternoon, so I assume her shop is open."

"Unless her shop is by appointment only. Some upscale salons require clients to call ahead. Give me the phone number. I'll make sure she's open."

Handing her Moira's card, he warned. "If she answers, don't give away who you are or why we're coming."

"Really, Detective?" She feigned innocence. "And here I thought I'd tell her we were on our way. Maybe even let her know we think she's a psycho killer." She grunted in disgust. "Could you give me some credit? While I'm not a trained investigator like you, I'm also not an idiot."

"Sorry. I'm being cranky today—shouldn't take it out on you. I need a break in this case, and Moira holds the key to solving this murder. I feel it in my bones."

Jillian noted the determined set of his jaw. She knew Ethan meant business. He wouldn't stop until he had answers. Moira would be no match for him, and Maggie would get the justice she deserved.

Jillian made the call, putting it on speaker. Expecting a phone to ring, a series of beeps and a recorded voice stating the number she had reached had been disconnected surprised her. Thinking she'd misdialed, she tried again. Same result.

"This isn't a good sign." Ethan scowled, causing furrowed lines across his forehead. "We're getting close to the address. Let's hope we have better luck there."

The GPS instructed him to turn left, taking them into an affluent subdivision with stately homes and manicured lawns. Sitting in the driveways were a pretentious array of high-end cars, trucks, and SUVs. This was no place for a business such as the one Moira had described.

Jillian said. "Are we lost?"

"Nope. I followed the GPS to the letter. Either Moira's business card is misprinted, or our mysterious friend is playing games with us. I'm inclined to believe the latter."

Did Moira miss an error on her business cards? Or was something devious happening here? Jillian usually gave people the benefit of the doubt—not this time. Her gut told her things were about to get very interesting.

Ethan parked by the curb and shut off the engine. He pointed at a resident pruning roses in his yard.

"Let's ask this guy if he knows Moira." Ethan climbed out of the car with Jillian in hot pursuit. The man smiled as they approached, his smile fading at seeing a police officer's badge.

"Good afternoon, sir. I'm Detective Harden with the Willow Springs Police Department. This is my—associate, Ms. Edwards. Could we ask you a few quick questions?"

"I ... I ... guess so." The man blinked behind his thick lenses. "I can't imagine what this is about."

"Let's start with your name."

"Oh ... um ... my name's Howard Lane. I live here with my wife and kids." He pointed to the house behind him. "Has there been another break-in on the street? The Andersons were robbed last year when they were in the Bahamas."

"No, sir. We're investigating a crime in our town a few nights ago. A lead brought us here to your street. Have you heard of a place called Body & Soul?"

"Can't say as I have." Mr. Lane scratched his head "What kind of business is it?"

"We were led to believe it was a salon offering body massage, tattoos, and spiritual guidance."

"The Homeowners' Association wouldn't allow something like that on our street. This is strictly a residential area. You said a lead brought you here. I think someone's pulling your leg, Detective."

"As you can see, we were given this address as Body & Soul's location." Ethan handed Mr. Lane Moira's business card. "There's obviously been a mistake. Sorry for wasting your time." He shook the man's hand and prepared to take the card back.

"Wait a minute." Mr. Lane peered at the card. "This could be the problem. This card has a misprint. *My* house is 1110 North Prescott, but there is a *South* Prescott on the other side of Stonefield. You might want to look there. The area is—how should I say it—a seedier part of town. Maybe you'll find this body salon there."

"Thank you, Mr. Lane. I appreciate your help. We'll let you get back to your roses."

"Can I ask a question?" Mr. Lane returned Moira's card. "Go ahead."

"What case are you working on?" Mr. Lane ducked his head, sending his glasses sliding down his nose. "I don't mean to pry, but I once thought of becoming a police officer. Things didn't work out for me—couldn't pass the vision test. I've had to be satisfied reading cop thrillers and mysteries."

"We're working on a hit-and-run homicide," Ethan said. "A woman was killed Friday night."

Mr. Lane sucked in a breath. "I saw the story in the paper. She was a pretty girl with her red hair and bright smile. There's a gal who works at the bowling alley down on Sycamore Avenue. For a split second, I thought it was her who'd been killed. I read the article and discovered it wasn't—said the poor woman was a teacher. Quite a coincidence, huh? Two women bearing such a striking resemblance living so close to each other."

Goosebumps broke out on Jillian's arms.

Coincidence? I don't think so.

"Mr. Lane, do you know this other woman's name? The one who works at the bowling alley?" Ethan remained in cop-mode.

"I've only talked to her a few times. The nametag on her uniform says Moira. Why? Could she be—wait a minute—the business card you handed me said Moira." He brightened at the prospect he might know someone involved in a murder. "Is the waitress involved in your case?"

"Possibly. Can you tell me anything else?" Ethan said.

Mr. Lane shook his head. "Not really."

"Would you have any idea how long she's worked there?"

"Not sure." Mr. Lane shook his head. "She's been there off and on during the three years I've been in the Friday night bowling league."

Ethan had one last question for their mystery-loving acquaintance. "Do you recall if she worked this past Friday?"

He's going to say no. I know it.

"Nope, she wasn't there. And Sheree, the other waitress, wasn't happy. She was called in when Moira didn't show for her shift."

"Thanks for your help, Mr. Lane." The men shook again. "Enjoy your afternoon."

"Good to meet you both. Hope you solve your case," he called after them.

They hustled to the car and didn't speak until they were inside. "Thank you for staying quiet. I'm sure it was hard for you." Ethan jotted a few things in his notebook. "Since our trip to the salon hasn't worked out, how do you feel about a bowling alley instead?"

"Lead on," she said. "This story keeps getting stranger and stranger. I'll follow wherever it takes us."

CHAPTER TWENTY-TWO

Ethan programmed his GPS for Sycamore Avenue. His clenched teeth alerted Jillian to his frustration.

Maybe talking about the case wil help him vent his anger.

"What do you think is going on with Moira? She said she has her own business, but we find out she's a waitress at a bowling alley. Do you think she holds down two jobs? I mean, I did it for five years, so it's possible. If not, why would she lie? There's no shame in waitressing. I paid my bills through college that way."

"Lies and half-truths mean a person is hiding something." Ethan stared straight ahead with a death grip on the steering wheel. "Moira wants people to believe she's something other than what she is."

"What is she, exactly? Grieving sister? Waitress? Business owner?" Jillian stared out the window at the landscaped yards speeding past. "Or murderer?"

"Let's hope we find those answers at the bowling alley. If we're lucky, Moira is working today. If not, maybe one of her coworkers will dish some dirt on our tricky friend."

The GPS signaled to turn right at the next stoplight. The bowling alley was a little more than a mile north and on the left. A huge billboard signaled their arrival—Benny's Bowling—where the balls are always hot.

"Oh, very classy." Jillian huffed, rolling her eyes. "Do you suppose Benny thinks he's funny?"

Ethan chuckled as he pulled into a parking spot close to the front door. The bowling crowd hadn't arrived yet.

They entered the poorly lit lobby and waited a few seconds for their eyes to adjust. The dark gray walls were a stark contrast to the autumn sunshine they'd come from. A bare bulb hanging from the ceiling gave off a dim light. Jillian struggled to make out a crooked metal coatrack, a small wooden table and chair, and a sign on the wall. Peering at the sign, she read, 'No children under the age of 17 allowed.'

Jillian pointed out the sign to Ethan, who said, "So, not a family-friendly place."

They moved through the lobby into the main part of the building, which like most bowling alleys, was quite large. This room contained the shoe rental counter, a good-size snack bar, and ten lanes for bowling. Unlike the lobby, fluorescent lights lit the room, revealing a smoky haze hanging in the air. The smell of stale, greasy food, warm beer, and unwashed feet assaulted their noses.

Several older gentlemen sat at the snack bar smoking cigarettes and drinking coffee, while no one used the bowling lanes. The old men hunched at the counter resembled Mr. Erickson as they eyed the newcomers with suspicious glares. Jillian figured he'd be right at home in a place like this. She did, however, have trouble picturing the rose-pruning, book-reading Mr. Lane hanging out here.

They had no luck finding an employee at the snack bar or the shoe counter, so they headed for the restaurant at the back of the building. A heavyset, bald man lumbered from the office and marched straight at them.

"Hey there, can I help you?" He took a smelly cigar from his mouth and smiled, showing crooked, brown teeth. "Is this your first time here?"

Ethan showed his badge, and the man stopped short. "I'm Detective Harden from the Willow Springs Police Department. This is my associate, Ms. Edwards. I'd like to speak with an employee, Moira Flannery."

He didn't stumble over the word 'associate' this time. Should I take this to mean he's getting used to my help?

"Huh, her." The man grunted. "Why do you want to talk to her? She do something wrong?" He puffed on his cigar.

"I need to ask her some questions. She could have information on a case I'm working."

Smooth, Detective.

"I'm surprised you cops didn't come asking for her sooner. Moira ain't been nothing but trouble from the day I hired her—late for her shifts or not showing at all, trying to stiff the other waitresses on their tips. She's also got a good-for-nothing boyfriend who hangs around here scaring my paying customers. Last time I saw her was Saturday morning. She came here begging off her weekend shifts, telling me some sob story about her twin sister being killed—didn't even know she had a sister. Said she needed a few days to tend to her affairs. I told her she could have until tomorrow. If she don't show for her shift, she's done."

"When did you hire Moira, Mr. uh ...?" Ethan waited for a name.

"Miller. Benny Miller. I'm the owner of this fine establishment." He gestured around the bowling alley. "Moira's worked here now and again for five years, I guess. She travels around a lot with her lowlife boyfriend. Here for a month or two, gone for weeks on end. Always comes back, though, wanting her job."

"Why do you keep hiring her back if she's so unreliable?"

As soon as the words were out, Jillian clamped her lips shut. She hadn't intended to jump into Ethan's interrogation.

"Aw, I'm an old softie." Benny blew cigar smoke in the air. "Plus, she's one of the best waitresses I have. All my regulars like her. When she's here, she works hard, never complains. The other girls told me she aged out in the system. You know, foster care. To hear them talk, life's been tough on Moira. I feel sorry for her, so I keep lettin' her come back."

Mr. Miller's version of Moira's life story varied quite a bit from the one they'd heard from her last night.

Jillian wondered which version was closest to the truth.

"Do your waitresses have spaces where they keep their personal items?" Ethan said.

"Not really, no. There's a pantry in the kitchen where they can lock purses during their shift. I don't allow them to bring stuff into work—distracts them from doing their jobs, you know. I even make them put away their cellphones."

"Would you have Moira's contact information? A phone number and an address?" Ethan fished for any clue.

"Sure, sure." Benny motioned for them to follow him to his office. "That's on her job application. She filled it out five years ago—don't know how accurate it is." He reached for the bottom drawer of a file cabinet and took out a folder labeled *Employees*. He rifled through all the papers. "Here ya go." He handed Ethan the application.

Jillian peeked at the paper. Moira's delicate cursive filled in the blanks on the form. The resemblance between Moira's and Maggie's handwriting startled Jillian. Probably a twin thing. Spooky.

Moira had written the same address and phone number from her business card, so no help there. Ethan handed the page back to Mr. Miller. He placed the paper back in the bottom drawer. "Did you find anything helpful?"

"Not really. We have the same information you do. She doesn't live at the address she gave you—we just came from there."

"She lied." Benny chewed on his cigar. "Why doesn't this surprise me? Moira wouldn't know the truth if it bit her on the ass." His cheeks reddened. He apologized for being vulgar. "Sorry, ma'am. I shouldn't cuss in front of a lady. My wife says I shouldn't cuss at all. You know." He pointed toward the ceiling. "He's always listening."

Jillian smiled, shaking her head. "No need for apology. I've let a few curse words slip from my mouth too." Her comeback brought a grin to Benny's face.

"Are any of your waitresses here? We'd like to talk to them." Ethan's gaze roved around the bowling alley.

"Sorry. The restaurant's open Thursday through Sunday. Those are our busy nights when we get the biggest crowds—league nights and all. The rest of the week, my regulars use the snack bar, which the missus and me can run on our own. You could come back tomorrow and talk to Paula. She's scheduled to work from four to midnight. Moira should be here for her shift too. Maybe you'll be able to talk to her in person—if she shows."

"We might stop by." Ethan wrote something in his notebook. "One last question and we'll get out of your hair."

Jillian stifled a giggle.

Hair—good one, Ethan.

"Would you know Moira's boyfriend's name?" Ethan's pen was poised, waiting to scribble another name on his list.

"Yeah, we all know the bum. Biggest loser you'd never want to meet—head to toe with creepy tattoos. Don't know why Moira stays with him. He treats her like dirt. Everyone says he's running around with several women behind her back."

"His name?"

"Oh sure," Benny said. "Dale Andrews—heard he's a mechanic down at Hank's Garage. I'd be shocked if the boy has worked a day in his life."

"Thank you, Mr. Miller." Ethan handed Benny his business card. "If you think of anything else, please give me a call."

"Sure thing, Detective. I'm happy to help the boys in blue." Benny shoved Ethan's card into his back pocket. "You never said when I asked. What's Moira done to get on the wrong side of the law?"

Jillian slid a glance at Ethan. How would he answer Benny's question?

"Let's say she may hold the key to solving a murder."

Benny choked on his foul-smelling cigar. "What? The girl is involved in murder?"

"I said she may hold the key to help *solve* a murder." Ethan repeated his statement.

"Moira may be many things, but she ain't a killer. She doesn't have a mean bone in her body." Benny defended his best waitress, pacing the floor and waving his cigar in the air. "I do not hire the criminal element here. That ain't good for business. She can't be involved in anything illegal."

"We still need to talk to her. Call me when she comes in." Ethan grabbed Jillian by the arm, leading her toward the door and their escape from the distraught Benny Miller, who followed on their heels.

"You bet I'll call. If she's broken the law, you can bet her scuzzy boyfriend talked her into it."

CHAPTER TWENTY-THREE

Getting away from the chatty Benny Miller proved a challenge. He offered drinks at the bar, half-price appetizers, and a free game. He even tried to enroll them in the next mixed couples' tournament.

"I bet you two'd make a great pair," he called after them.

Ethan nudged Jillian to keep moving for the front door where they made their exit. Dashing for the car, they collapsed in their seats with sighs of relief.

"I thought we'd never escape from Benny. He's quite a talker."

"Yeah." Ethan grunted. "I'd also hoped to interview the regulars sitting at the counter until they made themselves scarce—must not like talking to the police."

Yep, those guys were exactly like Mr. Erickson. Jillian bit her lip to squash the laughter building inside.

"What are you grinning for?" Ethan asked.

"Me? I'm not grinning." A bold face lie, since she could feel the corners of her mouth pulling skyward.

"Oh, give me a break. You're thinking about Travis and your big date. Don't worry, I'll get you home in plenty of time to get all dolled up."

"I was not. And it doesn't take me much time to get ready for a date." His teasing rubbed Jillian the wrong way. Before angry words were exchanged, a change of subject was in order. "At least this trip wasn't a complete waste. Creepy Tattoo Guy has a name—Dale Andrews. What do we do next?"

"We? There's no we, Jilly. I brought you on this adventure on the off chance we could talk to Moira. We didn't, so your part is done. This case gets more complicated by the hour. I won't put your life in danger again. Becca would kill me, not to mention your mom and dad, aunt, sisters, and Bryan." Ethan ticked everyone off on his fingers. "I'm taking you back to the bookstore, and you're going on a date with Mr. Wonderful."

His emphatic response didn't surprise her. She was ready with her comeback.

"Fine. Can we at least drive by 1110 *South* Prescott on our way out of town? I'd like to check if any part of Moira's story is true." She watched his knuckles whiten as he tightened his grip on the steering wheel.

"We'll drive by. Don't be surprised if we find an empty lot. Most everything Moira said has been a lie. Why would this be any different?" Ethan's frustration was palpable, taking up space in the front seat.

The shop did exist—sort of. The storefront window with 'Body & Soul' stenciled in gold, had been peppered with FOR RENT signs. No lights were on. They pressed their faces to the glass door, which revealed an empty space stripped of anything indicating it had ever been a salon.

"Moira may be a great waitress, but a poor business woman. The place is shut down." Jillian stepped back, relieved some part of Moira's story might be true.

What's wrong with me? Why do I care if Moira has a good side?

As soon as the question entered her head, she knew the answer. She didn't want anything to taint Maggie's memory.

"Judging from the cobwebs in the window, I'm betting this shop didn't close overnight. What I don't get is why Moira gave us her big sales pitch when there's nothing to sell. She must've thought I was a small town, naïve cop who wouldn't have her checked out." Ethan rubbed his temples, a pained expression on his face. "Let's head home."

"So, what's *your* next step?" Jillian shot him a saccharine smile.

"I'll check into Body & Soul's demise and run a background check on Dale Andrews. Won't be surprised if he has a rap sheet a mile long. Hank's Garage is off Route 36, so I'll make a quick stop on our way home. Like Moira, I don't expect Dale Andrews is working today."

"Sounds like you'll be busy. You should take something for that headache you have." Jillian handed him some Tylenol she took from her purse. "I won't ask you to tell me what you find out. You've made it clear I'm out of this investigation."

"I know what you're doing. Trying to guilt me into sharing information won't work. By law, I cannot share certain aspects of an investigation with the general public—"

"I am not the general public." Her tenuous grip on civility snapped. "I'm a victim in case you've forgotten. Someone almost ran me down in the street. I have a right to know what progress is being made to put my attacker behind bars. I'm not ignorant of the laws."

Those episodes of Law & Order she'd watched paid off.

"If you hadn't interrupted me, I would've said the law *does* require me to keep victims posted on new details of their case. I'll share what I can, Jilly."

"Oh—well—great. I appreciate being kept in the loop. The sooner Maggie's killer is behind bars, the better we'll all rest at night." She regretted jumping down Ethan's throat, so she offered an olive branch. "Thank you. I know you're doing everything you can to close this case."

"Haven't exactly done anything yet," he grumbled through gritted teeth.

"You will. I have faith."

"Glad someone does."

They made a quick stop at Hank's Garage. Ethan went in and left her waiting in the car. In less than five minutes, he climbed back in and slammed the door.

"I met Hank—nice guy. He confirmed no one named Dale Andrews works here—never has. None of his employees match the description of Creepy Tattoo Guy, either."

Yet again, the investigation ran into a dead end.

"I'm sorry. I wish Hank had been some help."

They drove home without speaking. The police scanner and Ethan's rhythmic drumming on the steering wheel provided quiet background noise. Those sounds must've lulled her to sleep because when she opened her eyes, the cruiser was idling in front of Whimsy & Wonder while Ethan entered info into the dashboard comp.

Jillian stretched and grabbed her cell phone from the seat. "I can't believe I dozed off—haven't been sleeping well." She dumped her phone in her purse. "Thanks for letting me go with you. Sorry we didn't find Moira. She's got some explaining to do when you do find her."

"She's not making it easy, but I'll track her down." The certainty she heard in Ethan's voice relieved her worries. She opened the car door.

"Hey." Ethan snagged her sleeve. "Have a good time on your date, and please call Becca in the morning. No one, especially me, will have a moment of peace until she's heard every detail. She's relentless in the pursuit of information she believes she's entitled to know." His face broke into a weary smile. "Sounds like someone else I know."

"Yeah, yeah. Very funny." She waved away his comment. "FYI—I won't need to call Becca. There will be breakfast guests at my kitchen table early tomorrow morning with coffee and pastries."

"Ah, your sisters and Becca will descend upon your place for the debriefing." He nodded. "Does Travis have any idea what he's getting himself into? Maybe we should have a Guy's Night to fill him in."

"Oh, yes, please. Another meeting of the minds. Just don't involve me in any more hairbrained ideas."

She shut the door and waved as he drove away.

Expecting to find Trixie hard at work, Jillian was surprised to find Aunt Grace sitting behind the counter reading the latest novel by her favorite romance writer.

"Hello, Kitten." Aunt Grace came around the counter to greet her. As she leaned to kiss her niece's cheek, the scent of freesia tickled Jillian's nose.

Grace was dressed in a different fashion, much more conservatively than her usual attire. A new style, her special occasion perfume—Jillian wondered what special occasion warranted wearing Jo Malone London today.

"Aunt Grace, this is a new look for you."

Grace did a slow, graceful pirouette, letting her niece judge the outfit from all angles. "Give me your honest opinion, Kitten. Does this pantsuit work for me, or is it too frumpy?"

She wore a sleek cut monochromatic navy jacket and pants with a crisp white shirt underneath. Accessories included a chunky pearl necklace and drop earrings, a bold gold ring, and, of course, her signature array of bracelets.

"Frumpy isn't a word I'd ever use to describe you, Aunt Grace. Everything you wear looks fabulous. I'll admit a tailored pantsuit isn't something I ever imagined you'd wear, but this style is very flattering. Dressed like this, you could be the CEO of a Fortune 500 company. What's the occasion?"

"Oh Kitten, don't be ridiculous. I could never run one of those big fancy companies." Aunt Grace blushed, shaking her head. "I've wanted to break out of my usual fashion rut for a while, and the lovely woman in the news, you know—our vice president—wears this style suit. I thought I'd give it a try. I do draw the line at her choice of footwear. No sneakers for this gal." She pointed to the navy kitten heels she'd chosen.

"You're amazing no matter what you wear, Aunt Grace."

"You're such a sweet girl. No wonder you're my favorite niece. Don't tell your sisters."

Jillian grinned. "We know you tell us all we're your favorite."

"Fine, you caught me. I'm guilty of loving all my nieces." She brushed hair from her eyes. "How was your trip to Stonefield? Any new information on Maggie's sister?"

"Nothing more than half-truths and questions, I'm afraid. Moira is a woman of mystery."

"She's not to be trusted," Grace said. "Her aura is dark. There is evil all around her. She's involved in Maggie's death. Ethan must find her soon."

Choosing not to address her aunt's ominous concerns, Jillian changed the subject. "Where's Trixie? Did she run out for an iced coffee? She loves those things."

"Trixie needed—"

The bell tinkled. A pint-sized customer standing in the doorway drew their attention. Jillian's heart soared. Liza, a former student, had stopped in. After a hug and a few minutes visiting, they scoured the store together for the perfect book to buy and three others the girl could borrow from the Lending Library.

"These are all wonderful choices, and you'll enjoy these two because the main character is a girl your age." Jillian tapped the books she'd set on the counter.

Liza promised to come back after she read them all, so they could discuss the books. She slung the gold tote bag with her newly acquired reading materials over her shoulder and waved goodbye. "Thanks, Ms. Edwards. I'll be back soon."

The store was now empty of customers. Jillian shifted her focus to her previous conversation. "Aunt Grace, you know you're welcome here any time, but I'm worried about Trixie. She's on the schedule to close the shop tonight. Is everything okay?"

"Everything's fine, Kitten." Aunt Grace fussed with the pendant adorning Jillian's neck. "Glad to see you wearing this today—just in case."

"And Trixie?"

"She ran a quick errand, so I filled in. She'll be back in a few minutes. Stop worrying."

"I'm not worrying. I'm detail-oriented. I like things scheduled, organized, and efficient. When everything is in its place, my store runs like a well-oiled machine."

"Yes. I know, Kitten. Organization is important to you— losing things has always driven you nuts." She patted Jillian's back, soothing the sting of her words. "I can assure you Trixie is not lost."

Grace's comment sparked a memory. "Have you come across a wrapped box anywhere in the shop?"

"Yes, Kitten. There's one behind the counter." Grace nodded to her left.

Jillian raced for the shelf, disappointed to find the books she'd wrapped this morning for a customer's phone order.

Maggie's box has to be here somewhere. Why can't I find it?

"Was it the box you wanted?" Grace wandered to the counter.

"No, I wrapped—"

The older woman's gasp stopped her short.

"Aunt Grace, what's wrong?" She searched her aunt's face for answers.

"I'm having a vision—you being late for your date, Kitten. It's quarter to five." Grace pointed at the clock on the wall.

Jillian sighed, the tension leaving her shoulders. "I have time. I want to hang out here until Trixie gets back."

"Why? Do you think I can't handle things without you? I'll have you know, young lady, I've held many jobs in my lifetime and was effective at each and every one." Aunt Grace puffed out her chest.

The bell above the door saved Jillian from anymore awkward discussion with her aunt. Trixie sailed through the door.

"Oh, hey, boss. Glad you're back. I ran to the post office to drop off a package—they close at five. Grace stood in for me." The words tumbled out in a nervous rush. "Hope that was okay."

"Of course, it's fine. And if you needed to step out, Aunt Grace is the perfect person to help us in the shop. No worries." Jillian hoped her choice of words would reassure both Trixie and Aunt Grace.

"Whew, thanks." Trixie faked wiping sweat from her brow. "I don't want to be in the doghouse the first week on the job." She plopped down on the stool behind the oak counter. "I'm back and will be until closing, so you ladies should go. You both have a gorgeous man to get ready for." She wiggled her eyebrows at them, laughing softly under her breath.

"That's right." Jillian smiled at her aunt. "Dr. Madison is taking you to some fancy French restaurant. Are you wearing your power suit on your date?"

"Heavens no, I'm wearing a little black dress I found on sale at Bella's Boutique." Grace shimmied her shoulders and wiggled her hips. "I want to make a good impression on my first official date with Robert. An accidental meeting at the Corner Deli doesn't count as a date. I hope you're planning to do the same thing, Kitten."

"Ooh, yeah, busting out the LBD. Very nice, Grace." Trixie spun on the stool to face Jillian. "What *are* you wearing? Do you have some sexy number picked out to make Mr. Hunky drool?"

"No, I won't be wearing anything like that this evening. Travis said to wear something comfortable, and a dress is not comfortable in my book." Jillian wrinkled her nose. "I'll go home now to get ready if you're finished giving me grief. Aunt Grace, you should do the same."

Without waiting for an answer, she went to claim her pups and head home. The anxiety this date had created dogged her steps all day. The thought of a warm shower made her smile—the perfect thing to soothe her ragged nerves.

She needed to look good, so she would feel good. Becca's advice reverberated in her head, so she repeated those words several times.

This may be my new mantra.

CHAPTER TWENTY-FOUR

Jillian pulled into her driveway a few minutes after five. Abbey and Hayley ran inside the moment she unlocked the front door and unleashed them. A few laps around the apartment convinced them nothing had changed in the hours they'd been gone. Satisfied, both dogs slurped from their water bowl while waiting for their mama to fill the food bowls with kibble.

"Enjoy your dinner, ladies, while I get ready for my date with Travis. You two seem impressed with him, and you're great judges of character. Here's hoping he's impressed with me."

Thoughts of her date caused rollercoaster-sized flip flops in her stomach. Her growing feelings for Travis were something she'd never experienced before—not even with Scott. Travis was different, special—something about him drew her in. Could she be falling for this guy? The very thought scared her.

What if he turned out to be a jerk?

She didn't want to put her heart out there only to have it broken again.

After a warm shower, a quick blow dry, and a light layer of makeup, Jillian slipped into the clothes Becca had helped her choose. As she looked at herself in the mirror, she liked the reflection staring back at her. Without any details on the date, she went on pure faith in Becca's ability to choose the perfect outfit.

At six o'clock on the dot, a knock at the door startled her slumbering pups and sent them scrambling to greet their guest. Shooing them back, Jillian took a deep breath before opening the door to the man who waited outside. Travis stood on her tiny porch, handsome in dark jeans and a light blue button-down shirt, which she noticed was comfortably untucked. He held a colorful bouquet in one hand and a large dog's leash in the other. He smiled.

Be still my heart.

Travis twisted and untwisted the dog's leash.

"Um, hi," he said. His companion, a black and tan German shepherd, let out a soft woof. A slight flush crept up Travis's cheeks when she invited them in. "I need to explain why Blaze is here first." He cleared his throat.

"I know how important your girls are to you. Blaze and I are tight as well. I figured if we're going to be dating—and I hope we are—we should make sure our pups get along. I planned this date with them in mind. I sure hope they like each other."

Jillian's pulse skipped a beat at the word *dating*. Travis's speech melted her heart. He'd included her girls on their date—the most thoughtful thing a guy had ever done for her.

"You're both welcome. Please, come inside." She stepped back, allowing room for man and dog.

Travis led his pup into the entryway, giving her the command—sit. Blaze responded by plopping her haunches on the tile floor. Sensing an interloper in their territory, Abbey and Hayley scampered up to the bigger dog. Jillian held her breath, wondering what all three canines would do.

The smaller schnauzers approached Blaze as a unified front. The bigger dog endured their scrutiny, her whole body quivering with excitement. Deciding the newcomer posed no threat, Abbey and Hayley wagged their tails and nudged closer to their new friend. Moments later, they darted down the hall, returning seconds later carrying toys and laying them at Blaze's feet.

Travis blew out a breath. "Bringing their toys is a good sign, right?"

"A great sign. Abbey and Hayley are possessive of their toys." Jillian pointed at the furry blue sheep and the spotted leopard. "Those are their favorites. If they're willing to share, they've decided Blaze is a friend."

"Great, let our date begin." Travis handed her the bouquet he'd been holding, a beautiful array in shades of cream, blue, and purple. Carrying them to the kitchen, she inhaled their scent. Travis followed.

"These are gorgeous, thank you. But two bouquets in one week? You're going to spoil me."

"Everybody needs spoiling now and then. Besides, your sister likes my business."

"Oh, I'm sure she does. Did she give you a hard time again?" She winced, waiting for the answer.

"Not so much. She's warming up to me."

From his vantage point in the kitchen where they chatted, Travis kept an eye on the dogs, who were playing a rousing game of tug of war with a fuzzy pink caterpillar.

"I'm glad they play well together. I would've been disappointed if 'man's best friend' ruined this man's plans for the evening." He ran a hand through his slightly damp hair.

Jillian stood at the sink, filling a crystal vase with water. From behind, Travis wrapped his arms around her waist and brushed her hair aside. He placed a small kiss on her neck. "I've thought of doing this all day. Too forward?"

Setting the flowers on the counter, she pivoted within his arms wrapping hers tightly around his middle. She touched her lips to his, depositing a soft, quick kiss. "Fine with me."

He needed no further invitation to return the kiss, his lasting a bit longer. His lips were warm, tasting of something salty. She felt the kiss all the way to her toes. With one hand, he rubbed a circle on the small of her back, making her knees weak and her mind go blank. He pulled back and sighed, placing his forehead against hers.

"Oh, my." Her legs quivered. She'd fall to the floor if he dared let go.

"I agree. Pretty good for our first date." He grinned down at her, an impish twinkle in his eyes. "I'm glad you didn't mind. I like to get the first kiss out of the way at the beginning of the date. Otherwise, you're stressing about it the whole evening, right?"

Before Jillian could express her agreement, something, besides her, caught his attention. "Do you get the sense we're being watched?" Travis glanced out the kitchen window. "I could swear I saw someone at the window."

"We are being watched." Sitting in the kitchen doorway were three pairs of beady brown eyes staring back at them. Abbey, Hayley, and Blaze scrutinized their humans, each dog cocking their head to the same side. Their pose would've made a great picture if Jillian's phone hadn't been in the other room.

"I think they're judging us." Jillian laughed at the furry trio. "Do you ever wonder what Blaze thinks of you?"

"Oh, she thinks I'm her manservant who caters to her every whim, which includes a bowl full of food twice a day, fresh water, plenty of treats, a daily run, and lots of belly rubs."

"Sounds a lot like my two. I'm the maid who cooks and cleans up after them."

The dogs didn't move, continuing to stare, making their humans jumpy.

"Maybe we should go." Travis stepped back, breaking contact with her. "We can load those three in my truck and head out—it's a thirty-minute drive to our date's destination."

"Are you sure we should take them? They're getting along well. Blaze can stay here with my girls until we get back."

"I planned our date with them in mind. Let's hit the road." Travis held out his hand to her and whistled for the dogs. "C'mon, tail-waggers, you can come with us."

Hearing the word *come*, all three dashed for the door. Abbey and Hayley waited while Jillian clipped on their leashes. Blaze sat at attention by Travis's side. The unusual quintet climbed into Travis's red truck—humans in the front and canines in the back.

"You drive a black SUV. Where did this truck come from?" Jillian slid into the spacious cab. She ran her hand over the supple leather.

"I have two cars—my black SUV and this truck. I drive the SUV back and forth to work because I can lock my gear and bedding in the back. On my days off, I like to drive this truck. Plus, it suits my purpose for our date."

"Speaking of." She fished for a clue. "Am I dressed for whatever we're doing?"

"Perfect." He winked at her. "Blue is a good color on you, by the way. What's most important is you're comfortable.

There won't be anyone judging you or your outfit where we're going."

"No hints, huh?" Jillian stretched, wiggling in her seat. "All right, I'll sit back and enjoy the ride."

Driving down the highway listening to the snores from the back seat, she talked about her trip to Stonefield, including the untruths Moira'd told.

"That woman has serious issues. She must be hiding something, otherwise why tell all those lies?" Travis said.

"Ethan said the same thing. He's been suspicious from the start." She shrugged. "I've considered myself a good judge of character—until now. Moira's secrecy and lying makes me question my ability to read people. I wonder too how well I knew Maggie. I mean, I didn't know she even had a sister."

Travis squeezed her hand. "Don't be hard on yourself or your friend. We can only know people as well as they allow us. Maybe Maggie had secrets, or maybe she felt uncomfortable sharing personal things. Whatever the case, remember her as the good friend you knew her to be."

There it was again—the fluttery sensation in the pit of her stomach. And the cause was sitting beside her, holding her hand. He knew exactly what to say and when to say it to ease her worries. How was it possible he understood her so well in such a short time?

The truck bounced down a narrow dirt road which seemed to lead nowhere. Wondering if he'd taken a wrong turn, Jillian remained quiet. She had vivid memories of her parents arguing on car trips when they were lost. Her father refused to stop and ask for directions. Male pride, her mother always said.

Travis made a sharp right. "We're here."

Here was an old drive-in theater Jillian remembered visiting as a kid. She'd heard the place shut down years ago. A few other cars were parked in the aisles, so it must be open for business.

"I hope you'll like this," Travis said. "A buddy bought the place. He's restoring everything to its former glory. The snack bar isn't open yet, so I brought dinner, drinks, and movie snacks. There's an air mattress, some pillows and blankets in back. I brought Blaze's bed for the pups. There might even be some snacks for them in the basket." He stopped his nervous rambling, avoided eye contact, and focused his attention out the window.

Is he worried I won't like this date?

"I love this." Jillian laid a hand on his arm, drawing his focus back to her. "What could be better than dinner and a movie with you on a beautiful fall evening?"

"Uh, two movies?" Travis shrugged, holding his palms out. "We're here for a double feature—two of Tom Cruise's lesser-known films. My friend—the owner— can't afford the prices on new releases yet, so he shows older movies and those less popular at the box office."

"Even better." Jillian climbed from the truck, opening the door to the back seat. "I'll take the dogs so they can do their business before the movie."

"Are you sure you can handle all three at the same time?" His face scrunched in doubt.

"Please. I've handled twenty-seven nine-year-olds all at once. Compared to them, these three are a piece of cake." She snapped her fingers.

Watching her walk away, Travis smiled and mumbled, "How did I get so lucky to have a woman like her come into my life?"

"You were at the right place at a wrong time." Her voice carried from a nearby grove of trees. "Before you ask, I used my super-teacher hearing. Yes, there is such a thing."

While she waited for the dogs, Jillian allowed her mind a few moments to wander— and wonder.

She couldn't believe all the planning Travis put into this date. Most guys she'd dated didn't pay attention to details. They flew by the seat of their pants. This was a nice change of pace.

Blaze's deep growl brought her attention back to the moment. The large dog stared into the thicket of trees, straining at her leash. The hair on her back was raised, her teeth bared. Her smaller pups closed ranks.

"What's the matter, girl? Some forest creature hiding in there?" Jillian followed Blaze's stare but saw nothing. She patted the dog's head, trying to soothe her. "C'mon, sweetie. Let's go find Travis." With a final stare into the woods, the canine allowed herself to be led away.

"Triple mission accomplished." She and the dogs returned to the truck. "They should be good for hours." Peeking at the supplies Travis had arranged in the truck bed, she whistled. "Wow, you've outdone yourself."

He'd placed blankets and pillows on an air mattress in the bed of his truck, so they'd have somewhere cozy to sit to watch the movies. He'd situated Blaze's bed by the tailgate, so the pups had room to stretch out.

Jillian marveled at the food he'd unpacked from the cooler—fried chicken, potato salad, coleslaw, and a box of Cate's best-selling cookies.

There was enough food to feed an army.

"How many people will be joining us?" she teased. "I hope you don't think I can eat all this. I mean, I have a good appetite, just not this good."

A sheepish grin spread across Travis's face. "Yeah, I might've gotten carried away. Did I mention there are movie snacks too?"

"Good thing we're watching a double feature," she said. "Maybe by the second show, we'll be ready for them."

Travis gave her two smaller pups a lift into the truck. Blaze hopped up on her own. Each dog got a chewy bone to keep them distracted from the food. With the furry ones settled, the humans got comfortable and filled their plates.

"Is this the potato salad and coleslaw from the Corner Deli? I love their food." Jillian spooned a serving of each onto her plate. Travis could only mumble, his mouth full of fried chicken. "Their food tastes good," she said, "because the Harrisons cook everything from scratch."

"I'm not a good cook." Travis admitted this truth. "So, I'm a regular customer there. Mrs. Harrison calls me 'handsome' and always tries to give me extra food. She reminds me of a younger version of my mom."

They ate their meal and chatted, enjoying the cool night air. The leaves rustling in the breeze and the company of an owl hooting from his tree provided nature's background music. This date was off to a great start.

"The first movie should start in five minutes." Travis checked his watch.

"Let's clean this mess." Jillian collected utensils from the takeout containers, closing them and stowing them in the cooler. Travis helped gather the trash and carried it to the nearest garbage can.

Attractive and he doesn't mind cleaning? Who is this guy?

Travis hooked the speakers over the bed of the truck and leaned on the air mattress, patting the spot next to him. Surrounded by pillows, warm blankets, and Travis, Jillian settled in for the double feature.

The first movie had sports and manly scenes for him with enough drama and romance to satisfy her. Small town football star falls for the cute All-American girl. Something interferes in their relationship, drama ensues. In the end, they're reunited. Everyone lives happily ever after.

Watching movies at the drive-in gave Jillian the chance to ask Travis questions without being shushed by those around them.

"Did you play any sports?" she said. "You know, like the lead character in the movie."

"I played football, but my favorite sport was baseball. My mom tells people I lived, ate, and breathed it. If I wasn't practicing or playing baseball, I watched games on TV. Three guys in the house constantly watching sports drove my mom crazy."

"You must've been good with all the practicing."

"Good enough—earned a scholarship to college. I thought my baseball days would end there. Instead, I had a great season my senior year and got drafted in the third round—sent me to a minor league team in Kentucky."

"You must've been better than good enough. Was minor league baseball as tough as they say?"

Her question received an incredulous stare from Travis.

"What? I've watched *Bull Durham*."

"Well, I'm no Kevin Costner," he laughed. "The movie's portrayal of the minor leagues was pretty accurate—terrible pay, long, brutal seasons played on crappy fields and unbearable bus rides. We had old equipment and hand-me-down uniforms. We dressed and showered in moldy locker rooms. Even for a bunch of guys, it was disgusting."

"Sounds awful." She wrinkled her nose. "Why do it?"

"Playing in the minors is a guy's shot at the Big Leagues." She sensed regret in his voice.

"Sounds like you miss playing. What made you quit?"

"A knee injury requiring reconstructive surgery. No team wanted a catcher with a bum knee." He shrugged it off. "My friend, Adam, has played in the majors for five years, so I live vicariously through him."

"I'm sorry your injury ended your baseball career—sounds like you would've been great if you'd had the chance to play in the major league." She reached over and squeezed his hand. "I've witnessed you in action as a firefighter. You're great at this job too."

Travis scooted closer, putting his arm around her shoulders. Jillian snuggled against his solid frame. His aftershave's musky scent wrapped around her like a warm hug.

She could get used to nights like this.

The loud opening soundtrack of the next movie began, drawing their attention back to the widescreen. Travis rummaged in the box he'd hauled from the back seat taking out popcorn, two sodas, Twizzlers, and some peanut M&Ms.

"I know we ate a big dinner, but I can't watch a movie without snacks." He handed her a soda and the peanut M&M's. Her mouth dropped open in surprise.

How did he know she couldn't refuse peanut M&M's?

"What's wrong? I thought you liked the peanut ones." He pulled the candies from her reach.

"I do. How'd *you* know they're my favorite?" She snatched the M&Ms from his grasp.

"You have a bowl on the counter at Whimsy & Wonder, another on the desk in your office, and one more on the coffee table in your living room. Why have three bowls filled with peanut M&Ms if they're not something you like?"

His thoughtfulness touched her. Not many men would've noticed or remembered the candy she'd put around her spaces. He won more brownie points as the night wore on.

He'd pulled out all the stops tonight.

The temperature had dropped at least fifteen degrees. Travis snatched a blanket from behind his back and draped it across their laps He opened the bag of popcorn, setting it between them. They settled in to watch the second show.

This film was an action movie with police chases, daring stunts, and a few loud explosions. While not her usual type of movie, Jillian enjoyed it more than she thought she would. Might have had something to do with the man sharing a blanket with her. As the final credits rolled, she glanced at her watch, not wanting this date to end.

She realized how late it was and knew they needed to wrap things up and head home. Travis reported for work at seven a.m. for his twenty-four-hour shift. He needed his rest. Despite his protests about the evening still being early, they packed the leftover snacks and deflated the air mattress.

Their sudden movements woke the girls, who needed a potty break before heading home.

"You did a great job with them the last time." Travis handed her three leashes. "I'll clean the mess we made here."

She wrapped the leads around her hand. "We'll be back."

"I'll be waiting."

Ten minutes had passed. Most of the other cars had pulled away when all three dogs ran back to Travis, trailing their leashes and barking like crazy.

"Hey, what's with you mutts? Did my date give you the slip?" Ruffling Blaze's fur, he tried to grab Abbey and

Hayley. They evaded his attempts, running around him in circles.

"Jillian," he called out. "What're you doing out there?"

No answer came. He put Blaze in the truck and attempted to corral the girls again.

"Quit playing around, Jillian." Travis's call met silence. "You're making me nervous."

Still nothing. Abbey and Hayley whined, herding Travis toward the trees.

"Let's go find your mama." Calling out her name again, he headed into the woods.

With their noses to the ground, the pups steered Travis away from his truck. They barked and howled deeper into the woods. He followed them, batting away low-hanging branches in his path. Abbey and Hayley led him to a clearing where the reason for their distress became apparent.

"Oh, no—Jillian!"

CHAPTER TWENTY-FIVE

Jillian's memory of events remained disconnected. Travis would tell everyone the story so many times she could recall his words verbatim.

"I followed the dogs into the woods and found Jillian lying there, face down in the dirt. I dropped to my knees and rolled her onto her back. She had an ugly cut across her neck. She was unconscious, but her breathing and pulse were steady. I tried to bring her around with no luck. Her pups knew something was wrong. They nudged her hand and licked her face until she opened her eyes. They managed to do what I couldn't."

The next part, she remembered. She'd heard Travis talking to the dogs.

"Good girls. You did a great job protecting your mom. I'll take it from here." Abbey and Hayley lay down as close to Jillian as they could, keeping watch.

"What happened?" She blinked. Her focus was fuzzy. "Why are we sitting on the ground?"

"I hope you can tell me. The pups ran back to the truck without you, scaring me half to death. Abbey and Hayley led me into the trees. I found you collapsed on the ground with a huge bump on the back of your head and a cut on your neck. Can you remember anything?"

Jillian struggled to retrieve even the tiniest memory of what had happened. She took a deep breath—an effort to slow her racing heart and concentrate her efforts. She calmed as flashes of memories came back.

"I ... I took the dogs to the grassy area. I heard a ... a noise." She pointed into the cluster of trees to her right. "They heard something and growled. I didn't ... there was no one—figured it was a wild animal. A man grabbed me from behind. He ... he yanked my head back and put a knife to my throat. I ... I guess I dropped the leashes. Oh my gosh—Blaze! Where is she?" Her voice quivered, growing stronger as she talked. Being wrapped in Travis's arms with her sweet girls by her side helped.

"Blaze is in the truck. She's fine." Travis brushed a loose curl from her face. "Can you remember anything else?"

"He said this was my last warning. No more questions or I'd be the next one dead. He drew his knife across my throat, and it burned. Blood oozed down my throat. I don't remember anything else—I'm sorry." She inhaled, steeling herself to move from the cold ground.

"Where do you think you're going?" Travis cradled her in his lap. "I can't believe I was a few feet away when he attacked you. I'd love to get my hands on him." Pressed to his chest, Jillian could feel the angry rumble as he spoke.

"Do you think he's still here?" Her frightened gaze surveyed the nearest trees shrouded in darkness.

"No, I'm sure he's gone. He knew I'd come for you." Travis gathered her closer, eliciting a whimper. He loosened his hold and massaged her arms. Lowering his face, he pressed a kiss to her forehead. "Let's get you to the hospital."

"I don't need a doctor, Travis. You can take care of me. Please drive me home." Her shaky voice betrayed her attempt at bravery.

Without saying a word, Travis stood, scooping her up in his arms. Her two tiny bodyguards fell in step with him. He carried her to his truck and placed her on the seat, tucking a blanket around her legs. He lifted Abbey and Hayley in next to Blaze, who wiggled with happiness at being reunited with her new friends.

Safe inside Travis's big truck, Jillian snugged the blanket tighter to ward off the chill she felt deep in her bones. She heard Travis's voice talking, only not to her.

How sweet. He's chatting with my girls.

Her eyelids grew heavy. The back of her head pounded and her neck still burned. Her eyes drifted shut.

"Oh no, you don't." Travis shook her arm, jostling her awake. "Keep those beautiful green eyes open."

"Hmm, what?" Jillian concentrated to put her thoughts into words. "I dozed off—I'm so sorry. Some fun date I am, huh?"

"You're a great date." Travis smiled, taking her hand. "However, the bump on your head has me worried. Please try to stay awake until you get checked out in the emergency room." He raised his hand to stop her. "This is nonnegotiable. You got hurt on my watch. I'm responsible. I should've been there to protect you."

Normally, the notion she needed protection would have angered Jillian, and she would've come out swinging. At the moment, she decided against it. This wonderful man had planned the most thoughtful first date imaginable. They hadn't expected their evening to end in the emergency room. The least she could do was cooperate, give him some peace of mind. Besides, she was too tired to argue.

"Fine. I'll get checked over if only to make you happy." She smiled, trying to alleviate some of his worries. "I've been called hardheaded many times, so I doubt a bump on my head could cause permanent damage."

Travis played the radio with the windows down, using the music and the cool air to keep her awake. He fired questions at her too. When they arrived at the hospital parking lot, Ethan's police cruiser waited for them.

"You called Ethan?" Jillian narrowed her eyes at Travis. Even that slight movement caused a pounding in her head.

"You bet I called him. You were assaulted." Travis banged his fist on the steering wheel. "You could have been killed. Ethan needed to know."

Stepping out of his car, Ethan approached the passenger side of Travis's truck. He wrenched open the door and whisked her out of her seat. He carried her toward the ER entrance with Travis in hot pursuit.

"Ethan, stop. This is ridiculous. My legs aren't broken. Put me down." Jillian struggled against his firm grip, flailing her arms and legs.

Ignoring her pleas, Ethan proceeded to the registrar's desk where he set her in a wheelchair. He flashed his badge and demanded his victim be taken care of ASAP. She'd never witnessed people race into action as fast as the nurses behind the desk. A police badge inspires a certain amount of obedience in people.

A nursing assistant pushed Jillian into a room and helped her onto a bed. One nurse wrapped a blood pressure cuff around her arm. Another examined her injuries while asking questions. Travis and Ethan jumped in providing answers for her.

The older of the two nurses wasn't intimidated by a police officer and his badge. Giving both men a hostile stare, she spoke in a no-nonsense tone.

"Gentlemen, I understand you're concerned. This woman does, however, appear capable of speaking for herself." She pointed at Travis. "And you. You've been in this ER enough times to know the rules. If you can't follow them, there's a waiting room down the hall to your left." Travis opened his mouth, snapping it shut when Ethan elbowed him in the ribs.

"We're sorry, um—" Ethan squinted at her ID badge. "—Nurse Freeman. We'll be quiet. I do need to be present in the room, if you're good with that. This patient is a victim of a physical assault."

"Mm-hmm." The woman pressed her lips together. "You need to step out for a few minutes while we get this poor girl into a hospital gown. I'll let you know when you can come back in. When you do, stay out of my way."

Travis and Ethan knocked into each other in their haste to follow Nurse Freeman's orders. Jillian laughed at them.

Not such tough guys after all.

The nurse's gruff demeanor changed with her patient. "Sweetheart, your bodyguards tell me you have that cut on your neck and a bump on the back of your head. Do you have injuries anywhere else?"

"No, ma'am, I don't think so." Her voice a mere whisper. Jillian was wary of this woman who'd put Travis and Ethan in their place with little more than a glare and a stern voice.

The nurse tsked. "Let me check your neck. If the incision is deep, you may need stitches. By the time we're done with that, they'll be ready for you in the CAT scan room."

Nurse Freeman prodded the neck wound, assessing the extent of the injury. She cleaned the cut. Jillian let out a hiss when the antiseptic hit the sensitive skin.

"I'm sorry. I know this stings." Nurse Freeman apologized.

"A little." Jillian sighed.

"You were lucky. The knife didn't penetrate too deeply. We can use surgical glue to close the gash." The nurse peeled off her gloves. "I'll let your two gentlemen come in and keep you company while I see about that scan." She signaled to the men waiting in the hall.

Travis closed the distance in a few steps, grabbing hold of her hand. Jillian leaned into him and rested her head against his side, closing her eyes. Suddenly, she gasped, startling both men.

"What's wrong?" Ethan rushed to her side. "Do you need the nurse?"

"Are you in pain?" Travis peered into her face.

"No." She tossed back the sheets. "The dogs are in the back seat of Travis's truck. We can't leave them out there."

"Whoa, where do you think you're going?" Travis grabbed hold of her shoulders, gently pressing her back on the bed. "The girls are fine. I called Bryan. He came and got them ten minutes ago. He'll keep them at his house until we're done here."

"And Blaze?" A tear leaked from her eye.

"Blaze, too." Travis wiped the tear away. "Those three pups are probably having a ball with Bryan."

Jillian relaxed back on the pillows and closed her eyes. Her whole body hurt. Her eyes prickled as more tears threatened. Someone placed a cool, wet cloth on her forehead, which soothed her enough for sleep to whisk her away. When she opened her eyes, Ethan was gone. Travis sat in the chair beside her bed, still holding her hand.

"You put the cloth on my head."

"I thought something cool would help your headache." He squeezed her hand.

Tears spilled down her cheeks. She couldn't hold them back.

"Hey, hey, what's wrong? Are you in pain?" Travis rubbed her arm. "Tell me what you need. I'll get it."

A commotion in the hall drowned out her answer. Raised voices and pounding feet headed in their general direction. A hand whisked back the privacy curtain. Jillian's parents and Aunt Grace rushed into the already cramped space. Everyone talked at once.

"Oh my goodness, Kitten. I warned you. Did the woman in my vision attack you?" Aunt Grace fluttered around the bed, fussing at Jillian.

"Hey, Peanut. You scared your mom and me to death." Her dad planted a kiss on her cheek. "You've been in good hands, I hear."

"Ethan called us. He said you'd been attacked and were in the ER." Her mom burst into tears and sobbed on her husband's shoulder.

"What's all this?" The ER doctor's arrival brought their disruption to a halt. "How did so many of you get in here? Hospital policy says no more than two visitors at a time."

"Hey, Doc." Travis and the physician shook hands, greeting each other like old friends.

"Good evening, Lieutenant." The doctor smiled. "Surprised you're in the ER tonight. Maybe you could shed some light on this." He motioned around the room.

"I brought my friend in after she was attacked. Her family heard she'd been hurt." Travis shrugged. "Can't tell you how glad I am you're working tonight, Doc."

"I understand you're worried for your ... daughter?" He glanced at Joy, who nodded. "At least two of you must step down the hall. There's a nice waiting room. Hospital policy."

After a quick discussion, Jillian's father and Grace left the exam room, leaving Joy and Travis to keep watch.

"I'm Dr. Pederson." He introduced himself. "I'll take good care of you." He manipulated the skin around the cut with his gloved fingers. Jillian sucked in a breath.

"Nurse Freeman will close this wound with special glue." The doctor prodded the bump on her head. "When she's finished, someone will get you for the CAT scan, so we can examine the goose egg on your head." Dr. Pederson patted her shoulder before leaving her with her mom, Travis, and Ethan, who'd snuck back in the room. The doctor hadn't objected when Ethan flashed his badge.

"Jilly, could I ask some questions while we wait for the nurse?" Ethan's request met with an objection from Travis.

Jillian pressed her hand to his chest.

"He's doing his job, Travis. I'm fine and want to help," she said. "Go ahead, Ethan."

"You told Travis a man attacked you." Ethan's eyes never left her face. "Any chance you can give a description?"

She shook her head. "No, he came from behind me. The only thing I saw was his knife."

"Can you describe it?"

"The blade was maybe five inches. The handle was black."

"Could you describe his hand or arm?

"No—wait, yes." She fought the headache building behind her eyes. "He was wearing red flannel—I think."

"Can you describe his voice? Or a smell?"

"He whispered in my ear, kind of slurred his words. His breath smelled like booze." The memory of his breath on her neck caused a shudder. "He reeked of cigarette smoke too—like the creepy guy from the bookstore."

The nurse stepped in with a supply cart, ready to take care of the throat wound. She chased Travis and Ethan out into the hallway, allowing Joy to stay. The men camped outside the door, talking.

"I'm done questioning Jillian. If you're good here, I'll go check on the forensics team I sent to the drive-in." Ethan cleared his throat. "You do know Bryan called her sisters? Her family will close ranks to keep her safe until I lock this guy away."

"I'm counting on it," Travis said. "You go. Do what you need to do. I'll stay here and make sure she gets home safe."

"You two should know I can hear you," Jillian called out from the exam room. "Teacher hearing—it's a real thing."

"Uh-huh, sure it is," Ethan mumbled under his breath.

"Heard that too."

Ethan continued, despite her eavesdropping. "You take her home. Becca will relieve you since your shift starts in a few hours. Her sisters will work out a schedule for the rest of the day. You need some sleep, LT—you look like something the cat dragged in."

"Gee, thanks." Travis scrubbed at the stubble on his face. "She won't be happy with us babysitting her."

"We have no choice. This guy is getting more violent by the day. He's made it clear he's coming for her. She isn't safe until he's behind bars," Ethan said. "Besides, I could never face my wife if something happened to her best friend. She'd make my life miserable."

"Becca's so nice, I can't believe she'd be spiteful."

"Let's hope you never do anything to incur her wrath." Ethan chuckled. "You're a big, tough guy—she's brought bigger men to their knees."

"Really? Duly noted—never anger your wife."

"Yep, don't poke the bear," Ethan winked at Travis.

"Becca wouldn't appreciate being likened to a bear." Jillian swatted at Ethan as the orderly pushed her past in a wheelchair. "Yes, I heard every word. You two underestimate the power of my teacher hearing. And you should know my silence will be expensive."

CHAPTER TWENTY-SIX

Jillian caught Travis pacing the floor of the small exam room. His head swiveled toward the door at the sound of squeaky wheels as they brought her in. Her mother sat in a chair by the window. Worn out from her ordeal, Jillian managed a tired smile in their direction.

"Hey, Travis. Hi, Mom. I must be a hot mess." She smoothed her hair, fussing with the bandage at her throat.

"No, you're beautiful," Travis whispered, a catch in his voice. He reached for her hand, helping her from the wheelchair back onto the bed.

"He's right, sweetheart. You look lovely as always." Joy took her other hand. "But what's more important is getting better and getting you out of here."

Jillian closed her eyes. Her breathing slowed, comforted by Travis's thumb stroking her skin.

"I'm going for some coffee. I'll let your dad and Grace know what's happening as well. Can I get you anything, Travis?" Joy said.

"No, thanks. I'm good."

"I'll be back in a few minutes." She grabbed her purse from the chair. She leaned down, delivering a motherly kiss to Travis's cheek. "Thanks for watching out for my girl."

Sitting in the quiet room, Travis muttered aloud. "How did he know where to find you?"

"He must have followed us from my house—maybe there *was* someone outside my kitchen window." She squeezed his hand, never opening her eyes. "Which means he watched us at the drive-in, waiting to catch me alone."

"What do you mean?" Travis leaned forward in his seat.

"When I took the girls into the trees the first time, all three of them growled at something in the woods. The hair on their backs raised. I thought it was a raccoon or a fox. I coaxed them away with a treat. So, not a wild animal— him." She let out a shuddering breath.

"Let's leave the worrying to Ethan. You need your rest." He settled back in his chair. "Doctor Pederson should be here in a few minutes."

Instead of resting, Jillian shifted in the bed, wide awake and staring at him.

Meeting her eyes, he made an apology and a promise.

"I'm sorry for not protecting you. I can promise it won't happen again." There was a tone in his voice, cold as steel. "We won't let you out of our sight until this guy is behind bars."

"While I appreciate everything you said, stop being an idiot." She yanked her hand away. "There's nothing for you to apologize for. You aren't responsible for what happened, and it's not your job to protect me." Changing her mind, she reached out, taking his hand back.

"I know you, Ethan, and everybody else have figured out a schedule of who's watching me for at least the next twenty-four hours. I'd fight you on this, but I'm tired and my head hurts, so you have a reprieve." She yawned and lay back on the pillow.

The doctor appeared in the doorway, clearing his throat as he entered. "Good news. All your tests came back fine. I'm having the nurse prepare your discharge papers."

"Thank you." Hearing she could go home put a smile on Jillian's face.

"You're welcome." He gave his patient specific instructions. "Go easy for a few days. Your neck will be sore. You may have headaches. I'm prescribing a mild painkiller and an antibiotic. We don't want your wound to become infected. I recommend you fill the prescriptions as soon as you can. We'll send you home with a few samples to tide you over until morning when Carpenter's Pharmacy opens."

"I'm taking her home," Travis said. "We'll put the prescriptions in their drop box on our way—they'll see them first thing when they open."

The doctor grinned at her. "Young lady, you'll get excellent care with this one. He's a good man and a gifted medic." He shook Travis's hand as he left the room.

Nurse Freeman brought the release papers and the prescriptions. After finishing her well-rehearsed discharge spiel, she addressed Travis. "I'll help this lovely girl get dressed. Go get your car and bring it around to the ER discharge door."

Giving the nurse a quick nod, Travis ducked out of the room. He passed Joy on her way in.

"You might have a faint scar on your neck which will fade with time. The tube of scar recovery gel I put with your medicine samples will help but be sure to also use sunscreen. Keep the wound clean and dry, change the bandage every day." The nurse checked the dressing one last time. "Don't be a martyr. Stay ahead of the pain by taking the medication on time. You'll thank me for it."

Nurse Freeman grabbed the bag of clothes from the closet.

"Your young man is very fond of you—I can tell. He's in our ER whenever his crew brings in a patient. Word gets out he's taken, there will be a lot of nurses with broken hearts."

"We've been on one date," Jillian said. "I wouldn't say he's taken."

"Oh, sweetie, I recognize a man who's falling in love when I see one. That boy is tumbling head over heels for you. No question. He's taken."

"In love? Oh no, I don't think so." Her fingers fumbled with the buttons on her cardigan. "We met a few days ago. People don't fall in love that fast."

Jillian snapped her mouth shut on hollow words.

Nurse Freeman sighed. "This world needs more love at first sight."

Is Travis in love with me? Am I falling in love with him?

"Thank you for taking such good care of my daughter," Joy said. "I'm relieved to know her injuries aren't as serious as we'd feared."

"I'm sure it was frightening to receive a call your child had been hurt." The nurse flashed Joy a sympathetic smile. "It doesn't matter how old they get. We still worry, don't we?"

The nurse retrieved a wheelchair from the hallway. "All right, Ms. Edwards. Let's get you out to your fella, so he can take you home."

"I'm capable of doing this on my own." Jillian waved away the chair as she climbed off the bed.

"Not on my watch. Hospital protocol." The nurse nudged her into the chair. Jillian sat, not having the energy to fight.

"Your dad, Aunt Grace, and I will take off." Joy kissed her daughter goodbye. "Text me when you get home, so I know you made it safely. Becca and Grace are spending the night with you. I'll be there in the morning."

Jillian questioned her mother. "You're on patrol duty tomorrow?"

"Could be." Joy shrugged and headed for the waiting area.

Nurse Freeman pushed Jillian to the door where Travis waited.

"You'll keep a close eye on our patient, correct?" The nurse winked at Travis. "I hear you kids are on a first date. Make sure this beautiful girl gets a spectacular goodnight kiss."

"Yes, ma'am." Travis thanked the nurse for all her help.

"Of course. Help is what I do." Nurse Freeman waved and returned to the ER.

Travis helped Jillian climb into his truck. "We'll stop on the way to drop off those prescriptions."

Her hand stopped him as he tried to shut the passenger door. "Bryan's house is on our way. Can we get the girls? I'd like them home with me. You need to get Blaze."

"Sure. Plan B. We'll drop the prescriptions, get the dogs, and take you home for a good night's sleep."

She rested her head back on the seat and mumbled, "Thank you."

After a quick stop at the pharmacy and an even quicker one at Bryan's, they headed for her house. Two vehicles were parked out front, and their owners waited on the porch. Becca vaulted down the steps and jerked open the truck's door.

"Thank goodness you're home safe. I've been frantic since Ethan called." She helped Jillian from the car with Grace hovering over their shoulders.

"Everything will be all right, Kitten. You're out of the hospital and home with the people who love you. Your aura is tinged with white—a good color for healing and protection." Grace stepped back, looking at Jillian with her critical eye. "Something is still off though—I'm sensing an evil presence—it feels nearby." Her head swiveled left and right, searching for said menace.

"Grace, let's get Jilly inside in case that evil is watching." Becca took the older woman's arm.

"No, wait. The evil is weakening. Maybe I'm getting vibes from these injuries he inflicted." Grace touched the bandage at Jillian's neck. "She's safe and protected—for now. You and Travis help her into the house. I'll get Abbey and Hayley, give them a lap or two around the yard." Grace opened the back door of the truck and came face-to-face with a new furry friend.

"Well, hello. There's an extra dog back here." Grace scratched the newcomer under the chin. "And who are you, sweet thing?"

"Her name's Blaze. She's mine," Travis said. "You can leave her in the truck. I'll take care of her in a minute."

"Nonsense. I'm capable of taking three pups around the yard for a few minutes. You all go inside." Aunt Grace herded the canines out of the car with ease. Jillian smiled at the sight of her aunt prancing around the yard in the little black dress and strappy sandals she'd worn on her date, juggling three dogs on their leashes.

Travis unlocked the door and took Jillian's hand to help her inside. She took one step into her living room and froze.

"No!" Her strangled voice was no more than a whisper.

Evil *had* paid a visit.

Her couch and comfy chair were upended. White cotton fluff obscured the living room carpet. Her grandmother's Tiffany lamp lay in pieces on the floor. The doors to her built-in bookshelves were ripped off the hinges, and the contents strewn around the room. The beautiful canvas above the fireplace had been slashed. She sucked in a breath, taking a step back. Travis caught her by the arms.

Peeking into the room, Becca gasped. "This cannot be happening! Why would someone do this?"

"Don't stand here discussing the damage. The person who did this could still be inside." Travis hissed under his breath. "All of you—take the dogs. Go to Bryan's. I'll let him know you're coming, and I'll call Ethan." He whirled Jillian around, giving her a not-so-gentle shove out the door.

She stumbled, grabbing the door frame for balance. "Wait—Cate and her family! The person who ransacked my apartment could've done this in their part of the house too." She headed for the stairs leading to Cate's kitchen. Travis blocked her way.

"I'll check on them as soon as you're out of here." He pushed her into Becca's arms. "Go. I'll meet you at Bryan's later."

Three women and three dogs climbed into Becca's SUV. Jillian glanced back. Travis stood on the porch making phone calls.

God, please let the man who did this be gone. Please keep Travis safe.

Jillian sat ensconced on Bryan's couch. Becca flitted around, fluffing pillows and tucking a blanket around her friend's legs. She offered a running commentary.

"Everyone wanted to be here when you came home from the ER. Your mom said we shouldn't all descend on you at once." She adjusted the afghan she'd arranged not two minutes before. "Your aunt and I volunteered for the first shift, so the others will be here tomorrow."

Bryan hovered in the doorway, watching Becca make a fuss.

"You need your medication," Becca said. "The pain pills might upset your stomach. Bryan, do you have something she could eat?"

"Um, maybe. Let me go check." He wandered off in search of food.

"I'll help him," Aunt Grace said. "If I know my son, he won't have much in his refrigerator or pantry—some chips, beer, frozen pizza. I'll find something for our girl."

Loud, frantic voices burst through the front door and surged their way into Bryan's living room. All three dogs rushed to greet Cate and Amanda. Jillian sighed. So much for waiting until tomorrow.

I love my family, but it's late. I'm exhausted.

"Quite a night, Jilly. Mom called—told us you'd been attacked. A few hours later, your date stomps on my stairs yelling, 'Anybody home?' Cate shook her head. "Travis showed us your apartment. I can't believe we didn't hear a thing, considering the mess they made. I told Wes we need to get a dog—a really big one." She put the blue box she'd brought on the table and wrapped Jillian in her arms. "Bryan's front door should be locked at all times. We walked right in and so could the lunatic who's threatening you."

"Where are Wes and the girls?" Jillian's heart raced. "Please tell me they're all right."

"They're fine. We bundled them off to Wes' parents' house." Cate released her grip. "They slept through the whole commotion."

Amanda spoke for the first time. Her voice vibrated with fury.

"This maniac stalks you, attacks you, and violates your house. When is this going to end?" She directed her anger at Becca. "Ethan better get busy and do his job."

Becca stiffened.

Jillian interceded. "Ethan is doing everything he can, Amanda. He'll catch this guy soon—relax."

"Relax? I don't believe I can when a psycho killer is coming after my little sister." She grabbed Cate's box from the table and stomped out of the room, cursing under her breath.

"In the meantime, you will not be by yourself." Bryan came back in the living room empty-handed.

Aunt Grace had called it. As usual, Bryan had no food in the house.

"Everyone's pitching in. We'll take care of you and the bookstore." Becca brought another pillow to the couch. "Let's see the nutcase get his hands on you again—not with all of us on guard."

"He sets one foot on my property, he'll live to regret it." Bryan paced, stopping each time he passed the front window checking for trouble.

"You plan to let him live?" Jillian stared at her big, strong cousin. She hoped a bit of humor would relieve some of the tension in the room.

"I make no guarantees." Bryan continued pacing.

Amanda came from the kitchen. "I threw together a late-night snack, so eat." She pointed at the meds Becca had set on the table. "You can't take those pills on an empty stomach, Jilly."

"Travis packed a smorgasbord for our date, so I'm not at all hungry. But those strawberries look good." Before Jillian could reach for one herself, Grace rushed to put a few on a plate along with two of Cate's sugar cookies.

"Here you go, Kitten. I'll make you some chamomile tea to help you relax, so you can get some sleep." Grace scurried to the kitchen.

"I'm still pretty wound up. Sleep may be difficult for the third night in a row." Jillian ate one of the smaller berries. "Has anyone heard from Travis yet?"

As if speaking his name conjured his presence, Bryan let him in the front door. Travis fixed his gaze on Jillian's face. His tired smile broke her heart.

"Glad you're following the doctor's orders." He dropped a quick kiss on her forehead and snatched a cookie from the plate. He broke it into three pieces and fed them to the pups.

"I'm glad you're here. What's happening at my place?" Jillian prepared for whatever news he'd brought.

"Ethan has the forensic techs scouring the place for fingerprints and any other evidence they can find. He'll release the scene later this morning. Then we can start putting your place back together."

"That will require a herculean effort." She swiped at the tears threatening to fall. "They destroyed the place. Everything is ruined."

"They're things, Jilly." There was Becca—the voice of reason. "Your renter's insurance will pay to have them replaced. Your safety—and the pups—is more important than things."

"Excuse me for sticking my nose into someone else's business. Bros have to look out for bros—Travis reports for his shift in a few hours." Bryan glanced at his watch. "He should get some sleep. We'll make sure our girl is safe."

"I don't know if I'll be able to sleep after—well, you know. I should get Blaze home though. Maybe take a shower to relax." Travis perched on the edge of the couch, putting an arm around Jillian. "I'll leave you in your family's capable hands." He pressed a soft kiss on her lips.

She drew him in closer. There were so many things she wanted to say to this amazing man—but not in front of everyone. "Thank you for a wonderful first date. I had a great time."

"Except for the part where you were attacked, ended up in the emergency room, and your house was vandalized," Travis said.

"Stop. None of that is your fault." She pressed her hand over his chest. "I want to hold onto the good memories from our date and let go of the bad stuff—at least for now. Can we try?"

"I'll give it my best shot." He leaned in, softly touching his lips to hers. Goosebumps broke out up and down her arms. She felt a slow warming of her face, knowing the others looked on with interest. She pushed back from Travis. He broke the kiss to gaze at her.

"Maybe this isn't the place to do this." Jillian nodded at the assembled crowd.

"This is the perfect place. Besides I'm following nurse's orders." He kissed her again, deeper and longer this time. Breaking it off, he grinned. "That's the proper way to end a first date."

Whoa, it sure is.

His kiss left her languid. Every inch of her body hummed.

Travis addressed the room, giving strict instructions for Jillian's care. "No strenuous activity. Medication every four to six hours to stay ahead of the pain. The full prescriptions should be ready soon after Carpenter's opens at eight. And lots of peace and quiet so she can rest."

"Yes, sir." Becca saluted. "Are those doctor's orders?"

"No, those are my orders," Travis snapped at her, repenting quickly. "Sorry, Becca. Rough night. I'm a bit on edge."

"We'll take good care of her, Travis." Becca wrapped him in one of her famous hugs.

Becca was the world's best hugger. She gave them away whenever the mood struck her. Travis might as well get used to receiving them.

He whistled to Blaze. "Call the station if you guys need anything. We can be here in minutes." He winked at Jillian. "Take care, beautiful." His furry companion followed him out the door.

"Did I hear Travis?" Aunt Grace returned from the kitchen. She carried the makings for her soothing tea.

"He's come and gone." Bryan took the tray from his mother's hands and set it on the coffee table.

"Oh, I'm sorry I missed him. He's the nicest young man." She sat and poured steaming liquid into a cup, adding a spoonful of honey. "Things will work out with him, Kitten. I saw it in my tea leaves this morning." She stirred, clanking the spoon against the cup. "I'm pleased my vision from a few years ago has come to fruition."

"What vision?" everyone except Bryan asked.

"I bet I know," Jillian said. "Your mom told Travis he'd meet the love of his life on a call. She now assumes I'm the answer. Am I right, Aunt Grace?"

Her aunt sipped her tea and smiled over the rim of her teacup. "Might be."

A moment of silence prevailed as no one knew how to respond to Grace's declaration.

Becca steered the conversation in a new direction. "Travis is gone." She plopped on the couch beside Jillian. "We're dying to hear your first date details—the juicier the better." She wiggled deeper in her seat, hunkered in for the story.

"There's my cue to leave the room. You ladies can gossip

and hear the sordid details." Bryan kissed Jillian on top of her head. "Goodnight, Cuz. The guest room is ready for you. Make yourself at home. *Mi casa es tu casa.*"

While Jillian sipped tea and nibbled a cookie, she regaled her rapt audience with every detail of the date, including the surprise of her dogs going with them.

"He knew exactly how to worm his way into your affections." Becca popped a juicy berry into her mouth. "Now we know why we didn't hear the pups inside. Good thing, considering what happened while you were gone."

"Yes, he's thoughtful." Grace gazed into her teacup. "Brave and daring, yet thoughtful and loving—explains his orange aura with vibrant blue splashes."

Amanda looked at the ceiling, and Cate stifled a snort at her aunt's rambling.

Jillian's wide yawn caught Becca's attention. She stood and clapped her hands.

"Show's over, ladies. Our patient is tired. We can hear the rest of the story another time."

Cate and Amanda left without argument. Becca led her charge to the guestroom with two pups following at their heels. Slipping on a pair of Bryan's sweatpants and a T-shirt, Jillian climbed into bed.

"Thanks for being here, Becca." Her eyes struggled to remain open, her voice laden with exhaustion.

"I wouldn't be anywhere else. Get some rest, sweet friend. This craziness will end soon." Becca shut off the light and tiptoed out of the room.

Not soon enough for me.

CHAPTER TWENTY-SEVEN

Jillian woke from a deep sleep with sunshine streaming onto her face from the part in the curtains. Throwing back the blankets, she stood and stretched, testing the stiffness of her muscles.

Hmm, not bad.

She leaned side to side to be sure. No crying in pain, so she began her day. First up—get the girls outside before they left a mess for her to clean up.

Careful with each movement, she grabbed the sweatshirt Bryan left on the chair, bracing for the cool autumn air.

"Rise and shine, ladies," Jillian called out to an empty bed, an empty room. "Uh-oh, how long have they been up and about?"

In search of the wayward pups, she found a surprise in Bryan's living room. Her mother sat on the couch with one dog cuddled on each side of her.

"Mom, what're you doing here so early?" She glanced about the room. "Where are Becca and Aunt Grace?"

"Becca left for the bakery. Your aunt has Thursday yoga class." Joy scratched Hayley behind the ears. "I've got this next shift."

"Becca doesn't have to be at Sugar & Spice until eight on Thursdays. Aunt Grace's yoga class doesn't start until eleven." Jillian flopped down beside her mom, taking Abbey onto her lap. "Why'd they take off before I got up? I wanted to thank them for staying last night."

"I don't know, dear. I guess they had things to do this morning." Joy's vague response set off warning bells in Jillian's mind.

Something smells fishy here.

Looking around, she discovered Bryan had no clock in his living room. "Mom, what time is it?"

"Oh ... um ... it's twelve-thirty." Joy quickly changed the subject. "Bryan will be here in a few minutes with lunch. Max heard what happened and insisted on sending food. Isn't he thoughtful?"

She hadn't heard a word past the time. "Twelve-thirty? In the afternoon? Mom, this is my day to open Whimsy & Wonder. How could you let me sleep so late?" Starting for the bathroom, her mother's no-nonsense voice stopped her.

"Jillian Saiorse Edwards. You're not going to work today." Her mother's tone left no room for compromise. "The doctor said you should take it easy for a day or two. You're going to rest and get your strength back. I'm here to make certain you do. Trixie will handle things at the store until you're back on your feet."

All the Edwards girls knew when their mother used their full Irish name, there'd be no arguing. She plopped on the couch, spreading the warm afghan across her lap. Her family's help would be accepted—today. Tomorrow would be a different story, though. She'd be back in her bookstore on Friday, whether they liked it or not.

"Fine. You win this round." Jillian huffed out an impatient breath. "I'll stay here like a good patient, but tomorrow I will go back to work."

"Not if I have any say in the matter," Joy muttered. "You won't be safe until this crazy person is locked behind bars. Ethan thinks it's best you stay away from work for the next few days. We can take your shifts at the bookstore."

Jillian ignored her mom's advice and changed the subject. "Speaking of Ethan, did you hear from him this morning? I need a few things from my apartment."

"He let me into your place earlier. I packed a bag of clothes, some personal items, plus a few things for the girls." She stopped any questions with a wag of a finger. "Yes, I got Abbey's medicine. Everything is here." She took one of Jillian's favorite Vera Bradley bags from behind her chair. "You're welcome."

The doorbell saved Jillian from giving her mom a response. Joy peered into the peephole with the dogs barking and prancing at the door.

She applauded her mom's efforts at safety. She took her job as Jillian's keeper to heart.

Joy opened the door to admit their visitor. Jillian laughed when she saw her cousin coming through his own front door.

"Bryan, do you always ring the bell at your own house?"

"I do when my cousin, who was assaulted by a lunatic, is staying here. I didn't want to scare you or Aunt Joy." He walked through the living room carrying a box of Styrofoam containers emitting the most appetizing aromas. Ethan followed him, an unexpected yet welcome guest.

"Come in, come in." Joy motioned everyone into the kitchen. "Bryan, whatever you've brought smells amazing. Knowing Max, I'm sure there's more than enough for all of us. I hope you'll both stay for lunch." Her mother— the consummate hostess—rattled around in the cabinets gathering plates and glasses to set the table.

"I can't stay, Aunt Joy." Bryan apologized. "We're slammed at McGuire's today with the lunch crowd. I promised I'd only be gone a few minutes. Max sent his famous barbecue chicken sliders and a few sides. He packed slices of lemon glazed blueberry pound cake for dessert. He wants to know what you think of this new recipe."

"Thanks for taking time to bring us lunch, Bryan. Please tell Max thank you too. We'll make sure he gets our critique soon." Jillian stood and gave her cousin a peck on the cheek.

"No problem. I wanted to check on you for myself." Bryan gave her a careful, one-armed hug. "How're you doing?"

"Better. I had a good night's sleep. Maybe a little too good." She glared at her mother. "Now, my lunch has been hand-delivered. Things are getting better and better."

"You scared us, Jilly. Behave yourself and listen to Aunt Joy. I'll check in with you later." He kissed his aunt goodbye, leaving them to enjoy their lunch.

"Ethan, you're awfully quiet," Joy said. "Grab a chair and join us for lunch. We have plenty to split three ways and still have food leftover."

"The food does smell good. I didn't have time for breakfast, so if you don't mind." He eyed the spread on the table.

"You sit here by me and help yourself." Joy placed serving spoons in all the take-out containers. The sight of the lunch buffet set Jillian's stomach rumbling. She hoped no one heard the noise.

After a few moments of enjoyable silence while they were eating, she asked Ethan all the questions rattling around in her head, which came tumbling out in a rush.

"What's happening at my apartment? Did the burglar leave fingerprints? When can I get in and start cleaning?"

"Take a breath, why don't ya?" He wiped his mouth with a napkin and put down his fork. He gave Jillian a pointed stare. "I do have some information for you. Maybe later in private."

Jillian knew Ethan well enough to know he wanted to protect her mom from the indelicate details of the case.

"I'm not as fragile and squeamish as most of you think I am." Joy pursed her lips.

"She's right, Ethan. Whatever information you have, you can share with both of us."

He took a quick sip of iced tea. "Whoever ransacked your place forced their way in through the window in the laundry room. They must've been wearing gloves because there were no foreign fingerprints. We've cleared the scene, so you can go back any time." Ethan reached for Jillian's hand. "Don't go alone—you're not safe there by yourself. You'll need help cleaning the mess anyway."

"What do you think they wanted?" Joy asked. "Did they steal her valuables?"

Like I have valuables.

"There's no way to be sure what they were after," Ethan said. "Jilly, you'll need to check—"

Jillian jumped in. "He wanted the box Maggie gave me. He says it's his, and he wants it back."

Joy and Ethan stared open-mouthed at her.

"How do you know he searched for a box?" Ethan asked.

"Something you said triggered the memory of something my attacker said last night." She used both hands to stave off Ethan's next question. "He knew Maggie had given me the box the night of the open house. Somehow, he knew she'd left without it. He assumed Maggie gave me the package, and I took it home."

"Is this the box you can't find?" He made a quick note in his phone.

"Yes," Jillian said. "He must've been angry when he didn't find it at my place." She ran a nervous hand over the bandage at her neck. "Oh my gosh, you don't think he'll try breaking into the bookstore, do you?"

"I'm surprised he hasn't already," Ethan said. "I'll have a patrol car sit on your store after hours. I don't think he'll try anything with customers coming and going during the day."

She breathed a sigh of relief. "Thanks, Ethan. I'd be devastated if he destroyed both my house and my shop."

"No problem. I have more news if you want to hear it."

"Of course, we do," Joy said. "Please go on."

"My contact at DCFS had some interesting answers for me. Maggie and Moira are, as claimed, identical twins and were placed into foster care when their mother died. They remained together in the system for a year as the department tried finding one family to adopt both girls. When this proved impossible, DCFS placed them for adoption separately."

"Moira told us the truth." Jillian shook her head in disbelief.

"Only partially," Ethan said. "Maggie got lucky, being adopted by a loving family from a small town in Ohio. Moira suffered a different fate. The records state she had a pathological tendency to lie, steal, throw tantrums, and hurt other children. The system couldn't place her in an adoptive home, so she remained a ward of the state—where she lived in eight different foster homes until aging out at eighteen."

"Her story breaks my heart." Joy sniffled into a tissue. "She lost her mother and her sister. She must've been a sad, confused little girl. Who could blame her for acting out? Such a pity they didn't find a family to take her in."

"She lied—told us she'd been adopted." The rise in Jillian's voice startled her sleeping pups. A reassuring pat on their heads settled them.

"Correct. Most of what Moira told us wasn't the truth. She landed in and out of juvenile detention centers as a teenager for various offenses. The most serious was when she attacked a fellow student and beat her unconscious."

Joy gasped. She reached for one of Jillian's hands.

Jillian's mouth dropped open as the questions poured out. "I don't understand. How could someone capable of such a heinous act be related to someone as sweet as Maggie? I mean, the two sisters couldn't be more different."

"That makes perfect sense, dear." Joy provided her own opinion. "Maggie was raised in a stable, loving home. She grew into a confident, educated young woman who had goals and worked to attain them."

"Moira, on the other hand, become a case number for DCFS." Ethan tapped his fork on his plate. "No stable home life, no parenting of any kind. Any skills she had were learned on the streets. Not surprising if you think about it."

Jillian's mind wandered to time spent with Maggie— hiking, shopping, watching movies, talking about books. Her musings caused her to miss something Ethan said. She caught the tail end of his sentence.

"Wait, what did you say?"

"I checked with the Stonefield Chamber of Commerce to verify Moira's claim to owning Body & Soul. This was false. A woman named Sheila Getty owned the business, which closed a year ago when she died in a boating accident on Lake Carlyle."

"Don't tell me Moira had something to do with her death." Jillian shuddered, thinking of her as a murderer. "Did she sabotage the boat?"

"No. Ms. Getty was an inexperienced sailor and got caught in a storm. Moira had been employed part-time at the salon for Ms. Getty at the time of her accident. According to the bank who owns the building, Moira thought she could step into Sheila's shoes."

"Busy girl. Tattoo artist by day, waitress by night," Joy said.

Jillian snorted, shocked at her mother's witty remark. "I'm guessing the bank set Moira straight, but not before she had those erroneous business cards printed."

"Moira tried keeping the business afloat for months after Sheila's unfortunate death. The bank asked her to evacuate the premises multiple times. She refused. They finally called the Stonefield police to evict her from the building. A cop buddy of mine said she was cuffed and stuffed, kicking and screaming, into the back of his squad car."

"Not a pretty scene." Jillian laughed, picturing an enraged Moira floundering in a police cruiser.

"Not very lady-like, either." Joy tsked, shaking her head. "Ethan, will you bring Moira in for questioning?"

"I'd love to talk to Moira, Mrs. Edwards. We found her car—silver with Georgia plates—abandoned in the woods behind Magnolia Manor. From the dents and missing mirror, it's the same car that attempted to run down Jillian in front of the bakery."

"Wonderful. You can arrest Moira for attempted murder." Joy sounded relieved the attacker had been caught.

"I won't be arresting Moira." Ethan shook his head. "She's dead. Someone slit her throat."

Jillian's hands flew to her neck, resting on the bandages.

"We found her body in the trunk of the car," Ethan went on. "The coroner estimates she's been dead ten to twelve hours. Someone killed her, shoved her body in the trunk, and dumped the car in the woods."

"That's awful," Jillian said. "No one deserves to be murdered and dumped like trash, not even her." She snapped her fingers. "You have to go after Dale Andrews. Arrest him for stalking and two murders—Maggie and Moira."

"Whoa, slow down, Jilly. We don't know Dale Andrews killed anyone. And I can't prove he's your stalker."

"C'mon, Ethan. Dale has to be the one. The way Benny Miller described him, he sounds like the same man Mr. Erickson, Mrs. Taylor, and I saw. He wants whatever Maggie gave me, and he's killed two people so far to get it."

Ethan blew out a long breath. "I don't disagree he could be our killer. Before I can bring him in for questioning, I need more than circumstantial evidence. My investigation into Maggie's death is far from done. Now, I also have to investigate Moira's death. We know she didn't slit her own throat. The murderer is still out there. Please don't let down your guard."

Jillian swallowed hard, realizing she hadn't thought this all the way through. Hercule Poirot, she was not.

"The key to this puzzle," she said, "is the box Maggie gave me. We need to find that thing. My tattooed visitor, whom *I believe* is Dale Andrews, wants it, so there must be something valuable inside."

"I ran Dale's name through our state database—nothing popped. Could be an alias. According to Moira's car registration, her last known address was a small town outside Atlanta. Maybe they met there. I'll expand my search to include Georgia and surrounding states."

"All this mystery and intrigue makes me tired. I can only imagine how exhausted you must be at the end of the day. Thank you for the job you do to protect us." Joy gave Ethan a kiss on the cheek.

"Just doing my job, Mrs. Edwards."

The trio finished their lunch in silence, digesting not only their food, but the information Ethan shared. Jillian was certain Dale Andrews had been her unwelcome guest at the bookstore. Was he also the driver who ran Maggie down in Jack's stolen SUV? Had he attacked her last night at the drive-in? If the creepy stranger was Dale, had he and Moira been working together, or had he acted alone? Could he have murdered his own girlfriend in cold blood?

All these questions made her head hurt. She needed some pain medication. Joy leaped to her feet and brought her the bottle.

"I could tell your head hurt by the way you squinted your eyes." Her mother shook two tablets into Jillian's hand and gave her a glass of water.

"I better go," Ethan said. "You need to get some rest, and I have a double murder case to solve."

"A double murder." Jillian walked him to the door. "This is Willow Springs, a quiet small town. How did this happen?"

"Murder can happen anywhere. Rest assured, solving these murders is my top priority."

"And you will." She stifled a yawn. "I wish I could help—however, I'm under house arrest. Warden Joy watches me like a hawk."

Ethan chuckled at her plight. "Relax. Enjoy having your mom pamper you. She thrives on taking care of her girls."

"I guess you never stop being a mother, no matter how old your children get." Jillian shrugged. "I'll humor my mom for a bit, but I won't impose on Trixie to carry the load at the bookstore."

"You poor, delusional girl." Ethan mocked her. "You must realize your entire family and best friend are plotting against you. They're not letting you near the store until the murderer is caught."

"I figured that was their plan. I'll give them today, no promises for tomorrow."

"Good luck with that. I'll tell Becca you're being a good patient. She's texted me five times since she heard I was coming over here." He called into the kitchen. "Thanks for sharing lunch with me, Mrs. E."

"Anytime, Ethan. You're always welcome at my table."

He gave Jillian a careful hug and took off. She hoped the next time she heard from him, he'd report the arrest of Maggie and Moira's killer.

Her head throbbed. She settled on the couch under a warm afghan. Her eyes grew heavy. She drifted off to sleep.

CHAPTER TWENTY-EIGHT

They sat in the bowling alley in Stonefield where they'd met Benny Miller. She and Travis were on a double date with Becca and Ethan, enjoying an evening of cheap bowling, bad food, and plenty of laughs. Jillian and Becca led the guys by only a few pins. The close game brought out their competitive sides. A bit of taunting, trash-talking, and teasing ensued, all in good-natured fun.

The mood changed when Dale Andrews stomped into the bowling alley. He dragged Moira across the floor by her arm like a rag doll and came straight toward them. Blood gushed from a jagged slash in Moira's neck. Dale waved the bloodied knife in his free hand.

"You." He pointed the knife at Jillian, then at Moira. "This is what I'll do to you if you don't give me the box." To drive home his point, he made a slicing gesture with the knife. Then he dumped Moira's lifeless body onto the floor.

While the women watched in horror, Ethan and Travis rushed at Dale, attempting to grab the knife and subdue him. Enraged, Dale slashed at them with the bloodied weapon, slicing out at them. Red streaks emerged across their chests, hands, and faces. Becca's terrified scream pierced the air.

Jillian woke from her dream. Sitting on the couch, she gulped in deep breaths, trying to slow her racing heart.

Her mother rushed into the room with a dishtowel swinging from her hand.

"Sweetheart, what's wrong?" Joy sat on the couch next to her. "I was in the kitchen and heard you shout."

"Bad dream."

"I'll say. You were shouting at Travis to stop. Stop what?"

She didn't want to alarm her mother. "I don't know, Mom," she lied. "Now I'm awake, I can't remember."

"Whatever it was didn't sound pleasant." Joy changed the subject. "Let's play backgammon or checkers—you know—as a distraction. Bryan must have one of those games stashed away somewhere."

Diverting attention from unpleasant subjects had always been Joy's specialty. When the girls were young, bad dreams, illnesses, and major disappointments had been dealt with by playing cards or board games. Even though she recognized her mother's attempt to take her mind off the problem at hand, she didn't think games were the solution. Nor did she feel like playing them.

"Thanks, Mom. I'd rather stretch my legs. Abbey and Hayley could use a few laps around the block too." Jillian scratched them on the tops of their heads. "I'll change my clothes and put on my shoes, so we can go for a walk." *Walk* was one of their favorite words. Hearing it sent them into canine histrionics as they raced for the door.

She pulled on a pair of jeans and a soft gray sweater and stared at her reflection in the mirror. The sterile white bandage stood out against her olive-toned skin. She grabbed a scarf to hide the gauze from prying eyes.

This is as good as it's going to get.

Her mother waited by the door with leashes in her hands.

"Mom, what are you doing?"

"Going for a walk with you and the girls. Put on your coat—chilly out there." Joy held out a fleece jacket.

"Why am I not surprised you feel the need to tag along?" Jillian said. "You're not letting me out that door alone, are you?"

"No, I am not. Someone needed mere minutes to cut your throat and knock you out." She put on her coat. "I'm not letting you go by yourself. End of discussion."

There was only one way Jillian would get out that door.

"Fine. Let's go."

Locking the door behind them, they each held a leash. Abbey and Hayley pranced in front, noses in the air and beards blowing in the breeze.

Jillian used nonstop chatter to distract her mother from the route she'd chosen. She steered the dogs down Washington, then Main, and turned down Sweetwater, headed in the direction of the bookstore.

"You're not fooling me, young lady. I know where we're going and shame on you." Joy shook her head. "Trixie will be offended if you check in on her. She'll think you don't trust her to take care of the store."

Offending Trixie was not something Jillian wanted.

Having had her plan thwarted, she considered her next move. She made a quick decision when she spied Mrs. Taylor working in her yard.

"Oh, Mom. There's one of my bookstore's neighbors. Let's stop and say hello."

Wielding a pair of pruning shears, Mrs. Taylor worked on dead-heading her rose bushes.

"Good afternoon, Mrs. Taylor," Jillian called out. "I'm happy you were outside as we passed by. I'd like you to meet my mom, Joy."

Mrs. Taylor placed the shears on the ground. She rubbed the dirt from her hands on the legs of her trim navy-and-white jogging suit. She extended a hand to Joy. "I'm pleased to meet you. Please call me Lizzie. All of my friends do."

"Is Lizzie short for Elizabeth?" Joy smiled warmly at the other woman. "If so, that would make your name Elizabeth Taylor."

"Yes, yes. I was Elizabeth James. Marrying my Thomas made me Elizabeth Taylor. I decided to go by Lizzie after our wedding. Didn't have to answer so many questions. Or listen to corny jokes."

"That's a lovely story," Joy said. "Not everyone can say they share their name with a famous movie star."

"Wouldn't it be nice to share her fame and fortune too?" Lizzie laughed at her own joke. "I'm teasing, though. I wouldn't have any idea what to do with all her money. At my age, my needs are simple. I'm happy here in my home, baking and gardening."

"Your roses were gorgeous this summer in those stunning shades of red and pink." Jillian smiled at her neighbor. "You have a natural green thumb."

"My Thomas was a horticulture professor for forty years at the college in Westhaven. He taught me everything there is to know about caring for plants. I owe all my beautiful flowers to him." A wistful smile crossed Mrs. Taylor's face, lasting but a moment. "Would you ladies have time for some iced tea and fresh lemon scones? I'd love the company." Mrs. Taylor motioned toward the house.

"Oh, we couldn't," Jillian said. "We have the pups."

"Sweetie, the invitation included them too. Your girls are welcome in my home. Thomas and I had dogs the entire time we were married. This," she pointed to her house, "is a dog-friendly zone. Please bring them inside." She started for the front door, expecting everyone, including Abbey and Hayley, to follow.

Mrs. Taylor led them into her kitchen. Like the rest of her home, the wallpaper had faded, the appliances were outdated, yet everything was spotless. Mrs. Taylor's 1960s' décor was a picture of time stood still. The kitchen table and chairs were the kind only found in vintage resale stores. The table had a red Formica tabletop, silver metal legs, and four matching chairs with cushioned seats. Four place settings of pink Carnival glass sat ready for guests.

Their hostess busied herself getting out matching pink glasses and filling them with ice. She brought the tea pitcher to the table and asked Jillian to pour. "My hands aren't as steady as they used to be."

Mrs. Taylor drizzled a sticky glaze on the lemon scones. She arranged them on a pink flowered plate that she placed on the table along with a smaller matching saucer filled with dog biscuits.

"I like having people over. I'm fortunate to have been outside when you came by. Please help yourself to a scone," Mrs. Taylor said. "Oh, look at these sweet girls sitting here waiting for treats. I'm giving them a biscuit—if you don't mind."

Jillian nodded her approval.

Mrs. Taylor patted their furry heads and handed them each a treat. Abbey and Hayley accepted the offered goodie and licked every crumb from the floor.

"Aren't you the sweetest things?" The older woman cooed at Jillian's girls. "Makes me miss my Molly. She was a blonde cocker spaniel Thomas and I found abandoned in a cornfield years ago. She was the best dog, friendly with everyone. We had her fourteen years. She passed away last spring—a few weeks before my Thomas. I think of them together, keeping each other company and waiting for me." She grew misty-eyed, lost for a moment with her memories.

The older woman snapped herself back to the present and spoke to Jillian. "I'm surprised you're not working, dear."

"My assistant, Trixie, is in charge today. I'll be back tomorrow morning."

"Hmm, don't be so sure." Joy sniffed, sipping her glass of iced tea.

"Mom, stop." Jillian hissed through clenched teeth. "Don't drag Mrs. Taylor into our disagreement."

"Lizzie, the wonderful pictures throughout the house tell me you're a mother and a grandmother." Joy nibbled on her scone, casting an innocent look at Mrs. Taylor.

Please don't go there, Mom.

"Why, yes. Thomas and I had three beautiful children who blessed us with eight wonderful grandchildren. I wish they all lived a bit closer."

"So, you know all too well what it's like to worry." Joy would not be deterred.

"Of course," Mrs. Taylor said. "You never stop worrying, even when they're grown and gone. You want them to be happy, healthy, and safe."

"That's right." Joy shot a triumphant smile in Jillian's direction. "I knew you'd understand my concern for my daughter." She launched into the story of the attack at the drive-in, the break-in at Jillian's apartment, and how it all related to the hit-and-run in front of the bookstore.

Mrs. Taylor hung on every word. She shook her head in disbelief, grabbing hold of Jillian's hand as if to protect her from harm.

"You understand why I don't think it's a good idea for her to work tomorrow. She needs more time to recover from her ordeal, and she could be in danger at the store." Joy finished the story, smug satisfaction written across her face.

Lizzie sighed. "You poor thing. This past week hasn't been kind to you. Your mother is right, dear. The best place for you is at home surrounded by your loved ones, so the awful man with the tattoos can't hurt you again. He's the one who's doing all this, isn't he?"

"Can't be anyone else," Joy said. "He's killed two people. He's not getting his hands on my daughter again."

"Two people? Not just the poor girl he ran down in the street?" Mrs. Taylor patted Jillian's hand harder and faster. "Your mother is right, dear. Stay home and be safe."

While touched by their concern, Jillian wouldn't let this lunatic keep her from running her new business and living her life. Besides, she knew she'd be watched like a hawk in her shop.

"Nothing will happen at the bookstore. Anyone who tries to hurt me will have to get past Ethan, Bryan, Travis, and the rest of my family. I'm in no danger while I'm at work."

"I hope the repairman got the store's back door fixed so your friend can lock everything nice and safe tonight." Mrs. Taylor reached for another scone, dribbling glaze across the table on the way to her plate. "You wouldn't want any surprises waiting for you in the morning."

"That's odd. Trixie didn't tell me there was something wrong. Or that she'd hired a repairman." Jillian frowned. "You saw someone fixing the door at my store today?"

"Yes, on my morning walk. A city crew had the concrete in front of your store blocked off, so I cut down the alleyway behind the houses. There was a man working on your back door."

"Did you speak with him?"

Mrs. Taylor thought for a moment. "Yes, we both said good morning. He said it was a nice day for a stroll. I agreed, mentioning how his job must take quite a bit of skill—working with tricky locks. He nodded and continued working. I went on my way."

"I wonder why Trixie didn't mention she'd called in a locksmith. Or why she didn't tell me there was a problem with the backdoor."

"I'm sure she didn't want to bother you with trivial details after what you've been through." Joy defended Trixie. "She's capable of handling things on her own."

"Yes, of course, she is. I couldn't run this store without her. But it's because of what I've been through that I should be kept in the loop about what's happening at my own store." This wouldn't be a problem if she hadn't been kept away from Whimsy & Wonder today. "Trixie would never leave the store unlocked at night. Something must've been out of whack when she opened this morning. What could've happened overnight causing the need for a repairman?"

"Trixie took care of whatever problem occurred," Joy said.

"I'm sure she did—just wish she'd let me know. We can't be too careful considering ... you know." Jillian ran a hand through her hair. "I'll be at work tomorrow, so I can—"

"Humph." Her mother snorted. "So you say."

Jillian ignored her mother's mutters. The three women spent the next hour sipping tea and sharing family stories until Mrs. Taylor's antique cuckoo clock chirped six times—a reminder Jillian and her mother had stayed too long.

"Goodness, look at the time. We'd better get moving." Joy stood and gathered the glasses and plates. "My other daughters and my sister are coming for dinner at six-thirty. They'll be worried if we're not there."

"Please leave the dishes," Mrs. Taylor said. "I can take care of those later when time presents itself. You two go, so you don't upset your family."

"No, please. Let us help you with this." Joy carried the dishes and set them on the counter. "You were so kind to invite us for tea. The least we can do is help you clean."

Together, they made quick work of straightening the kitchen. Jillian wrapped the remaining scones in plastic wrap and put the tea in the refrigerator. Mrs. Taylor washed the dishes and Joy dried. The entire kitchen looked spotless in less than ten minutes.

"Thank you for helping clean up," Lizzie said. "I don't move as quickly as I used to. This would've taken me much longer on my own."

"Thank you for the delicious tea and scones." Jillian coaxed the girls from under the table and clipped on their leashes. "And dog treats."

Abbey and Hayley each let out a soft woof—their own thank you to their hostess. Mrs. Taylor bent to scratch under their bearded chins.

"I've truly enjoyed our visit and hope to see you again soon, but if we don't head home right this instant, Jillian's sisters will call the police to report us missing." Joy shuddered. "We can't have that, now can we?"

"I'm sure your daughter's handsome young man won't mind getting called for you." Lizzie smiled at Jillian.

Mrs. Taylor had forgotten Ethan wasn't Jillian's young man. Once again, she didn't have the heart to correct her.

They arrived back at Bryan's at six-twenty to find their guests were early. Worried faces and insistent questions awaited them on the porch.

"Where have you two been?" Amanda tapped her foot as she struggled with a large cardboard box filled with mouthwatering smells.

"We thought something bad happened—again." Cate echoed Amanda's concern. "Poor Aunt Grace thought Mom had been dragged into it this time."

"I almost called Ethan to report you both missing." Becca hugged Jillian tight.

Only Grace remained silent, standing still with her eyes closed. Limp arms dangled at her sides. Her body language suggested she was in a trance as did the unintelligible muttering under her breath.

Joy shook her sister's shoulder. "Grace. What's wrong?"

Her eyes flew open, their focus zeroed in on one person. She took Jillian's face in her hands and spoke in a strangled voice.

"He's coming for you—he won't stop. There's blood on his hands. Give him what he wants, or he'll kill you."

Grace dropped her hands. Her eyes fluttered closed. Her legs collapsed and she dropped to the bench next to Bryan's front door. Joy rushed to her sister's side. Cate hurried inside for a glass of water. The rest of them stood in stunned silence, letting the eerie prophecy sink in. The color seeped back into Grace's face as she sipped the cool water.

"I'm sorry, Kitten. I hope I didn't frighten you." Grace met Jillian's eyes. "You walked toward me—bam— the vision hit. My prophecy is warning you. This man is furious with you. He'll stop at nothing to get what he wants."

"What man, Aunt Grace? Could you see his face?" She pressed for more details.

"The tall, handsome man with the red hair. The one who visited your store a few days ago."

Handsome? Jillian could think of a lot of words to describe Dale Andrews. That wasn't one of them.

"Please don't worry." She knelt in front of her aunt, taking her hands. "Nothing's going to happen. Ethan will catch this guy and arrest him."

"He sure will," Becca said. "Ethan will run this guy's name and description through every database they have. They'll get a hit soon."

"Why don't we go inside and have dinner?" Joy's suggestion received eager agreement from the others. "Something smells delicious. My nose tells me it's from La Casita."

"Ooh, La Casita." Aunt Grace's demeanor brightened at the mention of her favorite food. She hopped off the bench, scurrying for the door. "Let's move this fiesta inside. Please tell me there are margaritas."

CHAPTER TWENTY-NINE

Jillian smiled at the flurry of activity in Bryan's kitchen as everyone pitched in to unpack dinner. Joy pulled plates from the cabinet. Becca poured the jug of strawberry margaritas into a glass pitcher. Cate and Amanda transferred food from carryout bags to serving platters. Her family worked in sync—like a well-rehearsed dance—putting the meal on the table.

Jillian reached for the wide-brimmed glasses Becca would need for their beverages. Her mom, who was setting the table, swatted at her hands, batting away her attempts to be a part of the dance.

"Geesh. I'm not an invalid. I can help, you know."

"Enjoy the special treatment, Kitten." Aunt Grace folded napkins at each place setting.

"How long can I expect this special treatment to last?"

"As long as it takes." Joy raised her voice. "Dinner's ready. Everybody, take a seat."

An appetizer duo of mini chicken taquitos and fried papas rellenas kicked off the night's menu. For the main course, chicken and spinach enchiladas and beef and bean chimichangas with plenty of salsa and sour cream filled their plates. No take-out dinner from La Casita's would be complete without their signature vanilla caramel flan.

Squeezed around Bryan's kitchen table, the women kept their conversation light and breezy as they passed the food and drinks. The discussion steered clear of Aunt Grace's vision or the recent attacks. The goal of this dinner—relax, unwind, forget—if only for a short time, a killer had set his sights on Jillian.

Amanda entertained them with a story of an older gentleman who'd come into Blossoms & Blooms and ordered three dozen red roses.

Becca let out a long whistle. "That's thirty-six roses! Some lady will be surprised to get that delivery."

"Yes, it's a much larger order than my customers usually place, but it got weirder. This guy requested each dozen go to a different woman's address." Amanda paused and waited for their reaction.

"What?" Becca said. "He's dating three different women at the same time? I wonder if they know each other."

"No idea." Amanda shrugged. "He said they were wonderful ladies. He couldn't possibly decide between them. His face paled when I told him the total was over three hundred dollars. I bet he doesn't order flowers from me again."

"He should do the right thing and choose *one* of the women." Joy pursed her lips. "That's awful—toying with their affections, leading them on. He may have money, but he has no class."

"Aunt Grace, Dr. Madison didn't send you roses today, did he?" Amanda's pointed question spoke volumes. "The man in my shop could've been your date last night."

Everyone stared at Grace, who dabbed her lips with her napkin.

"Robert would never be dating three women at a time. He's a gentleman, not a scoundrel. Besides, he knows I prefer Gerbera daisies, which he hand delivered this morning." A smug smile crossed her face.

"Your good doctor must be a tall guy, dark hair going gray at the temples, light blue eyes." Amanda leaned in, her piercing stare focused on her aunt.

"Why, yes, he is. How did you know?" Grace pursed her lips. "I'm sure you've never met him."

"Where do you think he bought those daisies? I am the only florist in Willow Springs."

Having a physical description of Dr. Madison wasn't enough to satisfy the younger women. They grilled Grace for information about her new beau. She gave away no details.

"A lady never kisses and tells." However, the soft blush on Grace's cheeks gave her away.

"Ooh, there was kissing." Cate's teasing sent everyone into laughter.

This girls' dinner was in full swing when the doorbell rang. Becca sprang from the table and raced to the door, stumbling over the dogs as they scurried to greet new guests.

"Check the peephole," Joy called after her.

Becca returned, arm-in-arm, with three handsome male guests. "I found these hotties on your doorstep." All the men's faces turned red.

"Travis. Jack." She nodded to the third man. "What a surprise." Jillian rose to greet them as Travis introduced his engineer and his firefighter to her family.

"We cleared a call four blocks from here. Since we were close, I wanted to check on the patient. You're being well taken care of, I see." Travis gestured at the food on the table. "Looks like a fiesta in here."

"Come, sit down." Joy took Travis's arm, motioning to his crew. "We have plenty of food. You boys deserve a good, hot meal. We'll make room at the table."

"No, thank you, Mrs. Edwards," Travis said. "We can't stay—have to get back to the station in case another call comes in. I'm glad you're all here watching out for Jillian—at least until Bryan comes home from work."

"I'm here for the duration," Becca said. "Ethan's pulling an all-nighter on this case, so I'm staying here. We're having an old-fashioned sleepover."

"Jillian won't be alone until this guy is caught and thrown in jail. He's not putting his slimy hands on my sister again." Cate uttered the words, while everyone else murmured their agreement.

"See, told you they'd do this." Jillian nudged Travis with her elbow. "I'm being guarded like a prisoner in my own home—well, Bryan's home. No one will get anywhere near me with my guard dogs on duty. And I don't mean Abbey and Hayley."

Travis leaned in and whispered in her ear. "Knowing your family is keeping you safe takes a load off my mind." He pulled her close for a kiss. When it ended, he placed another brief kiss on her cheek. "I'll check in tomorrow when I get off duty. Stay safe."

Jillian walked the men to the door and made certain to flip the lock behind them. She leaned on the wall, allowing her heart rate time to recover.

Whew, that man can kiss. I feel it in every fiber of my being.

Everyone stared when she walked back in the kitchen.

"What?" She shrugged. "He was being nice and checking on me."

"Mm-hmm," they all said together.

322

"The boy is falling for you," Aunt Grace said.

"What—are you having a vision of my love life?"

"No, I have eyes in my head. I know a man in love when I see one." Grace pursed her lips. "And don't be cheeky, young lady. I'm correct more times than I'm wrong."

Aunt Grace and Nurse Freeman sounded a lot alike, knowing a man in love when they set eyes on him. Jillian wished she could be so sure. She dropped a quick kiss on Grace's forehead and whispered an apology. Dinner resumed, and the conversation became an inquisition of her recent date.

"We never finished hearing all the details of your date with Mr. Hunky," Becca said.

"Start from the beginning." Amanda moved her chair closer. "Don't leave anything out."

Her evening with Travis made for more pleasant conversation than the nasty business of murder. Jillian retold her story amidst her dinner dates' giggles, sighs, gasps, and questions.

After dinner, everyone helped clean up.

"Do you think Bryan will even notice we've used his kitchen?" Cate shook her head. "Everything is like brand new. The manufacturer's tag is still on the side of the fridge."

Grace sighed. "My son should slow down and enjoy life before it passes him by. Work, work, work. How's he ever going to meet a nice girl, settle down, and give me grandbabies?"

"Don't worry, Grace. There are plenty of women who'd like to get close enough to Bryan to make that happen." Becca stole a glance at Jillian. "I can think of a certain waitress at Manny's Pizzeria." Her voice trailed off, leaving Grace clamoring for information.

"Who's this girl you're talking about?"

Becca shared their recent encounter with Bryan's admirer.

"I remember her." Grace tapped a finger to her chin. "Bryan dated her his senior year in high school—cute girl, as I recall. My boy thought he was in love until she moved away. He met the next love of his life a few weeks later."

"Ugh, high school romances. They were the worst." Amanda wrinkled her nose.

"Maybe Bryan and this girl will reunite, fall in love, and get married. Wouldn't that be wonderful?" Grace clapped her hands.

"Aunt Grace, I don't think Bryan has any desire to reunite with her. As a matter of fact, he doesn't appear interested in getting married or having kids. You've met your son, haven't you? He's already married—to his restaurant." Cate patted her aunt's hand. "Maybe it'll happen someday. Be patient."

"Well, someone in this family is getting married soon." This pronouncement brought stunned silence. For a moment.

"Grace, what are you saying? No one in our family is getting married." Joy's eyes widened at her two unmarried daughters. "Are you?" Jillian and Amanda shook their heads no.

"The tea leaves say a wedding is near." Grace sipped her coffee. "They never lie."

All eyes were on the single ladies in the room. Neither of them said a word.

Joy cleared her throat. "Perhaps we should call it a night. Grace and I can take the dogs outside one more time. You girls wrap things up in here."

Grace snorted. "Wrap things up? That's one way to put it." She shrugged into her coat and handed Joy hers. "We know there are things you young girls won't say in front of your old mom and aunt. Make it quick though. I'm not standing outside all night—too cold out there." She snatched the door shut behind her.

"Quick—while they're gone—tell us the juicy details you left out." Cate begged Jillian.

"Yeah, spill it," Becca said. "With a guy as good looking as Travis, there had to have been more than a few G-rated kisses. You're holding back on us."

"I told you exactly what happened." She laughed at their disappointed expressions. "C'mon, you guys. This was our first date. Besides, it didn't end the way most first dates do."

"I'm bummed." Amanda's shoulders slumped. "I wanted something a bit spicier. Sam left yesterday on a three-week assignment. Since I'm not going on dates right now, I wanted to live vicariously through yours, Jilly.

"Sorry, ladies. The evening was great until the moment I was accosted at knifepoint. Bodily harm kind of puts a damper on a date."

Thinking of the psychotic murderer lurking in the dark at the drive-in had a sobering effect on their lighthearted banter. The four women stood staring at each other until Becca broke the silence.

"Group hug." They held onto each other for a few seconds. Breaking apart, they laughed so hard they cried.

Her mom and Aunt Grace brought Abbey and Hayley inside and unclipped their leads. Joy brought the evening to a close.

"Ladies, it's midnight. Our patient needs to take some meds and go to bed." When her directions were ignored, she cleared her throat and addressed the room again, louder this time.

"My goodness, it's getting late." She feigned checking her watch. "Jillian needs her rest, so get your coats. Becca, we're leaving her in your capable hands until tomorrow morning. You three ..." Joy snapped her fingers. "... it's time to go."

Amanda, Cate, and Grace followed orders. When Joy, as the matriarch of the family, said jump, they did. The sisters shared a hug before leaving. Aunt Grace embraced her youngest niece and held on tight, whispering a warning.

"You remember what I said," Aunt Grace murmured. "Keep your eyes and ears open and always have this close to protect you." She pressed a hand to the cold, metal cylinder hanging from Jillian's neck. Without another word, Grace left the apartment, the scent of her floral perfume lingering well after she was gone.

Jillian fingered the silver pendant. She'd forgotten she'd put the pendant on earlier.

Removing the necklace, she shoved it into her jeans pocket and prepared to face her mother.

Joy imparted one last piece of advice. "You may think you're invincible—you're not. Take care of yourself at work tomorrow, will you?"

"What makes you think I'll be at work? Everyone— including you—keeps telling me to stay home."

"When have you ever listened to us? You are and will always be a stubborn mule like your father. Please be careful at the store." Joy kissed Jillian goodnight, gave Becca a motherly hug, and left to drive Grace home.

"I love your mom. She knows you so well, yet still lets you make your own decisions even when they're stupid." Becca grabbed a blanket and a pillow from the wardrobe and settled on the couch. Jillian joined her.

"Gee, Becca. Why don't you tell me what you really think?"

"Fine, I will. But remember you asked. Don't get mad at my answer." Becca ignored Jillian's eye roll and proceeded to share her opinion. "You're making a huge mistake if you go to work tomorrow. Maggie's killer has made it clear he's coming after you and that stupid box. I don't understand why you'd put yourself in harm's way."

A soft knock at the door ended what would have been a ten-minute tirade.

Whoever this is—thank you.

"Let's place a bet. Who forgot what?" Jillian swept back her afghan, tossing aside her pillow. "I'm picking Aunt Grace left her purse. Becca?"

Becca had no bet to place. Her attention was on the white envelope someone had shoved under Bryan's door. She grabbed Jillian's arm.

"Stop! Don't open the door. And don't touch the envelope."

CHAPTER THIRTY

Becca made a phone call to Ethan. Jillian paced between the kitchen and living room, each time making sure the envelope hadn't disappeared and was still untouched. Becca sat on the edge of the sofa, gnawing on a ragged fingernail, a nervous habit since childhood. Neither spoke. They watched the clock above the fireplace—five minutes, ten, fifteen, twenty ticked by. Still no Ethan.

What's keeping him?

Jillian startled when a tap on the door broke the silence. Becca jumped from her seat, rushing to her friend's side.

"Hey, it's me," Ethan called. "Bryan's here too."

Jillian sidestepped the evidence Ethan had come to collect and opened the door. Bryan wrapped her in a tight hug, resting his chin on top of her head. Ethan's smile at Becca was replaced with his cop face as he snapped on a pair of latex gloves and retrieved this latest message from the killer.

He sliced open the envelope with his pocketknife. A small piece of paper fluttered to the floor. The message was visible to all in the same large bold font as the first note.

YOUR TIME IS RUNNING OUT.

Jillian slumped onto the couch, releasing the breath she'd held. "I'm so tired of these threats. When will they end?" She hadn't meant to speak this thought out loud. Now there it was, hanging in the air like fog on a spring morning.

Ethan locked eyes with her. "Soon. I promise."

"Are you kidding? All you've got is a promise?" Becca didn't hold back her emotions—not even for her husband. "She needs protection, Ethan. Get her a gun—a big scary one. She can keep it behind the counter at the store."

"Becca," Jillian snapped. "I run a children's bookstore. I'm not keeping a loaded gun in my store. I'll put a baseball bat behind the counter. And the girls will be with me. They're great watchdogs and can be fierce if they think I'm being threatened." She smiled at her sweet schnauzers cuddled together on a blanket on the couch. "So, they're not fierce now, but they can be."

"Great—a baseball bat and two small dogs. Yeah, that'll scare off a knife-wielding psycho." Becca's sarcasm and scowl were directed at her husband.

"She doesn't need a gun." Ethan shook his head. "A patrol car will watch Bryan's house tonight. Another will keep an eye on the store tomorrow. She'll be safe."

Becca rewarded his response with a jab to the ribs. "She'd better be."

"How about we all calm down? I'm not running scared from this nutcase." Jillian rubbed her forehead. "Now if you don't mind. My head hurts. I'm tired. If I'm going to work tomorrow, I need some sleep."

"I'll be home the rest of the night with them." Bryan nodded at Ethan. "I'll make sure everything is quiet here."

"Sounds good. Thanks, Bryan." Ethan kissed his wife goodnight and headed for the door. "The patrol car is parked out front. Call me if anything out of the ordinary happens, anything at all. And—"

"I know, I know. Lock the door and check the windows. I know the drill, Ethan. I am a detective's wife, after all." Becca blew her husband a kiss as he closed the door.

Becca flipped the deadbolt. "He'll find this guy, Jilly. I know he will."

Jillian hugged her close. "I know he's doing everything he can to get this maniac off the streets."

The women said good night and headed upstairs to the guest bedroom while Bryan prepared to sleep downstairs on the couch.

"Want to keep an eye on things."

As they put on their pjs, Becca mentioned the silver pendant. "Hey, I meant to say something before. Where'd you get the necklace you were wearing earlier?"

Grabbing her jeans from the chair she'd dumped them in, Jillian reached into the pocket and fished out the chain. "This? It's the amulet of protection Aunt Grace gave me after dinner the other night. She claims if I wear it at all times, I will be safe." She twirled the charm with her fingers. "I don't really believe in these things."

"You should wear it, Jilly. You never know." Becca shrugged. "I mean, what would it hurt?"

Jillian took a closer look at the cylindrical charm dangling from the chain. "Hold on a sec. You've got to see this."

She shook her head, chuckling.

"What's so funny?" Becca moved closer to get a look.

"Check out this so-called amulet." She shoved the necklace into her friend's hands.

Becca took the necklace and examined it closely. "Is this pepper spray? Your Aunt Grace gave you a tiny canister of pepper spray?"

"Bryan was right. He said she'd given me mace. I didn't pay that close attention. Can you believe my aunt thinks a bit of pepper spray is going to protect me from a lunatic with a knife?" Jillian shoved the necklace back into the jean's pocket. "If it were only that easy."

"You should wear the pendant." Becca's words echoed in Jillian's head as she drifted off. "What could it hurt?"

The alarm clock woke them at seven. Jillian remained motionless for a moment, gauging how her body felt after the events of Wednesday night. Her head didn't throb—check. Her neck didn't sting—great. Huge improvements since yesterday.

That sealed the deal. She would be at work today.

Becca sat up and stretched like a contented cat. "This is what sleeping until seven feels like—a luxury for someone who's usually at work by four-thirty." She grabbed her robe. "I'll take the girls outside. No offense, Jilly, you need a shower. You're a hot mess." Becca exited the bedroom, avoiding the pillow projectile aimed in her direction.

Jillian hopped out of bed and into the shower. Her head had been too sensitive yesterday to worry about her hair. This morning, she scrubbed her scalp and rinsed out the last remnants of dried blood. Washing away that reminder of her attack felt good. Despite the remaining tenderness, she washed her neck too. She'd need a scarf, so the new bandage she'd applied wouldn't show. She didn't want to answer questions from curious customers nor scare the kids.

She shrugged and slipped on the same pair of jeans she'd worn yesterday.

I didn't do anything to get them dirty.

She put on a soft pink sweater, added a striped scarf, and fixed her hair in a simple braid.

The smell of freshly brewed coffee assaulted her nostrils as she entered the kitchen. Becca leaned against the sink, staring out the window. The pups stood at their bowls, making happy grunting sounds as they crunched their kibble.

"The shower is all yours. Thanks for feeding my girls."

Becca whirled around and sloshed coffee onto the floor. "Oh, Jilly. You scared the pants off me." She grabbed some paper towels.

"Sorry—wasn't intentional. Why are you so jumpy this morning? Too much coffee?" Jillian smiled at her own joke. "I don't know how you drink that swill of yours."

"I'm fine." Becca shook off any concern with a wave of her hand. "You're the one with the problem. How can you not enjoy the nectar of the gods?"

Jillian wrinkled her nose as she put the kettle on the stove to make tea. "I prefer my Darjeeling with a drizzle of honey."

"Yeah, yeah. You drink your frou-frou tea. I'll stick to coffee." Becca grinned, shaking her head. "I can't believe you drink hot tea instead of coffee like the rest of us. What do you think—you're British royalty or something?"

"No, but you're being a royal pain in the—"

"Ah, ah, ah. No cursing. Swearing is frowned upon at the palace, Your Highness." Becca curtsied. Giving her best royal wave, she said, "I'm getting in the shower. I'll be ready to leave in less than twenty minutes. My job is to get you safely to the bookstore and that I will." Swallowing the last of her coffee, she placed the mug in the sink. "Can't waste one drop."

True to her word, Becca was back in the kitchen in under fifteen minutes. "Let's get you to work. You have books to sell. I have pastries to bake. Should we wake Bryan—let him know we're leaving?"

"Let him sleep. He doesn't leave for McGuire's until around ten o'clock." Jillian gathered her things for the day—laptop, travel mug full of tea, baggie of dog biscuits, and her purse. Juggling these items, she clipped leashes to the pups' collars and headed for the door.

"Gosh, do you think you have everything you need?" Becca held the door open for her friend.

Any sarcastic retort was cut off by the friendly officer who called out from the front of his squad car.

"Good morning, ladies. All was quiet last night." The young, clean-cut cop put on his hat. "I'll be heading out."

"Thank you for keeping an eye on things, Officer." Jillian smiled as she unlocked her car and climbed in. "Let's get this show on the road, Becca."

She backed out of Bryan's driveway. Adjusting her rearview mirror, she noticed a black SUV leaving the curb a few houses down. Heading north on Washington, the vehicle signaled the same turn.

"Um, Becca. I'm going to tell you something. Please don't freak out." She glanced in the mirror again. "A black vehicle has been tailing us since we left Bryan's house."

Becca whipped around and watched the car from the back window. The vehicle kept a safe distance, but could be following them.

"I'm calling Ethan." She yanked her phone from her purse, pressing her husband's number and putting it on speaker. Three rings and then straight to voicemail.

"Why doesn't he answer the phone?" Becca jabbed the red button, ending the call.

"Calm down, Becca. We're heading in the direction of a lot of businesses. Maybe the black car is headed downtown." One look at Becca told Jillian her friend wasn't buying this theory. "Fine. Try him again in a bit."

The black car tailing them suddenly hung a left onto a side street a few blocks before the bookstore. Jillian let out a huge sigh.

Were we being followed or is my imagination playing tricks on me?

CHAPTER THIRTY-ONE

Jillian unloaded her pups from the back seat. Juggling her bag and the two leashes, she struggled to unlock the door to the bookstore. After three attempts, she found success.

Whew, that wasn't easy.

She entered the cool darkness of her store and shouted over her shoulder. "Hey, Becca, would you lock the door after you come in? My hands are full."

On the phone placing another frantic, yet unanswered call to Ethan, Becca managed a wave in response. Ethan better answer soon.

Becca was running out of colorful language to shout at his voicemail.

After punching in the security code, she and the girls moved through the back rooms of the store. The soft white motion lights Bryan insisted on installing brightened their path. This morning, Jillian was thankful she'd listened to her cousin's advice. She kept her eyes open for anything out of place. Relief flooded through her when everything appeared to be as Trixie had left it.

She placed a new blanket and pillow behind the counter as Abbey and Hayley did their usual perimeter search of the store. The pups had the run of the place until they opened.

They loved sniffing out all the dark corners and checking every nook and cranny.

This morning, they found a granola bar a pair of small hands must have left on a bookshelf. Jillian caught them sharing the last tasty bite on the carpet in the Lending Library. Fearing the worst, she snatched the slimy morsel away and sniffed.

Thank goodness, it was peanut butter and not chocolate.

Jillian dumped the remnant in the trash and brushed off her hands.

She flipped a switch behind the counter. Soft music from the radio filled the rooms, creating a peaceful workplace—peaceful until Becca entered, sputtering and squawking like a wet hen.

"Four times. I've tried him four times. That man needs to answer his phone."

Slamming her purse down on the check-out counter, Becca grabbed a rag and proceeded to dust tables and shelves as if her life depended on it. "I left him a couple messages. He'd better call me soon."

"Relax, Becca. Maybe he's chasing down a big lead on this case. Or if we're lucky, he's making an arrest as we speak." Jillian tried to believe what she'd said was true.

"He'd better be." Becca's dust rag flew across the bookshelves in the Main Room. She attacked the offensive dust motes which dared land in her path.

"I'm going to grab some books to fill the empty spots on those shelves you're cleaning," Jillian said. "I'll be back."

"Great. I'll be down here still not talking to my husband." Becca huffed, blowing a stray strand of hair out of her face.

Enjoying the quiet, the organization, and the new book smell of her storage room, Jillian spent several minutes deciding which titles to take downstairs. Her thoughts wandered back to the suspicious black SUV. Had it really been following them, or was it a coincidence? After the past week, she wasn't taking any chances.

Better keep on my toes today.

Entering the Main Room with an armload of books, Jillian noticed Becca had ditched the dusting in favor of peering through the window onto Sweetwater.

"What's so fascinating out there?"

"Huh?" Becca whirled around. "Nothing. Just a handsome guy bringing us breakfast."

Three soft taps on the door wrenched Becca from the window. She flipped the lock to let their visitor in. Travis greeted her with a smile and coffee. He held a blue paper sack, which could only mean one thing—breakfast treats from Sugar & Spice.

"Good morning, handsome," Becca purred at Travis. "If you've brought me black coffee and a cinnamon roll, I'm leaving my husband and running away with you."

He arched his brows almost to his hairline. When he made no response to Becca's teasing, Jillian came to his rescue.

"Don't worry." She took the cardboard drink holder from him. "Becca promises to run away with anyone who brings her coffee and pastries. Ethan is aware of her weakness for caffeine and sweets. He married her anyway. I don't think he'll be coming after you for stealing his wife. I would advise you, however, not to make a habit of supplying her addiction."

She placed the coffee on the counter and greeted Travis with a kiss on the cheek. He dropped the blue sack next to the coffee and used his empty hands to go in for a real hug and bigger kiss.

"Knock it off, you two lovebirds." Becca cleared her throat. "Watching you play smoochie face is not conducive to enjoying my coffee."

"Jealous?" Travis grinned at her.

Becca snorted. "Puh-lease."

"I don't see your main squeeze coming here with your breakfast this morning." Travis's teasing brought a scowl to Becca's face.

Uh-oh, he stuck his foot in this one.

"All right, children." The teacher voice which had brought many of her students to attention rolled off her tongue. "Play nice or I'll write detentions."

Becca harrumphed but stuck out her hand to Travis. "Truce?"

He placed a quick kiss on her cheek. "Truce."

Jillian smiled at his sweet gesture.

Those two will be fast friends before too long.

Becca clapped her hands. "Okay. Loverboy is here for guard duty. I'm taking my breakfast and hitting the road. I assured Cate I'd be at the bakery as soon as my relief arrived." She grabbed her coffee and purse. "There are cookies, cupcakes, and tarts waiting to be baked, so I'm out of here. I hope you two can be trusted here by yourselves this morning. Don't forget, Ethan should be here soon."

"How're you getting to work? We came in my car." Jillian nudged Travis's arm. "Maybe you could drive her to work."

"No need," Becca said. "Ethan left my car parked out front last night. If I could borrow your big, strong man for a minute, I'd be grateful. I was looking out the window and noticed I've got a low tire. If it needs changing, I can't ever get those pesky lug nuts off."

"Sure. No problem." Travis squeezed Jillian's shoulder. "I'll be quick. Yell if you need me."

"For goodness' sake." She threw her hands in the air. "I'll be fine inside my own store. Nothing will happen in here. Go. Check Becca's tire. Stop fussing."

She would tell him about the note and the car tailing them when he came in.

Jillian watched them walk side by side, their heads together, deep in conversation. She doubted they were discussing her tire. Knowing Becca, she regaled him with the events of the last few hours. Jillian really didn't care what they discussed. She enjoyed watching her best friend and boyfriend hitting it off.

She froze.

Boyfriend? Was it too soon to call him that?

With her mind preoccupied considering the status of her relationship with Travis, she flipped the closed sign to open. A movement from behind caught her attention—probably the dogs. Before she could turn, a strong arm grabbed her waist. A large, calloused hand clamped down on her mouth.

"Don't bother screaming for your friends out there." A deep male voice growled in her ear. The same voice from the drive-in.

Jillian's heart raced. Panic welled inside her. How had he gotten in?

Her attacker shoved her forward, demanding she lock the front door. She flipped the deadbolt as instructed, then he yanked her backwards out of sight of the plate-glass window.

"I'm done playing games. I came for what's mine, and you will give it to me. If you try anything funny, like yelling for help, you can watch me slice those dogs of yours into pieces. Do you understand?" He dropped his hand from her mouth.

Tears sprang to her eyes. "Yes, I understand."

She would give him whatever he wanted to protect her—wait—why were the pups so quiet?

A chill ran up her spine.

"You give me Maggie's box, I'll leave the same way I came in." His raspy voice in her ear made her recoil.

"That's what this is about." She needed to keep him talking. "You killed Maggie for a box?"

"I want what's inside the box." He tightened his grasp, pinching the tender skin of her arm. She winced. "And I'm not the one who killed Maggie."

"If you didn't run down Maggie, who did?" She held her breath.

"Moira killed her, the freaking lunatic. Even stole a car to do it. Thought she could frame the owner for Maggie's murder." Her captor snarled. "She was an idiot."

"Moira killed her own sister. Why?" Thinking of Maggie, a lone tear made its way down Jillian's cheek.

"She got impatient. Moira wanted the box even more than I did." The man reached into his pocket, pulling out his knife. "No more questions. Where is it?"

Her attacker managed to stay behind her this whole time, keeping her from seeing his face. His menacing whisper sent goosebumps skittering down her arms. The cold steel of his knife pressed against her throat, piercing through the bandage and the already injured flesh beneath. She whimpered as a warm trickle of blood ran down her neck.

"Give me the box, and I might let you live." His cigarette, whiskey-tinged breath curdled Jillian's stomach.

She knew this maniac had no intention of letting her live once she gave him the box.

No witnesses left behind.

This attack felt like it had gone on for hours, when only minutes had passed. Travis worked outside, fixing Becca's tire, unaware of the danger inside. Ethan hadn't arrived yet.

She was on her own to figure a way out of this mess.

"Your name's Dale, right?" Her questions were meant to distract him, stall for time.

"Yeah, whatever. You can call me Dale if it makes you happy. Give me the box."

"I ... I put ... it's ... in my office. If you let go of me, I can get it."

"Do you think I'm stupid?" He yanked her back, pressing the knife deeper into her throat, making her cry out. "I let go, you run screaming for the door to get your boyfriend's attention. We'll go together. Now move."

He half-pushed, half-dragged her. Her toe caught on the rug. She bumped the counter which should've alerted her pups to the danger. Why weren't they barking? Or trying to protect her?

Jillian's blood ran cold.

He's done something to them. This needs to end. Now.

A plan formed as she allowed herself to be led away from the front.

Oh Lord, I can't believe I'm doing this. Please protect me from this madman.

"C'mon, keep moving," Dale snarled, yanking her back, farther from the window. He increased the pressure of his knife.

This is it. Either I make a move, or he's going to kill me.

A feeling of calm and peace washed over Jillian. She had faith things would be fine. Sliding her hand inside the pocket of her jeans, her fingers grazed Aunt Grace's pendant. She wrapped her hand around the smooth sides of the metal canister—salvation in a tiny silver cylinder.

Dale shoved her forward. She stumbled, knocked into the wall, and crashed to the floor. The noise of her fall garnered her dogs' attention at last. They staggered to investigate and found a stranger towering above their mama. Abbey and Hayley growled, their threats distracting Dale's attention for only a moment. That was all the time Jillian needed.

Good girls. Here goes.

Pushing herself to a standing position, she tugged the pepper spray from her pocket. Her sudden movement drew the lunatic's gaze. For the first time, she saw her attacker's face. Without hesitation, she emptied the entire contents of the canister in the direction of his head.

The man cursed. He released the knife, sending it clattering to the floor. He clawed at his face, falling to his knees. Tears streamed from his eyes and his nose ran like a river. Jillian stumbled away from him, dropping the empty canister from her trembling hands.

A crash of shattering glass filled the air as someone hurtled into the Main Room. The dark figure dropped and rolled among the broken shards. He leaped to his feet, gun drawn shouting, "Police. Don't move."

Ethan—thank God.

Footsteps thundered down the back hallway. Travis rushed in brandishing a tire iron.

"Jilly, what did this scum do to you?" Travis's weapon clattered to the floor, freeing his arms to crush her in a hug. He held on so tight, she could feel his heart racing in unison with hers. She leaned into him, his strength soothing her tattered nerves.

Loosening his grip, he stepped back and saw the blood on her neck. "He hurt you again. I'm going to kill him." Travis took a few steps toward the man who whimpered and writhed on the floor.

"Travis, don't." She snatched his arm. "He grabbed me, shoved me around. I'm fine. My girls are the ones who need help. He did something to them."

Abbey and Hayley were curled at her feet, not moving. She collapsed beside them, stroking their fur as she checked for injuries, listening for heartbeats.

Never taking his gun off the assailant, Ethan growled. "If you're so good, why is there blood on your sweater?"

"He poked the skin, reopened the wound. I'm fine—my girls aren't." She pointed at the man curled into a ball on the floor. "He did something. They need help, but you aren't listening to me, either of you." A sob caught in her throat, tears streaming down her face.

Travis sprang into action, scooping the two unresponsive dogs into his arms. "Ethan, I'll take Jillian and her girls to the vet—if you'll give us permission to leave."

The sound of approaching sirens wailed down the street. "Go. Get out of here. Sounds like the cavalry has arrived anyway," Ethan said. "I'll catch up with both of you later. I'll be busy here for a while."

Slapping a pair of handcuffs on his prisoner, Ethan read him his rights. "Dale Andrews, you have the right to remain silent. Anything you say can and will be used against you in a court of law."

Following Travis out the door, Jillian pointed to her attacker on the floor. "Ethan, that man isn't who you think he is."

CHAPTER THIRTY-TWO

Whimsy & Wonder had been open for business less than a week. Now, the doors were closed for who knew how long. The police would be there for hours collecting evidence to use against her attacker. The picture window would have to be replaced and the broken glass cleared away. The Main Room would require a thorough cleaning. Climbing into Travis's truck, Jillian glanced back on the scene. Her heart ached. The bay window wasn't the only thing shattered today.

Travis drove as fast as he dared to the Furry Friends Animal Hospital. Jillian notified the clinic they were coming. She spoke with Brooke, one of the techs.

"Don't worry. We'll be ready for your girls as soon as you can get here."

"Thank you." A sob caught in Jillian's throat.

Placing her phone back in her purse, she noticed a bunch of texts and missed calls.

My family.

Those would have to wait. The pups were her family too.

Travis rocketed into the parking lot. The doors flew open as they both hopped out. He cradled the pups in his arms and ran for the front entrance. Dr. Curtis met them.

"You two stay in here." He pointed to the small lobby marked *Dogs*. "Jessica will help me run the bloodwork, figure out what's wrong." He reached for Hayley, nodding to his vet tech to take Abbey.

The vet hustled the two limp dogs through the door marked 'Staff Only'. Travis sank into the nearest chair. Jillian paced the floor, twisting and untwisting the bloody scarf she'd removed from her neck.

When Dr. Curtis came back, his face gave away nothing.

"Are Abbey and Hayley okay? Did he poison them?" Her voice quivered.

"Their bloodwork showed no toxins which is good news. From their lethargic behavior, I'd hazard a guess your girls were given a large dose of some type of sedative. Those can't be detected through a blood test."

"How in the world did they get sedatives in their system?" Travis said.

"More than likely, it was put in something they ate," the vet said.

"Like a peanut butter granola bar left on a bookshelf." Jillian growled as fiercely as an angry bear.

Dr. Curtis advised keeping the dogs overnight for observation. While she hated leaving them, Jillian agreed with the doctor. She wanted what was best for her girls.

"They'll sleep off the effects and be ready to go home in the morning." The vet spotted the bandage on her neck. "You're bleeding. Let me take care of that for you. I don't normally work on humans, but I'm pretty sure I can handle this non-canine issue."

Jillian and Travis returned to the store to find the forensics team hard at work. Ethan was nowhere to be found.

"Detective Harden took his suspect in for booking," one of the crime scene techs reported. "I can let you retrieve your personal items, but then you'll have to leave, ma'am. Someone from the police department will notify you when the scene is clear."

Jillian tiptoed through the shattered glass on the floor, grabbing her purse and computer from behind the counter. Her heart beat in rhythm with each pound of the hammers nailing pieces of plywood across the window. She brushed a tear from her cheek and blew out a breath as the tech escorted her outside.

"You take care, Ms. Edwards. You've had a couple of pretty rough days." His kindness touched her heart, yet failed to lighten her spirits.

Her pups had been drugged. Her bookstore was in shambles. She wondered if this day could get any worse when a new thought struck.

I'm also homeless.

At least until her apartment was livable again.

As she stood on the sidewalk with Travis, the enormity of the week's events weighed on her. Her shuddering sigh captured his attention.

"What's wrong? Are you in pain? Please let me take you to the hospital to get checked out."

"A trip to the hospital isn't necessary. Dr. Curtis took care of me."

"No offense, he's a veterinarian. A dog doctor isn't quite the same as a human one."

"Don't be ridiculous. They've all taken anatomy classes and graduated from medical school. Any doctor who's good enough for my girls is good enough to take care of my neck wound."

"I'd prefer you'd let a human doctor check you over, but I can tell I'll lose that battle." He brushed a lock of hair from her cheek. "Instead, maybe we should let your family and friends know everything's fine with you and the girls. Although I'm certain they'll want to lay eyes on you for themselves."

Jillian couldn't believe how lucky she'd been when she met this kind-hearted man. Even during a crisis, he thought of others—one of the many qualities that made him a good firefighter. A flood of emotions threatened to overwhelm her. That's when it hit her.

I am falling in love with Travis—hopelessly and head over heels in love with him.

She'd have to deal with this revelation later.

Jillian drew in a deep calming breath. "Maybe we could meet for lunch at McGuire's. In all the commotion, I never ate breakfast. Could you call Bryan?"

"I'm on it." Travis reached for his phone.

She hadn't checked her own phone in more than an hour. Removing it from her purse, she wasn't surprised the screen was lit like Fourth of July fireworks with incoming texts and calls. "Looks like my family's heard about my morning—wonder how much they know."

"Given the Willow Springs Rumor Mill, they've heard it all." Travis punched in Bryan's number, putting it on speaker. He answered after only two rings with the usual greeting he saved for his buddies.

"What do you want? Some of us are busy working, you know."

Travis gave his gruff friend a condensed version of the morning and asked if it was too late for a family get-together. Without hesitation, Bryan sprang into action.

"You two get here ASAP. I'll take care of the rest. I guarantee everyone will be here by noon. Max is in the kitchen cooking for an army, so there'll be plenty of food."

Not realizing Jillian could hear him, Bryan continued. "Good thing the murdering lunatic is behind bars, or I might've killed him myself."

Jillian smiled. These guys were sweet, but their testosterone was out of control.

"Me and you both," Travis said. "Thanks, man. Be there soon."

"Give my cousin a kiss for me," Bryan said. He shouted orders to his staff. "Prepare yourself, people. My family's coming for lunch."

The line went dead.

Jillian gave the tech who escorted her out the store's alarm code. He promised he'd lock up when they were done. She could breathe easier, confident her bookstore was in good hands and her stalker was in police custody.

Maybe her life could get back to normal.

"Let's leave your car and take my truck." Travis caught her hand, his gaze drifting across the street. "Uh-oh, look who's coming."

Headed straight at them like a heat-seeking missile, Mr. Erickson was red-faced and yelling at the top of his lungs. Mrs. Taylor shuffled behind, chastising him for being rude.

Normal might have to wait.

"Hey, Book Lady." Mr. Erickson stopped short of running smack into her. "What the heck is going on at yer store today? First, there was all the gosh darn noise from them sirens. Now, we got cop cars and vans up and down the street. You said the store wasn't gonna disturb this neighborhood. What'd ya call this?" He waved his arms around at the offending EMS vehicles.

Mrs. Taylor put her hand on Mr. Erickson's arm. "Henry, you hush. This poor girl's been through a lot these last few days. She doesn't need you grousing at her, so mind your manners."

The old man grunted and wrinkled his nose. He spit slimy tobacco juice onto the pavement. "Yes, ma'am."

Jillian's mouth dropped open. She couldn't believe the old man had 'ma'amed' Mrs. Taylor.

She's having a good influence on him—must be serious with these two.

The idea made her smile. Mrs. Taylor would keep the churlish Mr. Erickson in line if anyone could.

"Good morning, Mr. Erickson. Mrs. Taylor." She hugged the sweet, older woman. "I'm sorry for the commotion. Everything is under control. The police are finished and should be leaving soon."

"What in the world happened here? How come yer front winda's all busted?" Like a dog with a bone, he wouldn't let it go.

"I'd love to tell you the whole story, Mr. Erickson, but we're in bit of a hurry. My family is expecting us for lunch." She paused, an idea to make peace with her cantankerous neighbor blooming in her mind.

"Maybe you'd both like to join us?" Jillian hoped they would accept her invitation.

They should know the truth about what happened in their own neighborhood, and they should hear it from her.

"Oh, we couldn't impose on your family." Mrs. Taylor tugged at Mr. Erickson's sleeve. "Let's go, Henry."

"Hold yer horse feathers," he said. "You're wantin' us to join you for lunch? Where you goin', and who's buyin'?"

Jillian smiled at the old man's hutzpah. "We're eating at my cousin's place, McGuire's. You're my guests—my treat."

Again, Mrs. Taylor attempted to decline her invitation. Mr. Erickson thwarted the effort.

"Count us in, Book Lady. I never say no to a free meal. We'll meet you there in a jiffy." He offered Mrs. Taylor his arm which she accepted. The two of them bustled across the street to his car.

"Do you think he's a safe driver?" Travis frowned, watching Mr. Erickson pull away from the curb.

"I have no idea and don't really want to find out. Let's hurry and get there first." Jillian climbed into the cab of Travis's big truck, sinking into the comfy leather seat. As she sat there with him, the weight of the world lifted from her shoulders. She leaned her head back and sighed.

I'll rest my eyes for a minute.

Travis shook her awake. "Jilly, we're here." He'd parked in a spot across from McGuire's. "You fell asleep, babe."

Babe. He called her babe. Goosebumps popped out on her arms.

"Again? I'm sorry I keep falling asleep when I'm with you. I swear, I'm a lot more fun than my recent behavior indicates." Jillian took one of his hands in hers and gave it a squeeze.

"You're a lot of fun, but today's been a rough one. Are you sure you're ready for this family gathering?" Travis helped her from the truck.

"Gathering? You mean inquisition." She smiled at Travis and patted his cheek. "They're my family. This will be—"

A loud noise coming down the street drowned her out. Mr. Erickson's 1982 dark green Buick Bonneville, badly in need of a new muffler, chugged to the curb. The elderly man stepped around to the passenger side and opened the door for Mrs. Taylor.

Nice to see chivalry is alive and well in Willow Springs.

Jillian grinned as the older couple crossed the street, arm in arm.

"We're ready for the lunch you promised, Book Lady." Mr. Erickson held the door for both women. "After you, purdy ladies."

"Thank you." She allowed Mrs. Taylor entrance first. "My family will be pleased to have lunch with such a polite gentleman as yourself."

A red flush crept under the collar of the old man's partially clean, only slightly wrinkled Oxford shirt. He ducked his head at the compliment and let the door swing shut on Travis.

"Polite gentleman? Yeah, right," Travis grumbled, grabbing hold of the door to keep it from slamming in his face.

"I can't wait for you both to meet my family. Although you've met quite a few of them already, Mrs. Taylor." Jillian led her guests toward the backroom.

The old man paled, taking a few steps back. "Oh, you did say you were meeting your family, didn't ya? Um ... well ... I don't do families. Nothing good ever came from mine, and I don't intend to become friendly with yours, Book Lady."

"Sorry, Mr. Erickson—a package deal. Free lunch *with* my family." Jillian shrugged, pursing her lips.

The old man's eyes narrowed. He shook a finger. "You drive a hard bargain, Book Lady. Never let it be said Henry Olaf Erickson ever passed on a free meal. My mama didn't raise no dummy. Let's eat."

Her entire family, along with Becca, Ethan, and Trixie, were seated at the table when Jillian entered with her special guests. After making the introductions, two more chairs appeared at the table like magic. Bryan took drink orders—an Arnold Palmer for Mr. Erickson and a sweet tea for Mrs. Taylor—leaving the women fluttering around

Jillian. Each one needed to make sure she was in one piece and unharmed. Her dad's booming voice rang out, thanking Travis and Ethan for rescuing his baby girl.

"You young men keep making a habit of saving my daughter from dangerous situations. To show my appreciation, drinks and lunch are on me." Her dad clapped them both on the back, shaking their hands.

Jillian's head snapped to attention. "Rescuing me? They most certainly did not. I had the situation under control when this one came crashing through my window like a ninja assassin." She pointed an accusing finger at Ethan.

"This one lumbered down the back hallway waving a tire iron like a crazed mechanic." She bumped Travis with her hip. "The canister of pepper spray Aunt Grace gave me saved the day. Those two came in after I had the killer on his knees."

"Pepper spray? I never gave you pepper spray. That stuff's dangerous," Grace said.

"Yes, you did, Aunt Grace. You gave me the necklace with the silver pendant, don't you remember? I emptied the entire canister in my stalker's face. He went down like a ton of bricks."

"I did not give you pepper spray. The cylinder held an atomizer filled with my secret recipe of essential oils and natural herbs. You were meant to spray it on yourself to ward off evil, to protect you. Didn't I tell you?"

Not pepper spray. That explains why I never sneezed or coughed.

She put her arms around her aunt. "The pendant did protect me. You saved my life."

"I did?" Grace beamed with pride. "Well, yes, of course, I did because I gave you the amulet."

"Please don't bottle and sell your secret recipe. Not after what that stuff did to my suspect's face." Ethan shuddered at the memory. "The medics said it was an allergic reaction—had trouble breathing. They gave him a shot of Epinephrine in the ambulance. By the time we got to the emergency room, his face looked like he'd been in a prize fight—and lost."

Max appeared, his arms laden with wonderful-smelling dishes—three kinds of burgers, sauteed fall vegetables, crispy potato skins loaded with toppings, and his famous grilled corn salad. Jillian's stomach rumbled as the food hit the table. Only the sounds of serving spoons scraping bowls followed by silverware striking plates prevailed for the next few minutes as everyone dug in to Max's delicious lunch.

Wriggling in her chair and sending several utensils clanging to the floor, Becca couldn't stand it.

"I can't wait another minute." She pointed her fork at Ethan. "Tell us what happened with Dale Andrews. And promise me he'll spend the rest of his miserable life behind bars."

CHAPTER THIRTY-THREE

Jillian's heart raced. Everyone wanted to hear the sordid details of his case. She wasn't sure she was ready, especially if something reflected poorly on Maggie.

Ethan took a swig of his drink and wiped his mouth with a napkin.

"The man I arrested this morning is not Dale Andrews."

This news elicited a gasp from a few and stunned the rest into silence. They stopped eating, put down their glasses and forks, and stared at him.

"We ran his fingerprints—found out his name is Colin Flannery. Records indicate he's Maggie and Moira's older brother." He slowed with those last two words.

More gasps and wide-eyed gaping.

"A brother? Did you know Maggie had a brother?" Becca spun around to gawk at Jillian, who shook her head.

"Colin sang like a sparrow once we confronted him with the truth. He went into foster care, like his sisters, when their mother died. He was thirteen. No one wanted to adopt a boy his age with the proclivity for crime he possessed. He bounced from one home to another until the age of sixteen when he ran away, disappearing off the grid.

"Years later, an accidental meet inside a holding cell in Atlanta brought Moira and Colin together again. They'd both been arrested for running scams on the elderly. Sitting in booking waiting to be taken to jail, one look and they knew—they'd each found a long lost sibling."

Ethan threw two mugshots onto the table, one of Moira and the other of Colin.

"My goodness, those two could be twins instead of Moira and Maggie." Joy studied the pictures closer. "No doubt they're brother and sister."

The photos were passed around the table.

"He's the tall, handsome man I saw in my vision." Aunt Grace tapped Colin's picture. "He also came in the store on Wednesday ... wanted books for his, uh ... daughter, I think he said."

Grace handed the photo to Mrs. Taylor who shook her head.

"No, dear. I think you're mistaken. This is the handyman I saw fixing the lock on the back door of the bookstore yesterday."

Trixie jumped from her seat, sprinting to Mrs. Taylor's side. "What man? I didn't hire anyone to fix the lock. There's nothing wrong with the door."

She squinted her eyes, examining the photo. "Hey, I've met this guy too. He stopped in last night a few minutes before closing. He wandered around the store—didn't buy anything. He thanked me and left."

"That must be when he planted the granola bar laced with sedatives Abbey and Hayley ate."

Jillian's declaration met a chorus of 'whats' and 'huhs'. Ethan's story took a back seat as she explained what happened, ending with their trip to the vet clinic.

"Dale ... Colin—whatever his name is—has no regard for life, human or canine." Grace closed her eyes and rubbed her temples. "He has a black soul and will pay for his sins one day. There are terrible things in his future."

"You mean like jail, Mom?" Bryan snorted, rolling his eyes.

"Bryan Aiden McGuire, don't you start with me." Aunt Grace scowled at her son.

Ethan cleared his throat. "If I may continue, the ladies are all correct. Colin admitted he came into the store on two different occasions to get a lay of the land, as he called it. He tinkered with the door yesterday in an effort to set his plan to break in this morning.

"You, Jillian, have one handy cousin. Bryan installed a lock the criminally-inclined Colin Flannery couldn't bust. What a shame you and your bestie couldn't be bothered to lock the door this morning." Ethan gestured at the two of them, shaking his head.

"Watch it, buddy. If you'd answered your phone the first time I called, I wouldn't have been distracted and would've remembered to lock the door." Becca cast an irritated glance at her husband, which he ignored. He continued with his story.

"Colin and Moira kept in touch through prison mail and met when they were both released months later. The duo traveled across the country, working odd jobs and scamming people out of money every chance they got. They fleeced one poor woman in Pittsburgh out of her life savings—close to half a million dollars. After each score, they'd live the good life until the money ran out, forcing them to concoct a new scheme."

"How in the world did they blow through all that money?" Travis asked.

"That's easy when a person has an addictive personality—Colin liked blackjack and high stakes poker,

Moira played the ponies. Money never lasted long in either of their pockets." Ethan took a bite of his second burger, washing it down with a swig of ice cold Pepsi.

"Is that why they moved to Stonefield? Because they'd run out of money and needed a new scam?" In her heart, Jillian knew the answer, but needed Ethan to confirm her suspicions.

"Yes. They moved to Stonefield two years ago and started a new con. They planned to cheat Moira's boss out of her business. When the woman died in an accident, things became even easier for the pair. At least for a while."

"Moira wasn't the grieving sister she pretended to be." Jillian rubbed her temples, a headache building. "She wasn't heartbroken at all. I'll bet they came to Willow Springs with a plan to scam money from Maggie too."

"Don't be ridiculous. She was a teacher. Everybody knows teachers don't make a lot of money." Amanda jumped in. "Sorry, Jilly. No offense."

"None taken—you can't argue with the truth."

"Colin saw Maggie's picture in the Stonefield paper a few months ago after she won some teaching award. They couldn't believe they'd lived so close for two years." Ethan paused, scratching the day-old stubble on his face. "And Maggie did have quite a bit of money. Or I should say, she'd soon have a lot of money."

"What are you saying? Maggie didn't have any money. As a matter of fact, she was swimming in school loan debt." Jillian narrowed her eyes, doubting this part of Ethan's story.

"Hang on. You don't know your friend as well as you thought." Ethan raised his hands, stopping her. "This whole mystery revolves around a key, a safe deposit box and some family money Colin and Moira wanted to take from Maggie."

"I never heard her talk of any family fortune. She struggled to make ends meet." Jillian knew for a fact Maggie budgeted her money each month, afraid of falling short of the funds needed for her bills.

"Colin and Moira came after Maggie because of a key and a few thousand dollars they thought she had." Becca took a deep breath, blowing it out in a whistle. "Wow, killing your sister for money, brutal."

"Yes, it is. There was no love lost between these siblings. Colin and Moira resented Maggie for the good life she'd had while they'd been forced to live within the system." Ethan downed his last swallow and signaled the waitress for a refill. "And it's quite a bit more than a few thousand dollars. Colin said she owed them. They were willing to do anything to get their hands on Maggie's money."

Max chose this moment to place dessert on the table—a breathtaking trifle with layers of red berries, lemon pound cake, and luscious whipped cream. He stared at the plates of untouched food.

"What's going on here?" His German accent became thick when angered. "No one is eating. You don't like my food?" He tossed the serving spoon onto the table.

Jillian rushed to his side, putting an arm around his shoulder. "Not at all, Max. Your food is delicious as always. We've been distracted with the details of Ethan's case—you know—my friend's murder." These last words came out in a reverent whisper.

"You." Max shook an angry finger at Ethan. "You keep people from enjoying their meal with such ugliness as murder. Humph." He stomped away from the table, swearing under his breath in German. The assembled party stared at Bryan. He waved off his temperamental chef's outburst.

"Max'll be fine. He'll cool off and come back with even more food. I would suggest we eat though while Ethan finishes his story."

Utensils were retrieved and dining recommenced while their attention remained on Ethan. He polished off his buffalo chicken burger and gobbled a few onion rings the waitress had just dropped by their table. His silence unnerved Jillian.

"I can't imagine how shocked Maggie must have been to encounter her siblings after all those years. And to find out they weren't nice people—awful."

"Not nice is an understatement." Ethan's tone dripped with contempt for their actions. "Moira got tired of waiting for her payday. She also didn't want to split the money three ways. She stole Travis's buddy's car and ran down her sister, hoping to frame him for the murder. This wasn't a spur-of-the-moment, temporary insanity kind of thing. She planned it out which makes her a cold-blooded killer."

"The man sitting in the driver's seat of the SUV the night of Jillian's open house had a beard. Mr. Erickson and Mrs. Taylor saw him, right?" Travis questioned.

Both the older guests nodded.

"How was Moira the one driving the car when it ran down poor Maggie?" Travis needed this hole in the story filled.

Ethan was happy to oblige. "Colin told us Moira was hiding in the backseat—she didn't want Maggie to see her. She hopped into the front seat when she watched her twin sister leave the bookstore."

"Dale ... I mean Colin told me Moira killed Maggie. I didn't believe him." Jillian shredded a napkin in anger. "She murdered her own sister—her twin."

Everyone remained silent, not knowing what to say or how to move on. Everyone except Ethan.

"Colin admitted the two of them broke into Maggie's house the night she died searching for a key. He was angry they didn't find it. He had no idea Moira had attempted to get into Maggie's classroom for the same purpose. According to Colin, Moira had the idea of befriending you, Jillian, and made her appearance here at McGuire's the other night, claiming she was devastated by her twin sister's death. She hoped you could lead them to the key."

Jillian's face was clouded with confusion. "Why in the world would Moira think Maggie had given me a key?"

"Maggie wrote of your friendship in her journal. Her siblings found and read it when they searched her place. They assumed she would have told her good friend her secret. Moira got nervous when you asked too many questions. She viewed you as a threat to her plans and decided you needed to be eliminated. Moira, not Colin, tried to hit you with her car."

"Moira ran down Maggie and tried to do the same to Jilly." Becca narrowed her eyes and muttered a threat. "Good thing she's already dead, or I'd have to go after her myself."

Ethan widened his eyes at his wife's outburst. "Hey, whoa. You okay, sweetie?" Becca took a few calming breaths and motioned for her husband to continue.

"When Colin found out Moira had gone rogue, he went ballistic. Tired of her out-of-control, reckless behavior, he decided to take her out and keep all the money to himself." Ethan polished off the last two onion rings on his plate.

"So, he slit her throat and dumped her in the trunk of her own car." Jillian sighed. "He did like that knife of his."

Travis leaned in, placing a soft kiss on her temple. He scooted his chair closer and put his arm around the back of her seat.

"Colin believed you were his only chance to get his hands

on the key. He stalked, threatened, and attacked you to get what he wanted." Ethan concluded his story and reached for another burger. He'd worked hard for the past twenty-four hours to close this case and deserved this meal, yet there were still many unanswered questions.

"Hold on a sec, can we go back to this mystery key?" Jillian said. "Maggie never gave me one. What made Colin think I had it?"

"Because of this." Ethan took a beautifully wrapped box out of a bag he'd stashed under the table.

Jillian gasped, startled to the point of toppling sideways in her chair. Travis caught her. "You found the gift from Maggie. Colin asked me for this thing over and over. How'd he know Maggie had given it to me?"

"Dale Andrews watched Maggie carry the box into your open house Friday night, but she came out without it." Ethan tapped his forehead with his finger. "Stands to reason, Maggie left the box with you inside the store."

"Wait a minute. You said Colin wasn't Dale Andrews. There really is a Dale Andrews?" Travis's puzzled expression mirrored those of the others gathered at the table.

"Yes, there is a Dale Andrews," Ethan said. "He was the creepy tattooed visitor at the bookstore last Friday. He sat in the black SUV the night of the party watching the guests come and go. He was Moira's good-for-nothing boyfriend too. They met at the bowling alley where she waitressed. They hit it off, started dating, and Moira insisted he be included in their money-making scheme."

Another mugshot hit the table.

"He's the scumbag Lizzie and I both saw sittin' in the car outside the Book Lady's store." Mr. Erickson sputtered around a big bite of onion rings and corn salad. "What was he doin'—casin' the joint? I heard 'em say that on a cop show I watch." He snorted, flecks of food flying from his mouth. Mrs. Taylor handed him a napkin.

"Sort of," Ethan said. "Colin didn't want Dale involved in their plans. Moira wouldn't take no for an answer. Colin gave Dale simple jobs, like watching Jillian's movements and reporting back. Explains why you noticed his car sitting outside the bookstore on several occasions." He smiled at the old man and his companion. "According to Colin, Dale took it upon himself to go *into* the store last Friday and threaten Jilly. Dale also helped Moira steal the car they used to run down Maggie."

"He's a dirty-rotten, low-down, no-good bast—"

"Henry, there are ladies present." Mrs. Taylor's stern tone stopped his tirade. "Manners, please."

"Sorry, ladies." Mr. Erickson gave the women a sheepish grin, winking at Ethan.

"We found Dale Andrews dead in his motel room," Ethan continued. "His throat had been slit like Moira's. Once he'd killed her, Colin saw no reason to keep Dale alive either."

"A real brother-sister murdering team." Jilly's dad pushed back his chair. He wrapped her in a protective hug. "I'm thankful my girl didn't become one of their victims."

Grace cleared her throat. "Thanks to my amulet of protection."

Her dad sighed and placed a kiss on top of Jillian's head. To Grace, he said, "Yes, even you have a good idea once in a while."

"Maggie's dead. Moira's dead. Dale's dead. So, Colin's plan was to get some key from Jilly and kill her too?" Amanda ticked the bodies off on her fingers. "Surely he knew he'd get caught when he tried to withdraw money from the bank."

"I don't think Ethan's dealing with the brightest bulb in the chandelier here." Cate nudged Amanda in the arm.

"You would be correct." Ethan agreed with the assessment of Colin's mental acuity. "His mother had shown him the key years ago. After her death, he became fixated on finding it. When he and Moira failed to get their hands on it, Colin became desperate. With nowhere else to search, he admitted Dale had been right—the key was inside the box."

"Colin kept demanding I give him the box, but I had no idea where it was." Jillian took the wrapped package in her hands. "Where did you find this?"

"I didn't. The forensics team found it after the murder when they searched your store. The tag read 'From Maggie', so they figured it might have some bearing on the case. They bagged it and brought it to the station where the box sat in evidence all week. I stumbled across it last night when I was reviewing evidence for anything I might've missed."

"I'm still confused." Jillian furrowed her brow. "Maggie never gave me any key."

"Maybe you should peek inside the box." Ethan removed the lid.

Jillian peered inside. A beautiful oval locket on a shimmery silver chain lay on the blue velvet. "This is lovely. What a beautiful gift." A tear traced its way down her cheek.

Thank you, Maggie. I'll treasure this always.

"Open the locket." Ethan's voice jolted her from her thoughts.

She opened the tiny clasp, and a small silver key dropped in her hand. A collective gasp filled the room.

Ethan reached into the box and removed a folded piece of blue stationery paper, offering it to Jillian.

"This is addressed to you."

With a trembling hand, she took it, leaving it folded.

Blue. Of course, Maggie used this paper. Blue was her

366

favorite color. She once said it reminded her of the things she loved—the sky, the ocean, and her Nana's eyes.

Jillian opened the letter, saddened by her friend's elegant handwriting gracing each line on the page. Though the words were blurred by her unshed tears, she took a deep breath and began to read. Unable to get past the first few sentences, she handed the letter to Travis, asking him to read it aloud.

Dear Jillian,

I've considered you my best friend for several years, so I hope I can impose on our friendship for a favor. Perhaps I'm being paranoid, but should something happen to me, I need someone I can trust to take care of the contents of this box.

There are many things, secrets really, I've never told anyone. Why? I'm not sure, but I'll share them with you now. I pray what I say won't change your perception of me.

When I was four, my mother died of brain cancer. I was adopted by a wonderful couple. I count my lucky stars I found a second mother (and father) who loved me. On the day I left for college, my mother gave me a locket belonging to my birth mother, with a letter she had written. Inside the locket was a key. The letter said the key opened a safe deposit box at Southern Illinois National Bank in our hometown. Inside the box, I would find bank papers for an account in the names of Colin, Moira, and Margaret Flannery. Colin and Moira are my biological siblings. I'll spare you the sordid details of my current relationship with them. Let's just say there were no tear-filled hugs when we were reunited with one another recently.

These bank accounts were opened by our paternal grandfather after our father was killed. We, my siblings and I, will be given access to the money in these accounts on my twenty-eighth birthday which you know is on December 22nd of this year. This is where the favor comes in.

If I'm unable, I'd like you to make sure my share of the money is put to good use. Please donate it to St. Francis to help cancer patients with their medical bills. The donation should be made in honor and remembrance of my mother, Katherine Marie O'Riley Flannery.

I know this is asking a lot, but I trust and respect you more than anyone else. You've always been so kind and supportive. Our friendship has often been a lifeline for me. I hope you can find it in your heart to grant me this last request.

Please keep the locket as a token of my gratitude. It would mean the world if you wear it, and maybe, sometimes, think of me.

Your friend,
Maggie

Travis read the letter to a captive audience. When he finished, there wasn't a dry eye in the house. The sound of sniffles, quiet sobs, and requests to pass the tissues broke the silence. Jillian was the first to speak.

"Poor Maggie. She knew her own siblings were out to get her. Why didn't she go to the police for help?"

"She did—once. There's a report on file. Maggie claimed her siblings were harassing her. Without any proof to back her claims, there wasn't anything the police could do." Ethan's brown eyes held sadness.

"I'll make certain Maggie's wishes for the money are followed." Jillian wiped an errant tear from her cheek. "With Moira dead, what happens to her part of the money? Can it be donated too?"

"I'm not sure of all the legalities here," Ethan said, "but the police department's lawyers are already in contact with the trustees' lawyers. Let's hope we hear good news."

"How much money are we talking about, Ethan?" Travis asked the very question Jillian had planned.

"Each sibling stood to inherit two million dollars."

A stunned hush followed this pronouncement.

Trixie slapped her palms down on the table, knocking her empty glass onto the floor where it shattered, garnering her an angry glare from the waitress. "Leaving four million dollars to donate?"

"Yes, and I'm sure St. Francis will be grateful for the money, if the law allows," Ethan said.

"I'll do everything within my power to make it happen." Jillian stared at the silver key lying on her palm. "For Maggie. And her mother."

"I do need this back." Ethan reached across the table for the key.

"But this is yours." He dropped Maggie's locket into Jillian's open hand.

Holding back a new stream of tears, she examined the beautiful heirloom. The front of the locket was engraved with a capital F in a graceful script. On the back, there was an inscription in what she thought was Irish Gaelic. It read, *Creideamh, gra agus teaghlach*. She showed the engraving to her mom. "Do you know what this means?'

Putting on her glasses, Joy studied the inscription. "My grandmother spoke in Gaelic, hoping we'd learn her native tongue. My own skills are a bit rusty, but if I'm not mistaken, it means faith, love, and family."

"Faith, love, and family." Jillian whispered the words as she placed the locket around her neck. "I'm glad Maggie found all three with her adoptive family."

The mood at the table had become somber as they took in everything Ethan shared. Everyone's eyes were downcast except for Jillian's. She gazed at the people she loved, giving silent thanks for each of them. A part of her grieved for everything that had been lost in the last week. Maggie, Moira, and Dale lost their lives. Colin would lose his freedom. She'd almost lost her life twice, and she suspected they'd all lost a bit of their trust in others.

Considerable time will pass before any of us will be able to look a stranger in the eye and not expect the worst.

In true Irish pub fashion, Bryan broke the solemn tone of the room by raising his glass in a toast. "To Maggie and her mother."

"To Maggie and her mother." Everyone clinked their glasses in salute.

Jillian raised her glass. "To faith, love, and family—may we always have plenty of all three."

"Oh, we will." Grace tipped her glass to the group. "There's much to look forward to as our family grows, all thanks to love and faith."

"How do you know this, Aunt Grace?" Jillian narrowed her eyes.

"I've seen it—in the bottom of my tea cup." She favored the room with an impish grin. "And the tea leaves are never wrong."

ABOUT THE AUTHOR

Jodi Casstevens-Short is a born and raised Midwesterner, proud University of Illinois alum, and a third generation educator. After thirty-five years as an elementary teacher, she retired to follow her dream of becoming a published author. She is currently working on many projects including a humorous memoir of her teaching career, several children's books, and Books Two and Three in her Willow Springs cozy mystery series. She lives in her hometown in Central Illinois with her firefighter husband and two sassy schnauzers, Riley and Finley. *Murdered by the Books* is her debut novel.